SC Fic 47/23   £3

Fiction Gift Aid
£
0 029310 020485

D1345171

EDWARD KANE

AND THE

PARLOUR MAID MURDERER

by

Ross Macfarlane QC

First Published in the UK in 2020 by
Scotland Street Press
100 Willowbrae Avenue
Edinburgh EH8 7HU

All rights reserved
Copyright ©Ross Macfarlane

The right of Ross Macfarlane to be identified as the author of this work
has been asserted in accordance with Section 77 of the Copyright,
Designs and Patents Act 1988

A CIP record for this book is available from the British Library.

Hardback ISBN 978-1-910895-481
Paperback ISBN 978-1-910895-498

This is a work of fiction. Names, characters, business, events and
incidents are the products of the author's imagination. Any resemblance
to actual persons, living or dead, or actual events is purely coincidental.

Typeset by Antonia Weir in Edinburgh
Printed in Glasgow by Bell & Bain Ltd

Illustrations by Lesley-Anne Barnes Macfarlane
Cover Design by Antonia Weir

To Lesley-Anne. My everything.

Contents

Advocate

Oxford English Dictionary.   Advocate: *"...a professional pleader in a court of justice..."*

Johnson's Dictionary – 1755.
"A'dvocacy. n.s. [from advocate.] The act of pleading; vindication; defence; apology: a word in little use..."

PART ONE: THE INSTRUCTION

1850: Edinburgh, Capital of Scotland

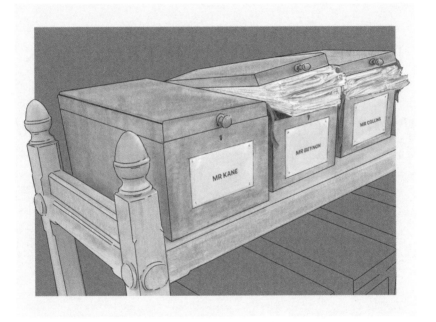

Chapter One

It was generally agreed that the public execution of Charles Makepeace had provided excellent entertainment for the twenty thousand men, women and children who attended.

On that day, the otherwise grey streets of Edinburgh had the atmosphere of a village fair where families and friends enjoyed a fine day out.

In the middle of the crowd, Edward Kane, Advocate, required to crane his neck to see the event. His manservant, 'Horse' (a nickname won at the Battle of Waterloo), stood beside him, holding Kane's hat and gloves.

This was the perfect spot from which to observe the hanging, except for the lady with the very tall hat directly in front of Kane.

Kane pointed to Horse, then pointed to the lady before him. Horse leaned forward, his head almost resting on the lady's shoulder. His thick Cockney accent cut through the otherwise Caledonian din: 'Scuse me, my dear,' he pointed to the offending piece of millinery, 'would it be possible to remove the tile from the roof?'

The lady looked surprised by the request, then offended, then resigned. She began, with a great harrumphing, the extrication of a seemingly infinite number of pins.

Horse made a slight bow to say: Thank'ee madam.

The lady shook her head violently. The tresses, which until that point been restrained by her hat were now free to range left, right and upwards, leaving Edward Kane's view now more restricted than before.

'I fear, Mr Horse, that we have progressed from the inconvenient obstruction of the frying pan to the total eclipse of the fire.'

'Well, Mr K, I could always ask her to take off her 'ead...'

Their exchange was interrupted by a loud murmur from the crowd. The murderer, Charles Makepeace, a.k.a. 'Black Charlie', was being led on to the scaffold.

Makepeace scowled at the crowd, baring a mouthful of uneven teeth like a row of winter chimneys. Yes. Men of all degrees were standing for him now. Women of all ages watched, some with half-smiles on their faces, some breathless with the excitement of his end, some visibly praying for the repose of his not-quite-departed soul.

Then there were the children in the crowd. Some dressed in their finery for the occasion, or asleep in their mothers' arms, some excited now and looking in his direction. And there were those other children on the streets. Whose parents were still lying in drunken stupors in the hovels they called home. A life of petty crime would be their daily fight against starvation. The time-honoured techniques: the dipping of pockets, the three card trick, the rolling of the drunken gentleman.

Makepeace smiled. The day of his death would be an anchor in the memories of others, a reference point in their personal almanacs: 'It was around the time that Black Charlie danced on air,' they would say. That memory, and only that, would be his lasting monument.

The trapdoor beneath Makepeace's feet opened.

For one so schooled in a lifetime of punishment and the constant threat of the noose, this development seemed to be a complete surprise to him. His eyes bulged in disbelief. The twisting and jerking fandango began, hands bound behind him punching against his lower back. The teeth grinding as if to resist the fatal pressure of his own body weight. The panicked cry as the irresistible wave of death washed over his gasps to reach the surface of life. And that dance, the dance on nothing but air. The dance on that open trapdoor, the void, Charles Makepeace's personal doorway to Eternity.

After a few minutes, the dance was done. Charles Makepeace's body at rest now and swinging and swaying gently at the end of a rope.

All the while, Edward Kane, Advocate, had his eyes fixed to the ground – witnessing nothing of what would become an infamous demise.

Mr Horse, on the other hand, was animated now:

'Well, Mr K, I knows you're squeamish and all, but you just missed a bloody good hanging. Time for a spot of luncheon, sir?'

The entertainment over, some of the crowd began to pack their belongings and make their way back; others watched the body sway in the breeze.

'No, Mr Horse. You may return to your quarters. I shall visit Parliament House – and my box.'

★★★

Footsteps away stood St Giles' Church and at the rear of that ancient site of worship was Parliament House, home of the Supreme Courts of Scotland.

Kane made his way through the festive crowds, walked along the covered porticos in Parliament Square and entered Parliament House.

It had been some 150 years since the Scottish Parliament in Edinburgh had extinguished itself to re-emerge, phoenix-like inside the greater body of the Westminster Parliament in London. It had left behind the old Parliament building that still bore its name, housing the Scottish Supreme Courts and the Faculty of Advocates Library.

The great Parliament Hall was busy today. The Supreme Court lawyers, the Advocates, were dressed for court in grey horsehair wigs and black gowns. They walked in pairs up and down that great hall: opponents on different sides of the case persuading and haggling with each other.

As Kane looked at those earnest promenading figures, he heard snatches of the business at hand: 'Five thousand Guineas – and expenses, of course...' 'I fail to see how the Pursuer can consider himself infeft....' 'Failure of consideration is clear...'

Kane stood at a fireplace and looked up at the magnificent Great Window. Intense sunshine glittered through the thousands of pieces of brightly-coloured glass and lent the hall a dreamlike quality. He had known this place all his life. As a child, Parliament Hall had served both as a courtroom and as a public market. Kane remembered visiting when, at the age of eight, hand-in-hand with his mother, she bought him his first pair of ice skates in one of the many booths there. When they had got home, Kane had entered his father's study and asked his father whether or not it was usual that in a single location, a judge should be sitting in one corner and a cobbler in the other. His father, until that point lost in a book, had puffed on his tobacco for a moment and then replied:

'That Justice should be dispensed in a public place is a noble and immemorial practice that has its seeds in the Forum of Ancient Rome. And that Forum where justice was first administered gave to the English language the word 'forensic' – a word that means 'of the courts', but it retains the odour of the common marketplace. I fear that the two meanings have been interlinked ever since that time. I hope, my son, that in your life to come, you will only ever require the services of the cobbler and never that of the Advocate. In my experience, the former will attempt to keep the shoes on your feet, while the latter will invariably oversee the removal of the shirt from your back.'

And with a satisfied puff of the pipe, his father resumed his reading.

Kane smiled. *Ah, father, father.* He walked out and into the main corridor, where a long row of small wooden boxes were lined against the wall. Each box had affixed a small brass plaque bearing the name of the Advocate to whom the box belonged. Advocates were a curious breed of lawyer. If you wanted an Advocate to do something for you, you drop the paperwork into the box and – whether they care for it or not – they are obliged to do it.

Kane looked into the box. Empty. Again. That receptacle of disappointment reminded him of a tiny, empty coffin. No work today. No work yesterday. The remedy today – as most days – would be coffee.

***

The Advocates Reading Room had all the appearance of the elite; but something of an unemployed elite.

Counsel of all ages and ranks mingled, chattered and regaled their brethren with their latest forensic triumphs and disasters. Advocates lounged in easy chairs or at tables, some reading newspapers, some puffing on their pipes of tobacco.

Kane sat, cup and saucer on his lap, finishing his coffee. His friend, Collins, listened attentively: 'I fear, my friend, that my larder will soon be as empty as my box. My apprehension is that, should some intrepid solicitor venture to place a set of instructions in my box, then I may mistake them for a leg of mutton and consume them whole.'

The friends laughed. Collins adjusted the arms of his horn-rimmed glasses:

'My dear Edward. Patience and fortitude! The readiness is all. For my own part, my condition was indistinguishable from your own and then...' he looked upwards and fluttered his fingers towards the ceiling '...like manna from heaven, the variation of a complex Deed of Trust found its way from another table to my own. And now the Collins household dines this evening – and dines well. Are there no crumbs from the Master's table?'

Collins was referring to any work that would be handed down from one senior Advocate to a more junior one.

Advocates in training spent nine months – without pay – 'devilling' with a qualified Advocate, learning the culture and practice of the profession. The would-be Advocate (the 'Devil') would, once qualified, likely receive a measure of pass-on work from his master or 'Devilmaster'.

Kane frowned: 'I regret to say that matters between my Devilmaster and myself have somewhat soured... but let us not dwell on that... Fortunately, he has restricted himself to The Law Room and so I seldom encounter him.'

The friends' conversation was interrupted when they realised that they had been come upon silently by Manville, the Head Faculty Servant. The Faculty Servants performed many functions for their busy Counsel, carrying messages, transporting papers, easing the Advocate's life from the demands of the public. And Manville ruled over them all.

Manville himself was, in the last analysis, something of a mysterious figure. He had served with her Majesty's Navy for a considerable period of his long life, and by consequence preferred the martial appellation 'Manville' to the more genteel 'Mr Manville'. As Faculty Servant, his duty to the interests of the Faculty was paramount. Nothing should interfere with the operation or reputation of that great institution. A young Advocate with his neck-tie improperly secured would be taken into a corner and entirely appropriately – if somewhat traumatically – rebuked by Manville. A Senior Member of Faculty being found semi-conscious and lying in a public street after an enthusiastic and liquid social event would invariably find Manville at his side, Hansom cab at the ready, declaring loudly 'It must be the influenza, sir'. And of the senior judges, Manville was a breathing encyclopaedia of those covert peccadillos and near-criminal events that can characterise the conduct of The Great.

Manville now stood at the table of the two young Advocates, waiting to be addressed. Kane looked up:

'Manville?'

The Faculty Servant leaned into them conspiratorially: 'Begging your pardon, gentlemen...'

'Yes?'

'...but, Mr Kane, I wonder if the Dean of Faculty could have a word, sir.'

Kane shrugged: 'With me?'

'With your good self, sir.'

The Dean of Faculty, Robert 'Rab' Lennox, was perhaps the greatest Advocate of his generation. Kane had had very few dealings with the leader of that great institution since passing Advocate and being called to the Bar two years previously. But for all his great powers of persuasion to jury and judge alike, the Dean was not known to be a warm individual. Not quite that he did not suffer fools gladly, rather that he did not suffer them at all. A remote figure, best appreciated from a distance. Being called into the Dean's Room was akin to being asked to attend at Mount Olympus. And the usual request for such an audience commonly meant one thing: a complaint had been lodged against an Advocate. Kane looked up again:

'Yes. Well, thank you, Manville.'

Despite the obvious message to depart, Manville stood stock still.

'Manville?'

'The Dean would like to speak to you, sir.'

'Yes, thank you.'

No movement. Manville spoke:

'I think that now would be an opportune moment, sir.'

Kane stood up and – in one effortless swoop – Manville removed the cup and saucer from the Advocate's hands, placed them carefully on the table and gently prodded the Advocate's back towards the door.

Still sitting, Collins smiled to himself and raised his cup as if in salutation: *'Ave Caesar, morituri te salutant...'*

★★★

Manville and Kane stood outside the door to the Dean's Room. A voice from inside called: 'Come!'

The Dean's Room was covered wall-to-wall in tomes from a hundred years of accumulated legal knowledge. Robert Lennox, Dean of Faculty, sat, like a large grey owl, quill in hand and puzzling over the papers in front of him. He did not look up, but continued to scratch his quill on the papers.

Manville made a cursory bow: 'Edward Kane, sir.'

Lennox did not look up: 'Thank you, Manville.'

Manville gave a short bow to the Dean, then to Kane and slipped away.

Kane stood unacknowledged by Lennox for what must have been three minutes before Lennox barked: 'Sit down, man – you're not in the headmaster's study, you know.'

Nevertheless, Kane had a sudden urge to stuff one of the many books down the back of his pinstripe trousers.

Lennox put down his quill, sprinkled some powder over the parchment, blew it off and looked up. He studied Kane's face for a moment: 'Oh, it's you.'

Kane – not knowing how to respond to this obvious truth – raised the index finger of his right hand, like a schoolboy proffering a tenuous answer: 'Yes, Dean of Faculty.'

Lennox stared at him: 'You have no idea why I've called you here, do you?'

'No, Dean of Faculty.'

'Of course not.'

The Dean got out of his chair and leafed through some papers on a nearby table. He pulled out a small bundle of papers bound with pink ribbon: 'Now, Edward....'

Edward, he called me Edward.

Kane should not have been surprised at this. It was a long-standing convention in the Faculty of Advocates that each member called the other by their Christian name. This underlined the collegiate nature of belonging to the Faculty of Advocates.

'Now, Edward, I'm hearing good reports of your work.'

'Thank you, Dean.'

'Good attention to detail, I understand.'

'Yes, Dean.'

'But a good Advocate is not a good Advocate if he exists merely on paper.'

'No, Dean.'

'A good Advocate is a master of the facts, a master of the law, a master of procedure.'

'Yes, Dean.'

'But more than that. A good Advocate is a master of persuasion.'

'Yes, Dean of Faculty.'

'However, you have virtually no experience of appearing in court. Is that correct?'

Kane sighed: 'Unfortunately, Dean of Faculty...'

Lennox held up his hand to stop the reply: 'It is my considered view, young fellow, that your obvious assiduity should be rewarded in the form of a set of instructions.'

The Dean held out the small bundle of papers.

Work. Work! And passed on from the Dean of Faculty himself. The corners of Kane's mouth twitched towards the ceiling.

'Of course,' said the Dean, 'there will be no fee paid for any work undertaken in this particular case...'

The sides of Kane's mouth pointed to the floor.

The Dean continued, 'You are aware, for example, of the operation of the Poor Roll.'

Kane took the papers: 'Certainly, Dean of Faculty. 'The Orphan, the Sick or the Lunatic', I understand to be the vernacular summation of those eligible for the provision of such services.'

'Indeed,' smiled the Dean. 'And I am inviting you, Edward, to participate similarly in a more gratuitous form of representation than would be usual. *Fiat Justicia*, Edward, *Fiat Justicia*. Let justice be done. The Faculty has a long tradition of assisting those who are without the means to do so themselves. This is a comparable species of case. *Pro bono publicae*, Edward.'

Kane had a depressing thought: the Dean may clothe the situation in as much Latin as he wished, but the inevitable translation was that he was expecting a great deal of work to be done for no pay.

'And, pray, Dean of Faculty, to which category does the party belong?'

'To which category, Edward?'

'The Orphan, the Sick or the Lunatic, sir?'

'Why, to none of these categories, my friend. 'Comparable', I said. You will undertake this enterprise as a service to me.'

'To you, Dean of Faculty?'

'These instructions have come for my attention, but since I am connected, by bonds of friendship, to certain parties within the matter, namely Sir Charles Irving, I am unable to accept the instructions here. Thus, I happily transfer them into your care.'

Sir Charles Irving? Kane had never met the gentleman, but it was well known that Sir Charles was responsible for a great deal of employment in the city through his ownership of various businesses and factories. His name was also synonymous with various acts of philanthropy. Sir Charles would be, perhaps, one of the richest men in Edinburgh. Then, why no fee here?

The Dean placed the papers into Kane's hands.

'Edward, while not actively involved in proceedings, I will seek to exercise a measure of control here. From a discreet distance, of course. I hope that that arrangement meets with your approval?'

What else could Kane say? 'Of course, Dean of Faculty.'

The Dean stood up to indicate that the meeting was at an end.

'Well, my friend, I am delighted that we have reached an accommodation on this difficult matter.'

Kane stood up.

'Thank you, Dean of Faculty. I perhaps ought to have asked: what is the nature of the case? Land? Trusts? Or an Interdict matter perhaps?'

'Oh no. When you have perused the papers, Edward, you will discover that you are representing the accused in The Law Criminal.'

'But, Dean of Faculty, I confess that I know little or nothing of that branch...'

'Yes. Did I neglect to mention, my friend, that the charge is that of Murder?'

***

'Murder, Mr K? Murder? And *you*, sir, you?'

Horse was frozen in the middle of brushing Kane's footwear, a shoe in one hand and a brush in the other.

'I'm bound to say, Mr Horse, that it would be of more encouragement to me if your incredulity could be more sensitively expressed.'

Horse resumed with the brush for a moment. And then: 'But did he do it, sir?'

'Sorry?'

'The gentleman in question, Mr K. Did he do the deed?'

Kane removed the bundle of papers from his bag.

'That, Mr Horse, should become apparent once I have studied this surprisingly thin brief.'

Horse continued to brush. Silently.

'Your silence is eloquent. If I had a penny to spare, Mr Horse, I might tender it for your thoughts on the matter.'

'Just minding my thoughts, Mr K. And – begging your pardon – but with you being this poor creature's only hope against the noose, sir, I hope, for his sake, that he's guilty.'

***

Kane's living quarters in the Old Town were by no means commodious, but the rent was suitably cheap. A large sitting room served as the main room, the study and the kitchen – the open fire used for cooking. The space off the sitting room was where Horse slept in the evening and where he kept the various mementos of his military service; and there was a small bedroom for Kane.

Kane pulled out the leaves of the great dining table and laid the instruction papers across it. The charge in the Indictment seemed to tell the entire story of the case against the accused:

..that you PATRICK MACNAIR did seize hold of the body of Martha Cunningham, throw her down a flight of stairs causing her to break her neck and did MURDER her...

The accompanying statements coloured in the rest of the picture:

The accused, Patrick Macnair, was a successful young corn merchant in Edinburgh. After military service, he had purchased a share in the local business and – through sheer hard persistence and an indefinable rough charm – he had now become a major supplier in the area. Despite his modest standing and connections, his wealth had brought him into contact with his social superiors at various events. On one such occasion, he had met Miss Cordelia Irving, the only daughter of Sir Charles Irving. Miss Cordelia Irving and Patrick Macnair formed an immediate relationship of affection and soon wished to be married. Macnair became a frequent visitor to the Irving family home at Heriot Row.

The deceased, Martha Cunningham, was a maidservant within the house at Heriot Row. Macnair came into frequent contact with her. On the evening in question, while Macnair was visiting the house, other servants heard voices, Macnair and the deceased arguing. They then heard a thudding noise and rapid footsteps. When they attended, they found the body of the parlour maid at the foot of the back staircase, with Macnair standing nearby. The Housekeeper, a Mrs Trent, saw Macnair leaning over the body. When asked what had happened, he said nothing and fled the scene quickly. He was later traced to his home and arrested. The accused made no reply to caution and charge. He was currently on remand at Calton prison and was refusing visitors.

Kane frowned. He looked over at Horse, who was now at the boot-polishing stage, cloth in hand.

'Well, Mr K. Have you had one of your 'eureka' moments, sir?'

Kane shook his head helplessly.

'Then, sir, only one thing for it. I'll put the kettle on.'

***

The rest of the papers revealed little information of any moment. The deceased, Martha Cunningham, was a seventeen-year-old girl. She had served the Irving family for some three years. She was pretty, spirited and coquettish. Some noted her as someone who neglected to respect her station at times, exhibiting an inappropriate familiarity with her superiors.

Poor child, thought Kane. *To have her neck snapped like a matchstick.* His reverie was broken by Horse:

'Mr K, sir, have a care to the time.' Horse pointed to a small marble clock on the mantelpiece. 'There's a particular young lady expecting you within the hour.'

Of course. Amanda! With the excitement of the events of the day, Kane had quite forgotten that he was expected to attend his fiancée, Miss Amanda Forbes-Knight, at three o'clock. The time was now approaching two-fifteen. Still, even with a change of clothing, one could walk to from the Old Town to Drummond Place at a relatively comfortable pace and still be on time.

'Mr Horse, I wonder if you would be so kind as to...'

Before Kane could finish, Horse held up a freshly laundered and starched shirt: 'My labours of this morning, sir. Knowing that you would like to be fresh as a daisy for your intended.'

***

Having divested himself of the black jacket and pinstriped trousers, Kane had, a little dandily, adorned himself with his starched shirt, wing collar, top hat, dress coat and walking stick. He walked down, pushing his way through the crowds into Edinburgh's New Town.

Making good time, he reflected on his first meeting with Miss Amanda Forbes-Knight. It was a crowded social event, but Amanda immediately stood out as the prettiest girl in the room. After being introduced, the small talk proved difficult (Amanda being no accomplished conversationalist) but Kane had reached into his fund of Latin learning: 'Of course, Miss Forbes-Knight, you do know the literal meaning of the name 'Amanda'?' The young lady shook her head. 'It means,' Kane continued, 'She Who Requires to Be Loved.' She giggled and nodded, and for the rest of that evening would lower her head and steal glances at Kane and smile. At their next meeting, a quieter affair, Miss Amanda recounted how, some years before, she had lost her mother. Kane told her that his father had also passed. Trauma creates its own kind of intimacy. The connexion was sealed, and after that date, Edward Kane – a young Advocate with prospects – was deemed an acceptable match for Miss Amanda Forbes-Knight.

However, engagement to Amanda came at a price. Amanda's father, Sir John Forbes-Knight was, by all accounts, Scotland's leading physician in the field of surgery. This universal acclaim had always surprised Kane, since, as far as he was aware, every patient of Mr Forbes-Knight appeared to end up dead on the table. Nevertheless, that august physician retained his place at the summit of his profession, amassing substantial wealth in the practice of the opening and closing of individuals. Sir John maintained and refined connections at the very highest stratum of Edinburgh society.

But he was a difficult man. Fiercely protective of two things: his professional reputation and his youngest daughter. And, whenever provided with the opportunity, he would remind Kane of the young Advocate's inherent unworthiness as a suitor.

Kane reached Drummond Place. Only a few decades old now, yet imposing and grand, as if the buildings themselves had always existed, lying in wait to be unveiled and emerge one day to proclaim their effortless superiority.

Kane mounted the stone steps of the exterior. He tugged the brass bell-pull beside the front door and could hear the jangling of the bell inside. Movement, then the door opened slowly.

It was the butler, Chambers. If one were to ask any random passer-by to draw a picture of a butler, then the result would always look remarkably like Chambers. Tall. Thin. Cheeks drawn. Head slightly tilted backwards. Nose forever pointing at five-past midnight. The eyes, hooded, slightly narrowed and always somewhat skeptical. There seemed always to be judgement folded into his conversation, but always polite. Polite as a block of ice. He acknowledged Kane with a slight nod: 'Good afternoon, sir.'

'Good afternoon, Chambers.' Kane went into the entrance hall and looked at the long case clock at the foot of the stairs. 'I hope I haven't kept anyone waiting, Chambers. The pavements did seem particularly populous today.'

'The hanging, sir. It draws the masses.'

'Did you attend, Chambers?'

'I do not attend these occasions myself, sir. The parlour maid and her particular friend relayed the facts. A satisfactory hanging by all accounts.'

'The crowd seemed to enjoy it, Chambers. I was there. You were not tempted to attend this one?'

'Like all popular events, sir, one's attendance results in the reek of a vulgarity best avoided. Shall I take your hat and gloves, sir?'

Kane handed over his hat, gloves and coat – feeling slightly insulted, but not being entirely sure by what.

Chambers placed the items in a coat recess in that great hall.

'If you follow me, sir, Miss Amanda is waiting for you upstairs in the drawing room.'

Kane followed Chambers up the winding staircase and into the three-windowed drawing room. There, sitting there like a perfect rose, was Amanda. She looked up, a beautiful smile spread across her face.

'My own Edward.' She stood up.

'Do not get up, my darling. I should be kneeling at your feet.'

With an imperceptible – but somehow obvious – look of disgust, Chambers spoke:

'If that will be all, Miss Amanda.' Then bowing to Kane on his exit: 'Sir.'

Chambers left them. Kane sat beside Miss Amanda on the love seat.

'You will forgive me, my darling, for my slightly moist state. I required to swim through veritable shoals of passers-by on the way here.'

'Of course,' sighed Miss Amanda 'the public event this morning. Dreadful. Perfectly dreadful.'

'Indeed. I did attend with my man Horse...'

Miss Amanda wrinkled her perfect nose. Horse was not a favourite.

Kane pressed on: '...and I confess that I could not watch that poor creature meet his fate.'

Miss Amanda gave a little laugh: 'No, my darling, you misunderstand me. I meant his crimes. Father says that we should dispense with hanging and boil such miscreants as Charles Makepeace in oil, as was the custom in Tudor times. Father loves all that Tudor rot. Can't get enough of it. Books everywhere. Boiling in oil, Father says that that was the deserved fate of the cook of King Henry the Eighth.'

Kane gave a weak laugh: 'It does seem, my love, a harsh penalty for a soufflé that did not rise...'

Miss Amanda punched his arm.

'No, you silly boy, for poisoning. The cook was boiled in oil for putting poison in the food. That's what Father said. And it does appear to be an apt and consign punishment.'

Kane gave a sickly smile: 'Ah. I see. 'Condign' punishment.'

It should be noted at this point that, while it is said that 'Love Conquers All', on many occasions, it simply 'Papers Over Cracks'. Miss Amanda, for all her many attractive qualities, was not known for her intellectual acuity. There was a moment of silence between them.

Kane ventured, to break the mood: 'Of course, your father is absolutely correct...'

'He is a surgeon, you know...'

'I can imagine that a range of condign punishments could be arranged for the various occupations and professions...'

'Indeed.'

'...and provide for even greater popular entertainment. For example, a rogue banking clerk could be bludgeoned to death with a golden block. Or perhaps asphyxiated with ten-shilling notes inserted down his throat.'

Any expected humorous response from Miss Amanda did not follow. She looked at Kane blankly. Kane soldiered on:

'Or, or, the landlord of the tavern – who watered down his beer – could be drowned in a vat of pure alcohol. Thus preserving his body as a pickled warning to others.'

Miss Amanda. Blank. She continued:

'Father says that the only people worse than the murderers or the cutpurses are those who defend them at criminal trial. The sheer vulgarity and theatricality of the Defence Counsel...'

Kane sighed: 'To be strangled with their own horsehair wigs, I wager...'

Miss Amanda looked blank. Then gave a little genteel laugh. 'Oh, you are a silly boy.'

There followed some fifteen minutes of billing, cooing and amorous conversation, interrupted only by the re-entry of the butler, Chambers.

'I hesitate to interrupt your intercourse, Miss Amanda, but Sir John has requested that I remind you that your lessons are about to begin. The pianoforte and singing tutor has already been in attendance for some ten minutes, miss.'

Miss Amanda got up suddenly. 'My goodness, Chambers. Is that the hour? I shall be there presently. I'll just escort Mr Kane down.'

'No need, miss. I should be happy to show Mr Kane the door.'

'Then I shall receive Mr Brookes in the music room.'

She held Kane's face in her hands for a moment: 'As Shakespeare said, my love: 'Panting is such sweet sorrow...'

Kane corrected her: 'Parting', my sweet, 'Parting' is such sweet sorrow'.'

Miss Amanda laughed carelessly: 'Oh, you lawyer, you!' – and then, like a whisp of fragrant smoke, she was gone.

Chambers led Kane silently down the stairs.

At the foot of the staircase, hat in hand and bundles of papers under his arms, stood an over-confident individual with a rather expansive moustache: the music tutor, Mr Brookes. A shock of hair appeared to be struggling free from a liberal application of oil on that handsome head.

Kane and Brookes gave each other a glancing bow as they passed and both murmured: 'Sir...'

Chambers spoke: 'Mr Brookes, if you would care to join Miss Amanda in the music room, she is now ready to commence her lesson.'

The gentlemen bowed again as Brookes bounded up the grand staircase.

Kane waited for Chambers to bring him his hat and gloves, but there seemed to be no progress on that front. Thus, he initiated a nervous conversation:

'And how is Miss Amanda progressing with her pianoforte studies, Chambers? She seems to have been concentrating on these for a good number of years now.'

Chambers sighed: 'Suffice to invoke the adage, Mr Kane, concerning the building of Rome and the duration of a single day.'

Kane thought to himself that, given the years-long duration of those music lessons, the city of Rome could have been built, destroyed and re-built with matchsticks.

'You will note, Mr Kane that I have not provided you with your hat, coat or gloves, sir.'

'It did strike me, Chambers.' Kane smiled and gave a weak laugh: 'Haven't sold them, have you?'

Chambers ignored the attempt at humour: 'Your visit is not yet at an end, sir. I have instructions from Sir John that once your meeting with Miss Amanda was concluded, he wished to speak you, sir, in his study. Forthwith.'

Kane sighed: 'Then, forthwith it is. Lead on, Chambers...'

***

'What the blazes is going on, Kane, what the blazes are you doing?'

Kane, who had only now entered Sir John's study – and somewhat sheepishly – was not aware that he was actively doing anything.

'I'm sorry, sir...'

'You should be! You should be!'

Sir John Forbes-Knight stood before the great window. Purple storm clouds threatened in the distance. Sir John's massive frame outlined against the astragal windows, his great grey, shaggy beard in furious action, he reminded Kane of an engraving of Moses coming down from the mountain – except here was a Moses incandescent with rage.

'The family, Kane. Did you spare a thought for the family?' His mouth was near-frothing, his eyes were bulging like baubles.

Kane waited for a respite in the torrent.

'Sir John – of course, I apologise for any slight to your family occasioned by my actions, but I am unaware of any conduct that would have led to such a conclusion.'

Sir John was silent for a moment, as if re-grouping his troops for the next assault. Then, 'Murder, sir.'

Kane shook his head: 'Of whom, Sir John?'

'Not of whom. By whom. That is the issue here.'

Kane stood. Stumped. Sir John spoke:

'You have taken instructions, sir, in a trial involving a murderer, have you not?'

The root and meaning of the great surgeon's anger were gradually emerging, like horse and four through a thick fog.

Kane breathed out: 'Ah...'

The giant surgeon was on him again: 'Well might you be speechless, Kane, that your want – nay, desperation! – to secure any legal instruction (for I am apprised daily of your 'prospects', sir) has led you to accept instruction from a notorious blackguard, a murderer – one Patrick Macnair...'

Somewhere within – in a quiet place insulated from that great bellowing –

something struck Kane as odd. Kane had only received the instructions from the Dean of Faculty that morning, and already...

'Do you hear me, Kane, do you hear me? If you lie down with fleas, young man, then you will invariably rise and begin to scratch, sir...'

...and in very private circumstances...

'...and that is more than a medical opinion, sir, which I am unquestionably qualified to render...it is a question of moral backbone...'

...but now, that intelligence appeared to be common knowledge only some hours later.

How did Sir John Forbes-Knight know about this?

'Do you think that my daughter wishes to be betrothed to a man whose daily efforts entail the frustration of justice itself...'

How did he come to learn?

Kane re-surfaced in time for Forbes-Knight's direct question:

'Well, Kane, what have you got to say for yourself?'

At this point Kane remembered the advice of his friend Collins, when discussing the crucial issue of persuasion: 'It is a cornerstone of the practice of advocacy that the good Advocate knows the Law, but the great Advocate knows the Judge...'

Kane looked at the great, trembling figure before him. What were the weak spots in that great fortress? Notions of vanity, perhaps? Or were aspirations of honour the chink in that great and angry armour?

'Sir John, I regret to say that you do me a great wrong. I have accepted these instructions, not for any personal or financial gain, sir, but for honour...'

The great figure raised its bushy eyebrows: 'Honour, sir? Honour?'

'As you are no doubt aware, sir, I was tasked with this enterprise only this morning and tasked by no other person than the Dean of the Faculty of Advocates.'

'I am aware of that, sir. The Dean himself was my visitor here, some thirty minutes ago.'

Ah – so that's how you knew...

'And, Sir John, that request having been made by the Dean himself for the sake of his own propriety...'

'His own propriety?'

'He has a personal connexion with the case, Sir John.'

'A personal connexion?'

'He has a friendship with Sir Charles Irving...'

'As do I...'

'The same Charles Irving in whose home the unfortunate events occurred.'

This seemed to spike the old surgeon's guns and he was silent for a moment.

Having hacked his way through the old man's anger for a moment, Kane had arrived at a clearing, only to find there was no clear path forward.

The great, angry, bear-like figure trembling before Kane stood temporarily stumped: 'And?'

'And...and...' Kane looked around the study in search of inspiration. His eye alighted upon a volume of Tudor portraiture. 'And, Sir Charles, I considered that I should follow the example of...'

'Yes?'

'...of Sir Walter Raleigh...'

'Raleigh? Raleigh?' Sir John frowned 'What the deuce has this to do with Raleigh?'

'Sir John – have you forgotten? When that great queen, Queen Elizabeth was confronted, in the city of London, by a pool of rainwater before her, and she could not easily pass, what did Raleigh do, sir?'

Sir John was proud to exhibit his Tudor learning: 'Well, Kane, Sir Walter Raleigh removed his cloak, sir, and placed it over that pool so that Her Majesty could progress over and through it without sullying herself or her footwear...'

'Precisely. Precisely, Sir John. And so have I prostrated myself, lain down – lain down with the fleas, as you would have it – so that honourable men (such as the Dean of Faculty and – no doubt, yourself, sir) may guarantee the expeditious progress of this unfortunate business while not being drawn into the mire of the whole dirty affair.'

Sir John seemed non-plussed by Kane's answer. He stood stock still, his brows knotted in complex calculation. His eyes narrowed and his nose wrinkled. And then, to Kane's complete surprise, the surgeon grabbed Kane by the hand and gave forth a loud peal of laugher: 'Haha! Capital, my friend, capital. Lennox is a wily fox, isn't he? Not the Dean of Faculty for nothing, old Lennox. So, you conduct the case, the trial is lost, the blackguard Macnair is hanged and justice is done. As you say, Kane, this is not the kind of occupation to which you are suited. It is a masterful stratagem, Kane, masterful. Haha – Lennox, the old fox...'

Kane managed to leave the old surgeon's study with his hand all but shaken off.

The butler, Chambers, led him downstairs, remarking as they descended: 'You appear to have left the master in a better complexion than you found him, sir.'

Their conversation was interrupted when Kane heard the sweet voice of a man singing, coming from the music room. The young Advocate raised his eyebrows and looked at Chambers enquiringly.

'That, Mr Kane, would be the singing voice of Mr Brookes, the music master. It is mellifluous to the ear. The first time.'

As they reached the bottom of the staircase and as Chambers was fetching Kane's coat and other outside garments, the front door of the house flew open.

Kane took a backward step as a vision, all oilskins and umbrella, shook her way into the hall.

'Oh, hello Edward – have you seen this weather?'

The voice belonged to Florence Forbes-Knight, Miss Amanda's older sister.

Florence or 'Florrie' was the eldest of the three Forbes-Knight sisters. Sir John often remarked that if he ever required to open her up in surgery, then he would find the word 'decent' stamped on her heart. No great beauty, perhaps, but warm. Fiercely intelligent, but never ostentatiously so. Florrie Forbes-Knight was, before all else, a friend for all seasons.

'Although, Edward, you already bear the stamp of someone who has recently survived a monsoon – have you come from Father's study?'

Kane nodded wearily.

'Father's not all bad, you know. It's just that his passionate enthusiasms can be somewhat mis-directed.'

Kane smiled: 'My survival on this occasion, Florrie, is due to a scant, but accurate knowledge of an episode of Tudor history.'

Florrie laughed as she shook her umbrella: 'That's the spirit Edward. My stratagem with Father is: when in doubt, be Anne of Cleves. Agree with everything the old man says, make a dignified exit and then quietly reap the benefits.'

At this point the silence was filled with the voice of Brookes, which came floating, beautifully, downstairs. Kane frowned and looked up.

'Yes,' said Florrie, 'Mr Brookes, the music master. I sometimes feel that the only difference between you and him, Edward, is that he is paid handsomely for exerting his attentions on my sister, whereas you are not.'

Kane looked up the staircase and laughed nervously.

Florrie smiled: 'Faced with such an incorporeal rival as Mr Brookes' music, Edward, you have every right to feel somewhat – how shall I put this – 'crotchet-y'.'

Kane felt the release of laughter and gave her a mock bow: 'Madam, I 'quaver' at your proposition.'

The two laughed. There was a momentary silence, and at that moment Kane felt the joy of basking in the warmth of their friendship.

★★★

'Begging your pardon, Mr K, but you looks like you been dragged for a good five miles by a coach and four, sir.'

It was after nine of the clock now and Kane was sitting, exhausted, in his chair by the fire.

'It has been something of a day, Horse. I confess that my head is spinning like a child's top at present.'

Horse handed Kane a full cup of liquid: 'Take this, sir…'

'What is it, Horse?'

'Glasgow Punch, sir.'

'Glasgow Punch?'

'Learned how to make it in the army, sir: sugar, lemon and large splash of rum.'

Kane relented and tested the concoction tentatively: 'You were somewhat sparing with the lemon, Horse.'

'There was no lemon, sir.'

'And the sugar is barely evident.'

'We soon ran out of that, sir.'

'And what did you use in its stead?'

'More rum, sir. Drink up.'

★★★

A distant watchman had called the time: 'Four o'clock and all is well.' Kane lay on his back with his eyes wide open, considering the events of the day.

A day like no other. The hangman's noose. The Dean of Faculty. A murder. His precious Miss Amanda. That infernal music master. And Florrie, dear, dear Florrie. He smiled and listened to the silence around him.

Four o'clock. Too late for the night, too early for the morning. An hour from now, the great city of Edinburgh would rouse from its slumbers and he would hear the hooves of the overnight travellers stilling at nearby inns; the clatter of the milk-man as he ladled his wares into the servants' jugs; the fishmonger loading his cart to deliver to the great houses down the hill in the New Town.

But all that Kane could hear at present was the sound of the gentle rain outside and Horse, moaning in his sleep in the adjoining room.

Horse was a man of good humour while awake, but when asleep, his mind would be threatened by all the horrors of battle. 'No, no, no... duck!... down, my lads, down!... out of the bleedin' way... no, Frenchie, not now, not yet...' Stuck on that spinning carousel in his sleeping hours, Horse would emerge apparently none the worse, refreshed for the day ahead.

Then a single thought blotted out all others, causing Kane to stiffen. A murder trial. Kane had never even seen a murder trial.

I have no idea, no idea what I'm doing...

Chapter Two

Morning. Blinding light as the shutters clattered open.

Kane opened one eye and stared into the dizzying void. Then he heard the voice of Horse:

'Morning, Mr. K. And a fine one it is, sir. All that rain last night, sir – washed the city clean. Here's your hot water, sir – I'll leave it on your dresser.'

As Horse came into focus, Kane could see his outline place a bowl of water on a small dresser in front of the mirror.

'What time is it, Horse?'

'Twenty after seven, sir.'

The pale, flat sunlight struggled through the small windows.

'I'll put on the breakfast while you compose yourself, sir.'

Horse shuffled off, and Kane got up and sat on the side of the bed. Had he slept at all? It hardly felt like it.

Kane removed a chamber pot from under the bed and relieved himself. He could hear Horse whistling in the adjoining room, stoking the fire, clattering the pots and pans and preparing the breakfast things.

Kane went to the mirror. *I look older today,* he thought. He washed his hands in the bowl, unwrapped a towel and went through his shaving kit. He lathered up the soap, lathered up the shaving brush, stuck out his chin and spread the cloud of lather around the lower half of his face. *What about a moustache? Would Amanda prefer me with a moustache?* He took out the razor from the towel, opened it into a wide 'v' shape and began to scrape his face carefully with the blade.

Kane heard the sizzling of breakfast in the pan on the fire in the other room. There would be sausages and yesterday's bread, but toasted and strong tea (the only kind that Horse appeared able to prepare – 'It's the army sir, it does things to a man...').

The young Advocate got dressed and went into the sitting room, where Horse was shepherding three large sausages from a huge frying pan onto an old china plate. Horse looked up and regarded Kane: 'You looks very spruce, sir, very spruce, I say. Tea is on the table.'

Kane sat at the table. The same table that served as his study in the evenings, but now adorned with a crisp white tablecloth, a knife and fork neatly set out for breakfast, and a huge pot of tea in the centre.

'Let me pour you a cuppa, Mr K. Good way to clear them cobwebs.'

Horse set down a cup and saucer on the table and poured the tea – somewhat parlously, thought Kane – from a height, the tea bubbling as it filled the cup.

'I'll just get some milk...'

Horse went over to the window, threw it open, poked his head out and retrieved a cracked white jug from the windowsill. The jug had been covered with a small block of wood, underneath which was a chequered cloth. Horse removed the cloth, sniffed the contents of the jug and pondered for a moment. Then he sniffed again, gave a slight shrug and returned to the table.

Pouring some milk into Kane's cup and stirring in the white globs, Horse smiled: 'Well, sir, I've tasted better and I've tasted worse, but this'll do you no harm.'

Kane sniffed at the cup: 'Is the milk-man late in his rounds, Horse?'

'Milkman's been and gone, sir. But we had a bit if a tussle today because he was looking for this month's money, Mr K. I told him that we'd settle up at the end of the week, 'But,' says he, 'the equation is now very simple: no money equals no milk.' So I says to him: 'Don't give me no Pie-Fagorrases Ferum here. Ow dare you. You should be paying me to get your produce into the china cup of the Advocate what lives here, you cheeky blighter!' So he starts swinging his great big ladle about and he says...'

'I'm sorry to interrupt you here, Mr Horse, but you need continue no further. I have understood the general drift of the conversation.'

'Very well, sir.'

Kane took a sip of his tea. His eyebrows raised sharply.

'I note that there is no diminution in the strength of the tea, Mr Horse.'

Horse looked proud: 'Thank you, sir.'

Kane's eyes searched along the surface of the table: 'Could I trouble you for some sugar?'

'No sugar, sir.'

'No sugar?'

'Well, sir, the story is this: so I was standing at the grocers, sir, and I says 'I'll have some sugar', and the young grocer's boy – a cheeky wretch at the best of times – he says: 'Oh, no you won't. Not until we see the sillar.' So I says 'See the sillar? See the sillar? Wot you talking about, lad? Can't you speak the Queen's English?' And he says: 'The money, the money – you're in Scotland now, you English bun. Learn the language...' So, I grabs him by the neckerchief – like this – until his face, I swear it was turning blue, Mr K – and I says...'

Kane raised both hands to halt the narrative: 'No, no – Mr Horse – you need not proceed. I have your meaning.'

A silence between the gentlemen. Then Horse spoke: 'The long and the short of it is – there ain't no sugar.'

Kane raised the cup to his lips and took a sip. Either the beverage was improving or his tastebuds were growing gradually numb.

'No milk. No sugar. I fear, Mr Horse, that the time has come to consult your friend Mrs Ratchett.'

Horse appeared to have an infinite number of 'friends'. One of whom was Mrs Ratchett. And Mrs Ratchett was the particular friend of the Jewish gentleman, Mr Isaacs. And Mr Isaacs was a pawnbroker. And – as Horse would remind Mrs Ratchett when negotiating a fair transaction – the existence of Mrs Ratchett was an (as yet) unknown fact to Mrs Isaacs, the pawnbroker's wife.

'I fear that time has indeed come, Mr K. And Mrs Ratchett, as you are aware, sir, is the very soul of discretion.' Horse held out his open hand to Kane. 'Your Hunter, if you please.'

Kane took out his Hunter pocket watch from his waistcoat pocket and examined it with some sadness. The watch had belonged to his father and to his grandfather before. On the day that Kane had graduated from the University, his father presented him with the watch and chain, held him by the shoulder and said:

'Edward. I give to you the timepiece that belonged to my own father. And with it, I offer you the same advice he rendered me: Do not squander your time. Do not scatter its precious moments carelessly. Of the many resources in life, Time is one of the few properties that we cannot replace.'

Dead now, his father, these four years. The physician had no adequate explanation other than the old man's heart had 'Stopped like a clock.'

He handed it over to Horse, who smiled: 'Usual terms, sir?'

Kane sighed and nodded.

'What can I say, Mr K – God bless the Annual Pledge. You'll have it back in no time, mark my words – once we get things turned around, sir.'

Kane nodded without much enthusiasm, when their exchange was interrupted by a rather timid knock at the door. Despite the gentleness of the sound, its unexpected occurrence gave both gentlemen a start.

Kane looked at the small marble clock on the mantelpiece: 'Five past eight. Are we expecting anyone, Horse?'

'Not as I know, sir.'

Another timid knock.

'I suppose we had better answer the door, Mr Horse.'

Horse thought for a moment, then picked up the long bread knife from the chopping board.

'I s'pose we better had, sir.'

Horse tucked the bread knife into his belt and made his way towards the door. He stood for a moment, before opening the door quickly and violently.

The door opened to reveal a rather tiny, elderly gentleman dressed for business. A bald pate with streaks of greasy hair flattened down, round spectacles, he was holding his hat in one hand and a briefcase in the other. He stood, quivering slightly, looking for all the world like a startled mole.

Horse glowered at him: 'Yes?'

The Mole narrowed his little eyes and spoke: 'Mr Kane?'

'What do you want? You ain't a debt collector, are ya?'

'Mr Edward Kane?'

'Who wants to know?'

'Mr Kane, my name is Whittle. John Whittle. I am to be your instructing agent, sir.'

An 'instructing agent' – a solicitor. A lawyer who would assist Kane in a law case (and give him work).

Horse looked at him with suspicion: 'What case are you on about?'

Whittle looked around him, before whispering:

'The unfortunate matter in Heriot Row, sir. The regrettable demise of the parlour maid. I am reluctant to name names, sir, in so public a place, you will understand....'

'You mean the murder...'

'The very same, sir.'

There was a moment of silence, then The Mole spoke up again: 'You will forgive me, Mr Kane, but you were not quite what I was expecting...'

Horse clutched Whittle's shoulder and dragged him out of the hallway: 'Shut yer pie-hole and get in here.'

The next few moments entailed the introduction of Mr Whittle to the real Edward Kane (to Whittle's patent relief) while Horse – in what appeared to be a single motion – removed their guest's coat and hat, sat him down at the table and poured him a cup of tea.

Whittle gave a nervous little laugh: 'Your man is very expeditious.'

Kane nodded: 'Ex-military, Mr Whittle. Waterloo, in fact.'

Whittle eyed Horse up and down: 'I have heard it remarked that if every man who claimed to have fought at Waterloo were assembled in one place, then the numbers would far exceed the population of India...'

Horse eyed Whittle, picked up the stale loaf and produced the serrated bread knife from his belt: 'Would you like something cut, sir?'

The Mole involuntarily put his hand to his throat and muttered: 'No, thank you, Mr Horse.'

'You can just call me 'Horse', sir. That was the name that Wellington give me hisself, sir. At Waterloo, sir.'

There was something of an embarrassing pause, then Horse followed up: 'And I didn't see no Indian gentlemen there at the time. I'll leave you to your business.' Horse strode off to his room.

Whittle reached into his briefcase and produced a bundle of papers bound in pink tape.

'I thought, Mr Kane, that you would appreciate the balance of the papers in this case. A very disturbing incident, I must say. And there appears to be no clear account that might exonerate our client.'

'Have you met the client, Mr Whittle?'

Whittle frowned. 'I was able to have a very brief meeting at the police office, sir, but I am bound to say that Mr Macnair was not the easiest of clients.'

'How so?'

Whittle thought for a moment.

'I have worked in the law now, man and boy, for some 45 years, Mr Kane. I have been entrusted with the affairs of clients of all stations, from the meanest bairns' part to the executry of the nobility. But no case has ever troubled my mind in quite this way.'

Whittle was silent for a moment while he collected his thoughts:

'You see, sir, in all my experience of these matters, I have never seen such an accused. Mr Macnair wishes to say nothing.'

Kane put down his cup: 'As is his right, sir. No man requires to incriminate himself.'

'More than that, Mr Kane. The accused simply refuses to give instructions in his defence.'

'Then he is accepting of his guilt.'

'No, sir. He refuses to state his innocence or guilt.'

'Is there the touch of the lunatic about him, Mr Whittle? Do we doubt his capacity?'

'Not at all. I doubt that I have ever met a more sane man in my life. Although, I do hear him mutter – often – under his breath, sir, 'Second to none. Second to none.'

'Very curious.'

'But he presents as a fine, upstanding man. A soldier, sir, who served his country. Also, a person of great mercantile acuity, resulting in considerable means and substantial holdings in property.'

The irony was not lost on Kane, that in order to defend a person of considerable means and property, the young Advocate would require to pawn his own watch.

'And yet, Mr Whittle, we have his case from the Poor Roll. Very curious.'

Whittle frowned: 'I beg your pardon, sir – the Poor Roll?'

'Yes, we are instructed to conduct the matter without fee, are we not?'

'Not in my case, Mr Kane. The fee will be substantial by my reckoning.'

'But, sir...' Kane tried to recall the terms of his clandestine conversation with the Dean of Faculty. Best, perhaps, to leave this matter for a private talk with the Dean.

Kane put his cup onto its saucer: 'In any event, Mr Whittle, what is the next stage in these proceedings?'

'Well, you will require to consult with the client, of course, sir. At the very least, to ascertain if you can obtain clearer instruction in the matter.'

'Where can we find him, Mr Whittle?'

'He has been remanded, Mr Kane, in the Calton.'

'The Calton, Mr Whittle?'

Whittle stood up and closed his briefcase.

'The Calton Jail. I understand, Mr Kane, that it falls within the vagaries of human nature that certain individuals deny the existence of Hell. I would respectfully suggest that they have never visited the Calton Jail. Would tomorrow afternoon be convenient?'

***

Later that morning, Kane resolved to go and watch a murder trial, if he could. Outside the courts at Parliament House, he noticed a group of Macers – the gentlemen who carry the ceremonial Mace into the courtroom to tell the world that the court was now in session.

They stood, smoking their pipes and laughing together.

'Excuse me, gentlemen...'

The Macers looked round and gave him a small bow: 'Mr Kane, sir.'

'I was wondering. I should like to view a criminal trial today. Preferably a murder. Is there a courtroom that you could recommend?'

A silent wave of humour fell over the group. Kane explained: 'As research, gentlemen, for my study purposes.'

One of the older Macers, Andy Andrews, answered him.

'Begging your pardon, Mr Kane. Our amusement was not directed at you, sir. We we're just discussing the trial that's lately finished.'

'With a conviction?'

'No, sir – with an acquittal. 'Not Proven', sir.'

In the legal world of Scotland, there existed a range of options for the jury in a criminal trial: Guilty; Not Guilty; or Not Proven. When a jury returned a verdict of 'Not Proven', the accused was acquitted and walked free.

'Yes, Mr Kane, Not Proven. Didn't take the jury long to come back, sir. By the Court clock, I counted five and thirty minutes.'

'Then the facts must have favoured the accused, Mr Andrews.'

The old Macer smiled: 'Don't know about the facts, sir. The gentleman accused threw another gentleman out of a window. From the third storey landing, sir. Not an appealing sight once he arrived on the pavement, I understand.'

'And, pray, Mr Andrews, who was the Defence Counsel in the case?'

Another ripple of good-humoured laughter spread along the group.

'That would be Mr Norris, sir. N. P. Norris.'

The group laughed and one of them muttered: 'It's N.P. alright!'

Norval Peter Norris, Advocate, had become perhaps the foremost criminal law counsel of his time. The clerks had lost count of the occasions on which they had recorded the initials of N. P. Norris, beside the ultimate verdict of the jury: 'N.P.' for 'Not Proven'.

Andrews pointed towards Parliament House.

'Mr Norris will be in the Reading Room, sir, if you'd like to consult further. He does like a pipe after his exertions.'

Kane bowed his thanks and entered Parliament House.

Kane entered the Reading Room and looked around. Among the Counsel reading their newspapers, drinking their coffee and chatting, was Norris. He was sitting alone at a table by the window, sucking on a long pipe.

A little anxiously, Kane approached him: 'Norval?'

Calling a very senior member of the bar by first name was always odd at first.

N. P. looked up, startled, with a face that told Kane that he was not entirely recognised.

'Norval,' Kane pointed to his own chest 'Norval, it's Edward Kane.'

N. P. stood up and smiled. 'Of course. Of course, it is. I apologise, Edward. You found me deep in thought. Please join me.'

Kane sat down, tentatively.

'I apologise if I have interrupted your thoughts, Norval.'

'No. No. Thank you, Edward. I was musing on the trials of our saviour, Jesus Christ.'

'The trials?'

'You will recall from your studies, Edward, that Our Lord appeared before a number of different judges before verdict and sentencing...'

Kane nodded.

'...before being sentenced to his own gallows: the cross. He appeared, first before the Sanhedrin court of the Jewry, then before the Roman Governor, Pontius Pilate. And what was Pilate's question to Christ, Edward? Do you recall the question of Pontius Pilate?'

This was not the conversation that Kane had been expecting. 'Not offhand, Norval.'

'Pilate asked: 'What is truth? What is truth?'

N. P. sucked on his pipe and muttered to himself: 'What is truth?' He snapped out of his reverie and smiled. 'And so, young Edward, how goes it at your end of the Scottish Bar?'

★★★

Four o'clock in the morning, and Kane could hear the ringing of the great clock at St Giles' Church again. His mind was vexed with the business of the day. He lay there, his mind wandering half in and half out of sleep: *What a curious fellow old N. P. is. He appears to spend his working life frustrating the ends of justice, and his private life ruminating upon the meaning of truth. Small wonder that he appears somewhat detached from this world at times.*

The church bell again. Four and thirty. The moonlight was insistent through the gaps in the shutters now. Better to get up and work, Kane conceded.

He got out of bed, picked up the large, hooked stick that opened the shutters. The moon, like a large, silver florin, illuminated the bedroom.

Kane pulled on his nightcap, dressing gown and slippers. He lit the candle in the holder beside his bed and went into the sitting room.

He had retired wearily after 10 o'clock the previous evening and had left the Macnair papers spread across the table. But as he looked now – nothing. The papers had vanished entirely. Kane stood perplexed, candle in hand, and, on turning round, he was suddenly aware of a blade at his throat.

Horse's face became immediately apologetic.

'Oh, Mr Kane, sir. Begging your pardon, sir. I heard a creeping noise, and you being such a sound sleeper, Mr K...'

'You can perhaps remove the bread knife from such proximity to my throat, Mr Horse.'

Horse lowered the knife.

'Of course, sir. I do apologise, sir. But you can't be too careful...'

The two men looked at each other in the light of the single candle.

'Mr K. – it's that bloomin' case ennit! You can't sleep because of that Macnair case.'

'I confess, Horse, that it troubles me.'

'There's something just plain rum about it, Mr K. That's what's vexing you. Just plain rum, I say.'

Kane sighed and nodded; then pointed at the bare table.

'What happened to my papers?'

'Piled neatly on the chair here, sir. Done it before I retired. Need the table clear for the breakfast cloth in the morning, Mr K.'

'You get back to bed, Horse. I'm going to work here for a couple of hours.'

'Not at all, Mr K. You do your work and I'll put on a brew. You know me, sir. Never needed much sleep.'

It was true. Horse appeared to exist comfortably on four or five hours, perhaps in avoidance of the Waterloo nightmares.

And so, Kane sat at his study-dining table while Horse started the business of the morning. Lighting the fire, boiling the water, stewing the tea. He smiled as he handed Kane a tin mug: 'My old army cup, sir.

Thought you'd like it this morning, you being under siege and all.'

Kane tasted it. Surprisingly consumable. 'Mr Horse, do I detect both fresh milk and a dash of sugar here?'

Horse nodded.

'Did Mrs Ratchett come through, then?'

'Not yet, sir. But there's a new barmaid at the White Hart Inn. She has a soft spot for the military, Mr K. And very obliging, Mr K, if you take my meaning – at least until Friday.'

***

In a week of surprises, another one lay in store that very morning. Shaved, dressed and 'very spruce' (as Horse would have it) Kane arrived at the Advocates Library to find that someone had left him some work to do.

The brief solicitor's letter of instruction presented terse compliments to Counsel and requested Counsel's Opinion on a land boundary dispute.

Ah, two people with limitless funds who wish to best each other over a piece of land worth no more than tuppence! thought Kane.

Large pieces of parchment outlined areas of ownership; hand-written deeds documented changes of title; scrawled dispositions laid out blurry rules concerning the uses of and burdens on the land.

Kane smiled. This was the kind of Law in which he felt comfortable. That said, it was complex material, not the type of work that could be concluded in a day. However, the fee would be welcome and would secure both the outstanding tradesmen's bills and possibly even the recovery of the family fob-watch.

Kane's thoughts were interrupted by the voice of Collins, who nodded towards the large bundle of papers in Kane's hand. 'Well, my friend, you look as if you have obtained gainful employment at last.'

Kane smiled.

'Collins, if you are now at liberty for tea and conversation, then I will recount the acquisition of not one, but two new cases.'

And with that, the two friends made their way into the Reading Room.

***

Collins was attentive to the unusual narrative of his friend. And while listening to that account, Collins pored over the various land documents provided to Kane for the Opinion of Counsel. Half reading, half nodding, sometimes muttering a throaty 'Mm-hmm' of agreement. Ears and eyes always focused, tight lips, frowning with concentration.

Kane was nearing the end of his account: 'So – in the course of 48 short hours, my friend, my fortune appears to have stood on its head.'

Kane was glowing with excitement, but Collins appeared troubled.

'Collins, my dear, you ought, at least to feign happiness at my own good fortune. You of all people understand my recent pecuniary privations.'

'I apologise, Kane, for my somewhat saturnine response to your tale, but I was expecting you to address a complication to your narrative – but that seems to have escaped you.'

Kane was a mixture of hurt and puzzled: 'I regret to say, my friend, that your meaning is far from clear.'

Collins looked anxious: 'As I understand the facts, Edward, you now hold instructions in two separate matters.'

'Yes?'

'One: your defence of the Pannel, Patrick Macnair, accused of the murder of a parlour maid at the home of Sir Charles Irving...'

Kane: 'Yes.'

'...and two: the more recent instruction for you to provide a legal Opinion on a dispute concerning an area of land.'

'That is correct.'

'And who owns the land, Edward?'

Kane examined his cursory letter of instruction. No indication of ownership from that. He rummaged through the papers and retrieved the final land Disposition.

The land was owned by Sir Charles Irving.

***

'Edward Kane, you disappoint me!'

Robert Lennox, Dean of the Faculty of Advocates, stood with his back to Kane and looked out of the window. He turned around suddenly:

'You must learn to be more robust, man. Not wend your way in here every time you have the fragment of a concern.'

'Dean of Faculty...'

'Hold your tongue.'

The Dean had not completed his rebuke. Kane held his tongue.

'You cannot imagine, sir, you cannot imagine the constellation of concerns that fall to be determined by the Dean of the Faculty of Advocates...'

Kane suddenly regretted seeking the Dean's guidance.

'Do you hear me, Kane? Do you hear me?'

Such was the volume of the Dean's remonstration, Kane mused that it was now possible that the population of Glasgow could hear him.

'The ingratitude, sir, the ingratitude, when I have elected you to represent the murderer, Macnair...'

A hopeless affair, now funded by myself...

'...and, by way of recompense, I suggest your name for this!' Lennox pointed to the pile of papers for the land dispute.

Ah. So that is how these instructions came into my hands...

'...and all that I receive in return, is the sight of you, unpacking your heart like a common drab. Get out of my sight, Kane. Get out. Go and do your duty...'

Kane remained seated.

'Are you deaf, man?'

'I beg your pardon, Dean of Faculty, but I wished to clarify a certain matter with you. When you conferred the murder papers on me, and I thank you for those, you stated that it was comparable to the Poor Roll, and yet, it appears...'

'How dare you, you insolent cur. I said no such thing. Get out of my sight, before I have Manville throw you out. Get out!'

And with that, the Dean turned his back on Kane again and began to study the papers in his hands. But Kane noted that those hands were trembling now.

But an awareness of Manville standing at the door told Kane that the meeting was over.

***

'Who would have thought, Mr K, who would have thought that there would be so many good-looking women in Hell.'

Kane and Horse stood in the courtyard of Calton Jail. Far from the hell predicted by Mr Whittle, this resembled a small, pleasant village where a great number of women seemed to come and go, some carrying tiny babies.

Kane nodded: 'I wonder the extent to which, Mr Horse, the fairness of their feature led to the ultimate abandonment of their character.'

A small clump of ladies were now cooing and waving flirtatiously in the direction of the Advocate and his manservant. Horse bowed back at them.

'Mr Horse, what are you doing? Do you know those ladies?'

'Oh, no, sir.' Horse pointed to his face 'I just have a wery friendly mug, sir.'

Kane regarded his manservant's face. Broken nose, cheeky smile from a mouth lacking the full complement of teeth. Friendly as a snarling guard dog. Yet in a curious twist of human nature, the more battered that Horse's face became, the more desirable he seemed to be.

Kane's musings were interrupted by the sound of panting. Mr Whittle had not been at the front gate to meet them as planned, but now came bustling towards them.

'I am so sorry, gentlemen. I do apologise. My carriage...'

Horse cut in: 'We thought you was stuck, sir. Maybe stuck in India...'

'...my carriage had been carefully arranged for our meeting, but as you will be aware from your own travels here, an incident in Leith appears to have spilled over into the route to the prison here, and consequently...'

Horse interrupted The Mole: 'We walked, sir. We just got 'ere.'

Whittle's face was covered in incredulity: 'Walked, sir. Walked?'

Of course, they had walked. Negotiations had not yet been concluded satisfactorily with the pawnbroker's particular friend, Mrs Ratchett, and thus funds were spared in the journey between the Old Town and the prison.

The walk itself had not been onerous, although Calton Hill proved a substantial ascent immediately before the prison. At its summit stood Calton Jail. Beautiful, imperious and often mistaken by visitors to be Edinburgh Castle.

Kane spoke: 'It was such a fine day, Mr Whittle, we thought that we should walk in some of God's good air. And a very pleasant stroll it was too, sir.'

Whittle was not listening now. He was looking at his surroundings with patent disgust on his face.

'As I advised, gentlemen, Hell on earth.'

Despite this fixed view, a small clump of women were now smiling and giving fluttery waves of their fingers in Whittle's direction, while he was sneaking horrified glances in return.

Horse took his chance: 'Those ladies, sir. Seem to know you. Know you well, sir.'

'Don't be ridiculous.' The Mole sweated now.

'They do seem wery familiar with you, personally, if you do not mind me saying so, sir.'

Kane interrupted Horse's fun: 'Well, Mr Horse, our instructing solicitor, Mr Whittle, has already explained that, in his time, he has required to represent a number of different clients ranging from the nobility to the deserving poor. No doubt one of these ladies has benefitted from his services at one time or another.'

Horse leered: 'Thank you, sir. I was just thinkin' that somebody had rendered somebody a service here...'

At this point, they were interrupted by a brutal-looking prison warder: 'Youse looking for something, gents? A wee short time with these ladies here, maybe? I can do you a good price for the three of them...'

The Mole began to splutter: 'How, how dare you...'

Horse studied the warder's face: 'Johnny? Johnny Brand? My old friend. How you been, my boy?'

The warder looked surprised, then: 'Horse, ma old pal, Horse. I heard you were deid...'

'Yes, and I heard you was 'andsome. Turns out we was both wrong, eh?'

The warder bent over with laughter. 'Ah, ye huvnae changed, huv ye? Same old Horse! Is that you back in the jail again, boy?'

Whittle thought: *Again?*

'No, no, Johnny, me old friend, I am the wery pillar of respectability now. I am now accompanying these fine gentlemen – a law agent and an Advocate, no less...'

The warden suddenly grabbed The Mole's hand and started shaking it vigorously. An honour, sir, never met an Advocate before.'

Horse smiled at Kane but did nothing to correct him.

'And, Johnny, we have come for to see our client, a Mr Macnair.'

'You mean Paddy Macnair?'

'That's the gent.'

'Mr Patrick Macnair, 'The Parlour Maid Murderer?'

'Who's been filling that head of yours with rumour and nonsense, Johnny?'

'Well, that's what it says in all the newspapers...'

Horse sighed: 'And since when, Johnny Brand, since when did you learn to read?'

The warden shuffled uncomfortably and looked at his feet.

'Well, that's fur me to know, Horse. Fur me to know. But, even the prison chaplain here says that it was printed plain as day, in black and in white, he says, in The Scotsman newspaper itself, so it must be true —

'Patrick Macnair – The Parlour Maid Murderer'. So put that in yer pipe, Mr Horse, and you have a smoke of that!'

'Oh, Johnny, my Johnny. I have missed that great mind of yours.'

The warder beamed.

'But enough of this chatter, me old friend. Lay on and take us to that famous woman killer, then.'

'Alright. If you gents would follow me, I'll take youse to his billet. It's not what youse might call swanky, but I've seen worser. I've told him there was visitors on the list, so he'll be expecting you.'

Kane and The Mole were led on by the warder. Horse, following on, gave the group of smirking women a cheery (if somewhat leery) wink.

★★★

Patrick Macnair, The Parlour Maid Murderer, was not quite what Kane was expecting.

Macnair was bent double, muttering to himself. The small cell had bare walls, a wooden cot in the corner with piss-pot under the bed. Underneath the barred window stood a chair and a desk with a black, battered bible on top.

'He disnae say much, gentlemen. And when he does, it doesn't mean a lot. I'll fetch ye some chairs.'

The warder left them. They stood for a moment, but Macnair appeared oblivious to their presence.

The Mole attempted to break the ice: 'Mr Macnair? Mr Macnair? It's me. Whittle. Whittle, sir. From the Police Office. Where you were charged, sir.'

This evoked no response. Whittle turned to Kane and Horse and shrugged. 'As I was telling you, sirs.'

Horse looked at Kane for permission.

'Would you mind, sir?'

Kane nodded.

A pause. Then Horse barked an ear-shattering command.

'Soldier! Stand to attention for your betters!'

In a single action, Macnair was on his feet, ramrod-straight-backed and facing forward.

Horse bellowed: 'Let me present to you, Mr Edward Kane, Advocate. Here to question you with the intention of aiding your cause, soldier. Don't you forget that.'

Macnair addressed the company for the first time: 'Yes, sir.'

Kane didn't quite know what to say to what now appeared to be the toy tin soldier before him: 'You may, eh, you may...'

He looked towards Horse for help in the matter. Horse barked: 'At ease soldier. Sit down, man.'

Macnair seemed more humanly animated now.

'Apologies, gentlemen. You find me in the depths of despair, I confess.'

He spoke to Kane direct: 'Allow me to fetch you the chair, sir.'

And with that, he removed the chair from under the desk, wiped the seat of it with his sleeve, and placed it beside Kane to sit on. Again, Kane was not quite sure of the protocol of the situation, but soon felt Horse's hands on his shoulders – pushing him down on to the chair.

'Thank you, Mr Horse...'

Macnair peered at Horse's face for a moment: 'Horse?'

Horse was quick to cut this off: 'Mr Kane, here, is going to represent you – out of the goodness of his heart, I must say – and I wants you to be particularly polite to his questions. Understand me, soldier?'

Macnair nodded.

Horse continued: 'Now, sit down on yer bunk, man, and do as yer told.'

Macnair slumped down on his bunk and seemed, initially, to be intent on resuming his bent-double posture, but a violent clearing of Horse's throat soon brought him back to the upright position.

Kane spoke to him gently.

'How are they treating you here, Mr Macnair?'

Macnair thought for a moment and then: 'Well enough, sir. Well enough. I was in the service of his majesty for a time, and so the rough billeting is not unfamiliar.'

'In the service of his majesty?'

'Royal Scots Greys, sir. Second Dragoons.'

'You are very thin, sir. Are they feeding you adequately?'

Macnair smiled: 'Adequately enough. If you care for a diet of porridge.'

For the first time, thought Kane, here in this small attempt at humour is a glimpse of the successful man of business, of boyish charm, perhaps, a certain twinkle in the eye, a glimpse of the suitor of the daughter of a knight of the realm.

'You understand why we are here, Macnair?'

The gloom descended again. 'I understand why you are here, Mr Kane, and I thank you for your interest in my welfare. The larger question is how you come to be here in the first place. I have instructed no defence.'

'If you truly did murder the parlour maid, Macnair, I can appeal for clemency on your behalf. There are perhaps mitigating circumstances...'

'I have no defence to offer, Mr Kane.'

'Then, if I you are accepting of your guilt...'

'I fear, Mr Kane, that you hear, but you do not listen.'

Kane motioned to Whittle, who produced some of the case documents from his briefcase.

'I wonder if I might clarify some of the more obscure factors of the case with you.'

Kane read through the papers. 'Yes, here. At least one of the witnesses...'

Macnair quickly interrupted him: 'There were no witnesses present at the event, sir.'

Kane ploughed on: 'Of the witnesses who heard the events, the cook, a Mrs Bolton, said that even after you had thrown the unfortunate girl down the stairs that you continued to speak to her. Is that correct?'

'I have no comment to make.'

'Were you in some sort of dispute with her, Macnair?'

'No.'

'Had she survived the fall, Macnair?'

'I have no comment.'

'What did you discuss?'

'I have nothing to say.'

'I hesitate to ask, sir, but was there, perhaps, an improper connexion between you and the unfortunate parlour maid, Mr Macnair?'

'I have no comment.'

'Did she, perhaps, threaten to reveal a tryst to your fiancée, Miss Cordelia Irving.'

'I have no comment to make.'

'Is that perhaps the truth of it, Macnair?'

'Ridiculous, sir. I love miss Cordelia more than life itself. I would never, never, I say...'

'And so, when the parlour maid threatened to disclose your murky and illicit connexion, sir, you took hold of her and you threw her down that staircase...'

'Fantasy!'

'Because you were in danger of being blackmailed, Macnair, was that not it?'

'I have no comment to make...'

'You have neither confirmed nor denied that you were the malefactor here, sir.'

'Stuff and nonsense...'

'And if you were being blackmailed, Macnair, the jury might understand that. It was an unfortunate accident. You were trying, perhaps, to restrain the young girl, she struggled and she fell. Was that it?'

Macnair thought for a moment. Then shook his head: 'No. That is not how it transpired, sir.'

'Then what did you speak about, just before the girl died, Macnair? After she had come down the stairs?'

Macnair sat. Lost in thought.

At that point, the silence was broken by a clattering noise. The warder,

Brand, had finally returned carrying two chairs on one arm and one chair on another.

'Yee'd think that there would be nothin' but chairs in this place – but think again.'

Macnair stood up. 'Warder, I thank you for your pains here, but I'm afraid that these gentlemen are leaving. And they are leaving now.'

★★★

Before the gates of the great Calton Prison, Kane looked down at the winding streets of Edinburgh, seeking an answer along the smoky rooftops.

Whittle broke the silence.

'Well, sirs, you now see for yourselves the challenges that I described to you.'

Kane nodded. He felt as if his arms and legs were rooted to the spot. *There must be an answer here.*

The Mole examined his fob watch: 'I note the time, gentlemen. I am afraid that I have other, more pressing, business to which I must attend.'

Horse made a sideways glance at Kane: more pressing than the prospect of the gallows?

'And, fortuitously, here are two coaches approaching. I shall secure one for each of us.'

Behind Mr Whittle's back, Horse made a cut-throat sign to Kane that indicated that the expense of such a coach was not entirely in accordance with that day's budget.

Kane raised his hand: 'Please, Mr Whittle, do not trouble yourself...'

'No trouble at all, sir. No trouble at all.'

And with that, Whittle proceeded to wave down the two coaches.

Behind Whittle's back, Kane saw Horse mimic a clenched fist and an imaginary – but completely satisfying – assault on the person of The Mole.

But before the hiring of the cabs could be confirmed, Kane heard a voice call his name.

'Edward? Edward?'

Kane looked round at the prison gates, and there, outside, stood Florrie Forbes-Knight.

She waved, accompanied by her companion, Miss Black, and the two ladies approached.

'Edward! I thought it was you! What on earth are you doing in Calton Jail?'

'At the risk of being branded pedantic, Florrie, I am on the outside of the prison.'

'I am relieved to hear it.' She smiled.

'And before we embark on a more detailed discussion of the relative blackness of pots and kettles, why am I finding Miss Florence Forbes-Knight in the curtilage of this notorious establishment?'

'Oh, Edward, I do like it when you are so... so grandiloquent!'

Kane began to blush now.

'Every inch the eloquent Advocate that appears in our highest courts.'

Kane looked at the floor: *not lately*.

'Miss Black and I...' Florrie indicated the lady on her left, 'I'm sorry, have you met Miss Black?'

'I don't think that I have had that pleasure.' Kane removed his hat and gave a little bow. 'Edward Kane. At your service, miss.'

Miss Black gave a curtsey.

Florrie continued: 'And this is his man, Mr Horse...'

Horse tapped his head with his right index finger and gave a little bow: 'Ma'am.'

'Well, my dear Florrie...'

But Florrie's question was interrupted by The Mole, who had now secured the services of not one, but two cabs.

'Excuse me, ladies. Mr Kane, your carriage is waiting.'

Kane sighed. Then Florrie spoke. 'Oh, I'm sorry, Edward. Miss Black and I were about to make our way back into the New Town.'

'I suppose, then, that we could give you a ride in our carriage...'

Horse sighed and raised his eyes to the sky at the sheer expense.

Florrie motioned to the great vista of Edinburgh below them. 'Oh, Edward, it is such a beautiful day, we thought that we might travel on foot...'

Horse jumped in: 'Begging your pardon, miss, but there are some streets on the way that a respectable person like yourself should not cross. Not cross alone, that is. Me and Mr Kane here would be happy to be your chappy...your chappy...'

'Chaperones, Mr Horse?'

'That's it, miss. Chappy-rones.'

Kane gave a nervous laugh: 'I'm afraid Florrie that Mr Horse's major experience of French is... shooting at them.'

Florrie smiled: 'Chaperones! What a splendid idea! Miss Black – we have been entertaining angels unawares.'

The Mole remained standing there – with his two cabs at the ready. Horse turned to Whittle. 'And you, sir, can tell that cabbie to sling his hook as well.'

Whittle attempted to harrumph his displeasure, but the party had already turned to leave.

★★★

It was such a beautiful day as they walked into town. Kane and Florrie walked as a pair in front, while Horse entertained Miss Black just behind them.

'And so, Florrie, I am still ignorant of why a Forbes-Knight daughter was seen in the midst of the deprivation of the Calton Jail?'

'I promise to tell you, Edward, if you promise to tell me why you were there. I did not take you for – as my father would have it: 'One of those blackguard Criminal Defence Counsel'.'

Kane smiled and gave a short bow: 'No – I insist – ladies first...'

'Very well, Edward. My own visit there was prompted by Matthew

25: 'I was sick, and ye visited me; I was in prison, and ye came unto me...' Curious, is it not, that we commonly narrow our attention to the prohibitions of Scripture while avoiding those active commands to do good.'

Kane was touched by Florrie's speech and didn't quite know what to say. He blurted:

'Well, judging from the individuals we encountered in the courtyard, Florrie, they did not appear to require food or clothing. Indeed, they appeared intent on persisting in certain forms of gainful – if somewhat dubious – employment...'

Florrie stopped: 'Edward, you are so naive. Do you imagine that those poor creatures would so depend on such an occupation if they could read? If they could write? If they could practise a trade?'

Kane began to blush.

'Oh, Edward. I am sorry. I have embarrassed you.'

'Florrie, it is merely the consciousness of my own stupidity that rushes into my cheeks at these moments.'

'Father despairs of me, you know. He says that I shall never marry. Too shrewish, apparently. Too plain and, quite simply, too bookish. And I reply that it is neither shrewish nor bookish to express an opinion on matters.'

'I have first-hand experience of your father's displeasure.'

'Father doesn't believe that women should have an opinion at all. But I told him, 'The Lord created Eve to be the helpmeet of Adam. Eve would be of no practical use to Adam if she were simply to remain quiet at all times, would she?'

'An excellent point, Miss Forbes-Knight.' Then, with an affectionate smile: 'Although it was a pity about all that apple business, wasn't it?'

Florrie stopped in her tracks. Then, on seeing Kane's beaming face, teasing her now – she promptly dug him in the ribs.

'And so, my dear Edward – in answer to your impertinent question – Miss Black and I, and a group of others, attend at the gaol to provide lessons such as reading and writing to those poor unfortunate creatures and to the innocent children imprisoned with them.'

This was a complete answer, and Kane could think of no appropriate riposte, so the friends walked along in silence in the sunshine.

As they approached the Great London Road, Florrie spoke: 'It was the Parlour Maid Murderer, wasn't it? That's why you were at the prison, Edward. You were visiting Patrick Macnair, whom the press have named 'the Parlour Maid Murderer'.'

'How on earth...?'

'It was Father. Father was holding forth at the breakfast table. He told us all about it. Of course, he wasn't at all happy at first, but he seems entirely sanguine about it now. Apparently, you are to represent the poor fellow at the murder trial, and a good hanging is guaranteed soon afterwards. Father's words, not mine.'

'Well, your father's estimation of my abilities...'

'Don't worry. I have long accepted that Father considers himself the sun around which all other concerns must orbit.'

'He can assuredly exert a great quantity of heat.'

'But rest assured, Edward, now that Father is convinced that you will play a part in the ultimate hanging of the felon in question, then he considers you 'a capital fellow'.'

The party of four reached the Great London Road and began to head west.

'Are you allowed to speak of it, Edward?'

'Of what, pray?'

'Of your dealings with the notour murderer, Patrick Macnair? He seemed pleasant enough to me.'

'You have had dealings with him, Florrie?'

'We have been introduced. Socially. He did not seem like a killer at the time. Charming, yes. Trying to better himself – that was obvious, and should be commended. But a murderer?' Florrie shook her head. 'But please, Edward, do not feel you must betray any confidences of your meeting with him.'

'Florrie – if only there were confidences to betray. The fellow is perfectly mute on the matter.'

'Then he has not confessed?'

'Neither confessed, nor denied.'

Florrie stopped again: 'Then what are you to do?'

'What indeed?'

At that point they heard a squeal of laughter from behind them. Horse was regaling Miss Black with stories of his army days.

Florrie motioned towards Horse. 'Your man appears to have a way for entertaining ladies. Miss Black seems quite taken with him.'

Kane smiled: 'Mr Horse is simultaneously the most transparent and the most mysterious individual I have ever met.' They walked on, enjoying each other's company.

Then Florrie ventured: 'Is that not part of the mystery with Patrick Macnair?'

'In what sense?'

'On the occasions on which I met him, one could not fail to notice that he was charming.'

'I could believe so.'

'No woman in the room was safe from his outrageous flattery.'

'Including yourself, Florrie?' asked Kane with a smirk.

'Oh, not me, Edward. He could do better than me. And he knew it.' Kane shook his head. It struck him that a lifetime of living in the shadow of a prettier, younger sister had left Florrie blind to her own loveliness. But he said nothing.

Florrie continued, narrowing her eyes in concentration. 'My own theory is that here we have a man from the lower orders. After a great deal of hard work and application, he finds himself in an exalted position upstairs. But, all the while, he retains something of an appetite for downstairs...'

'The maid, you mean?'

'I saw that poor creature on a number of occasions – the Irvings are near neighbours. A pretty girl, rather coquettish and – by all accounts – very obliging.'

'You are not the first to say that.'

'The gossip – and it is no more than gossip – is that Macnair killed her in a frenzy of what the French would term 'Crime Passionelle'. Might that be the answer here, Edward?'

Kane pursed his lips. 'Florrie, of the few words that I extracted from the fellow, there was a complete denial of such a suggestion. In any event, I am given to understand that his intended is no less comely in appearance.'

'Oh – Miss Cordelia Irving.'

Florrie was silent, then smiled: 'Edward, have you met Miss Cordelia Irving?'

'I can't say that I've had the pleasure.'

Florrie mocked the low, purring voice of a femme fatale: 'Cordeee – lia Irrr-vinggggg.' Florrie laughed: 'Oh, Edward, my poor Edward. I have this sudden vision of Cordelia Irving as a very bright flame. And of you, Edward, as one more poor moth...'

Chapter Three

The following morning, as Kane was sitting at his spot in the Advocates Library, one of Manville's men brought him a little note.

'It was brought by a messenger boy. From the solicitors, sir. He says he'll wait for a response.'

Kane unfolded the note:

> *Dear Sir*
>
> *Sir Michael Coates v Sir Charles Irving*
> *Our client: Sir Charles Irving*
>
> *We should be grateful if you could attend a consultation with Sir Charles in respect of our letter of instruction of 15th inst.*
> *Would a time of seven o'clock this evening be convenient? Our Mr Malcolm will be at our offices to receive you at that time.*
> *We await your reply by return.*
>
> *Yours faithfully...*

And the note was signed by the Mr John Malcolm, Senior Partner, Malcolm and Co.

Kane crossed out the writing and scribbled at the bottom of the page:

I shall attend as instructed.

Yours etc.

Edward Kane, Advocate.

He handed the note back to the servitor and tried to resume his work.

Seven o' clock in the evening? The offices should be closed at that hour. But, of course, when one has an extremely wealthy client, no doubt making certain demands, then what does it matter what it is o' clock?

★★★

'Seven o' clock, Mr K? Seven o'clock? What kind of heathen works at seven o'clock?'

'Well, Mr Horse. As the adage tells us: 'He who pays the piper will call the tune'.'

'The bloomin' cheek of it, Mr K. Of course, I will have to accompany you. To make sure it's not a trap, and all.'

Kane laughed. 'A trap? Horse, I hardly think that Sir Charles Irving, a Knight of the Realm, is lying in wait for a humble Advocate.'

'I've heard things, Mr K.'

'No successful man is without his detractors, Horse.'

'No, sir. I mean under-the-table sorts of things. I mean, how do you think he made all that money? It's him should be in jail, sir.'

Kane had heard murmurings of the appalling conditions in the factories owned by Irving. Some of the workers had begun to call the main factory, 'the workhouse'. It was also said, in the deepest of whispers, that Sir Charles had his 'favourites', girls in their mid-teens, whose duties tended to be lighter and who seemed to have more money to spend at the end of every week.

The young ladies in question – whom Sir Charles had named 'The Sea Nymphs' – were taken into Sir Charles' office on a daily basis for some twenty minutes of 'personal instruction'. This, ostensibly, was to improve their knowledge of Scripture. Martha Cunningham, the deceased parlour maid, had been such a Sea Nymph, transplanted from the factory to the family home at the request of Sir Charles.

'My dear Horse, if every transgression of our nobility were brought to account, then I fear we should have to build a prison on every street corner, but the plain fact is this: I am entrusted to represent the interests of Sir Charles Irving in this land dispute. It is my bounden duty to do my utmost in that respect.'

Horse harrumphed.

'And... and I fully intend to present myself at the offices of his law agents at seven of the clock this evening. Alone. So, may I suggest that you, Mr Horse, more intently press your friend Mrs Ratchett to conclude a reasonable bargain in respect of my timepiece.'

Horse turned around and looked out of the window. It was growing dark.

'So you won't be needing me or me Aunty Betty, then?'

'Mr Horse, have the rest of the evening to yourself. It will be a welcome break from the mystery and madness of this case.'

Horse nodded, smiled and savoured the words: 'Mystery and madness, sir. Mystery and madness. Very good. You can use them words to the jury just before they hang him.'

**

Kane arrived at the solicitors' New Town offices on the stroke of seven. It was dark by this time, and on approaching the building, he was dismayed to see that the offices appeared to be closed, with no light in the windows.

He pulled on the front doorbell and heard it ring deep inside the building. No immediate sign of life within. He rapped on the door with the tip of his walking cane. Nothing. He bent over and peered through the letterbox. A light glowed in one of the inner rooms. A door opened, and Kane could see a tall gentleman, dressed for business, holding a candle and now coming towards the front door. The door opened with a rustle and jangle of keys.

The tall man, like a scrawny eagle, peered down at Kane. His voice dripped with entitlement: 'Are you Kane the Advocate?'

Kane doffed his hat and nodded.

'Come in for a moment. I'm John Malcolm...' he pronounced it 'Moll-cum' '... the senior partner here. How do you do, sir.'

They did not shake hands, as was the custom for Edinburgh solicitors and Advocates.

Kane gave a slight bow: 'Edward Kane, at your service, Mr Malcolm.'

Inside the solicitor's offices, it was clear that the building had shut up shop for the night. An empty, cold feeling now filled the great space. Kane looked around at the grand entrance and made polite conversation: 'These are very commodious surroundings, Mister Malcolm.'

Malcolm nodded, but proceeded to retrieve his coat and hat from a series of coat pegs in that great atrium.

Kane gave a little laugh: 'Would it not be more conducive to sit by a warm fire within, Mr Malcolm, than to require to wear our outdoor coats during the consultation.'

Malcolm gave a disapproving look: 'The consultation will not be here, sir. It will be at the home of Sir Charles. At Heriot Row.'

'But, I thought from the letter...'

Malcolm retorted somewhat sniffily: 'A close examination of the letter, sir, would have shown you no such thing. I do hope that the quality of your written work exceeds your general powers of observation.'

And with that, Malcolm exited and waited for Kane to follow.

Outside the offices, Malcolm produced a great key and locked the door on that repository of Edinburgh's Old Money secrets.

After the short walk to Heriot Row, Malcolm led Kane not to the front door, but to the alley that served the back of the house.

'You appear surprised, Mr Kane.'

'I confess, Mr Malcolm, that I have never before entered such a house through the tradesmen's entrance.'

Malcolm shook his head impatiently: 'Mr Kane, do not delude yourself that you are invited here as a guest of Sir Charles. You and I are both here on a footing of master and servant. Your wig and gown may endow you with a special status within our courts, sir, but in this gentleman's home you are no less an employee than the cook, or dare I say it, the parlour maid.'

And with that, Malcolm gave the back door of the great house a loud knock, in an odd rhythm.

Whispering behind the door was quickly followed by an elderly lady's head, which popped out to study the faces of both Kane and Malcolm before the door slammed shut again. More whispering, then the door opened at a more leisurely pace. This time, it was the butler, a certain Mr Hand with a narrow cadaverous face and pale long-fingered hands. He greeted both of the visitors with a reserved civility.

'Mr Malcolm, please come in. And I presume that you are Mr Kane? Let me take your hats and coats, gentlemen.'

The pallid Mr Hand led both gentlemen up a narrow, stone back staircase.

'If you would follow me, gentlemen. Sir Charles is expecting you in the study.'

On what Kane calculated to be the second floor, Hand led them through a door which revealed a glorious warm fire. Sat in front of the fire in a comfortable armchair was a man who appeared to be asleep. The gentleman – whom Kane assessed as some eighty years old – wore a brocaded dressing gown and slippers, and a pipe lay smoking in the ornamental ashtray on a small table at his side.

Hand crept to his master's side and gingerly touched the old man's shoulder: 'Sir Charles? Sir Charles?'

The old man opened his eyes gradually, unsure of where he was. As the old gentleman surfaced from sleep, his entire demeanour began to change. The gentle, wrinkled face began to convulse with spasms that shut and open the eyes rapidly. The mouth began to clench and open, with teeth bared, then lips pursed. The head began to shake, as if shaking off an invisible adversary. The whole process was like a clear glass bottle being filled up with dirty water.

The old man coughed and spluttered for a moment, and then the real Sir Charles Irving emerged. Strangely younger now, more vigorous, lustier.

He waved them in: 'Come in, gentlemen, come in. Sit down.'

Two seats had been placed before the old man's chair for Kane and Malcolm. Malcolm spoke:

'Sir Charles, may I introduce...'

Irving waved him away: 'Yes, yes, of course. You'll be Kane, the young Advocate...'

'How do you do, sir...'

Irving coughed into a handkerchief: 'Yes, yes, we can dispense with all that.'

Sir Charles leaned forward in his chair: 'Now, what's the answer, Kane, what is the answer?'

Kane was taken aback now. His inability to answer largely stemmed from the fact that he had no idea what the question was.

'Well, Sir Charles...'

Malcolm threw him a lifeline: 'Sir Charles, the letter of instruction posed a number of different and complex questions for Counsel to consider. To which question do you refer?'

The old man scowled and waved his handkerchief: 'Damn your eyes, man – the only question worth a fig here: are we going to win or are we not? What is your answer? Win or not?'

Kane considered for a moment, then: 'In a word, Sir Charles: Not.'

The old man uttered a spluttering laugh: 'Of course not! An idiot child could tell you that. Of course we could never 'win', in that very narrow sense. But the remaining question is this: to what extent are we able to make the other party's life a misery, eh? My old adversary, Sir Michael Coates. To what extent can we drag this case through the courts and make a victory of sheer inconvenience? The single sleepless night of an adversary is worth a king's ransom.'

'Is that entirely proper, Sir Charles?' ventured Kane.

'Are you deaf, man? Are you deaf? I'm not asking you what is 'proper' – I'm asking you what is legal...'

Kane sat in silence, increasingly uncomfortable.

'Mr Kane, I have acted for Sir Charles these many years and what I understand him to be asking sir is this:'

Malcolm counted on his fingers:

'First, does Sir Charles have any prospect of success in the matter, no matter how slim and secondly, if such a prospect exists, and he wished to press that claim to the utmost...'

Kane looked over and saw Irving smiling and nodding vigorously.

'...to the utmost, sir, then what would be the appropriate procedure, given every crucial fact in the case may have to be examined thoroughly in the ultimate course of a proof?'

Kane pondered Malcolm's questions, all the while musing that he had never seen such dirty work performed with the appearance of such clean hands.

They sat in silence while Kane considered. The moment was broken by Irving: 'Well, that will be all, gentlemen. Go away and think about it and we will consult again. Mr Malcolm, if you retire for a moment with my man, Mr Hand, then he will pay you immediately for your services to date. Oh, and we'll pay the young fellow here too. We'll call it a down payment on a future relationship, shall we, Mr Kane?'

Malcolm rose from his seat and smiled: 'That would be most welcome, Sir Charles.'

'Mr Hand, take Malcolm here to the safe in the basement. Young Mr Kane can remain with me.' He leered at Kane. 'Don't want too many people knowing exactly where the treasures lie, do we? Malcolm knows. But then, Malcolm, you know everything, don't you?'

Malcolm gave a small bow and left with Hand.

Kane and the old man sat before the fire in silence.

The study was very pleasing. Several portraits hung on the walls, some with faces bearing a likeness to Sir Charles. A pair of antique pistols hung above the fireplace. Books of all types, some obviously very rare, filled the ornate bookshelves. A small, but exquisite, antique Davenport desk sat in the corner of the room, although it was dwarfed by another huge, rugged oaken desk that lay covered in papers and ledgers.

The old man spoke: 'You are admiring the small Davenport writing bureau, Kane.'

'I am, Sir Charles. It is very unusual.'

'No doubt, it would make a fine addition to your own study, young fellow?'

Kane smiled and nodded, remembering his own desk – an old dinner table from which he had recently eaten watery mutton stew.

'I won the desk in a wager, you know.'

'That was fortunate, sir.'

'Oh no, Kane, oh no – there was nothing 'fortunate' about it. You see, I am fond of a bet, but I would never gamble.'

Kane had no idea what as to the old man's meaning, and politely told him so.

'You see, young fellow, gambling involves a measure of uncertainty. My own approach is to remove any area of uncertainty – and then place the wager. Do you catch my meaning, sir?'

'I think that I grasp the principle, Sir Charles, but removing every uncertainty would surely prove an impossibility.'

'Look around you, Kane. Look around you. Everything you see, everything you know about me, my status, my possessions, my very wealth – all accumulated from a life where I have removed all possible uncertainties – and then I make my move. Do you understand me?'

The old man stared at Kane. Kane tugged at his collar and gave a nervous laugh: 'You do keep your study uncommonly warm, Sir Charles.'

Irving sat back in his chair.

'I have been somewhat indisposed of late. And that has rather slowed me down, I regret to say.'

They sat in silence.

'So, you like the desk, do you?'

'It is certainly a remarkable piece, Sir Charles.'

'Then, it is yours. I shall have it delivered to the Advocates Library for you.'

'That is impossible.'

The old man looked vexed at being crossed.

'I apologise, Sir Charles. What I intended to say was that, in my professional capacity, I am not permitted to accept gifts from those instructing me.'

'Stuff and nonsense, Kane. I am a regular donor of such gifts to various other members of your Faculty...'

'That would be a matter for them, Sir Charles. The Dean of Faculty prohibits...'

Kane's objection was interrupted by the old man's loud laugh: 'The Dean of Faculty? Why, sir, he is one of the main recipients of my largesse!' Irving was dismissive now: 'Old Rab Lennox- 'Dean of Faculty' – I knew him when he was an apprentice.'

'Even so, Sir Charles...'

'Even so' – my eye, sir. Do you think that Rab Lennox became Dean of the Faculty of Advocates by kissing babies and smelling roses? You are even more naive than I was told, Kane...'

A warning bell struck inside Kane: *Than I was told...?*

'Now you're a clever enough young fellow, Kane, but here is a lesson for you. Be very careful to choose who your friends are, do you hear me? And then be a friend in return. That is how this world turns. I do you a service and you do me one in return. Do you understand? However, if you are not my friend, Mr Kane, then... I need say no more.'

The old man didn't look at Kane directly, but stared into the fire for a moment, then:

'Now, my friend, this other fellow, Macnair, 'The Parlour Maid Murderer'...'

Kane looked up, surprised.

'I'm afraid, Sir Charles, that I cannot...'

The old man shouted over Kane.

'Don't interrupt me, Kane, do you hear? Do not dare interrupt me.'

Kane fell silent and Irving continued, quieter now, but with an unnerving intensity:

'He is a blackguard of the first order. And he is obviously guilty. I was there that night when he threw my poor Martha, that poor girl, over the banister. Can you imagine the terror.'

'I'm sorry, Sir Charles.'

'On that same staircase there, where you ascended yourself tonight. My poor Martha. She was... she was special to me...'

The old man paused and stared into the fire.

'Gone. Gone in an instant. Neck snapped like a twig when she landed. God rest her soul.'

In his head, Kane ran through what he had read of the case: 'And her last words, Sir Charles...'

'Her last words'? What the deuce do you mean, man, 'her last words'?'

'The girl's last words. She said something to Patrick Macnair before she died. After the fall.'

Irving considered for a moment, then: 'Who told you such nonsense?'

'It was in my statements, Sir Charles. From your household.'

The old man leaned forward in his chair: 'And who in my household, sir, would have said such a thing?'

Kane decided that a lie to protect the cook, Mrs Bolton, was for the best: 'I have quite forgotten, Sir Charles. Doubtless, I am mistaken in the matter. Perhaps I have commixed the facts of this case with those of another.'

Irving's eyes narrowed, as if making a mental note: 'No doubt, Mr Kane, no doubt.'

They sat in silence. Then Kane spoke: 'Mr Malcolm appears to be taking a considerable amount of time to conclude the business with your man, Hand, Sir Charles.'

The old man stared at Kane: 'It is a long drop from here to the basement, sir.'

Kane was conscious of a sudden change in the atmosphere of the room, akin to a large stone dropped into still pool of water.

'Who is this?' The voice belonged to a young woman in her mid-twenties. Kane looked up, and there, standing in the doorway was possibly the most beautiful woman that Kane had ever seen. Raven hair. Large eyes that seemed to glisten in the firelight. A mouth that called to Kane's mind a cherry that was ripe for plucking. Or kissing.

The old man smiled. 'Come in, my darling. Come and meet our illustrious guest.'

The young lady entered the room with a certain swagger and looked Kane up and down. Kane suddenly had the feeling that he was being viewed rather like a dead rat that had been found on a dinner plate.

Sir Charles waved his handkerchief at Kane: 'This, my dear, is Mr Edward Kane, the Advocate.'

Kane stood up and gave a shallow bow: 'How do you do.'

'Oh Father, I thought you said he was a guest. And it transpires that he is just another one of your employees.'

She held out her hand to Kane. Not to be shaken, but rather to be kissed. Kane, somewhat clumsily, obliged. And then stammered: 'And who, who might I ask...'

The girl began to laugh in a low, purring voice that was familiar to Kane in a way he could not place: 'Of course, you have no idea who I am have you?'

Kane smiled weakly. The old man obliged: 'I apologise, Mr Kane, may I present to you my daughter, Miss Cordelia Irving.'

Of course, I ought to have known.

'And, Father, where is Mr Hand? I have been ringing for attention for a good few minutes now and nothing! Am I expected to do everything in this house myself? Am I expected to make tea? Or would you prefer,

Father, that I should don an apron and scour like a scullery maid?'

'The servants have been discharged for the evening, my darling.'

'Nonsense. I saw that useless old harridan Mrs Bolton, the so-called cook, skulking about near the kitchen earlier.'

'There was business to discuss, my dear, and we required a measure of privacy.'

'And so, another cold collation for supper. And where on earth is Hand?'

'He is tending to the fees of Mr Malcolm...'

The girl groaned: 'One more exhibit from the Irving collection of waxworks...'

Irving looked at the girl and smiled, then spoke to Kane: 'You must forgive my daughter's high spiritedness, Mr Kane. We lost her mother when she was very young, and I have rather indulged her since.'

It struck Kane that this was the first trustworthy thing that Irving had said in the whole of the evening.

The girl slumped into a chair beside Kane and she stared at his feet.

'Your boots are filthy. Did you know that? And old. Are you poor?'

Kane looked at his footwear. It had seen better days.

'Don't you have a man, or something to keep them clean? Or, or, is it perhaps you can't afford the polish? And your collar – is it frayed? Do I detect a fraying? Are you perhaps merely a pauper masquerading as a gentleman, sir?'

Kane looked at the old man: 'Well, Sir Charles, I appear to have been found out.'

Irving rebuked his daughter, but gently: 'Darling, please remember who you are. Mr Kane is our... our...' The definition of Kane's status eluded him at that point.

He turned to Kane: 'Sometimes, I fear that we shall have to return her to finishing school and demand a return of the fees.'

'But it's so tedious here in Edinburgh, Father. Now, London that is a place of excitement. Or what about America?' She turned to Kane: 'And what about you, Mr... Mr... what did you say your name was?'

'Kane, miss, Edward Kane.'

'What about you, Kanemiss? Don't you find Edinburgh incredibly tedious? What type of law do you practice, anyway, Kanemiss?'

Sir Charles stepped in: 'He is assisting with the land dispute, my dear.'

The girl gave a theatrical groan: 'Oh no. The never-ending battle between Father and old Michael Coates. So dull. What we need in this city is a good murder, don't you agree, Kanemiss?'

She smiled condescendingly at Kane and he was struck by a thought. Here was someone who presented as – it had to be conceded – very beautiful indeed. But inside, somewhere at her very core, there was something rancid. A beautiful, rosy apple, but a lovely fruit with a rotten core and a slithering worm inside.

Kane saw the old man's eyes glisten at that moment, and he hissed: 'But my dear, don't you know you are in the presence of a man who is representing a notorious murderer as we speak.'

The girl was staring at Kane intently now, searching his features for something of the Learned Counsel for the Defence in that modest demeanour. Then she laughed: 'Oh Father, you are such a tease!'

'I am perfectly serious, my dear. Mr Kane, tell her the identity of your infamous client.'

Kane didn't know what to say at that point or whether, indeed, he should speak at all.

Sir Charles Irving leaned forward in his chair and barked: 'Spit it out, man – who is the blackguard?'

Kane looked directly at the girl: 'I hold instruction to represent Mr Patrick Macnair.'

Cordelia blanched.

The old man sat back in his chair and laughed: 'Do you hear that, my love? This young buck here is the thing standing between your beloved and the noose.' The old man smiled and rubbed his neck.

The girl studied Kane's face again. She tried to laugh, but failed. And now, her whole being appeared to shrink, sucked in from inside like water escaping down an open drain. Her eyes were hot and wet now as she spoke: 'Have you seen him?'

Kane did not answer.

'Have you seen him, Mr Kane?'

'Yes, miss.'

'And how is his... his demeanour?'

'Well, miss, as you will have seen for yourself...'

'For myself? For myself, Kane? Do you think that I would abase myself to mingle with the... with the class of people who are incarcerated there?'

'Apologies, miss, I rather presumed...'

'Then don't. Don't 'rather presume' anything.'

She was silent for a moment, staring into the fire, then: 'If you could see my heart, Mr Kane. Shattered into a thousand pieces. The man I loved. Meddling with a common wretch of girl. A parlour maid. And how does that make me look? Well, as the adage tells us: you can take the boy out of the gutter, Mr Kane, but you cannot take the gutter out of the boy.'

And with that Mr Hand returned. Alone. He held an envelope in his hands.

'Ah, Mr Hand,' the old man grinned 'You have been sorely missed. Not least by those in want of common necessities, such as tea.'

In all truth, Kane did not wish to stay for tea. His apprehension, however, proved unfounded when it soon became apparent that he was not being invited.

But where is Mr Malcolm?

'Now, Mr Hand,' the old man looked up, 'Mr Kane and I have had our little chat, and I think that it is fair to say that he remains ambiguous in certain areas of our discussion...'

Hand nodded: 'Shall I extinguish both candles, sir?'

'Regrettably, yes, Mr Hand.'

Kane had no idea what was going on now. Mr Hand went to the

window, where a double-headed candelabra stood, bearing two flickering candles.

Mr Hand licked between the thumb and index finger of his right hand and, methodically, he snuffed out the first candle, then the second. As the second candle was being extinguished, Kane thought that he saw Cordelia Irving give a slight shake of the head.

'Now,' grinned the old man 'your presence is darkened, Mr Kane, when it could have been so bright.'

Kane shook his head: 'I'm sorry, Mr Hand, but where is Mr Malcolm?'

'Gone, sir. He had other important business to attend to. However, he left this letter for you, Mr Kane. I think that you will find the contents to your satisfaction.'

Hand gave Kane the letter bearing the words: *Edward Kane, Advocate*.

Kane, puzzled, thanked Hand and put the envelope in his inside jacket pocket.

Then Sir Charles gave Mr Hand a nod, and Hand said:

'That concludes the meeting tonight, Mr Kane. Let me show you to your coat.'

And, rather perfunctorily, thought Kane, the butler took him by the arm and assisted him from the room. The old man did not bid him farewell, nor did the girl, who was still staring into the fire.

When they had scaled down the narrow back staircase and reached the tradesmen's entrance once more, Hand left Kane for a moment to retrieve his coat and hat.

When Hand left his sight, Kane took the envelope from his jacket pocket to peek inside.

Ready cash, and a great quantity of it. Enough money here to retrieve his watch and to live on for a month. Six weeks, perhaps. Kane heard Hand returning and hastily put the envelope behind his back.

As Mr Hand was helping Kane on with his coat, 'I trust that the contents of the envelope meet with your satisfaction, sir?'

Kane smiled: 'It does seem a disproportionately generous consideration for such little industry on my part, Mr Hand.'

'Loyalty, Mr Kane. Sir Charles always rewards loyalty, sir.'

Mr Hand held open the door for Kane to leave.

***

On nights like this, Edinburgh deserved its nickname 'Auld Reekie'. The chimney stacks smeared the sky with smoky clouds and cast a dismal gloom over the narrow, winding streets. Kane pushed on towards the Old Town, over Princes Street, then up to The High Street. The night was getting colder now, and the quicker way home was through a small, unlit alley.

A voice emerged from a dim doorway, 'Scuse me, sir. Huv you got a light?'

Kane looked around and in the darkness, he could make out the figures of two men behind him. Peering through the gloom, he could see that one was tall and thin. The other, deeper in the shadows, small, round and squat. Standing beside each other, the total effect was of a letter 'b'. The tall man had the reek of alcohol about him.

'I beg your pardon?'

The tall man spoke: 'A light, sir. Me and my friend are gonnae have a pipe, sir, but we need a light. Have you got a match?'

'Well...' Kane patted his coat pockets. A small scrunching sound revealed a box of matches in his right-hand pocket. Kane produced the box and handed it over.

'Much obliged, sir. Nothing like a good pipe, eh?'

The tall man placed a long pipe in his mouth. He removed a match from the box and struck it, a sudden flash in the darkness, but then the match blew out immediately.

The squat man, still standing in the shadows, now spoke in a grating voice.

'Look at that. Look at that. Snuffed out in a second, sir, that flame. Fragile as a parlour maid's neck.'

And with that, the tall man snapped the spent match in two, flicked it away, then opened the box again.

'Ye see. That's what happens here, eh? One match disnae work, ye snap its neck in two and try another, friendlier one. Know what I mean, sir?'

Kane had no idea, but gathered the impression that it would be better to leave the scene. And leave now. He gave a short bow:

'You may keep the matches, gentlemen, and I bid you a very good evening.'

The tall man spoke: 'No, sir, no. There's no hurry here, Mr... eh... sir. Will you have a pipe with us, sir? Just a wee pipe.'

He placed a lit match into the bowl of the pipe, the flaring flame disclosing a face that resembled a weasel. The man puffed and puffed; small clouds of smoke rose from the pipe. He shook the match out and held the pipe out to Kane.

'Ye see! Have a wee, friendly pipe with us, sir.'

Kane considered, then: 'I'm grateful for the kind invitation, my man, but I'm afraid I am expected elsewhere...'

Kane tried to move on, but was suddenly aware that the squat gentleman had taken him by the arm. When he looked back up, the sharp point of a knife was being held at this throat. The squat man manhandled Kane for all of five seconds, swiftly manoeuvring both of Kane's arms up his back.

The tall man spoke: 'You sound like an educated fella, but I think you need a wee lesson here in who your friends are...'

Kane wanted to give an appropriate retort, however, all that he was conscious of was the pressure of the pointed knife blade digging into the soft flesh of his throat.

A moment of stillness was interrupted by a voice from the darkness:

'Scuse me, gents. Have you met me Aunty Betty?'

Kane breathed a sigh of relief at the voice. A Cockney brogue. Mr Horse.

The interruption was far from expected by the two men in the alley.

They stood frozen for a moment, then the tall man spoke: 'Whoever ye are, ye have no business here. Get away before ye come tae harm. I mean it...'

The voice continued: 'I was just wonderin' if you had met me Aunty Betty?'

The tall man continued: 'I know your type – get your arse away fae here, ya Mary, before I put my boot right up it!'

There was a moment of silence. Then: 'Well, gentlemen, since you 'ave not 'ad the pleasure of the acquaintance of me Aunty Betty, let me introduce you.'

Kane shut his eyes tight and tried to lower his head. He knew what was coming. 'Aunty Betty' was Horse's affectionate name for his nine-inch iron truncheon.

The tall man became the first to make her acquaintance, when she removed, with remarkable efficiency, any remaining teeth that he possessed. He dropped his knife and began to stagger towards Horse, resembling the final, uncertain stages of a spinning top.

Aunty Betty, noting his approach, and being a creature averse to risk, then paid a swift, but definitive visit to his left temple. His eyes pointed towards the sky, as his long, straight body, fell – in a slow and stately motion – down into the gutter.

Horse arose to give 'Aunty Betty' a formal introduction to the round, squat man, but that individual, having declined the invitation, could be heard running (with some difficulty, given his shape) along the cobblestones.

Kane exhaled: 'Oh, Horse, what a stroke of luck.'

'Luck, Mr K? Luck had nothin' to do with it. Been shadowing you all night, sir. And I seen these two geezers dodgin' about near Irving's house, lookin' up at that gent's windows all night. Then you left, sir, and it were obvious that they was up to no good.'

Kane remembered the lights snuffed out in the window. Horse looked down at the man in the gutter.

'So I thought, sir, that Aunty Betty might need to make an appearance, if you know what I mean.'

'What are we going to do with him? We can't very well leave him here.'

'He'll be alright, sir. He'll wake up with a sore head, no teeth and smellin' of piss, but he'll be alright. Anyway, the fat boy will come back and get him. Trust me, Mr K, they need each other. Now let's get away, before the Old Bill turns up and starts asking too many questions...'

★★★

Fifteen minutes later, Horse had Kane sitting in a comfortable chair at home in a dressing gown and with a cup of Glasgow punch in his hand.

'I'm bound to say, Mr Horse, that it does taste better with sugar.'

'A good medicine, sir – to calm the nerves.'

Kane took Horse through the events of the evening at the home of Sir Charles Irving ('Very curious, Mr K') and then came to the grand finale: 'And so, Mr Horse, I looked inside that envelope to find a sizeable amount of ready cash. Enough, my friend, to sustain a struggling young Advocate and his man for four to six weeks. Hand me my coat, Horse.'

Horse handed Kane his coat.

'And – miraculous to relate – enough also to retrieve a certain family timepiece from, shall we call it 'the hock'.'

Kane smiled as he reached into his inside coat pocket. And fumbled. And he searched the other side of his coat. And he fumbled some more. And went through the various pockets of the coat. Nothing. He placed the coat on his lap and looked at Horse.

Horse took the coat back.

'Looks like you been rolled, Mr K. The little fat fella who was running away, he's took all your cash is my guess. Well, the drinks will be on him tonight, sir.'

Kane's face fell.

'Buck up, Mr K. Look at it this way, we're no worse off this evening than we was this morning.'

Kane gave an audible sigh and nodded.

'And tonight, Mr K, we got the Glasgow punch – so drink up, sir. Drink up.'

***

Early the following morning, at his desk in the Advocates Library, Kane was poring over some of the land deeds when one of Manville's men approached him.

'Yes?'

'A visitor for you in the Hall, sir.'

'A visitor?'

'Yes, sir. He asked me to give you his card.'

The servitor handed over a card that bore the introduction:

Inspector Mackintosh of the Detective.

Kane left his desk and went out into the great Parliament Hall. It was a busy Tuesday morning, and the Hall was filled by a dozen Advocates in wig and gown, discussing their cases for the day.

His attention was drawn to a small gentleman in a thick coat and a bowler hat standing beside a granite statute. The gentleman sported a large, bushy moustache that was too big for his face. He was examining the statue with great concentration. This was being done through a pair of eyeglasses, the thickness of which reminded Kane of the bottoms of wine bottles.

Kane ventured: 'Inspector Mackintosh, I presume?'

The little man peered towards Kane and extended his hand: 'Mackintosh, sir. Just Mackintosh. At your service.'

'Edward Kane, Advocate, sir – at yours.'

'Was just looking at the statue of the sick man here, sir.'

'The sick man' mister, er, Mackintosh?'

Mackintosh of the Detective peered at the inscription on the granite statue and read: 'It says here that he was sick.' He looked up at the statue. 'Maybe that's why he had to pose sitting down, sir.'

'I rather think, Mackintosh, that it says 'Sic Sedebat' which I understand to be Latin for 'This is how he used to sit.' An explanation, perhaps, of the sitter's rather informal pose...'

Mackintosh narrowed his eyes and nodded sagely: 'Very clever, sir, very, very subtle, if I may be so bold.' He examined the head of the statue: 'Still, he has the face of a notorious villain...'

'Mackintosh, it is, in fact, a statue of Sir Walter Scott...'

Mackintosh did not look surprised, but nodded his head sagely again: 'Very subtle sir, very, very subtle...'

Kane enquired as to the purpose behind Mackintosh's visit to Parliament House as the two gentlemen paced up and down the great hall.

'Reports, Mr Kane, sir, reports that there was a disturbance in a lane near here.'

Kane's remembrance of Horse and 'Aunty Betty' brought on sudden nerves.

'But when the constable attended, sir, all he found was a great deal of blood and a collection of teeth, recently extracted it would appear.'

Kane gave a tentative laugh: 'Then I fear, Mackintosh, that someone is in need of a dental surgeon, not an Advocate...'

'But the old lady, who lives above the scene, sir, says that she looked out and witnessed a commotion involving a gentleman, like yourself, sir and some other gentlemen and she heard the shouts of an Englishman at some point in a dispute that appeared to relate to that gentleman's great aunt.'

'And why have you come to me, Mackintosh?'

'It is known that you live nearby and have your own man, an Englishman with the soubriquet 'The Horse', sir.'

Kane stopped walking.

'I am afraid that your efforts are in vain, sir. I know nothing of the matter. I was, in fact, at the home of Sir Charles Irving for a considerable part of the evening. I am happy that you confirm that position with Sir

Charles himself, Mackintosh. You will appreciate that I am very busy.
Good day, sir.'

Kane began to leave. But Mackintosh spoke:

'Begging your pardon, My Kane. You have perhaps seen through the
pretext of my visit to you. It is Sir Charles that I wished to speak to you
about. It will take very little time, sir, if you'll indulge me.'

And so, they resumed their walk.

'You will perhaps have guessed, Mr Kane, that, in reality, I wish to
speak to you concerning Patrick Macnair, the Parlour Maid Murderer.'

Kane frowned: 'The repetition of an allegation does not make it true,
Mackintosh.'

'Not saying it does, sir. Just using the common shorthand. You'll have
seen it in the newspaper yourself.'

'I confess, Mackintosh, that the more I read of what is alleged to have
happened, the more I fear that a fair trial becomes impossible.'

'But you and me, Mr Kane, you and me got the real paperwork for the
case. We know what really happened, eh?'

'Maybe you do, Mackintosh, but I am still at a loss in a number of
areas.'

'Such as, sir?'

Perhaps the small man in the bottle glasses was more acute than he
first presented.

'Well, Mackintosh – you are of the Detective. Perhaps you can tell me.'

There was a moment of silence, then the little man grinned: 'I've been
rumbled, sir. Let me be square with you...'

Mackintosh looked into Kane's face now.

'...it would be helpful if you would just tell me, sir. Did he do it? I
mean, has he told you he done it?'

Kane was startled at this new directness.

'Mr Mackintosh, the secrets of the Catholic confessional are no more
protected than the privilege that exists between the Advocate and the
accused.'

'Begging your pardon, sir, but if he done it and he's going to admit to it at the trial, then I can stop thinking on it. The wife, sir, Mrs Mackintosh, she says that I'm a-tossin' and a-turnin' every night with this one. So many questions we don't know the answers to.'

Kane nodded: 'We are in a similar position, you and I, Mackintosh. I, too, am haunted by that unfortunate girl's last words.'

'Her last words, sir?'

'Yes, when...' But when he looked down at Mackintosh, the detective's face was entirely blank.

Mackintosh persisted: 'Martha Cunningham's last words? I'm afraid, sir, that...'

'You have studied the materials before you, Mackintosh?'

'Religiously, sir. But no mention of last words, Mr Kane. No doubt, something that Mr Macnair told you himself?'

Odd. The information was in the paperwork and Mackintosh, despite his tossing and turning on the case, had missed it?

'But, of course, Mr Kane, you can't confirm that.'

They walked on in silence, then Kane said: 'And what is the fact that haunts your very sleep, Mackintosh?'

Mackintosh thought for a moment, then: 'The father, sir.'

'The father?'

'Yes, sir. Who is the father?'

Kane stopped and they both stopped walking: 'I confess, Mackintosh, that you have stymied me completely, now. What has Martha Cunningham's father to do with it?'

'No, Mr Kane. When I say 'the father', I mean of course, the father of the child that was being carried by that poor, dead parlour maid. She was expecting, Mr Kane, expecting a child. But you'll know that from your own papers. The question is: who was the father? Are you feeling unwell, sir? You have turned quite pale...'

PART TWO: THE FAMILY WAY

Chapter Four

Collins looked grim: 'Expecting a baby? But Edward, surely that information would have been in the materials provided to you?'

Kane sat. The tea on the table before him was cold and undrunk.

Behind his horn-rimmed spectacles, Collins narrowed his eyes: 'Are you sure that you did not just miss it, my friend, *per incuriam?*'

Kane was insistent: 'Collins, I could no more fail to notice such a fact as to fail to notice Noah and an ark full of animals floating up and down the Cowgate!'

'And who provided the statements in question?'

Kane thought for a moment: 'The Dean of Faculty.'

'No, I mean, sir, who prepared the statements themselves? The statements that provided such imperfect instruction.'

'That would be a certain Mr Whittle, my instructing agent.'

'And who is paying for the instruction on this matter?'

'In my case, Collins, no-one. *Pro bono pubicae* and all that.'

'Yes, yes – but I recall you saying that your solicitor, Mr Whittle, is in funds.'

'Yes?'

'Then, who is paying Whittle?'

Kane knotted his eyebrows and considered: 'Well...I suppose I rather assumed that Macnair himself was funding his defence...'

Collins laughed and shook his head: 'Edward Kane, Advocate, you thought that the gentleman who refuses even to provide the barest whisper of a defence is prepared to pay handsomely for it. Oh, Edward...'

Collins got out of his chair and looked out of the window of the Reading Room. Kane sat up:

'Collins, my friend – what are you doing?'

'Edward, I am just looking out of the window, in the expectation that I might catch sight of Noah and an ark full of animals...'

This gentle teasing ceased when Collins became aware of the presence of Manville, Head Faculty Servant, at the table. His approach, as always, had been near-imperceptible.

Kane sat up and nodded: 'Manville...'

'Mr Kane...'

Silence, then Kane spoke: 'Is it the Dean of Faculty?'

'Yes, sir.'

'Does he wish to speak to me?'

'Yes, sir.'

'Now?'

'Yes, sir. If you would care to follow me, sir.'

★★★

'Kane – are you capable of doing nothing right?'

It struck Kane that Rab Lennox, Dean of the Faculty of Advocates, would be easily ascertainable in a dark room on account of the sheer luminosity of his red face.

'Sir Charles is very unhappy, Kane. Very unhappy. I give you a simple – yes simple – land dispute and you decide to look it in the mouth.'

It struck Kane as being highly unlikely that one could look a land dispute in the mouth. *A horse, perhaps. Yes, a horse, but...*

'Are you listening to me, Kane?'

'Yes, Dean of Faculty.'

'What is the issue, Kane?'

'Well, Dean of Faculty, in terms of linking one title to another...'

'No, no, no – not the land nonsense – what is your issue?'

A sudden exhaustion fell over Kane. At times like these, he wished that he had followed his father into the Church. At least there, hellish scenes like this were reserved for the afterlife.

But before Kane could answer, Lennox got out of his chair and stood looking out of the window.

'And the Macnair murder. How is that progressing?'

Why has the Dean linked Sir Charles' land problems with the Macnair murder?

'I confess, Dean, that it may be a case outwith my competence...'

The Dean turned around, smiling now. His smile had all the sincerity of an alligator:

'Nonsense, Edward. Nonsense. Part of the calling of the Advocate, Edward. The hopeless cause. We have all tholed such cases. The pretence of a defence, then the final – but just – determination. Have you consulted with Macnair?'

'Yes. Briefly.'

'Capital. And did he state a defence?'

'He will state nothing, Dean. He refuses completely to be drawn on the events.'

'Ah, a clear sign of his guilt. You can rest easily, Edward. And sleep soundly. No need to study the scant paperwork. Nothing that you can do can save the blackguard. Nor should it. The penalty for murder is death. He knew that, in the very act of throttling that poor girl...'

Throttling? Where did that come from?

He looked up. Manville was at the door. The Dean had his back to him again and was looking out of the window.

'Thank you, Edward. That will be all.'

***

Kane sloped back into the Reading Room. No sign of Collins now, but in the corner, at a table, in the usual place, sat 'Not Proven' Norval Norris, smoking his pipe. Kane lacked the energy for conversation and began to leave, when Norris called his name.

'Edward...'

Norris ushered him into the empty seat across the table.

'Edward, my dear fellow, how goes it?'

Kane slumped down.

'Norval, if I am to be perfectly honest, then I confess that I am all at sea.'

Norris nodded and sucked on his pipe.

'It is a serious business, Edward. The death of a pretty, young parlour maid. The downfall of a successful man of business. The newspapers do not lack the ink to tell the whole lurid tale.'

There was a silence between them, then: 'Norval, I have no idea what is going on. And all that stands between Patrick Macnair and the gallows is me.'

Norval puffed on his pipe for a moment.

'Cui bono'

'Cui bono?'

'The first question in any case, Edward – 'Cui bono' – who benefits from what happened?'

Kane thought for a moment. The obvious answer was Macnair himself: an illicit connexion with a girl of a low class; her pregnancy; her threats to reveal their liaison. The unmasking of Macnair would be a nail in the coffin of his engagement to Miss Cordelia Irving, and any prospect of social position would be dashed forever. Only the death of the girl would resolve all of these issues. Kane's consideration was interrupted by Norris:

'Who else was in the house that night?'

'A number of people, I understand. The girl, Macnair, Sir Charles, Miss

Cordelia, the cook, in fact, the entire serving staff...'

'And the butler?'

'Yes, a certain Mr Hand. I understand that he was there, although I don't recall seeing any statement from him.'

'Curious...'

'In what way, curious?'

'The butler is the eyes and ears of every great house. He is the almanac of every coming and going. And you have nothing from him regarding the events of the evening?'

'Nothing.'

Norris sat back and puffed on his pipe.

'Well, my young friend, it appears that you have a mountain to climb, but let us look upon the bright side here. As I understand from you, there were no witnesses to the event itself. People attended at the body soon afterwards and found Macnair there already. But who is to say that he was even there when the event happened? If the other onlookers rushed to the scene, then why not Macnair also?'

'But Norval, he was heard arguing with the girl immediately before the event...'

'How do they know that it was his voice?'

Kane thought for a moment. The statements were silent on the issue that it was Macnair's voice for sure.

'For example – where was the butler, Mr... Mr...'

'Mr Hand.'

'Yes, the mysterious Mr Hand. Where was he at that instant?'

Norris began to mock-declaim, as if to a jury: 'And what was Mr Hand's own relationship with the deceased girl. That poor, unfortunate girl who was completely in the power? The power of Mr Hand...'

Kane began to feel some of the tug of Norris' talent for persuasion. Oh, for a fraction of his ability in this case.

'Edward – look at your papers again. By my reckoning you have, at a rough calculation, half a dozen other possible suspects in this case.

Create – in the mind of the jury – a chair. An empty chair. And then place someone in that chair. Someone other than Patrick Macnair.'

***

'I fear, Edward, that you do not love me any more.'

Kane sat forward in his chair: 'But why, my sweet?'

Miss Amanda attempted to strike a noble pose: 'You take no interest whatsoever in my Art.'

The greatest surprise to Kane of this declaration, was that Miss Amanda had not expressed any interest in art of any kind until this very point. He faltered:

'Of course, my sweet lambkin, of course I am interested. I have often remarked... I have often wished to remark that you have the soul... the soul of a Bohemian...'

Miss Amanda hugged herself and giggled: 'Oh, Edward, the creative fire that burns within. It must out, my love – it must out!'

These words sounded oddly unlike her, Edward thought.

'And so, Father is very keen, very enthusiastic that I display my talent. To the world.'

Kane nodded enthusiastically: 'Of course, my pet. You could perhaps rent gallery space and exhibit. That's what all the real... all the more seasoned artists do...'

'Edward, have you lost your senses? What are you talking about?'

'Your paintings, my darling. Your artwork. Exhibiting your considerable talent to the world.'

'But, Edward, I do not paint.'

Kane felt his mouth move, but no words were coming out.

'It is my singing voice, silly.' She was shy suddenly: 'Mr Brookes says that while my piano is extremely, extremely accomplished, it is my voice that reveals my true genius. That reveals my very soul. 'Song', he says, 'is your canvas.' Her face was seraphic now with joy. 'My voice is my art.'

'Well...' Kane was struggling to find the right words. 'Mr Brookes is certainly very accomplished himself. I have heard his voice and it...'

'It is divine, Edward, so he should know. He said that I should not reveal my great talent to anyone at present because there are still some minor aspects that require a measure of schooling; however, I told Father what Mr Brookes had said... why are you smiling, Edward?'

In truth, the encounter between Sir John Forbes-Knight and the platitudinous music master is something that Kane would have paid ready money to witness, had he possessed any.

'I am just so happy for you, my darling.'

'...and so I told Father what Mr Brookes had said and Father summoned him to the study and demanded of Mr Brookes that he now prepare me to give a public concert.'

Kane earnestly wished that he could place his pocket handkerchief into his mouth unnoticed.

'And when, my darling Amanda, when are we to we expect this public debut. Next year, perhaps?'

'Goodness, no, my darling. At the end of the month. Immediately after that horrid murder trial of yours.'

***

Kane was exhausted by the case papers. Now, he could possibly recite them by rote. It was akin to tallying up the same group of numbers again and again, and expecting a different result.

He had tried to consult with Macnair again, but Macnair had refused to see him. Horse said that he would speak to his friend at the prison and try to arrange it whether Macnair wanted that or not.

Kane sat at his desk in the Advocates Library. Inside his head, a dull drum started to beat. Maybe a change of scene would lift it.

Kane entered the great hall. Busy as usual. Kane stood before one of the fires and warmed his open hands before the flames.

One of the Advocates walking up and down was the Dean of Faculty. And walking beside him was Sir Charles Irving. And scurrying behind them, Mr Whittle.

'How on earth do you survive here, Mr Kanemiss? It is so cold I can almost see the breath before me.'

And Kane looked around at Cordelia Irving.

'It's just Father. One of his many suits against his old enemy, Sir Michael Coates. They were great friends once, you know. But when love turns to hate, well...'

Kane stood aside to allow Cordelia a greater share of the fire. She seemed different today. Less brittle.

'Am I allowed to ask how preparations are going for the trial, or is that a secret?'

'I am taking every step possible...'

'Has Patrick said how it happened? Why he did it?'

Kane looked at the floor and shook his head.

Miss Irving looked into the fire: 'If it hadn't been Patrick, it would have been someone else. She was a bonny girl. And didn't she know it. And she was – how shall I put this – free with her favours. The way that she had with all men, young or old. The landed gentry and the butler. She would hand them something and then, just at the point of release, hold on for that fraction of a second longer than necessary. And the man looks up. And she smiles. And that smile is clear: 'Would you like to....'

Kane shuffled, uncomfortably: 'Certainly, the paperwork suggests...'

Cordelia laughed: 'Oh, poo the old paperwork. The girl had charm, and no paper can catch that. Like one of those sea nymphs...' she nodded over to her father now '...that my father is obsessed with.'

Kane looked at the floor again.

'Oh, don't think that I haven't heard the rumours, Mr Kane. It's all scurrilous nonsense, of course. Most likely the invention of Michael Coates. No. Father idolises...no, that is not correct...Father 'idealises' women. Apparently, that is why I am named 'Cordelia' – so that I might prove to be the best of daughters. As in that old Shakespeare play. And don't get me started about Father's views on Shakespeare and all that rot about him being Christopher Marlowe...'

At that point, Sir Charles Irving, in the middle of Parliament Hall, looked over and noted that his daughter was speaking to an Advocate at the fireplace. He stilled his companions and made his way over. There was something in the old man's gait, Kane noted, eloquent of a person carrying an illness. Irving was peering towards them, as if trying to ascertain the identity of the Advocate in question.

'Ah, it's Mr Kane. Good morning to you, sir.'

'Good morning, Sir Charles.'

'I would have thought that you would be busy with the important – and lucrative – work that I have entrusted to you, rather than sprawling here like some over-fed cat before a fire.'

'Well, Sir Charles, I understand that even Hercules took a rest between his near-impossible labours.'

Sir Charles laughed: 'Well said, my friend. Very droll, very droll indeed.'

Cordelia spoke: 'We were just discussing Shakespeare, Father. And my name.'

The old man looked at Kane: 'You have children, Mr Kane?'

'No, sir. But I hope to one day.'

'A piece of advice, my young friend. Do not pin your hopes upon your children. This one here,' he nodded towards the girl, 'I named Cordelia. In retrospect, I ought to have named her 'Goneril'.'

The old man gave a feeble, wheezy laugh.

'Oh, Father,' the girl retorted, 'it's such an uninteresting play in any event. An old man wandering around in a storm, with only a clown for company...'

Kane had a sudden image of Sir Charles and The Mole wandering around Parliament Hall.

The old man spoke: 'I apologise, Mr Kane, for my daughter's lack of appreciation of the finer arts.'

They were interrupted by the frantic beckoning of Mr Whittle, who was urging Sir Charles to re-join Lennox.

'Ah. The hour has come. A piece of advice, Mr Kane. There is important work to be done. Don't dawdle. Or, if you must, then try not to dawdle so visibly.'

And with that, the old man limped off.

They watched Irving join the others in silence. Cordelia looked into the fire. They stood for a long time. Then: 'Do you believe in Hell, Mr. Kane?'

'I beg your pardon?'

'Do you believe in the fires of Hell? Eternal damnation and all that?'

'I... I cannot say that my mind has dwelt long on the question.'

'You are not a person of faith, Mr Kane?'

Kane laughed: 'My father was a Minister...'

Then Cordelia joined him in that laugh: 'Then you are every inch a 'Son of the Manse'. I would have thought that your catechism would be impeccable, Mr Kane.'

'Miss Irving, my father loved God, not in some remote fashion, but rather as a son loves a father. He also loved language. I well recall a sermon in which he dissected the mind of the atheist. 'The letter 'a' in the word 'atheist',' my father preached, 'does not represent a rejection of God, but, rather it reflects the very absence of God. Just as the letter 'a' in the word 'amoral' denotes the absence of morality. The 'a'-theist lives an existence without God, akin to a world without a sun, where the soul is a merely a frozen landscape.'

'Your father must have been a very powerful speaker, Mr Kane.'

'He would have made a fine Advocate, I do not doubt that, Miss Irving.'

Cordelia looked into the flames again. 'Do you think that that girl is in Hell? The parlour maid, I mean?'

'Who can say?'

'I mean to say that, if the girl was as wanton as she presented – and, of course, she was with child at the point of her death...'

Kane wondered if he was the only person in Edinburgh who hadn't known this fact.

'...and if she was so steeped in sin. Then it would be straight to Hell, would it not?'

Kane shrugged.

'But what would happen to the baby, Mr Kane? Where would the soul of the unborn child go?'

Kane stood silent for a moment, then offered. 'As I understand it – from my 'catechism', as you would have it – an unbaptised child would spend eternity in Limbo. A place that is neither Heaven nor Hell.'

Cordelia Irving pondered this. 'What an exquisite kind of torture for the dead parlour maid. Either she spends eternity in Hell, never seeing the face of her only child; or in Heaven, for all eternity still, never, ever seeing that little face. A species of Hell in itself. Thus, in either event, Edward – may I call you Edward?'

Kane nodded, although surprised at the sudden intimacy and intensity of the conversation.

'In either event, Heaven seems no greater reward in those circumstances.'

'I'm bound to say, Miss Irving...'

'Call me Cordelia...'

'I'm bound to say...' Kane paused for a moment, then: '...Cordelia. That you present an exceedingly morbid disposition in this matter...'

The girl chuckled: 'Father says the same, all the time.'

She looked into the fire for a time longer, then:

'I lost my mother on the day of my birth. I never saw her face, nor she mine. I keep a small portrait of her – here.'

Cordelia Irving held up a locket that was hanging around her neck on a golden chain. She opened the locket to reveal a miniature portrait.

'They say it is a good likeness. The physician told father that he could not save both the mother and the baby – and that he had to make a choice. Father chose the baby. He was convinced that I was to be a boy, you see.'

Kane studied the portrait: 'She was very beautiful.'

'Thank you. I hope one day that I will see her face-to-face. In the afterlife.'

Kane was at a loss as to how to respond appropriately. He smiled: 'Amen to that. Very beautiful. And I see a strong family resemblance in you.'

'Why, Edward Kane, kind sir, you have just paid me an unwitting compliment.'

Kane felt his cheeks flush. He looked at the floor.

'Edward, I must apologise to you.'

'For what?'

'For the other night. At Papa's house. I was teasing and cruel to you.'

'It is of no matter...'

'No. I apologise. Father has so many lawyers and notaries and Advocates in the house, all dancing attendance on his latest vendetta. I rather took you for just another stuffed shirt.'

'There is nothing to apologise for, Cordelia.'

They smiled at each other.

'And your return home. When you left Papa's house. It was a safe journey, I presume?'

Kane paused before answering: 'It was... well, I survived to tell any tale, as you can see. Why do you ask?'

'It's just that Father said that you were living in a less salubrious part of the city. Just curious.'

At that, Sir Charles Irving joined them once again: 'Ah – and so we live to fight another day. I must say, Kane, that your Dean, Lennox, is certainly worth his corn. The man is a magician. He is able to produce a veritable wall of bricks from the merest suggestion of a straw. On days like today, seeing such unhappiness in the enemy camp, it feels good to be alive.' The old man rubbed his hands together in the direction of Sir Michael Coates.

He looked at Cordelia and Kane, '...and what have you two been chattering about that you are so... so cosy?'

'Father, I have just been apologising to Mr Kane for my unacceptable behaviour the other evening, and by way of recompense, I am inviting him to our home – for tea.'

***

'Tea, Mr K? Tea?'

'It would have been rude to say no, Mr Horse'

'Beggin' your pardon, Mr K, but have you gone soft in the 'ead?'

'I appreciate your concern, Horse, but...'

'What's come over you, sir? I mean she's said to be a good-looking woman, I'll give you that, but...'

'That has nothing to do with it.'

'Then what has it got to do with, sir? One day, the Irvings send out men to cut your throat and the next day they're asking if you'd like milk and two sugar. It don't make any sense. It's a bleedin' madhouse over there.'

'Mr Horse, there is no evidence that Sir Charles was behind the robbery.'

'I looked up at that window, sir. I saw those candles go out.'

'Well, sometimes a candle going out is just a candle going out...'

'But how does it look, sir? What with you, the only thing standing between that poor devil Macnair and the hangman, and there you are with your feet under his table canoodling...'

'Don't be ridiculous, Horse...'

'...canoodling with his woman. Trying to avoid the noose? Looks like you're tightening it around his throat.'

And with that, Horse scooped the half-full dinner plate away from under Kane's nose and clanked it into the sink.

'I hadn't finished that, Mr Horse.'

'No? Well, we don't want it to go spoiling your tea, Mr Kane, do we?'

***

The busy weeks went on and the day of the trial was approaching. Whittle's messenger finally arrived at the Advocates Library bearing a number of outstanding papers requested by Kane, the bulk of which –

upon examination – added nothing of substance to the case.

There had been the medical report of the police surgeon, Dr Stanton. In his view, the girl was some three months' pregnant. He noted other small injuries, abrasions to the arms, scratches to the neck and face, possibly from contact with sharp stone stairs on the back staircase. The cause of death, a broken neck, near instant as a result of the tumble and fall.

'Edward? Edward?'

Kane emerged from the papers to find another Advocate standing at the desk: Jonathan Hunter.

'Edward, may I have a word?'

Jon Hunter was an individual in the Faculty who was universally respected. That rare concoction of good breeding, impeccable manners and unforced charm, allied to a sound common sense meant that he was often the first port of call for a reliable opinion on any matter, legal or personal. It was commonly agreed that Jon Hunter was guaranteed high office later in his illustrious career.

They walked up and down Parliament Hall.

'Edward, just to tell you that today, I was, as it were, 'tapped on the shoulder' by the Lord Advocate.'

Kane understood instantly that such a 'tap on the shoulder' meant that the Lord Advocate, the head of Scotland's prosecution service, had recruited Jon Hunter to be one of his prosecutors of serious crime.

'Jon – I am delighted for you. It is an honour.'

'Thank you, my friend. I am humbled by the appointment.'

The friends walked on.

'Now, when the Lord Advocate appointed me, he said that he did not wish my first criminal trial to be a particularly onerous one.'

'Very sensible, Jon.'

'And so, he has assigned me to the trial of Patrick Macnair...'

This information made Kane stop in his tracks.

'...which, the Lord Advocate assures me, will be somewhat akin to the shooting of a great number of fish in a very small barrel. Shall we discuss the matter?'

***

'Success, Mr K, success!'

Horse directed Kane's view to the dining table. It was covered with a starched white tablecloth, and on the table was a jug of fresh milk.

'And, Mr K, a nice cut of meat for dinner.'

'Excellent work, Mr Horse. I assume that your friend, Mrs Ratchett, finally yielded a satisfactory price for the watch?'

'Very satisfactory, Mr K, very satisfactory. The tradesmen is up to date now and I even had the serving girl at the White Hart smiling – but the money was only a part of that, sir, if you catch my meaning.'

'Excellent, Mr Horse. I have almost completed the next tranche of work for Sir Charles, and so we will see if that results in an equally handsome remuneration.'

'And next time you gets it, My K, me and me Aunty Betty will see you home. Don't want no candles snuffed out again, do we, sir?'

Kane smiled ruefully and shook his head.

'And another thing, Mr K. I was chewing the fat with Mrs Ratchett, as you do, and she told me something very curious.'

'Yes?'

'First of all, Mr K, a question for you. The dead parlour maid, the one Macnair has been stuck with, what did she look like?'

Kane could almost recite the description by rote now.

'Seventeen years old; small; auburn hair; very pretty; coquettish...'

'Coquettish'? Don't know what that means, sir.'

'It means 'flirtatious'...'

Horse tapped his finger on his nose and laughed: 'Oh, I do know what that means, sir.'

'...to all men, apparently. Young and old, high and low. And with that, a certain lack of knowing her place.'

Horse was now stroking his chin between his index finger and his thumb.

'Why do you ask, Horse?'

'Well, as you know, if you want the best price off the pawnbroker, Mr Isaacs, then you talk to Mrs Ratchett first and she looks at the merchandise and she gives the all-clear.'

'Yes?'

'So a visit to Mrs Ratchett saves the – begging your pardon, sir – embarrassment of being seen going into Mr Isaacs' establishment.'

'I understand.'

'Then, Mrs Ratchett's house sees some pretty rum people visit there.'

'I do not doubt it, Mr Horse.'

'People, who you would think wouldn't struggle for a bob or two – but there they are in Mrs Ratchett's house selling off the silver. So, Mrs Ratchett tells me that about a week before your friend Patrick Macnair croaks the little girl, a pretty, young thing about sixteen comes to see Mrs Ratchett trying to flog a couple of old candlesticks...'

'Yes?'

'...and very nice candlesticks, too. But a bit tarnished now. Looked as if they had not been used for a number of years. Maybe been in the attic, sir.'

'And so, perhaps would not have been readily missed.'

'Exactly, Mr K. So Mrs Ratchett says to the girl: 'Where did you get these, my lovely?' And the girl is not pleasant. 'Mind yer own beeswax,' she says 'Is there siller in these or not?' And Mrs Ratchett looks at the girl and she looks at the sticks and she says 'Get out of here, before I give ye a good hiding. It's not stolen goods we want here.' And she cuffs the girl around the earhole and throws her out the door.'

Kane pondered for a moment, and spoke: 'Then we have a young girl matching the description of the parlour maid, Martha Cunningham, and she is desperate for money just days before she...'

'Correct, sir. Just days before she snuffed the old candle. Mrs Ratchett says that the girl reeked of desperate.'

'We can probably assume the reason why she required the money so desperately, Horse.'

'Of course we can. The thing is, that if she had just told Mrs Ratchett that she was in the family way, then Mrs Ratchett – well, she served as a young nurse at Waterloo, sir. She knows a thing or two about the human body. She might have been able to assist the girl with her... with her predicament, sir.'

'The whole affair is unfortunate.'

'But what about this, Mr K? So, Mrs Ratchett looks out of her winder – to make sure the girl has left the common stair and all – and what does she see? She sees that girl join a man, sir.'

Kane's heart began to sink.

'And, Horse, did that man fit the description on Patrick Macnair?'

'No sir, it was an older bloke. Quite well-turned out by the sound of it...'

'Sir Charles?'

'No, Mr K. It weren't Sir Charles. She knows Sir Charles by sight, sir. Most people do in this town.'

'Then who?'

'She doesn't know who, sir. All she says is that he was tall, pale and snooty. Big, long fingers. Looked like a walking corpse, she said.'

Kane thought for a moment, then:

'Horse, that is an excellent description of a certain butler, Sir Charles' butler Mr Hand...'

***

'Well, Edward – what do you think?'

Miss Amanda was glowing. She was showing off the new dress. Kane found it rather dazzling: 'Well, my darling. It is very... very... pink, is it not?'

'It is perfectly of the mode, Edward. And Mr Brookes feels that it would be the perfect dress for the programme that he is devising.'

'It is certainly very eye-catching.'

'He has also suggested that precious jewels could be hired and sewn into the fabric, so that the outfit would positively shimmer under the footlights. Can you imagine, Edward!'

'It all sounds very impressive, my darling. But, er, how does the singing part progress?'

'Wonderfully well, my sweet. Mr Brookes says that my performance will never fully take flight until I reveal my talent to an audience.'

Miss Amanda held her hands apart.

'Like a rare bird, where my talent is one wing and the adoration of the audience the other. And together...' Miss Amanda put her hands together as if in prayer and then fluttered her fingers. '...and together, we fly.'

'Mr Brookes certainly has very singular powers of expression.'

'Oh, Edward, Mr Brookes is so preceptive. To take someone like me, someone who already has what he has described as 'primitive' talent and to transmute that into something akin to genius.'

She gave a little laugh: 'Oh, listen to me. These were the words of Mr Brookes, Edward, not my own. But enough of me, Edward. What do you think of my talents?'

Before Kane could answer, their congress was interrupted by the butler, Chambers.

'I hesitate to interrupt these important proceedings, but Sir John has requested the presence of Mr Kane in the study, Miss Amanda.'

'Oh, Father is such a fusspot! He is forever asking me when you are going to make something of yourself, Edward, so that we can be married. And I have told him 'Papa, perhaps that we shall have to forego an ordinary existence and live the life of the artist.'

Chambers the butler gave a little cough. 'Again, I hesitate to interrupt The Life Aesthetic, Mr Kane, but Sir John is waiting...'

Kane got up from his chair and gave Miss Amanda a small bow: 'If you will excuse me, my darling.'

But, by this time, Amanda was busily examining the fabric of her dress: 'Yes, jewels...'

***

On the way to the study, Kane broached the subject with Chambers: 'Chambers, you have heard Miss Amanda sing, have you not?'

'Not willingly, sir.'

'But she receives music tuition constantly.'

'That is so, sir.' The butler's curt response did not admit of any further enquiry on the matter.

'And you must have heard her play the piano,'

'Yes, sir. Her playing of the piano is easily distinguishable from that of her tutor.'

'Her style, you mean, is very different?'

Chambers did not answer immediately. 'Her compliance with what is written on the page is, perhaps, not as assiduously observed as that of her teacher.'

It took Kane a moment to interpret this, and then: 'You mean, Chambers, that she still plays the wrong notes.'

'Those are your words, Mr Kane.'

And then something struck Kane. A question that could be asked only of this person: 'Mr Chambers?'

'Yes, sir.'

'Are you acquainted with a Mr Hand? The Mr Hand who is in the service of Sir Charles Irving?'

A pause, and then: 'I am, sir.'

'And what are your thoughts about him?'

'In what respect, sir?'

'As a matter of generality.'

'Mr Hand is a good and faithful servant to Sir Charles, sir. However, as I understand it, if one is young and of the female sex, then best, perhaps, not to find oneself in his presence alone. But then, it is not uncommon for a servant to follow in the footsteps of the master, is it?'

★★★

Sir John was sitting behind a desk covered with clutter. He waved Kane in: 'Come in, come in, young fellow. And how are you, my young Raleigh?'

Kane smiled, remembering the narrow escape from their last conversation.

'Very well, thank you, sir. You wished to see me?'

'Yes, sit down, sit down...'

Kane sat across the desk from Sir John. The old surgeon's bushy eyebrows and beard assumed a sombre expression.

'Now, young man, it is time that you and I had a candid conversation. I'll come straight to the point, Kane. You are not good enough for my daughter. There. I've said it.'

Any words that Kane had prepared in his head had been suddenly wiped clean like a schoolboy's slate tablet.

'Well, Sir John, I...'

'Lost for words, are you? Not a particularly fine advertisement for your trade as an Advocate then, eh?'

'I confess, Sir John, that this is not the conversation I had expected...'

'Stand back and take a good look at yourself, man. You are meant to be an outstanding orator and pleader in our courts...'

Kane struggled, 'Sir John, I must protest...'

'Protest all you like, young fellow. Let me make it plain...'

Kane wondered if it could be made any plainer.

'...you have no breeding and you have no money. That is the sum and substance of it. The possession of one of those is commonly the cure for the lack of the other. Look at that blackguard Macnair. His head for business took him into houses where he had no business to be. As for you, Kane, well, you are a likeable enough young man, but, as a prospective husband for my youngest daughter, you just won't do... To put it more bluntly...'

'Sir John, I am not sure that it would be possible to put it more bluntly...'

'Well, I have made my point, then. Feel free to leave as soon as you like. No need to speak to Amanda. I will tell her that you have been called away on business. An unlikely excuse in your case, I fear, but she is so wrapped up in this singing business that she will not suspect.'

Sir John stood up and offered Kane his hand: 'Good luck, Kane. You're a decent young chap. And you'll make a fine husband. To a school mistress or the like...'

After a brief shake of hands, Kane staggered from the study. On his way down the staircase, he was met by Florrie.

'Goodness, Edward, are you feeling quite well?'

Kane shook his head. Florrie looked concerned: 'It's Father, isn't it? Shall we sneak down to the kitchen and we can pour you a glass of water?'

★★★

Midnight in Parliament Hall. Edward Kane paced the great hall, trying to untangle his thoughts. The lamps in the hall burned low, and the great open fires glowed, crackled and shifted in the near-darkness.

Kane had long since given up attempting to make sense of the Macnair case. A feeling of helplessness fell over him.

And then, a voice: 'Welcome to The Law Criminal, Edward.'

Kane surfaced from his thoughts to see a smiling 'Not Proven' Norval Norris.

'I wager, Edward, that you have never been kept awake until this hour by the perusal of a contract or the like.'

Kane laughed, happy at the company: 'Then you, Norval, must be a veritable insomniac.'

'Oh, no, Edward. I only walk the length of the hall at this hour on the occasions when I fear that my client is innocent. I assume that that is the reason for your own perambulation now.'

Norris joined Kane's walk as he detailed his concerns about the case. Norris would nod, stop for a moment, take a puff of his pipe, consider, then walk on.

'You see, Edward, I understand that the evidence against your client appears very strong. But it is only one side of this great story.'

'Given Macnair's silence, I struggle to see the other side, Norval.'

'The man is presumed innocent, Edward. There does not require to be another side. It is for the Crown to prove its case against him, beyond reasonable doubt. Remember that 'empty chair' we spoke of, Edward.'

Kane stopped walking and concentrated. He looked Norris in the face. Norris puffed on the pipe.

'Here is an idea, my young friend. I am in the middle of such a trial. A chap allegedly poisoned his wife. But – fortunately for the accused – the late wife might have been carrying on with a number of other gentlemen, for example, her employer, a pharmacist named Dr Brown. I am to cross-examine this Dr Brown tomorrow morning. Come and have a look. Let's see if we can't get my client out of that chair and Dr Brown into it instead...'

***

'And you, sir, are a philandering scoundrel!'

Norris was shouting now. The tall gentleman in the witness box folded his arms in defiance and retorted: 'And you, sir, are deluded.'

'Deluded'?' Norris gave a wry smile and faced the fifteen men in the jury as he asked the next question: 'Is it 'deluded' to say that you knew the deceased, Mrs Ferguson very well, Dr Brown?

'That is not in dispute, sir. But I am not accused of killing her by poison – your client is.'

Norris pressed on: 'It is not 'deluded' to say that Mrs Ferguson was employed at your pharmacy, is it?'

'Yes, she was employed there, sir.'

'It is not 'deluded' to say that Mrs Ferguson and you often toiled in that pharmacy, later into the evening, after that establishment was closed to the public...?'

'There are a great deal of preparations that must be made in advance...'

'Oh, I don't doubt that, sir...' Norris grinned at the jury members now '...preparations, such as making sure that the door was bolted first...'

The jury members started to laugh.

The witness was angry now: 'I resent the implication, sir.'

Norris turned around quickly and faced the doctor: 'You resent what, sir? If the premises are meant to be closed to the public at that hour, then there is no shame in locking the door, is there? Or is there something that you would like to tell us?'

The doctor was tempted to speak. But changed his mind, then shook his head.

Norris pressed his advantage: 'You see, doctor, I put a simple, everyday scenario to you – the securing of work premises – and your mind immediately turned to more salacious thoughts. Are you blushing now, sir?'

The jury members leaned forward to examine the doctor's face.

'Are these 'deluded' questions bringing back certain uncomfortable memories for you, Doctor Brown?'

The witness shook his head.

'Let me turn to other matters, doctor.'

'Yes.'

'You yourself are a widower, yes?'

'Yes.'

'No woman at home.'

'That is correct.'

'And only Mrs Ferguson at work.'

'Yes.'

'Alone with you. In the evening.'

The witness was silent for a moment, then, reluctantly: 'Yes.'

'In a workplace where the contents include many items under lock and key.'

'Yes.'

'Because they are, simply put, poison.'

Dr Brown paused, then: 'They are medicine.'

'Let me ask you about something else, doctor.'

'Yes.'

'You are a widower?'

'I have accepted that.'

'Because your wife died.'

The doctor's confidence appeared to be returning now: 'If you think carefully about your question, sir, it will be obvious that the status of widower requires for that unfortunate event to occur.'

Norris faced the jury again as he answered: 'Oh, Dr Brown – I have thought very carefully upon that question. As I understand it, your wife fell ill before she died...'

'Yes. What of it?'

'What of it, indeed, Dr Brown?'

The witness seemed molten with rage now and pointed to the accused in the dock: 'I would remind you sir, that I am not the one who is on trial here.'

Norris smirked: 'Not at present, Doctor Brown. Not at present. Thank you.'

And he sat down with a smile.

Amongst the jury, some men shook their heads and folded their arms.

★★★

'And was his lordship expecting you, sir?'

The old lady and Kane stood at the front door of Sir Charles Irving.

'I received a note from the solicitor, Mr Malcolm, that I should attend this afternoon.'

'Well, ye'd better come in, then.'

Kane entered the large atrium of the house. The furnishings were certainly opulent, perhaps too much so to be in entirely good taste. Every choice – rug, lamp, table, coat rack – proclaimed the owner's pride in his prosperity a little too loudly.

Kane removed his hat and coat and gave them to the old lady.

'I was rather expecting to see the butler, Mr Hand.'

'Aye, Mr Hand has been called away, but just for a wee while. One of the tradesmen has been light wi' the meat delivery. And Hand is away to put a flea in his ear! Mr Hand likes things just so.'

'And who might you be, madam?'

'I'm the head cook, sir. I shouldnae really be answering the door, but I was just passing, like, when the bell went.'

'Ah – you must be Mrs Bolton!'

The old cook became guarded, then: 'I was just passing, sir. I'll get one of the maids to tend to you...'

'No, no, Mrs Bolton. I am Edward Kane, the Advocate. I am the one who is to defend Patrick Macnair.'

The old lady looked puzzled for a moment, then: 'Yer awful young-lookin' for an Advocate...'

'I am at the outset of my profession, Mrs Bolton.'

'And how is the boy?'

'Macnair?'

'Aye.'

'Mr Macnair is... he is bearing up.'

Mrs Bolton smiled: 'That boy is a cheeky midden! Aye – and one for the ladies as well. And he'll no' be wantin' for company in the Calton, I'm telling ye.'

It had not struck Kane before, but it was now obvious to him that there would be an easy flow of female company for Macnair within the Calton Jail – at an extremely agreeable price.

'Mrs Bolton, you were there that night. The night when the girl...'

Mrs Bolton sighed: 'Aye, ah was, sir. The night ma wee Martha got her neck broke. That was another wee scamp, that girl. Mony's the time I told her "You've got to know your place, hen, or you'll come tae grief."'

'You sound as if you were very fond of her, Mrs Bolton.'

'She was like a wee daughter to me. I had my own bairns, Mr Kane, but I lost the three of them to the sickness when they were babbies. The cholera, the doctor said. A wee girl and two wee boys. They were just babbies. My wee babbies. My first, Maria…' and at this point the old lady made the sign of the cross and blessed herself '…and then wee Edward – same name as you, sir… and my youngest babby, Richard. I didnae hae them for long, sir. Wee Edward would have been…'

She paused to study Kane's face.

'He would have been about your age now, sir… aye, your age… my wee Eddie…'

The old lady stood in silence, in wearied resignation of a sadness that had haunted her heart for decades. Kane looked into her face and saw the traces of someone who had been beautiful in youth, but whose features had been erased by sadness and loss.

'If ye wait here, I'll ring for the girl and we'll see if the maister is ready for you, Mr Kane.'

Kane interrupted her: 'Mrs Bolton, I saw the statement that you gave…'

'Och, I spoke to lots of folk, sir… I didnae ken what I was saying half the time. I was so upset.'

'But you heard Martha speak. After the fall…'

'I telt you – I didnae ken what I was saying.'

'Mrs Bolton, you seem to have been the only one to have heard the girl speak.'

'Maybe I heard it, maybe I didnae… it was like a lunatic asylum, the hale thing. There's men shoutin' and women squealin' and squalkin' and dresses swishin' and doors bangin' and I look out and there's Macnair wi' that guilty look on his face and all hell breakin' loose…' And at that point, the old cook began to cry.

'Sorry, sir, she was like a daughter to me. My wee Martha…'

Kane reached into his pocket, produced a cotton handkerchief and gave it to the old lady. She thanked him, took the handkerchief and immediately blew her nose on it.

'Mrs Bolton, I am content that you keep the handkerchief...'

Tears were streaming down the old lady's face: 'Dinnae be silly, son. I'll have it laundered and sent up tae the Advocates for you.'

The exchange was interrupted by a man's voice calling from downstairs, summoning Mrs Bolton. Kane thought that he recognised the voice, but he couldn't quite place it.

'Excuse me, Mr Kane.'

The old cook opened a nearby door and shouted down: 'Haud yer horses – I'll be there in a minute.'

Then she turned to Kane: 'I'm telling ye, this place is as busy as Princes Street the day. I could be answering that door all day. What with you and the other fella – the one doon the stairs now.'

'The other fellow?'

'Aye, what do they cry him again? Eh – Mr Mackintosh. Mackintosh of the Detective.'

***

'I thought I heard a voice, sir.'

Mrs Bolton had taken Kane down to the kitchen area where the back stairs ended. Where Martha Cunningham's body had come to an abrupt halt. And there – on his hands and knees – was Mackintosh of the Detective.

Gone was the bowler hat and coat. He had also divested himself of his jacket and was now kneeling at the foot of the stairs, in his waistcoat and shirt-sleeves. When Kane reached the foot of the stairs, Mackintosh was putting his thick glasses back on to focus on Kane's face.

'You'll excuse me not shaking hands, Mr Kane. Sometimes, you have to look at the locus yourself and do the job right.' Mackintosh removed his thick glasses again and held them at a distance from his face, down towards the carpet on the stairs.

'These old eyeglasses are very, very good for the magnification, sir. The threads of this carpet are as large as green beans now.'

Kane watched Mackintosh examine the fibres for a moment.

'And what, Mr Mackintosh...'

He was soon corrected: 'Just 'Mackintosh', sir.'

'And what – 'Mackintosh' – do you hope to find in a thick layer of carpet some weeks after the event?'

Mackintosh stood up and thought for a moment.

'Sir Charles must be very rich indeed that he can lay such a fine piece of carpet on a stone stair used only by the servants...'

The old cook, Mrs Bolton, spoke: 'The master takes very good care of us. This used to be the carpet on the main staircase upstairs. But Miss Cordelia said that it was too old-fashioned, so a new one was ordered and this one was put on the back stairs.'

Mackintosh shook his head: 'Better not tell my wife that, or she'll be here daily looking for any other scraps. So, Sir Charles takes very good care of you?'

'Aye, sir. Especially the young lassies.'

Mackintosh and Kane shot an immediate glance between themselves. Kane spoke:

'And what about Mr Hand? How does he get on with the young ladies?'

'Why don't you ask me yourself, sir?' said Mr Hand, who was now standing at the kitchen door.

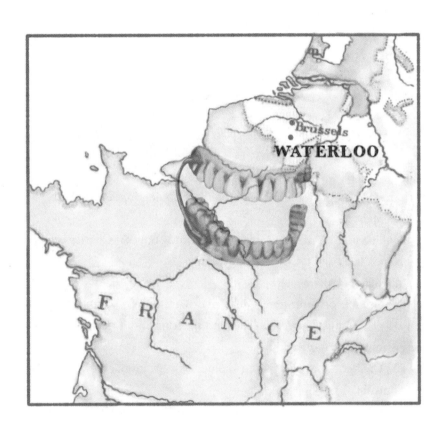

Chapter Five

'Are you simple-minded, Kane? Is there something wrong with you – up here?'

Standing in front of the fireplace of the study now, Sir Charles pointed to his own head and twirled his index finger.

'Not that I am aware, sir.'

'Because I invite you here – into my own house – one of the great houses of Edinburgh, and you're found skulking about near the kitchen asking impertinent questions.'

'Sir Charles, I was making polite conversation with Detective Mackintosh.'

'Detective? That fool is more deluded than you are. He has as much chance of recognising a clue as a blind man in a coal cellar.'

'Father...' Cordelia Irving stood up now. 'Father, Mr Kane is our guest...'

Sir Charles turned his ire on his daughter now: 'Stuff and nonsense! He will never be our guest. He is as much our guest as that filthy sweep who dreeps into this house down the chimney.' And with that, the old man began to cough uncontrollably into a handkerchief.

Cordelia looked worried.

'Father has been poorly these last few months...'

The old man was furious: 'You stupid girl. That is no business of a stranger.'

Cordelia fell silent. Sir Charles turned towards Kane.

'You are wondering why I called you here?'

Kane looked around himself: 'I am more wondering, sir, why my instructing agent, Mr Malcolm, is not present. I am not permitted to conduct business if he is not here...'

The old man smirked: 'Well, he does not require to be here for me to dispense with your services, does he? You have been a great disappointment to me, young fellow. I have offered you the hand of friendship. In your humble position, sir, I have offered you the world. And you throw that offer back in my face...'

The old man was ranting now. Kane's mind began to wander. As he stood in the study, he looked into the face of Sir Charles and an image appeared in his mind. His own father's study. There were countless books there. His father had collected different versions of The Bible and had read the New Testament in the original Greek. Sometimes, when Kane had been a small child and allowed to play in the study, he would sit on the floor surrounded by some of those old books. His father would sit at a great desk, working on that Sunday's sermon, smoking his pipe: now gesticulating, now trying certain phrases out loud. Kane would sit on the floor on the rug, four or five years old, with a small piece of charcoal and pieces of scrap paper, and he would draw lines and shapes. Once, his father had left The New Testament in Greek on the floor. The young Edward Kane, his tongue placed between his teeth in an exercise of fierce concentration, carefully copied all the shapes, the strange triangles and the bisected ovals on the title on the cover:

Ἡ Καινὴ Διαθήκη

When the young Edward's father looked down and realised that his prodigy had produced the words 'The New Testament' – and in Greek letters, no less – he gave an almighty laugh, scooped up the boy and flung him up into the air and then caught him again with a warm hug. Of course, that event found its way into the Minister's next sermon (as many, perhaps more mundane family moments would, in order to make some scriptural point or another) about the understanding of God's Word.

But why that memory now?

Sir Charles Irving continued to shout. Kane could see and hear the old man ('...you have no idea who you are dealing with here...') but some part, some inner part of Kane had become detached from the whole event, and his mind continued to wander.

No, that's not it. That's not it at all.

The memory that he was trying to conjure was a completely different one. Still in his father's study. But younger now, maybe aged three. It was one of the books. A small bible, made for children, perhaps. With illustrations. Kane clearly remembered one of the illustrations: Jesus being baptised by John the Baptist. Jesus in the river with his long, brown hair that never seemed to get wet; John the Baptist looking wild-eyed; and the dove, the beautiful, radiant white bird coming down. And everybody seemed so happy to see it. Even at that young age, Kane wondered why people did not welcome other birds in Edinburgh the same way, but would shoo them away impatiently.

But not that. Not that memory, but yes, that book.

Later on in the book there was an illustration of the story of Jesus on the mountain being tempted by the Devil. The illustration had always frightened the young Kane. It was the combination of two elements: the unreadable face of Jesus and the evil face of Satan. *Is it really temptation if you don't want what is being offered to you in the first place?* Kane would ponder that in years to come when he would think of that inscrutable face. But now, he located the reason for the memory. The illustrator had caught a certain expression perfectly. The Devil's face, in offering Jesus the whole world and everything in it: and Satan looked confident, but desperate; threatening, but brittle; smiling, but clearly tormented. And now, submerged under the stream of invective spewed out by the brittle old man before him, the face of the Devil in that child's book was the face of Sir Charles Irving today. And then Kane had the sudden, certain realisation. The furious and immediate demands, the coughing fits, the hollowness in the old man's eyes: Sir Charles Irving was dying.

***

'You're a better man than I am, Mr K. I would have lamped him one...'

Horse held up a clenched fist and held the knuckles near Kane's face.

'Thank you, Mr Horse You can take the fist out of my face now.'

'I'm just so angry for you, Mr K, after all that's happened and you doing all that work and losing all that money.'

Kane reminded Horse that he hadn't precisely lost the money. It had been taken from him at knifepoint.

'But at least, Mr K, you'll have the money you're owed for the work you done for him after you got robbed.'

Kane sighed: 'I'm afraid not. He said that the money in the envelope was also a payment to account for the work to be done. I'm afraid that that particular well appears to be dry.'

'Well, sir – can't be helped. But, anyways, I've put out the word, Mr K, about the two blokes what fleeced you.'

'Put out the word?'

'There's a nice young lady friend of mine, and she works at the Surgeon's Hall up the road, in Nicolson Street there...'

'And?'

'And, what with all them doctors and the like hanging about the place, she says that one or two of them doctors is doing a lot of teeth-pulling and such these days.'

'I'm afraid, Horse, that I have lost the drift of your meaning...'

'Well, sir, you'll remember that the night you was set upon, I came to your assistance with me Aunty Betty...'

'I remember it well...'

'And me Auntie relieved the big tall fella of the rest of his teeth?'

'Vividly...'

'Well, I was doing a bit of thinkin' here, and I thought, if it was me:
Right – I've just come into a bundle of money. What do I do now?'

'Yes?'

'I thought: I'll 'ave a jar...' Horse mimicked drinking beer, '...and I'll
get myself a decent piece of steak.'

'Sounds like an excellent pastime, Mr Horse.'

'So, I'll be standin' there, Mr K, with a good, strong beer in me hand
and a good thick steak on me plate. But, here's the problem....'

Kane attempted, without success, to conjure the memory of the taste
of a good, thick steak...

'The bloke wot rolled you that night. He's got all that money – but he
can't eat the streak – because he's got no teeth!'

'And so?'

'And so, you gets the teeth made, Mr K. You gets yourself some
'Waterloo Teeth'...'

Now, it was acknowledged that Mr Horse had served as a lad, and
served with distinction, at the Battle of Waterloo in 1815. And it was
never challenged – nor should it be – that he was given the nickname
'Horse' by the Duke of Wellington himself. And sometimes, when he
was deep in his cups, Horse would regale and horrify in equal measure
with his memories of that great victory. Tales of bravery and cowardice,
and of the strange things that men do in battle.

One such tale concerned the collection of dead men's teeth. The
bodies of the dead soldiers lay across that plain and were soon set upon
by the natural forces of decay. But Horse's story was of a different kind of
scavenger. Groups of camp followers, low men, would scour the scattered
corpses searching for good teeth to remove and to sell. Set into dentures,
these teeth would be offered to the rich. The Battle of Waterloo, with
some fifty thousand dead, led to a nice glut in the teeth economy of what
came later to be known as 'Waterloo Teeth'.

'So, Mr K, I was asking me friend, Mrs Ratchett, about this and she says that you can still get a decent pair of them old gnashers for a couple of quid.'

'That would seem a substantial amount of money for the man that we're taking about, Mr Horse.'

'Not if he wants to eat the steak, sir. I got Mrs Ratchett on the lookout for anybody who wants to buy some, and I've got me little girl at the Surgeon's Hall on the lookout for anybody who wants them fitted.'

'Well, Mr Horse. That seems a sensible precaution. And, on the subject of food, what culinary delights do we have in store this evening?'

'We got a nice mutton broth poured over some of yesterday's bread, Mr K. Can't be too careful with them old purse strings at the moment...'

***

'And the peace of God, which passeth all understanding...'

The Minister stood in the pulpit of the great High Kirk of St Giles and raised both hands, seeking blessing from above.

That sermon, thought Kane, was precisely like the peace of God in that it had passed all understanding.

The Minister's polished monotone filled the grey space, while Kane looked around. Many of the usual attenders, the poor, some close to tears, sat with their heads bowed. And the wealthy and worthy of Edinburgh sat, as if attending a play, luminous in their finery.

The problem, thought Kane, of having a Minister as a father is that, once you have been exposed to several hundred sermons – as Kane had – then the sermon structure was all too apparent in the hands of a clumsy preacher.

Kane's mind wandered. His thoughts turned to Miss Amanda. Kane had thought that, after a few years at the Bar, he would have made those inroads to establishing himself and being able to provide for his fiancée. Yet here he remained. Social connections appeared to be the surest method of securing instruction and – as Sir John Forbes-Knight had painfully reminded him – Kane had none to speak of.

Even his good friend Collins – a veritable almanac of every available legal remedy – had found it difficult to establish himself.

Kane squeezed his eyes shut. *The Parlour Maid Murderer.* Not precisely the type of case that Kane had hoped to establish his reputation. Every person he had spoken to had presumed the guilt of Patrick Macnair.

Kane's eyes wandered around the congregation, resting on a couple of restless young chaps, who seemed somewhat out of place. And that man – over there – looked familiar, but his head was bowed. *Was he praying – or asleep?* And that enormous, colourful and excitable lady at his side. Nudging him now, nudging him awake. *That must have hurt!* He's jolted up. *Inspector Mackintosh!*

Mackintosh awoke with a start. The first thing that he was aware of was the glowering face of his wife. Her lips pursed, her enormous eyes staring and wide, she looked like an outraged owl. Mackintosh mouthed the words 'Apologies, my dear' and resumed his pretence of attention to the Minister and the sermon, the premises of which seemed no further advanced.

Mackintosh bowed his head as if in prayer, but, all the time, his eyes were scanning the congregation. He was new to the church, but he already knew a number of the congregation by sight, some worthy, some less so. Mackintosh wondered what a ne'er-do-well like Willy Cullen was doing in here today? From that big Irish Catholic family. Macintosh made a note to keep an extra eye on him – just in case he 'bumped into' some of the wealthier parties on the way out.

And behind him, Jamie Garden. Mackintosh had never seen Cullen and Garden work as a team before. He thought that he had best make his presence known. Mackintosh gave a loud cough. Cullen and Garden looked over a little too quickly. Mackintosh smiled over at them. Cullen and Garden exchanged looks with each other, then – despite the Minister being in only the foothills of the sermon – both men rose from their seats and pushed their way to the front entrance.

As Mackintosh was looking back, he realised that he himself was being looked at – by Edward Kane.

There was that slight jolt of recognition as eyes met eyes, then Kane gave him a gentle smile, as if to say: 'Will this sermon never end?' Mackintosh looked at the Minister, then at Mrs Mackintosh, then back at Kane. Trapped. Kane bowed his head and began to shake lightly, suppressing the urge to laugh out loud.

***

The sermon having finally extinguished itself despite its attempt to achieve eternal life, just outside the church entrance, Mackintosh introduced Mrs Mackintosh to the young Advocate.

The lady, dressed in her Sunday best, with her wide eyes and bright blue bonnet reminded Kane of a startled parrot.

'My dear, this is Edward Kane, Advocate. As I was telling you, Mr Kane here will be defending Patrick Macnair.'

Kane tipped his hat and made a bow, and the lady curtsied.

'Yours, ma'am.'

'Pleased to make your acquaintance, Mr Kane. But here's the question: did he do it?'

Mackintosh interrupted this unexpected interrogation: 'My dear, my dear, please...'

'I only ask, Mr Kane, I only ask because – look at my husband. He can't sleep a wink with all his tossing and turning, all of the night, Mr Kane. And he can't eat, either – take a good look at him, wasting away to nothing...'

To be obliging, Kane took a good look at Mackintosh. Mackintosh was essentially the shape of a Christmas pudding, but Kane did not relay this observation.

'I am heartily sorry, madam, but this is a case that vexes us all. And I am happy to admit that I, too, have been losing sleep. Your husband and I appear to be engaged in a joint enterprise: to discover the truth of the matter. And our investigations are found wanting.'

'But did he do it, Mr Kane? Has he denied it?'

'I fear, madam, that those may be two separate issues...'

Mrs Mackintosh flipped up her parasol in disgust: 'Oh, you lawyers. You have an equivocation for everything. Well the sooner that the scoundrel is tried and hanged, the better.'

She looked beyond Kane for a moment, gave a little wave to another lady across the way, and then turned to her husband: 'Mackintosh – I see that Mrs Phillips would like to have a word. I leave you here with your legal friend. See if you can't talk some sense into him.'

And with that, she turned on her heel and was gone down the street.

The two gentlemen did not speak for a moment, then Mackintosh broke the silence: 'You'll have to excuse my missus, Mr Kane. She's a very passionate woman. Very passionate. And she does worry about me.'

Kane smiled. 'Mackintosh, who were the two young lads who left in a hurry during the sermon?'

'A couple of the local boys, sir, Jamie Garden and Willie Cullen. Well-known faces to the local officers around here, sir. Nothing for you to worry about. Most likely they were being kept at the police office at the side of the building first.'

'Not faces that I recognise.'

'Perhaps not the model of the regular church attender, sir. Me and the wife have just started here at Saint Giles ourselves. Mrs Mackintosh said there'll be a better class of Christian here, sir.'

It struck Kane that that would have been an excellent title for one of his father's sermons.

Mackintosh continued: 'And, as she reminds me, Mr Kane, there's a reason why every home keeps rat poison. Get rid of the pests and keep the plague off the streets. Look at those two young fellas. Jamie Garden – a dangerous idiot. The worst kind. The one who thinks that he's the brains of the outfit. And the big lad, Willie Cullen...'

Mackintosh pointed to his head.

'Nothing at all up here, Mr Kane.'

'They looked harmless enough, Mackintosh.'

'Aye, sir. They're harmless enough until one of them has a knife at your throat. I'll bet my pension they'll be up to no good, the two of them, tonight. They'll be dead, the two of them, before they reach twenty, that's my prediction. And good riddance to them.'

Kane sighed and looked towards where he had recently witnessed the hanging of Charles Makepeace.

The gentlemen's conversation was interrupted by a woman's voice: 'Perhaps education is the answer?'

The men looked round, and there was a smiling Florrie Forbes-Knight.

The gentlemen tipped their hats.

'Sorry, miss, didn't see you there.'

'And would your opinion have been any different, had you seen me?'

The detective shook his head: 'Not mine, miss. In my game, we don't teach rats the alphabet. Education? They don't seem to have a problem with their 'rithmetic when they're counting the money they've stolen.'

Mackintosh gave another bow and nodded towards his wife, who was now across the street, gesticulating wildly to him.

'Now, if you'll excuse me, odds are that I'm about to be schooled for something myself...'

Florrie and Kane watched Mackintosh waddle across the road, greet his wife timidly, and dodge the attention of Mrs Mackintosh's wayward umbrella before the couple dandered away down the street.

Kane smiled and turned to Florrie:

'And what brings you here, Miss Forbes-Knight? I don't recall seeing you at Saint Giles before?'

'I was in one of the other chapels. I'm not ashamed to say, Mr Kane, that I have been trying on – for want of a better phrase – a number of different churches in recent weeks.'

'You make it sound like choosing a new hat.'

'The similarities, I would have thought, would be obvious. In the first place, one is looking to achieve a good fit and, further, if one makes the wrong choice, then that is likely to result in a persistent headache.'

Kane laughed.

'And of the limited prerogatives available to my sex, Edward, I understand that one of those is that I may change my mind. On that basis, I confess, on some days I wake up Moderate and on others positively Evangelical.'

'Then I bow to the lady's prerogative.'

Kane gave a mock bow and Florrie a pretend curtsey.

'Anyway, Edward, I knew I'd find you here, if only because Saint Giles is the patron of the leper colony and, in our household at the moment, well...'

Kane frowned: 'Your father had some harsh words for me, Florrie.'

'He was very distracted that day. Of course, it was not helped by the fact that he had been visited by Sir Charles Irving that morning...'

'Before or after my visit?'

'Oh, before. I rather think that your fate had been sealed as soon as Sir Charles entered father's study. What on earth did you do to that old man that he is so agin you?'

Kane thought for a moment, then: 'I refused to be bought. Like a new hat...'

'But you acquired the headache, nonetheless.'

The two friends stood and smiled.

'Anyway, Edward, I have something for you.'

Florrie reached into the folds of her coat and produced a letter.

'It's from Amanda.'

Kane took the letter and stood looking at it for a moment. Florrie placed her hand gently on his arm: 'Would you like to be alone when you read it?'

Kane shook his head and opened the envelope. He removed the pink, scented letter and read its child-like handwriting:

My darling, darling Edward.

You must excuse this moist peace of paper. It is full of the imaginary tears that I have wanted to cry since Papa (CRUEL Papa) has separated us.

Papa said that we must part because you are a failure. I have told Papa that I know that you are a failure, but that I retain a deep affection for you despite your many and obvious shortcomings.

My concert is at the end of this month. Mr Brookes says that the concert will be called 'The Epiphany', because on that date the world will see my true talent revealed.

We have ordered a great number of jewels that will be sewn into my dress, because Mr Brookes says that they will sparkle under the lights and amaze the audience as I sing.

Mr Brookes also says that Papa should consider the rental of halls in London and also in America because of the demand that will surely follow after my Edinburgh debut.

And so, my darling Edward. All is not lost yet. When I find my fame perhaps I could make a great deal of money and I could provide for us both in a way that you cannot. Perhaps you could give up your career as a failed lawyer and assist me in mine? Mr Brookes says that I will need someone to carry the heavy trunks containing my costumes. That way, you could be assured of a regular income and we could still see each other from time to time.

I write these words more in sorrow than in anguish.

Yours sincerely

Amanda Forbes-Knight

p.s.
Please come to see my concert. Please bring friends, if you can. Unfortunately, there can be no discount on the admission price just because we were formerly engaged.

Kane let his arm drop, still holding the letter. Florrie shook her head: 'I've read it. I helped her with some of the spelling. 'Epiphany' proved particularly problematic. How are you feeling, Edward?'

Kane held up the letter again and smiled ruefully: 'I confess, Florrie , that I do not know if this communication is a letter of goodbye or an offer of employment.'

Florrie shook her head: 'I don't think that Amanda knows herself.'

Kane nodded. He stood and looked at Florrie: *What a beautiful, mournful smile she has.*

The two friends stood silent as the church building emptied its parishioners onto Parliament Square, which was soon filled with the chatter and bustle of families and friends.

And then, above those voices, Kane heard a more familiar one: 'Mister K, Mister K...'

Pushing his way now through the throng was Horse. When Horse saw that Kane was speaking to Florrie, he gave the lady a short bow, then: 'Sorry to interrupt, Mister K, sir, but I think we found him.'

'Found him?'

Horse attempted to relay the information in cryptic fashion. He pointed to his mouth: 'The bloke with the teeth, sir – or should I say without the teeth, sir. The tall, skinny one. The one what wants the steak, sir...'

At this stage of the narrative, Horse winked, pursed his lips and tapped his nose.

Kane looked puzzled.

Horse slowed down now: 'He has been and gone and seen a certain lady... what is the particular friend... of a certain Jewish gentleman... who likes to have in his safekeeping... for example a valuable family watch...'

Kane nodded: 'Ah!'

'Well, sir, a certain wery tall gentleman has recently purchased a pair of gnashers that previously had belonged to a dead soldier in a field in Belgium, sir.'

There was silence for a moment, while Kane took this in.

Then Florrie spoke: 'My, Edward! You do live an interesting life...'

'And where is that gentleman now, Mr Horse.'

'Well, sir, he haggles the teeth down to 30 bob and he demands a written receipt in case them gnashers don't work.'

'Yes?'

'And in that written receipt, Mr K, he has given his name and his address as proof of the purchase.'

Horse retrieved a crumpled piece of paper from his coat pocket and handed it to Kane. Kane unfolded it and read the name Billy Brown and an address in The Cowgate.

'So – he lives five minutes' walk from here, Mr Horse.'

'He does indeed, sir. I thought that I'd go and visit him tonight, sir. And that I might take me old Aunty Betty with me. I think she'll want to meet him again. Now if you'll excuse me.'

Horse gave a low bow to Florrie and made off.

Florrie watched him go: 'Well, Edward, whatever might be said of your man, Horse, he certainly seems to hold a great affectation for his elderly aunt.'

Edward smiled: 'Yes. They're very close...'

***

'Shut up, ye idiot!'

'Jamie – who'll hear me up here? Look!'

Standing in the moonlight, high upon the rooftops of Heriot Row, Jamie Garden and Willie Cullen could see the lights of the Old Town tenements and the distant glow of lights in Fife.

'Anyway, it's after eleven – who's up at this time?'

Jamie and Willie crept along the rooftops, checking each little roof hatch as they went. The 'M' shapes of the roofs afforded them an easy passage along the valleys of roof tiles and gutters covering the long street.

Garden turned around to challenge Cullen: 'Are ye sure that it's one of the ones along here?'

'I told ye – my uncle worked up on the roof here last week. We should see the wee roof-door any minute. He said he left the hatch unlocked. So that we can just dreep down intae the house and take what we want. He's put a chalk mark of an 'x' on the outside hatch. Keep going...'

Garden shook his head: 'You'd better be right. What house was it again?'

'Ye know – the wee auld fella's house – ma uncle says that the place is just packed wi' jewels and golden candlesticks and stuff – the auld fella – I think they cry him 'Sir Charles. Sir Charles Irving'. Ha! Here's the door here...'

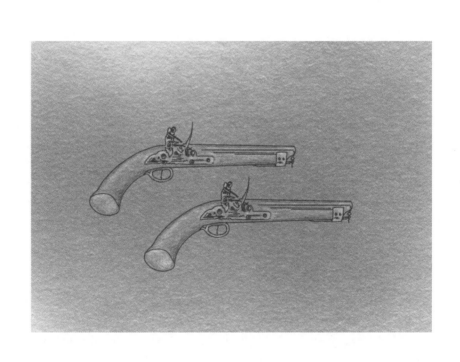

Chapter Six

'Jesus, Mary and Joseph – you'll wake up the dead wi' that loud knocking. Have ye seen the time? I've told ye, sir – he's not here the now and I'm not expecting him back this night.'

Horse stood at the door of the dingy tenement as he was tongue-lashed again by Mrs Malone, the landlady, in her Irish brogue.

The pawnbrokers' receipt for the Waterloo teeth had revealed an address in the part of Edinburgh largely populated by Irish immigrants and labourers. Horse was trying to contain his temper.

'No, madam, you told me earlier that he might be back by now...'

'Well, he's not here. And if he's not home by this time, then I'm not expecting him now. I am not Billy Brown's keeper, I keep tellin' ye that, so make yourself scarce or I'll call the constable on yeez...'

The old lady stood shivering in her shabby coat, holding up her candlestick and peering through the gloom. Horse was certain she knew more than she was saying. But there was more than one way to skin this cat. Horse gave the lady a low bow.

'I'm sorry to be a pest, madam, but I've got some very important news for him. And it's about the inheritance...'

The old lady's interest was piqued: 'The inheritance?'

'Yes, the inheritance. You will have seen for yourself, madam, that he 'as just received the first instalment of that very inheritance from his aunt...'

The old lady stood in silence while she considered this. Then nodded: 'He did pay his arrears in full last week, sir. But not a single peep about any inheritance to speak of...'

Horse flew the kite a little higher: 'It would be obvious when you think about it, madam. New clothes?'

The landlady nodded. Horse sighed.

'New teeth?'

Mrs Malone smiled in realisation: 'I knew there was something different about the boy. Just couldn't put me finger on it...'

Horse patted the outside of the breast pocket of his coat, where his Aunty Betty was kept: 'I've got the balance of the business in me pocket here, madam. And I need to deliver it to him, personal, like.'

The landlady was obviously swithering now.

Horse put on his hat: 'Well, madam, if he ain't here, he ain't here. I'll just take all this money back to where it come from. The will says – specific – that if he can't be found, then the money goes straight to the church...' he turned around to go.

'No – wait, sir. Who did you say the money was from?'

'Er, from his recently deceased auntie...' The string of Horse's kite was now parlously stretched: 'From his poor old auntie, a woman very much like yourself, Mrs Malone, from the Old Country. Worked like a dog she did, every day of her life from the age of eleven. And now all that money goes to the priest instead of her flesh and blood. It's a bloomin' liberty if you ask me. But that's The Law for you, ennit? Goodnight, madam. Sorry to trouble you.'

The old lady was conflicted now: 'The Auld Country? Billy Brown never the once mentioned an auntie in the Auld Country. Whereabouts in Ireland was she from, now?'

'Well, madam, she was, er, she was...'

Horse's mind suddenly resembled a fresh, white bedsheet, blowing on a washing line. Horse had never in his life visited the Emerald Isle of Ireland – and found himself running through various folk songs that he would hear the Irish

soldiers sing in the barracks. There had to be some place names in there.

Ah, but they had been good on the fiddle and the whistle, but the songs...the songs...the place names...

The white sheet flapped in the wind.

Horse hummed to himself: 'Oh, Peggy Gordon, you are my darlin'/ Come sit ye down upon my knee...' – no place name there...

Those Irish soldiers - they loved their singing and their fighting and their whiskey. What about 'Whiskey in the Bar' - or was it 'Whiskey in the JAR'? The words and even the tune of that song seemed to be different every time they sang it. How did it start?

'As I was going over...' - Yes! - 'the Cork and Kerry mountains...'

Horse cleared his throat, then: 'I believe, madam, that the deceased auntie came from the vicinity of the Cork and Kerry mountains.'

The old lady smiled:

'I had a cousin meself who married a fisherman from Bantry...'

Horse nodded sagely: 'Ah. Bantry...'

'You know – where they catch all them little pilchards...'

Horse nodded even more sagely: 'Of course, all them little pilchards...'

There was a silence between them, then Mrs Malone uttered the words: 'Do you know The Doric Tavern?'

'I do indeed, madam.'

'Ye'll find Billy Brown in there. And if he's not there, they'll tell ye where he is.'

Horse gave a low bow: 'I thank you madam. You have done Mr Brown a great service. I will see that he gets what he deserves.'

'No excuses for the rent being late now!'

'Indeed not, Mrs Malone, indeed not. And I have another small bequest here for his little friend...'

'His little friend?'

'You know, the little, fat bloke what Mr Brown hangs about with. Oh, by all accounts, they do have some very jolly times together...'

Mrs Malone thought for a moment. 'I did see him with a wee fat fellow. But only the once.'

'In the last week or so?'

'Yes, sir. Before he came into the money. He was at the front door lettin' all the heat out of the house -and I shouted 'Billy Brown – were ye born in a barn?' I looks and there's a wee fat fella there, and he hands Billy a long envelope.'

'And did you hear what they were saying?'

'No, sir. But I did hear Billy say, 'Thank you, Dode' when he took the envelope.'

'Thank you... what?'

'Thank you, Dode'. It's what the Edinburgh folk call 'George'.'

'Dode?'

'Aye, and when the wee stout fella gets away from the door, I says to Billy: 'And who was yer wee friend, then?' And Billy says 'Fat Dode? Fat Dode is nobody.' And he starts to laugh.'

Horse considered this for a minute, then asked: 'And did you see what was in the envelope what was handed over?'

Mrs Malone looked somewhat abashed for a moment, then said: 'Well, ye have to understand, sir, that Billy Brown was a good few weeks behind with the rent...'

'Yes?'

'So when he goes out that night, I goes up to his room, ye know, to see if there's any washing to be done – because that's part of the room and the board...'

'Yes?'

'And, as I'm going about picking up the clothes, I sees that envelope and on the front there's writing – but crossed out – and it says 'Mr George Soutar, Esq'.'

'George Soutar...'

'And I'm thinkin' to meself – that must be the wee fat fella, with 'George' and 'Dode' being the same and all. So I takes the envelope and I opens it up, because, ye know, it might have some of the rent money in it...'

'And?'

'Isn't there a bread knife in it. Just a long bread knife. But no money, or anything like that. And I'm thinkin' to meself, 'What's the use of a breadknife when you haven't even a loaf?''

Horse thought back to the night of the robbery. It was a bread knife that had been held to Kane's throat during the attack. He gave a low bow:

'Mrs Malone, I am very much obliged to you. You have done your civic duty proud, madam, and I will now go to these gentlemen and pay them out good and proper.'

Mrs Malone glowed and curtseyed. And Horse gave a doff of his hat – and hurried in the direction of The Doric Bar.

★★★

'Shhh! What's that noise?'

Jamie Garden and Willie Cullen stood frozen in the long dining room belonging to Sir Charles Irving.

'x' had marked the spot of entry on the roof hatch, and now they were creeping along the dark staircases and rooms of that great Edinburgh house.

Jamie Garden had been brought up in Edinburgh, but his grandmother had been one of the cooks in the grand estate at Hopetoun House, out by Queensferry. As a child he would often visit there with his mother and, when the master was away, his grandmother would sneak him into the lavish rooms – 'But dinnae touch anything, son, or the butler will ken.' – and the boy would stand and wonder at the candlesticks, the rugs, the paintings, the gilded chairs, the chandeliers, the books, the pianoforte, the long, long dining table that would seat – how many? – thirty? Forty? One day, he vowed to himself, he would sit at such a table.

His grandmother would take him into the library: 'Ye see all them books, son. That's the only difference between us and them. The rich fowk ken whit's in all them books and we dinnae. That's the only difference. So, work at your books, son.'

And Garden had worked at the books. He was soon the best reader in his class at school. But what of it? He was surrounded by fools. Teachers had suggested that he take up an appropriate apprenticeship – perhaps working as a bookseller's apprentice? But why would he do that? He was bound for greater things.

Better to hide in plain sight among the fools around him, periodically writing letters for them or reading letters from home to those illiterate Irish who now swarmed the streets of Edinburgh. He would write their replies for them. For a fee.

Garden had developed a standard formula he could recite in his sleep. A tale of streets paved with gold and a brighter tomorrow in the beautiful city of Edinburgh.

Sometimes, as he was reading this stock narrative reply back to the labourer in question, he would look up and see the tears form in that great navvy's eyes at the picture that he had painted.

And the word spread: if you wanted something done 'with the reading and the writing' – you came to Jamie Garden.

All of those small fees for the work done amounted to a tidy income for Garden. But that was not enough.

Willie Cullen would be the brawn to Garden's brains and, if necessary, Garden's defence to the gallows. If all went wrong, then Garden could come to an arrangement with the Crown, give evidence against Cullen and walk away a free man.

Cullen whispered now in his low, Irish tone: 'D'ye hear that, Jamie. Some fella's doin' a power of shoutin' now in that other room. Listen.'

The two intruders listened carefully. Judging from the voices they could hear, there seemed to be some kind of intense argument between an old man and an old woman.

Culllen laughed and whispered: 'Ah – listen. The auld girl is giving the auld fella as good as she's getting by the sounds of it!'

Garden and Cullen did not leave the expansive dining room for fear of being discovered. So Garden quietly pulled up a chair and sat down. A secret, silent, unwelcome guest at Sir Charles Irving's table.

Cullen was listening at the door now and quietly chuckling: 'Jamie, Jamie – ye should hear what the auld dear is saying to him. Sure, she's got the goods on the auld fella. I'd give that auld witch a belt if she spoke to me like that, I tell ye.'

Cullen slumped down onto a chair at the dining table beside Garden. Then he smiled and began to rummage through the stolen items in his bag. He produced a solid silver salt cellar and pepper pot.

Garden frowned: 'What the blazes are you doing, Cullen?'

'Well, Jamie, I thought that since we're sittin' at the table of them great people, then it would be rude not to eat with them.'

And like a child at an imaginary tea party, Cullen began nodding and talking to other guests: 'Oh, yes, milady...'

Cullen began to drink his imaginary tea from an imaginary teacup, holding the imaginary handle between his thumb and index finger and pointing his pinky towards the ceiling.

'What's that you say, milady? His lordship hasn't given you a good seeing to in a good long while? And could I do you the pleasure? Well, I'll certainly consult me social diary, now.'

And Garden watched and smiled, in spite of himself.

'And this here venison wants a good deal of seasoning, don't it? Could you pass the pepper, please?'

And Cullen took the solid silver pepper pot and sprinkled the white pepper liberally over the dining table.

Garden put out his hand: 'Stop it, you fool...'

Cullen laughed.

And then Cullen felt the white pepper dust enter his nose and the sneeze was now inevitable. Like a great runaway train approaching from a tunnel, nothing was going to stop it. Cullen half-closed his eyes, gave a short intake of breath, curled his top lip over his teeth, tilted his head backwards and...

Garden jumped up, got behind Cullen's head, placed the crook of his right arm over Cullen's nose and mouth and – when the sneeze came – it was barely audible.

Garden hissed: 'You idiot – you'll get us both hanged.' He kept his arm over Cullen's face until Cullen nodded.

Willie Cullen, looking sheepish, whispered: 'Thank you, Jamie. Yer a grand man to have on side.' Then gave an almighty, violent sneeze.

The argument in the other room stopped, and Cullen and Garden heard footsteps coming towards the dining room.

★★★

'What do you want, Horse?'

The barmaid – her face a study in skepticism and disappointment – stood with folded arms at the front door of The Doric Tavern, blocking Horse's entry.

'Now, is that any way to talk to your favourite Englishman, Josephine?'

Horse had tried the door, but it was locked. However, a quick look through the window revealed a number of patrons, by candlelight, still enjoying their drinks.

The barmaid mock-scolded him: 'You've put me off Englishmen for life, ye toe-rag. Ye haven't been here for months...'

'I told you that night, my dear, I'm a bit of a wanderer, I am.'

The barmaid smiled and shook her head.

'Anyhow, my dear, I'll not stop long. Just looking for my old chum, Billy Brown...'

The barmaid looked puzzled now: 'Billy Brown? I've never seen you with Billy Brown.'

'I've just recently made his acquaintance, like. Since he come into the money.'

'I know – he's spending it like water, as well.'

Horse gave a silent groan. The barmaid continued: 'Well, you've just missed him. He's away with one of the girls.'

'Where to?'

'I don't know – likely to get a bit of private time with her, to get away from the likes of you, ya cheeky scamp.'

Horse rubbed his chin for a moment: 'And what about his little friend. The fat one. Goes by the name of 'Dode'? 'Fat Dode'?'

The girl thought for a moment, then: 'Nah – can't say that I've ever heard of him.'

Then she smiled and cocked her head. 'You comin' in or not, Mr Horse?'

***

Sir Charles Irving and Mrs Bolton stood at the dining room door. Both held up their candles and scanned the room.

The old man screwed up his face and sniffed the air: 'What the deuce is that smell?'

Mrs Bolton sniffed, then: 'Pepper?' She went to the dining table and ran her finger along the scattered white pepper. 'Look at this mess, Charlie. Mr Hand will have something to say to that maid, I'm telling ye.'

Irving was silent for a moment. Then, almost cheerfully: 'Well, Mrs Bolton. That can wait for the morning. Now, I've said all I have to say about the expense of the meat stocks. I have kept you too long from your bed, madam. I will lock up my study, and then I will retire.'

The old man and the cook closed the doors of the dining room. Their voices and footsteps faded into the darkness of the great house.

Wrapped inside the darkness of the long, thick curtains of the floor-length windows, Jamie Garden and Willie Cullen did not stir. Cullen popped out his head and hissed: 'Jamie? Jamie?'

Garden emerged and shook his head: 'You see what nearly happened there.'

'Sure, it was what me barber calls 'a close shave'.'

'Any closer, Willie, and that shave would have cut your throat...'

Cullen held out his enormous shovel-like hands.

'Any closer, Jamie, and I would take them old folks and I'd wring their necks like two auld chickens.'

Garden shook his head: 'Get your bag and let's get out of here...'

***

Twenty-five minutes to midnight. Kane sat, exhausted, at his desk in the Advocates Library.

One small ray of hope had been the envelope that had been waiting for him in his work box, scrawled with *Mister Eddie Kane Esq., Advocate.*

On opening it, however, he found that the contents comprised a washed, starched and newly-ironed handkerchief. The old cook, Mrs Bolton, had made good her promise to return it. There was the accompanying note:

Dear Mister Kane

Sir, I hope you do not mind me calling you 'Eddie' on the envelope. That was the name of one of the bairns that I had lost. He would have been about your age now. Who nose, maybe he would have turned out a gentleman like your goodself.
Thanking you.

Agnes Bolton (Mrs. widow.)

p.s. Speak again to Mr Hand. He nose more than you think.

Kane thought of this note as he was perusing the Macnair papers again.

'I see that this case has made sleepwalkers of all of us...'

Kane looked up from his papers, and there stood a smiling Jon Hunter.

The Law Room of the Advocates Library had been empty at nine o' clock in the evening when Kane had set down his papers.

'I apologise, Jon – I didn't see you.'

'I myself am working in the main library. I did pop my head in earlier, but you were absorbed in your papers, so I left you to it…'

'The trial is next week.'

'I am very well aware of that. And I have read these papers now, on so many occasions, that I have started to dream about the events.'

Kane laughed: 'Then, perhaps, Jon, you can explain to me what actually transpired on the evening in question.'

'I shan't lie, Edward. From the Crown perspective, the case appears simple. Open and shut, you might say. Is it not time, my friend, for Macnair simply to admit as to what he did and to throw himself on the mercy of the Court? Is that not the only way to avoid the gallows?'

And there, at that late hour, in the candlelight of the Law Room, Kane saw something in Jon Hunter's face that he had never seen before. Hidden under the smile and the friendly conversation, there was an undercurrent of something more fragile. Something resembling fear.

Kane realised that this whole case, like a disease, was beginning to infect everyone who came into contact with it: himself, the Dean of Faculty, Jon Hunter. Even Inspector Mackintosh of the Detective was probably lying awake at this hour with the events of the night in question spinning in his head.

But, thought Kane, why should Jon Hunter be afraid? And then it struck him: this case would define Hunter's success or failure as an Advocate. One of the most notorious cases of its day, fish in a barrel – how could he possibly lose? But if he did not secure a conviction in this straightforward case, the most straightforward of cases, he would be discarded into the ranks of the tried, but ineffectual. Dumped into the land of the failures. Kane suddenly felt sorry for Jon Hunter.

'Oh, Jon – do not think that I have not tried. Taking instructions from the chap Macnair is an impossible proposition. I visit him, and the first thing that I see is that he is bent double weeping over the dead parlour maid, and the next I hear – from Sir Charles Irving's old cook, so less – is that Mr Macnair is likely cavorting with ladies of the night – every night – in the precincts of the old Calton Jail.'

Jon Hunter smiled and shook his head.

★★★

Jamie Garden whispered now to Willie Cullen: 'Have you got everything?'

'Me sack is so heavy, Jamie, I can hardly lift it. It was like emptying out Aladdin's cave down there.'

Creeping up the back stairs now, the two intruders came to the open ceiling hatch that led to the void area at the top of the house.

'Now, Willie, you just give me a punty up, I'll get into the hatch, you can hand me up the bags, then I'll give you a hand up.'

They put their bags down gently and silently. Cullen crouched below the ceiling hatch and cupped his hands in front of him. As Garden put his right foot into Cullen's hands, an old man's voice came from the darkness:

'I think you missed one of the candlesticks...'

★★★

'That, my lovely, was a very large helping of a very pleasant gin. It was a shame to put the water in it.'

Horse wiped his mouth with his cuff. The Doric Tavern barmaid smiled knowingly: 'Well, Horse, you know me. I hate to disappoint...'

She nodded towards the clock on the mantle.

'And that's me finished at midnight. And I'll have to walk home now. At this hour. In the dark. If only I had a big, strong man to keep me safe...'

★★★

When the matches flared and the lamps were lit, the first thing that Jamie Garden and Willie Cullen saw, was that Sir Charles Irving had a pair of pistols pointed straight at them.

Irving stood flanked by Mrs Bolton on one side and Mr Hand on the other.

'Were you actually under the impression that you could hide those great, filthy navvy boots behind curtains made of silk?' the old man crowed. 'The question is what to do with you now. And please be assured that these pistols, although they appear antique, are entirely capable of blowing a hole in your head.'

Garden sprang into action: 'My sincerest apologies, Sir Charles. What we did was not right. My friend, his uncle was working on the roof here last week, and he left a tool up on the roof and we came back to get it for him, that's all. And we saw your roof hatch open, so we came down to close it. And temptation got the better of us.'

Sir Charles stood still and silent considering the explanation. Garden took this as an opportunity to persuade further:

'I swear to you, Sir Charles, I swear that we are both honest men. It was a moment of folly, sir. And I swear to you that there will be no repeat of this if you let us go. Upon my mother's life, sir.'

Irving frowned: 'And what is your name, boy?'

Garden thought quickly. This was no time for the truth: 'Bobby. Bobby Peel, sir.'

'And the entire enterprise was not planned?'

'Just a moment of folly, sir.'

Sir Charles was silent for a moment, then: 'In that case, Mr... 'Bobby Peel'... then why did you and your companion here (whose name, no doubt you'll tell me, is something resembling 'Billy Pitt, the Younger') on this entirely spontaneous visit to my home both carry these large sacks?' Sir Charles cocked his head and indicated the two sacks filled with valuables.

The jig was up. Time for Jamie Garden, always the chameleon, to assume a different colour for survival. He nodded and smiled: 'Well, sir you have us there. It has to be admitted, sir. You have us there.'

What was it that Willie Cullen had said when he had been listening at the door to those old people arguing? 'The old woman has got the goods on the old fellow.' That was worth a try here.

'Well, Sir Charles. Apologies, but we couldn't but overhear all that arguing with you and your good lady wife here...'

Mr Hand, the butler, who had been silent until now, spoke out: 'This lady is the cook, you insolent rogue.'

Garden shook his head: 'And that makes it worse, doesn't it? The cook knows things, Sir Charles. And so do we, now...'

Of course, Garden had no real idea what he was talking about. But the chance remark made by his companion could perhaps be parlayed into an agreement not to have the police sent for. With a little skillful handling, there might even be a profit to be turned here.

Jamie Garden smiled. This was Jamie Garden at his best. Jamie Garden who could talk his way out of anything. Jamie Garden who was destined for great things.

And with that, Sir Charles Irving took his pistol and he shot Jamie Garden in the head.

***

'Where were you last night, Horse? I looked into your quarters when I arrived home and there was neither sight nor sound of you.'

Kane sat at the kitchen table, one hand holding a fat sausage on a fork, the other a cup of steaming hot tea. Horse sat on a little stool by the open fire, toasting bread.

'And what o'clock might that have been, sir?'

'I confess, it was past midnight.'

'I was out and about, sir, doing the necessary.'

'It is difficult to imagine, Mr Horse, any 'necessary' that requires to be done at that hour of the night – or should I say 'morning'.'

Horse smiled and had a vision of the Doric barmaid, Josephine.

'You would be surprised, Mr K, very surprised at the sort of things what need seeing to in the middle of the night.'

Kane drank his tea and said nothing.

'Anyways, sir, I got the net is closing in on them two warmints.'

Kane nodded: 'Our two friends, who so kindly relieved me of Sir Charles' envelope. At knifepoint.'

'Them's the ones, sir. Now, the tall, lanky one – Billy Brown is the name – I just about got him last night. But he was off with one of the girls spending your money, sir.'

Kane thought for a moment. *At least my money is out on the town enjoying itself...*

'I'll 'ave him in the next couple of days, no doubt about that, Mr K. I knows where he lives, I knows where he drinks, I knows who his friends is – we'll 'ave him by next week at the latest...'

'Excellent, Horse.'

'And I'll see how much money he's still got from the wad they nicked off you, sir.'

Horse now removed the slice of bread from the toasting fork and laid it onto a small plate on the table in front of Kane, who began to spread with his butter knife.

'But the other bloke, Mr K. The other bloke is a different story.'

'The more rotund gentleman?' inquired Kane.

'That one, sir. He's vanished like.'

'Very mysterious, Mr Horse,' said Kane, munching on the toast.

'No, no, that's not what I mean. How can I put it?'

Horse thought for a moment.

'Some people, they are always there, and you know they are there, but you don't know they are there. Do you know what I mean, sir?'

Kane shook his head: 'I'm afraid, Mr Horse, that the mystery deepens.'

'Like, you go into a public house, sir, and you look around you for a familiar face. And you don't find nobody you know, sir. And you leave. And all them other faces in the pub, sir. You just forget them.'

Kane nodded and sipped from his teacup.

'Well, this other fellow, the small round one – George Soutar or 'Fat Dode', they calls him – he's one of them faces in the pub. He don't even exist until you know him, sir.'

Kane nodded and chewed on his toast: 'Horse, Edinburgh is a great city with the heart of a small village. Someone will know him. That face will emerge. And when it does...'

Horse laughed: 'Oh, Mr K – it's like looking for a bloke what jumps in puddles and makes no splash...'

A rap at the door interrupted their laughter.

Kane raised his eyebrows: 'Is it my imagination, Mr Horse, or has there been a recent increase in the early morning business at our door?'

Horse placed the toasting fork in his belt, opened the door and there stood Inspector Mackintosh.

Mackintosh tipped his bowler hat: 'Good morning to you, sir. Mr Horse, I presume?'

'Who's asking?'

'I am Inspector Mackintosh of the Detective. Is your master at home, Mr Horse?'

'He's just finishing his breakfast, Mr Mackintosh...'

'Just 'Mackintosh', Mr Horse, just 'Mackintosh'. I am sorry to disturb you so early, sir.'

'Not at all. It's like Princes Street here every morning. Come in.'

Horse led Mackintosh into the kitchen, where Kane was finishing his toast. Kane dabbed his mouth with his napkin and stood up from the table: 'Mackintosh, good morning to you. Come in and sit down. Would you like a cup of tea?'

'Thank you, Mr Kane, but I don't think that we'll have time for tea.'

'Sorry, Mackintosh, I'm not quite...'

'There's been a shooting, sir. At the home of Sir Charles Irving. One dead. One clinging to life...'

★★★

Mackintosh had a carriage waiting. As the carriage headed on towards the Royal Infirmary at High School Yards, he explained that a call had come for police assistance around one o'clock in the morning to attend at Heriot Row. When officers arrived, they found what appeared to be the bodies of two young men on the upper level. Both had been shot in the head.

Kane frowned and turned to the detective: 'Mackintosh, I am deeply grateful to you for informing me of these events, but I am afraid that a more mundane question troubles me at this juncture: why have you chosen to share this information with me? Why am I the one accompanying you to the hospital?'

Mackintosh didn't look at Kane. He looked out of the carriage window. 'The truth, Mr Kane. The truth. You and me seem to be the only ones interested in it. The whole affair with Sir Charles Irving and Patrick Macnair and now a shooting of two young ne'er do wells in a great house...'

The detective looked out onto the cobbled streets as the carriage sped towards the hospital.

'The affair is like a swirling fog, sir. And you and me are the only ones trying to see clear. Other people, the Irvings and the Macnairs and the like, the fog suits them. Let them hide in their great names or their big houses. But you and me, Mr Kane, we want the truth. When I was told about all of this, the shooting and all, Mr Kane, you were the first person that came to mind.'

'Mackintosh, I am... I am flattered...' And before Kane could conclude his thanks, the carriage pulled up outside the hospital building.

***

'You'd better hurry, gentlemen. Mr Moss says he doesn't expect the patient to live.'

The nurse led the pair up a winding stair and pushed through a great door until Mackintosh and Kane found themselves not in a hospital ward, as expected, but in what appeared to be a large lecture theatre, filled with a murmuring crowd.

Kane addressed the nurse: 'I apologise, Miss, er, Miss...'

'Nurse Parker.'

'I apologise, Nurse Parker, but we are here in connection with William Cullen...'

'Shh!!!' – an angry hiss came now from a gentleman in the back row of the auditorium.

The nurse rolled her eyes, then indicated down towards the front of the lecture theatre. Before she promptly turned and walked out the door.

Kane and Mackintosh removed their hats and took two empty seats at the end of a row at the front of the auditorium. Around thirty other gentlemen sat around them, some with pens and notebooks at the ready. In the area below, lying on a table, was an unconscious Willie Cullen, his head swathed in bandages.

'And so, gentlemen, if I may have your attention...'

The voice belonged to the surgeon, Mr Robert Moss, FRCS MBBS. Bald as a coot, in a grubby frock-coat, Moss held up a scalpel in his right hand to begin the demonstration.

'And for those of you who were unable to attend at one o'clock this morning...' A titter spread across the auditorium '... I can inform you that this young buck was brought in with a gunshot wound to the head. He was thought dead, until signs of life were spotted in the carriage taking him away. And so, he was brought here. And when I opened up the back of the young chap's head, I found this.'

And Moss held up between his fingers a small silver ball.

'Now, this charming trinket appears harmless enough, perhaps. But it is a very different story when fired – at close range – by one of these.'

Moss now held up a pistol.

'A New Land Pattern pistol, nine-inch barrel...'

Kane whispered: 'That's one of the guns Sir Charles had above his fireplace...' Mackintosh nodded silently.

Moss clicked the gun and continued: '... A weapon guaranteed to ensure very good spark, but perhaps very poor accuracy...'

Moss nodded down towards the unconscious Cullen.

'And so, by all accounts, this young fellow and his friend were making an inventory of the family silver – at midnight mark you. Problem is: it was someone else's family and someone else's silver...'

Laughter, hooting and stamping now from the audience.

'... thus the aggrieved owner marked his disapproval by shooting them both in the head. I'm bound to say that the other fellow was less fortunate. He was shot here...'

Moss pointed to the centre of his forehead between the eyes.

'...and following the sparks and the loud report, such a silver ball would have killed him instantly. On examining the body, I noted the powder burns between his eyes. Moral of that story - if you wish to kill an intruder with one of these notoriously unreliable pistols...' Moss held up the gun '...then ask him, politely, to stand still first. And this chap here....'

Moss pointed down to Cullen.

'... appears to have had a different experience. I am informed that he attempted to reach for a weapon behind him, and so the owner of the pistol let off a shot, catching this young fellow on the back of the head...'

Moss turned Cullen's head gently so that the back of the head was exposed to the audience. He began to remove the bandages to reveal the bloody mess.

'We see here the wound at the occipital region. The point of entry and the direction of travel are in accordance with the history given...'

And with that, Moss ran the scalpel down the head of the sleeping Willie Cullen, and blood began to spurt over Moss's frock coat.

Kane was shocked, not because of the levity of the speaker in such a grave situation, but, rather at the colour of the blood itself. It was such a vivid red, such a colour as he had never seen before. A colour radiant and vibrant, Kane thought that it must be the colour of Life itself.

Meanwhile, Moss gave a cursory nod and the blood was being hurriedly cleared away by two gentlemen with cloths standing around the table. Moss placed his fingers into the breach in Cullen's head.

'You see, the signs are that the internal bleeding would not stop, possibly because I missed a splinter of that deadly silver pea inside his head. Let me see...'

Moss's hand rummaged around inside Cullen's skull. It reminded Kane of someone searching for a ha'penny inside a deep pocket.

'Ah! I have something now. Either the outstanding part of the missile, or a piece of this poor chap's shattered cranium. Either way – better out than in!'

And with that, Moss produced a small bloody fragment of something indistinct. The men around the table busily mopped up. Moss dropped the item into a bowl of water and scrubbed it with a small brush. He held the object up to the light.

'And so, gentlemen – the mystery is solved. A tiny part of that small sphere had been overlooked and was still lodged in his skull.'

And then, nodding to the gentlemen around the table: 'You can close him up now, thank you.' The gentlemen began the process of sewing up Wille Cullen's head.

Moss stood to face his audience: 'Now, gentlemen – any questions?'

A somewhat earnest, bespectacled young gentleman in the front row raised his hand.

'Yes?'

'Mr Moss, what is the prognosis for this young man now?'

'Thank you, Mr Fairley, in a case such as this it is impossible to say. Given the extent of his injury, he will more than likely die.'

'But you have removed the offending fragment, sir.'

'We have done what we can, Fairley. By rights, he should be dead already.'

Moss stood over the sleeping Cullen.

'And the site of the injury makes all prediction futile. The brain, like the heart, is a mysterious organ, gentlemen. He may recover. He may not. It is in the lap of the gods.'

★★★

Robert Moss leaned back in the chair of his office and sucked on his pipe. His frock coat still bore the bloodstains of his morning's endeavours.

Mackintosh frowned: 'But when, Dr Moss...'

He was gently rebuked by the surgeon: 'Mister Moss, if you please...'

'Apologies, sir. Mr Moss, when will I be able to question the lad?'

The surgeon sucked on his pipe. 'Perhaps the day after tomorrow. Perhaps never. You heard what I said in the lecture. It is no exaggeration to say that his spirit hovers between life and death at present.'

There was silence again in the surgeon's office until he said: 'And, in any event, what do you hope to gain from an interview with the boy? I have examined him thoroughly. If it is your intention to demonstrate that the boy is an Irish navigator resident in Edinburgh to get his spade-like hands dirty, then, gentlemen, I venture that you do not require to wake him.'

Nurse Parker entered the office abruptly.

'Begging your pardon, Mr Moss. You are required in the ward.'

The surgeon rose from his seat.

'Well, gentlemen, no rest for the wicked, I'm afraid. Thank you for attending this morning, and I am sorry that I could be of no greater assistance.'

He nodded to the nurse, who briskly ushered Mackintosh and Kane out of the door.

As the they were walking silently along the long corridor, Mackintosh spoke: 'Well, Nurse Parker. I wonder if I might express my thanks to you for your assistance today?'

Nurse Parker nodded impassively and led them on.

Mackintosh continued: 'Oh, that poor lad there on the operating table. Not going to make it, they say.'

They kept on walking, towards the exit.

'And his poor mother and father. I'll have to break the news to them. And when I do, do you know what they'll ask me?'

Nurse Parker raised her eyebrows and turned her face towards

Mackintosh to receive the answer.

'They'll say to me: 'Mackintosh, you're a detective. Tell us: what were the boy's last words?''

Nurse Parker slowed down her pace: 'I'm not really supposed to be speaking to people who are not family...'

'But I am a detective, Nurse Parker...'

The nurse shook her head: 'Well, he didn't make much sense when he was admitted. Barely conscious, and babbling... nonsense, I suppose.'

She thought for a moment, then: 'Pass the salt,' he said that clearly.'

'Yes?'

Nurse Parker knotted her eyebrows in concentration now: 'And something about – and it sounds like a fairy story – 'the old witch' or 'the old deer'.'

Mackintosh considered this: 'The old witch'? 'The old deer'?'

'Yes. And they 'got good' or 'got goods' for an 'old fellow'.'

Mackintosh processed this, smiled and then tipped his hat: 'Nurse Parker, it has been my great pleasure to speak to you and I can assure you that his family will be very grateful to you for this.'

The nurse – unaccustomed to such fulsome praise – began to blush and gave a shy curtsey.

When Mackintosh and Kane left the building, Mackintosh broke into a wide grin.

'There you have it, Mr Kane. Straight from the horse's mouth, sir.'

Kane shrugged.

'The boy's last words, sir.'

'A fairy story from his childhood, perhaps? A wicked witch and an old deer aiding an old man. Perhaps one of those folk tales by the Brothers Grimm?'

Mackintosh smiled: 'This was no fairy story, Mr Kane. It answers something that has been troubling me. Why did Sir Charles Irving shoot the boys? There was no need.'

Kane thought for a moment: 'To prevent their escape?'

'No-one was trying to escape, Mr Kane. You heard the what the surgeon said in there. Jamie Garden got it in the head. With that old pistol, you'd have to be standing still to get that done to you.'

Kane shook his head.

'No, Mr Kane. Those boys knew something they oughtn't to know. Maybe heard something? And that's why they got shot.'

'So what do we do now, Mackintosh?'

'We wait for the boy to wake up.'

'And if he fails to regain consciousness?'

Mackintosh shook his head: 'We are all in the hands of the Good Lord, sir. But we'll plough on regardless. And, of course, you have other matters to attend to, sir.'

Kane looked puzzled.

'The trial, Mr Kane. The trial of Patrick Macnair. Next week, is it not?'

Kane nodded.

'I hope you don't mind me saying, Mr Kane, but you seem awfully calm about the prospect.'

Kane sighed. Calm? No. He located the appropriate word to describe his state of mind: Helpless.

***

'Horse – what on earth is that you're holding?'

Horse held a rolled-up piece of parchment.

'It's a bill poster, Mr K. It was stuck to the wall next to the Assembly Rooms in George Street, sir. I thought you'd like to see if for yourself, sir.'

'And why, Mr Horse, would I wish to see a bill poster formerly attached to a public wall? What possible interest could...'

Kane's protestation was silenced when Horse unrolled the poster in one motion. The first thing that Kane noted was the name of his erstwhile fiancée, Miss Amanda Forbes-Knight. The remainder of the poster was somewhat hyperbolic in fashion:

*'EPIPHANY. The Directors beg to announce that MISS AMANDA
FORBES-KNIGHT will perform the WORLD PREMIER in the form
of a number of UNFORGETTABLE DRAMATIC and MUSICAL
RECITALS...'*

'You look puzzled, Mr K.' Horse rolled the poster back up.

'I think, Horse, if you had told me some three weeks ago that I
would soon be defending a notorious murder, relieved of my amorous
obligations and then invited to a public engagement designed to exhibit
the 'unforgettable' musical talents of Miss Amanda Forbes-Knight, then I
would have told you that you were...'

'A crack-pot, sir?'

Kane smiled: 'Let us be charitable and choose the word 'mistaken', Mr
Horse.'

Horse held up the poster: 'Are you going to attend, sir?'

Kane sighed: 'I have been invited. By 'the diva' herself. Her letter did
seem apprehensive about possible numbers. She invited me to bring a
friend. I will invite Collins. Thus, Mr Horse, you shall secure two tickets.'

Horse tapped the rolled-up poster against the palm of his hand.

'You do not approve, Mr Horse?'

'Sounds like a bloomin' waste of two bob to me...'

And at that – as had become something of a custom of a morning at
the Kane residence – there was a loud knock at the door.

Kane raised his eyebrows to enquire of Horse who it might be. Horse
shook his head: 'Wait here, sir. If it's somebody looking for money, then...'

'Please just answer door, Mr Horse.'

Kane heard Horse's voice and the voice of another man that he didn't
recognise. He couldn't make out the terms of the conversation.

After a couple of minutes, Horse entered, followed by an emaciated
man of about twenty. The young chap was thin and wiry as a pipe cleaner.
He looked all around him with more than a common interest. The long
strap of a canvas satchel was stretched over his shoulder and in his hands,
he held a crumpled hat and a rectangular, flat piece of cardboard. Horse

spoke:

'Mr Kane, this is a Mr Simon...' The young fellow gave a low bow:

'Culp, sir. Simon Culp.'

'Simon Culp, Mr K. And Mr Culp here has come to draw you...'

'Mr Kane, Mr Kane – it's an honour. It will be an honour for me to draw – from life – to illustrate the man who defended the notorious Parlour Maid Murderer.'

Kane was somewhat overwhelmed by this sudden introduction, and so, he did what all well-bred people do in these situations: he offered his guest a cup of tea. The invitation was quickly accepted.

'And... I don't suppose there's any toast left?' Culp framed his question in such a piteous fashion that Kane had to smile. He turned to Horse:

'Mr Horse. I should be grateful if you could employ your talent on the toasting fork for our young friend here?'

'A thick slice would be appreciated,' ventured the young artist.

Horse – not at his happiest at this turn of events – moved towards the larder, and Kane thought that he heard him mutter something along the lines of 'A thick ear is what you'll get.'

'Well, Mr Culp, I am flattered by your attention, but I fear that I am a far from worthy subject for the exercise of your art.'

'Oh, no sir. On the contrary. The Parlour Maid Murder has captured the common imagination. The whole of the city of Edinburgh appears to be talking about it.'

Kane pondered for a moment the difference between the words 'fame' and 'notoriety', while Horse now held a piece bread against the flames of the fire. Culp continued: 'My aim, sir, is to make a sketch of the court proceedings. For posterity.'

Culp lifted up the long cardboard box which had been resting on his lap. 'I have some samples of my previous work here for you to see, sir.' He opened his bag and took out some of his work.

Meanwhile, Horse – who was toasting the bread at the fire – was also now craning his neck to look behind him to see the drawings.

'Oooooh, careful – careful!' Culp exclaimed in Horse's direction and pointed to the now-dark bread at the end of the toasting fork – 'We don't want it burned now!'

Horse removed the toast from the end of the fork and – with what could not be described as good grace – plonked it onto a small side-plate in front of the young artist. The young man looked at the piece of toast with an enthusiasm eloquent of someone who was not likely to eat again for some time.

There was a silence while Culp considered the food before him. He looked at Kane: 'I don't suppose... you have any butter?'

Kane looked at Horse with raised eyebrows. Horse headed to the larder.

The young artist spoke: 'You see, Mr Kane, you see, what I really want my work to show is the truth...' Kane recalled his conversation with 'Not Proven' Norval and the words of Pontius Pilate.

The philosophical conversation was broken by Horse slamming down onto the table a small plate containing a negligible knob of butter.

Culp looked delighted and licked his lips. 'Ooooh – thank you, Mr Horse.' And he proceeded to butter the toast in a considered fashion, filling each tiny crater in that thick slice of toasted bread.

Kane spoke: 'Well, I am sorry to disappoint you, Mr Culp, but I am afraid that I cannot help you. I do not seek fame, but am simply carrying out – to the best of my ability – the duties to which I am bound by my profession.'

Culp nodded amiably and munched his way through the last of his toast. He reached for his teacup.

'That is quite understandable, Mr Kane. In fact, that was the expected response. But, in fairness to you, sir, I wanted to get a good look at you at close quarters and memorise your likeness. And I have done that now.' He drank from the cup, then: 'The plain fact is this, Mr Kane, you are defending The Parlour Maid Murderer. You are now a public figure. And at the trial, next week, I will draw the truth for all to see...'

Kane interrupted him: 'You will draw your version of the truth, sir.'

The young artist smiled, stood up, retrieved his bag, hat and cardboard box and gave a small bow.

'I will draw the truth from my perspective, Mr Kane. That is all an artist can do. And may I thank you for a very convivial breakfast. And, Mr Horse, thank you for a prodigiously strong cup of tea.'

***

'I am not sure if that is permitted, sir. And what did you say your name was?'

Nurse Parker looked apprehensive as she was confronted by the insistence of the small fat man before her. He spoke with a grating voice: 'Cullen, Miss. Joseph Cullen. I am Willie Cullen's uncle...'

Nurse Parker frowned. The anonymous-looking, round gentleman before her did not resemble in any way the boy who was lying unconscious in the hospital ward.

'You understand that your nephew is seriously wounded, Mr Cullen?'

The fat man's face assumed a grave aspect: 'Oh yes, miss...'

'I am not sure what you hope to achieve by seeing him...'

He spoke quickly: 'I have brought him these, miss', and he produced from his pocket a string of rosary beads. 'I had them blessed by the priest, miss. I will hang them at the end of poor Willie's bed, and I will pray over him for a while. If that is not too inconvenient.'

Nurse Parker considered the beads for a moment, sighed, and then: 'Follow me, Mr Cullen.'

And so it was that George Soutar, 'Fat Dode', was led to the beside of the unconscious Wille Cullen.

***

'Ye missed, him, Horse. Billy Brown? He was just here last night.'

Bridie, the barmaid at the White Hart Inn gave a laugh as Horse squeezed his eyes tight shut and punched the palm of his hand.

'What's the matter, Horsey, Horsey? Does he owe ye money?'

Horse said nothing. Bridie smiled and reached over the counter of the bar and ran her index finger along the knuckles of Horse's hand: 'Ye see, Horsey. If ye would just came in here every night tae see me, then ye widnae miss him, would ye?'

'Will he be back tonight, then?'

Bridie shook her head. She removed her hand. Horse sensed that she knew something but was not saying.

'If I came in here every night, my lovely Bridget, I'd carry you up them stairs and you'd soon know all about it, my dear. No other beggar would get served that night, I'm telling ya.'

Bridie smiled and warmed again immediately.

'So, my lovely, if the bold Billy Brown ain't here tonight, then where am I gonna find him?'

'How should I know?'

'Because, I knows you, my love, and I knows that you know something, and you ain't tellin' yer old pal, Horse here...'

'Why should I tell you anything, ye scallywag?' She shrugged and smiled as she polished a glass. Horse cocked his head and raised his eyebrows.

The barmaid shook her head and laughed: 'Och, he said not to tell anybody because he said that people was looking for him. I thought it was the polis he was talking about – not you. There's that public house in Tollcross, next door tae the post office. Run by that old woman. It disnae have a name, 'cause it's no' got the paperwork and that, but you ken the one I mean, Horse?'

'I know the one...'

'He said he was meeting somebody there. Tuesday it was.'

'Did he mention a time?'

'I think it was after one...'

It made perfect sense. The drinking den run by old Mrs Bennett – by reputation, no stranger to the law. But somehow, the law never seemed to catch up with her. Just the kind of pub to frequent if you knew that people were looking for you.

***

George Soutar had removed his hat and had assumed a concerned expression. Nurse Parker held a pencil and paper and looked at her notes:

'Now there are a number of things that we do not know about him, Mr Cullen, and you – being his uncle – can perhaps help us with that. For example, how old is he, exactly?'

Fat Dode looked carefully at the boy's swollen, bandaged head. And then he volunteered an answer: 'Fourteen?'

Nurse Parker looked up from her notes: 'Fourteen? The doctor thought he was around twenty.'

'He was always big for his age.'

The nurse shook her head: 'And do you have a current address for him?'

'He was always on the roam, that one. Hard one to pin down, if you know what I mean.'

'But you are his uncle, sir. Yes?'

'Yes. But he is my wife's nephew, not mine. You would have to enquire of her, miss, the detail of the lad.'

Nurse Parker looked again at her notes and frowned: 'But your surname is the same, Mr Cullen.'

Fat Dode looked non-plussed: 'What, miss?'

'Your name is Cullen and his name is Cullen.'

'Yes?'

'So he would be your nephew. If he were the nephew of your wife, then he would have a different name. Possibly her maiden name.'

There was a pause, while Fat Dode processed the logic: 'Yes, miss. My wife's maiden name was Cullen as well.'

Nurse Parker was staring now at the man unravelling before her. Then he spoke: 'You know. Big Irish family. We all end up marrying each other.'

At that moment, Nurse Parker resolved never to let this visitor anywhere near her patient.

'Well, Mr Cullen, if you just follow me to the waiting room, then we will examine your credentials, and then you can spend time with your nephew.'

Fat Dode was sweating now: 'No need for that, miss. Just a flying visit. I just need a few moments alone to pray over the boy, you understand.'

The nurse smiled a smile without warmth: 'I am sorry, Mr Cullen. I don't make the rules. I will just call for assistance and then we can see what we can do for you, sir.'

With that, George Soutar's aspect darkened, like a mask falling from his face, and he growled: 'Listen to me, you drab. Just let me see the boy for five minutes and there won't be any trouble.'

Nurse Parker was not cowed: 'Trouble? Oh, I'm sorry, 'Mr Cullen'. I did not realise that there was to be trouble. That is why I carry this bell – so that the very large police constable who is attached to the ward can deal with any such unpleasantness. Let us summon him now, shall we?'

And with that, she took the bell and rang it so vigorously that all of the other patients in the surrounding beds looked up as did the nurses at the end of the ward.

George Soutar quickly pulled his hat over his head with the brim down over his face and headed quickly for the exit. The young nurse watched him go. And then she was approached by an angry-looking hospital Matron.

'Nurse Parker, Nurse Parker!' said the Matron 'Why on earth are you ringing the lunchtime bell at this time? It is barely eleven of the clock.'

And now, for the first time, Nurse Parker looked concerned: 'Apologies matron,' she nodded towards the unconscious boy on the bed, 'but I fear that this young man's situation is more grave than we realised.'

***

'I really do envy you, my friend.' Collins sat, teacup in hand and smiled at Kane.

'Then, my dear Collins, I fear for your sanity.'

'No, no, Edward. What I mean, more precisely, is that I admire your fortitude. You and I sat here a short number of weeks ago beweeping our outcast state, and then...'

Collins stopped suddenly in mid-sentence and looked above Kane's head. Kane pondered for a moment, then: 'It's Manville, isn't it?'

Collins nodded.

'And he is standing behind me, isn't he?'

Collins nodded again and began to sip from his teacup.

Kane rose from his chair: 'Then, lay on, MacDuff...'

***

As Kane had learned from previous encounters, the best strategy for dealing with the Dean of Faculty, Rab Lennox, was to keep one's head bent low until one could ascertain whether the weather was to be stormy or fair. Sitting in the Dean's room, as far as Kane could tell today, the sky was clear with only a small chance of rain.

'You have been very quiet, Edward.'

'I have been listening to you intently, Dean of Faculty.'

'No, no – I mean that you have been very quiet of late. You undertook to keep me apprised of developments in the Macnair case – and yet, I have heard nothing from you, sir.'

If required to give a full report of the frenzy of events since meeting Macnair, Kane would be capable of speaking for hours, at some points holding back tears. But what bearing did any of these events have on the only issue at stake: did Macnair murder Martha Cunningham or did he not?

'Dean of Faculty, if I have not reported back, it is because there is nothing to report.'

Lennox nodded and looked pleased: 'Capital, capital. I mean to say, of course, that I am delighted that you have kept me informed where relevant and have not troubled me with the fripperies that often attend these matters.'

'I have met with Macnair the once, Dean. He refused to provide instructions. I am no further forward since the day of instruction.'

Lennox rose from his chair and went to the window, his back to Kane.

'Then, Edward, on the day of the trial, you will inform the Court that you do not hold instruction in this matter. The Pannel, Macnair, has refused to give you such instruction, despite your repeated requests. You will then ask the Court for leave to withdraw from acting in the matter. Lord Scott, in the chair, will grant your request...'

Lord Scott? How does he know that the trial will be heard by Lord Scott?

'...and you will cease to act in the matter. And the case will proceed. A trip to the gallows for Macnair. And justice will be done.'

Then, Lennox turned around and smiled at Kane.

'Thank you, Edward. That will be all.'

★★★

'Edward Kane – dashing young Advocate – you look glum, sir!'

Collecting his hat and coat from the Faculty servants, Kane was encountered by an unusually cheerful Norval Norris.

'Is it the butterflies, Edward? They have free run of the stomach in advance of every trial.'

Kane pondered that mere butterflies would be welcome. In his case, the sensation was more akin to being devoured gradually by rats.

Kane sighed: 'Norris, I fear that whenever I am exposed to your gifts, sir, that I am made even more conscious of my own shortcomings.'

Norris laughed, good-naturedly: 'Edward, you have already laid out the facts of the Macnair case. Much of it makes no sense. How, for example, how could a girl whose neck has just been broken then enter into a conversation with her own murderer? It simply makes no sense. There is a truth in this case, Edward, but someone is hiding it.'

Kane pondered for a moment: 'But what if that truth leads to the conclusion that Patrick Macnair is, indeed, the Parlour Maid Murderer?'

Norris placed his hand on Kane's shoulder: 'Then, my young friend, you will just have to find a different truth, won't you...'

★★★

'Edward. Edward?'

As he was heading towards the exit of Parliament Hall, Kane looked around and saw a smiling Cordelia Irving, beckoning him towards the fireplace.

He approached and doffed his hat. Cordelia smiled: 'Why, Edward, I almost did not recognise you, you look so... so... serious. Is this the face you assume when you are making those grave and learned submissions?' Cordelia pulled an exaggerated stern expression so comical that Kane had to smile.

'And so, Miss Cordelia Irving, to what do we owe the unalloyed pleasure of your company in these hallowed halls?'

Cordelia laughed: 'Can't you guess, Edward? It's Father and one of his innumerable vendettas. I swear that that man gets worse as he gets older.'

They both laughed.

'Oh, and if you wish to cite me to attest to this truth,' she raised her right hand, 'then my full name is Cordelia Imogen Irving...'

'Imogen?'

She put down her hand.

'Another attempt by my father to populate the entire world with Shakespearean names.'

They laughed together. An observer might have mistaken them for friends.

Then the conversation came to a natural stop. There was a period of a few seconds of silence between them as there appeared to be no immediate or logical starting point for resumption of their conversation. In that moment, Kane looked into the face of Cordelia Imogen Irving and she looked back into his. And he became aware now of something overpowering his senses. Something basic, something deeper than human civility. Like a small animal being overcome by the musk of a nearby predator, he felt frozen to the spot. Helpless and waiting and trembling, but all the while, consenting to be consumed whole. Cordelia Irving's eyes, hot and wet, seemed to examine every detail of Kane's face. But each look, each change of focus felt like a gentle caress. And at that moment, Edward Kane would have done anything she asked.

She broke the spell: 'I suppose you heard of that business that happened at home?'

'I was shocked to hear it.'

Cordelia laughed: 'Not as shocked, I think, as the two ruffians who were shot in the head.'

'A most regrettable incident. One dead, one clinging to life.'

'Regrettable? I agree. But the regrettable aspect, Edward, is that Father did not simply kill them both outright. I did say to him: 'If you are going to shoot someone in the temple, father, then at least have the good grace to do it more than once.'

Cordelia Irving laughed. Kane smiled politely.

'In fact, Edward, if you examine today's newspapers, you will find that our home is now being referred to as 'The House of Death'.'

She laughed again, but this time her laugh more resembled a kind of controlled shriek. Again, as she carefully considered his face, Kane felt somewhere deep inside a dark, irresistible undertow.

'Oh, Edward, I do so enjoy our little chats. You are such a lovely boy. Like an anchor of goodness in a sea of... of... I don't know...'

The thought was interrupted by the voice of Sir Charles Irving: 'Cordelia, Cordelia – what the deuce do you think you are doing?'

The old man was striding towards the fireplace.

'And why on earth would you be speaking to this person?'

Cordelia smiled: 'If you are referring to Mr Kane here, then I would remind you of two things: one: this is his place of business; and two: I consider Mr Kane to be a friend. In fact, he was in the process of offering an expression of regret concerning the recent events in our home.'

The old man nodded and grinned: 'It is a mystery to me that the extermination of a brace of vermin may be considered newsworthy.'

Cordelia laughed: 'Oh, Father, you are incorrigible.'

The old man looked up abruptly. 'But enough of them. They have, no doubt, woken up in Hell by now.'

Kane spoke: 'Sir Charles, I understand that the younger of the two is, in fact, still alive.'

A look of shock registered on the old man's face. But he soon collected himself and studied Kane's face.

'Then, Mr Kane, I predict that he is not long for this earth. I would place a bet on that – and I never gamble.

There was silence as the old man stared into the crackling fire. He was smiling, but Kane saw the obvious tremors now that shook the old man's arm.

★★★

The lamps of the hospital ward had been lowered as the day had come to a close. A pleasant sort of weariness now filled Nurse Parker from bottom to top. The tiredness of a job well done. The guarantee of a sound sleep to come that evening.

At the front entrance of the infirmary, night was coming down quickly now as she looked out onto High School Yards and beyond. A thick blanket of fog appeared to be covering much of the city. Was that the smoke from the chimneys of Auld Reekie, the great city of Edinburgh? Or was it the thick mist that would come in from the sea - the sea haar? Either way, Lily Parker would require to watch her step tonight. Keep to the main streets and avoid mischief. Walk home, but keep under the lamplight. Up the hill first, towards South Bridge, towards the university...

At the portals of the Old College of Edinburgh University, stood George Soutar. Watching the nurse emerge from Infirmary Street, pulling up her collar against the cold, Soutar pulled down the brim of his hat and began to walk behind her.

The soot and the fog swirled and closed around them as they walked towards the south side of the city.

***

'Mr K?'

The voice was whispering, but insistent.

'Mr K – wake up. Wake up, sir.'

Kane awoke with a start: 'Uh? Horse? What time is it?'

Kane looked around him and had the sudden fear that he had gone blind, such was the blackness around him.

'Sorry, Mr K, it's half past-four, sir.'

Kane was still groggy: 'Morning or night?'

'Morning, sir.'

Kane sat up in bed and began to mutter sleepily: 'What's the matter?'

'Nothing is the matter, sir. But there's work to be done.'

'At half past four in the morning, Horse? Have you taken leave of your senses?'

Horse did not answer at first, but Kane heard the clattering of the bedroom shutters being opened, which did little to dispel the gloom in the room.

'Sorry to rouse you, Mr K. But we got business this morning. Business up the hill. And there's a certain gentleman I wants you to meet.'

Kane was thoroughly convinced now that this whole event was a dream. And so, he went along with it.

'Of course, of course, Mr Horse. Business up a hill with a stranger at half-past four in the morning – what could be more natural, sir?'

Kane lay back down on the bed.

A few moments later, he was aware of his shoulder being held and being shaken in a manner that could not be described as gently.

'Mr K. Mr K. You have to get up, sir.'

'Dear Lord, is there no end to this nightmare?'

Kane opened one eye and was now aware that a candle had been placed before a mirror and that the room was now considerably brighter.

'I've filled your wash-bowl, sir. Steaming hot water for a good close shave. And I've got the kettle on for a nice cup of tea. I'll sort out some breakfast, and I'll tell you what's-what on the way there.'

Kane sat up on the side of the bed now. He felt his feet on the cold stone floor. It took a moment for him to take in what he was being told, and then he said: 'On the way where, Horse? On the way where?'

'To the prison, sir. We are going to pay a visit to Patrick Macnair.'

Kane thought for is moment.

'At five o'clock in the morning.'

'Today's a special day, Mr K. A good time for a visit. And we're taking a special guest in with us today, sir. So, get yourself sorted and we'll get out. I've got a cab coming at six.'

A cab? thought Kane. The expense. *This must be a dream.*

Chapter Seven

Six-fifteen a.m. There was silence between Kane and his man now as he pondered the task before him. The streets were still quiet at this time of the morning, and the only sound that could be heard was the clatter of the horses' hooves on the cobbled streets and the creaking of the carriage.

The thick sea haar had not yet lifted from the night before, and the city of Edinburgh looked like a dream. Emerging from the mist at the top of the hill was Calton Jail. Majestic and brutal.

As they approached the prison gates, Kane began to make out a figure standing at the entrance. At first he thought it was a woman, but the form of a man wearing a kilt gradually became complete on approach; a tall man; military bearing; powerfully built; aged around sixty years; his back ram-rod straight; small moustache; a face that, Kane perceived, would stand for no nonsense.

The carriage came to a stop outside the prison gates. Following a brief haggle concerning the fare, Horse jumped down and strode over to the gentleman standing at the gates, seized his right hand with two of his own and exclaimed: 'The Dog! The Dog!' The gentleman did not seem surprised by this greeting but, instead, himself cried: 'The Horse! The

Horse!'

Kane, following behind, was not quite sure if this encounter should be taken as an amicable reunion or the initiation of a public brawl.

Horse turned back to Kane: 'Mr Kane, sir, allow me to introduce you to my old mucker here, Regimental Sergeant William McNaughtan, commonly known – with the greatest of respect – as 'Mad Dog McNaughtan'.'

The gentleman gave a salute with a force of energy that tempted Kane to salute in return, but Kane's proffered his hand for the traditional handshake instead.

McNaughtan spoke with a deep English accent, forceful, every inch the army Sergeant. Kane could see why he and Horse would be such good friends. McNaughtan took Kane's hand.

'Mister Kane, sah!' He said loudly. 'A pleasure, a veritable pleasure to meet such a distinguished personage as ye-self, sah. The Horse here 'as explained your predicament. And I 'ave come for to assist you today.'

Kane bowed: 'And I shall be very grateful for your help, Mr McNaughtan. Shall we proceed?'

The parties went to the front gate of the prison, and Horse pulled on the great bell-pull.

The gentlemen waited. The pulling of the bell appeared to have had no effect on the sleeping prison. Kane was about to suggest that it be pulled again, when he heard the clanking of keys from the inside. The small door, carved into the middle of the larger gate, creaked open and out popped the head of the warder, Johnny Brand.

Horse chided him cheerfully: 'You took your time opening that bloomin' gate, Johnny, didn't you? You been at the drink again?'

Brand waved in the three visitors: 'Stop your nonsense, Horse. You know what's happening today. We've got to get the whole thing set up and tested, you know, for later.'

Johnny Brand noticed the third visitor. He nodded towards McNaughtan: 'And who's your pal here? What is this? An army reunion?'

McNaughtan first cocked his head to one side, then in an incredibly quick motion, as if he were caching a fly in his fist, his hand darted out towards Brand's face. He secured Johnny Brand's nose between his index and middle fingers and squeezed it tight. Brand gave out a little helpless squawk, as he was pulled to the ground. McNaughtan looked down on him, twisting Brand's nose as he spoke: 'And at this point, my son, I would likely stick me dagger in yer eye. Fancy a bit if that, do ya?'

Brand attempted to shake his head, although the vice that secured his nose made this somewhat difficult. He looked, rather pathetically, towards Horse.

Horse shook his head and sighed: 'Well, Johnny, did I forget to introduce me friend here? Say hello, then, to Regimental Sergeant William McNaughtan. Known affectionally by all and sundry as...'

'Mad Dog McNaughtan.' Brand's nose had been released from captivity, but he was still kneeling on the ground.

McNaughtan smiled, but deep inside his eyes, there seemed to be a kind of inexhaustible fury: 'Oh, no need to kneel, my son. Get up.' Brand cowered on the ground, uncertain of what to do. McNaughtan bared his teeth and growled: 'Get up, I said.'

Brand sprang up from the ground and, Kane noticed, appeared to stand to attention.

McNaughtan offered his hand: 'Very pleased to make your acquaintance, Mr Brand. And do you mind if I offer you a piece of friendly advice, son?'

'Yes?'

McNaughtan cocked his head: 'Yes' what?'

Brand thought for a moment, then: 'Yes, sir.'

'My advice is this, Mr Brand: good manners costs nothing. You understand me?'

'Yes, sir'

'Good boy. Now, the prisoner Macnair. Where is he?'

'In his cell, sir.'

'Does he know we're coming?'

'No, sir.'

'Good. Then time for a little visit.'

***

Fat Dode Soutar felt chilled to the bone. How long had he been standing here now? Hours. Still, it was all excellent preparation. Now he knew the street, the building, the occupants. This is where the nurse lived. It had been careless of him not to get the job finished with the boy in the hospital. And the nurse got a good look at him as well.

Walking home, that nurse had kept to the main streets, to the lamplight, to the more populated areas of the city. Did she know that she was being followed? Standing outside her lodgings now, he began his preparation. When the street was empty, when there was no-one in the common stair, when her room-mates were out of the house, when she would open the door innocently. That's when it would happen. And afterwards, he would ransack the rooms for anything of value. This would look just like a straightforward robbery. And then he would dump the stolen items into the water at Leith Docks at midnight. Nothing would connect Soutar with the event. Nothing would be left to chance. He put his hand in his pocket and felt the rough bristles of the rope inside. It had served him so well in the past. But not today. Soutar looked up at the sky. Was that the dawn about to break? As he held that piece of rope tightly in his hand, Fat Dode Soutar walked towards town and, in a matter of seconds, was lost in the mists of the thick Edinburgh haar.

***

'Is that the dawn about to break?' Edward Kane stood in the courtyard of Calton Jail and looked up at the sky.

Horse smiled and nodded towards Mad Dog McNaughtan: 'If I knows this man, sir, something is about to break.'

Johnny Brand stood fumbling with the keys at the cell door. He tittered nervously as McNaughtan stared at him: 'Sorry, gents. Quite a few keys here on the old bunch...'

The rattling of the keys and opening of the cell door had an effect on its occupants.

Patrick Macnair sat up in bed, leaning on his elbow, screwing up his eyes and blinking into the half light of the open door: 'Johnny, is that you?'

Brand laughed nervously: 'Mister Macnair – got some visitors for you...'

Macnair lay down on his back on the bed and laughed lazily: 'Well, unless they have come in with the milk – or brought us some more gin – you can tell them that their services are not required.'

Kane thought that he heard the voice of a woman, chuckling. It transpired that he was mistaken. It was, in fact, the sound of two women. When Kane's eyes became accustomed to the darkness in the cell, he became aware of two forms in the bed beside Macnair. Both ladies were in a state of undress and were clearly still under the influence of drink from the night before.

There was a silence in the room for a moment. And then the cell was filled with the booming voice of Mad Dog McNaughtan:

'Get. Aaaaap...'

Kane saw something that he had never seen before. As if operated by an invisible hand, Patrick Macnair's body appeared to be seized and placed upright on the floor before the visitors. Macnair started to shake his head, as if shaking off a nightmare. He stood there at attention. Entirely naked.

'Look at you, son,' McNaughtan barked, 'what a state...'

Macnair responded, almost automatically: 'Yes, Mr McNaughtan.'

The Mad Dog spun around and addressed Johnny Brand, the warder: 'You! Brand!'

The warder cowered: 'Yes, sir.'

McNaughtan indicated the ladies on the bed: 'Get them two trollops out of here.'

Brand scuttled across the floor, picking up female garments as he went, muttering: 'Come on, Maisie. Come on, Daisy. Be off with you now, girls. Time you were off...'

When the ladies scampered off, clutching their clothes to them, McNaughtan walked around the naked Patrick Macnair in slow circles, like an unhappy god inspecting a defective Adam.

Macnair spoke: 'I apologise, Mr McNaughtan....'

The Mad Dog screamed at Macnair: 'Did I say you could speak, soldier? Did I?'

'No sir.'

'Then shut your bleedin' mouth – or I'll shut it for ya. You understand?'

'Yes, sir.'

'I remember the very first time I seen you, Macnair. What was it? Ten years ago?'

'Yes, sir.'

'You thought you was a lady's man then, but I soon made a soldier out of you, didn't I?'

'Yes, sir.'

'Took me a while. Took me a good while. But you was a good soldier, Macnair.'

'Yes, sir. Thank you, sir.'

'And look at you now, 'Paddy' Macnair. Flabby, drunk, in jail – bloody useless...'

'Yes, sir. Thank you, sir.'

'Now get some clothes on your back,' McNaughtan motioned to Macnair's nakedness. 'Sight of that is enough to put me off me breakfast.'

Macnair moved across the room, picking up discarded items of clothing.

'Now sit down,' McNaughtan ordered.

Macnair obeyed the order.

'Alright – what's the motto of our regiment, boy?'

Macnair thought for a moment, then started 'Nemo me impune...'

He was quickly interrupted by McNaughtan: 'Nah, nah – not the bleedin' foreign one, son! I mean the one in the Queen's English.'

Macnair spoke the motto: 'Second to None, sergeant, Second to None.'

McNaughtan stared at Patrick Macnair for a long time and said nothing. It seemed as if Macnair was being melted away under the intense glare of his old army sergeant. The old soldier nodded towards Kane: 'I got your lawyer here, Macnair. The thing is, that he is trying to help you, son. He has to go into that battle for ya. And he needs bullets in his gun. You got to plead either Guilty or Not Guilty.'

Macnair exhaled, as if his very life force was ebbing out of him. He looked up at the old sergeant: 'I can't.'

McNaughtan persisted: 'Second to None, boy – Second to None! If you disgrace yerself, Paddy, ye disgrace all of us. If you killed the girl, then own up. I tell ya – I done things I'm not proud of, but I don't run away from them. When me and the Horse there was fighting alongside Wellington himself, I spied the French boy with the drum – and I killed him. I killed the boy playing the fife an' all. No need for it. But it was the Mad Dog in me wasn't it? And I thought they was all the enemy. But I put me hands up.'

Macnair had his head in his hands now and he was shaking violently.

'Second to None, Paddy, Second to None. If you didn't do it, then go down fighting, my son. Give the Advocate Mr Kane here the bullets to put in his gun. He can plead Not Guilty for you. But if you did kill that little girl, then let him plead Guilty for you. If that's the truth, then put your hands up. There's honour in that, Paddy.'

Macnair seemed frozen to the spot. Only his eyes moved, and they moved rapidly from side to side as if he were trying to dispel an evil thought from his mind. And then, he looked up at his old sergeant and spoke softly: 'I plead...'

'Yes?'

'I plead... Not Guilty.'

The old soldier smiled and placed his hand on Macnair's shoulder: 'Well done, son, well done – Second to None...'

★★★

As Kane, Horse and McNaughtan were leaving the prison, escorted to the door by (a now conspicuously mannerly) Johnny Brand, they were met by a group of women. Some of the women were sobbing. In the middle of the group, Kane saw Florence Forbes-Knight. She had her arms around an elderly lady and appeared to be consoling her. Kane gave a timid wave to attract her attention.

Florrie looked up, saw Kane and motioned for him to wait for her. She released her embrace of the old lady and then held her by the hands, speaking words of comfort. The old lady nodded and repeatedly dabbed her eyes with a handkerchief. Florrie nodded, then gently moved away and towards Kane.

Kane smiled as he greeted her: 'Florrie, we seem to be destined to meet with increasing regularity – but in captivity. I hope that this is not some fateful warning for our friendship...'

Kane's smile was not reciprocated on this occasion. Florrie just shook her head, obviously upset.

'My dear Florrie. Whatever is the matter?'

She was close to tears, but spoke: 'You do not know what is to happen this morning, Edward?'

Kane then recalled that Johnny Brand had alluded to getting something set up and tested. He shook his head.

'Edward, there is to be a hanging today.'

Kane did not know how to respond, so asked: 'Where?'

'Here. In the prison. Later this morning.'

Kane let the fact sink in, and then motioned towards the group of women: 'And who are these ladies?'

'The family of the poor unfortunate. The lady that I was consoling is his mother. He is the only son of the family.'

Again, Kane was at a loss for words, and rather blurted out: 'The young man must have done something terrible. To be condemned to die, I mean.'

'He killed his intended. They were engaged to be married, but she formed an association with another man. He confronted her. She did not deny it...'

It struck Kane that in those particular circumstances, a plea of clemency was likely to be effective and a hanging averted, with a punishment of Life Imprisonment imposed as the obvious alternative.

'And at trial, who was his Counsel?'

'Someone called Frederick Carr.'

Kane was aware of Frederick Carr's reputation. The Advocate seemed to alternate between two different personalities: 'Fearless Freddie', relentless champion of the underdog. Passionate, articulate and persuasive. Or 'Careless Carr', lazy, uninterested and apparently oblivious to the fact that someone's precious life was in his hands. Which Freddie was likely to appear on any day was largely dependent on how much alcohol had been consumed, either the night before or that very morning.

Kane ventured: 'And how did Freddie... how did Carr perform at trial?'

Florrie shook her head: 'Apparently, on the first day, he was full of fire and on the second, he presented as nursing a bad headache, as if all of the fire had been doused overnight.'

Kane mused that this was likely an accurate description, the bright flame of passion being drowned in a sea of fine claret.

Again, Kane was at a loss for words: 'I'm sorry, Florrie. I venture that the men of the jury thought: 'An eye for an eye'.'

'And I venture that one day the entire world will wake up blind.'

Kane mock-scolded her: 'Miss Florence Forbes-Knight! As long as this world has you residing in it, then that will never be the case.'

Florrie had tears in her eyes now. She placed her hand on Kane's arm, to thank him for the compliment, and she looked into Kane's eyes. Had one asked Kane for words to describe his feeling at that moment, then the feeling was simply akin to discovering a welcoming face in an unfriendly crowd.

Florrie composed herself: 'But, Edward, you will have other concerns at present. You are here concerning the parlour maid incident.'

Sweet Florrie. She was the only one who did not immediately call Macnair 'The Parlour Maid Murderer'.

Kane sighed and nodded.

'Edward, I do pray for you, you know that.'

'I confess, Florrie, that I feel crushed at times.'

'Then perhaps, Edward, the prayers are the only thing keeping you on your feet.'

Edward took her hand: 'Then keep praying, my dear Florrie, just keep praying.'

At this point, they were interrupted by the warder Johnny Brand: 'Sorry to disturb you, Mister Kane, but there's still a power of work to do this morning, and...' He motioned to the group of ladies, crying in front of them.

'Of course, Mister Brand. Apologies for any delay.'

Kane smiled at Florrie and Florrie smiled back. 'And good luck with the trial, Edward.'

'Thank you, Florrie.'

'When is it due to start?'

Kane frowned. The rude awakening at four thirty that morning and the subsequent events had rather muddied his thinking.

'The trial? Of course. The trial begins... tomorrow...'

The trial was tomorrow and all of a sudden, he had a man facing the noose who was now pleading Not Guilty. Kane had no evidence and no witnesses. He was suddenly conscious of the stiff, highly-starched, tight-fitting collar around his own neck.

***

'Do you think it was something you ate, Mr K?'

Edward Kane looked up from the bucket, shook his head, then immediately crouched over and was violently sick again.

'My own theory is that when you think of the particular cut of meat and you feel sick, then that was the thing that made you sick, Mr K. So, we both had the mutton tonight, sir...'

Kane looked as if he was about to burst into tears at this point – then promptly vomited again.

'... mind you, Mr K, we both et the same thing. Now that I think of it, that rice pudding looked as if it was on its way out...'

This observation was followed by more copious vomiting.

'... although, begging your pardon, sir, I don't think it's the food here is what's done it.'

Kane looked up from the bucket. His face ghostly white now, he dabbed the sides of his mouth with a tattered piece of cloth:

'And what, Mr Horse, in your considered medical opinion, is the cause of my affliction?'

'Fear, sir.'

Kane looked into the bucket and had no reply.

'Fear, Mr K. I seen it dozens of times. Just before we went into battle. Grown men. Good soldiers. Better men than you and me. Weak as kittens, sir. Emptying their guts into a bucket.'

Kane pushed his lips and nodded.

'I confess, Mr Horse, that I do feel as weak as a kitten.'

'Trouble is, Mr K. In about ten hours, you go into battle and the bloke what you're defending has taken all the bullets out of the gun, sir. More fool him, Mr K.'

Kane nodded and thought for a moment.

'What time is it, Horse?'

Horse looked at the clock on the mantelpiece: 'It's a quarter after nine, sir.'

Kane put his head into his hands.

'Then I had best look at those dashed papers again, hadn't I?'

Horse shook his head: 'Mr K, begging your pardon, sir – but if you stare at them papers any longer, you'll look make a hole in the middle of them.'

Kane was resigned and nodded his head.

'Best thing, sir, is a good night's sleep.'

Kane laughed in a rather hollow fashion.

'There is no likelihood of that, Mr Horse.'

'I thought you'd say that, Mr K, so I have prepared for you a little concoction that has proved very useful to me in the past.'

'You have missed your vocation, Horse. You should have been an apothecary,' Kane remarked, his voice not entirely devoid of sarcasm.

Kane covered the bucket and went into his bedroom. When he emerged some minutes later wearing his nightgown, nightcap and bedsocks, Horse was standing in the pantry area, a smile on his face and a cup of liquid in his hands. Kane pointed at the cup.

'What is it?'

'It is, Mr Kane, a potion of my own devising. I calls it 'Dreamless Sleep'. Now, into bed with you before you drinks it.'

Kane smiled and went into his bedroom.

'Into bed, sir, if you please.'

Kane got into bed and under the covers, looking up at Horse: 'Is that satisfactory, Mr Horse?'

Horse handed him the cup and ordered: 'Drink. Rather a curious smell, so down in one gulp if possible.'

Kane obeyed. The cup now emptied, he handed it back to Horse, waited for a moment, and then said: 'And so, Mr Horse, you claim...'

And then Edward Kane, Advocate, was suddenly unconscious on the eve of his first murder trial and slept soundly for the next nine hours.

PART THREE: THE TRIAL

Chapter Eight

'Is something on fire?'

Kane peered through the large, noisy crowd as he and Horse approached Parliament Square.

'With a bit of luck, Mr K, the courts have burnt down and you got more time to find you a case, sir.'

Kane shook his head. This was a bad idea. The sleeping draught of Horse's devising had ensured a long and dreamless sleep (necessitating, it must be said, a prolonged period standing over the chamber pot in the morning), but Kane mused that when Rip van Winkle had woken up, he must surely have had the kind of dull, thumping headache that now afflicted Kane.

Breakfast had been initially refused. However, Mr Horse – a veritable encyclopaedia of pre-battle preparation – had arranged a slice of toast and a cup of prodigiously strong tea and stood over Kane who was ordered to chew slowly and drink up.

And now, as foggy as Kane felt, he was pushing through the crowd to the courts at Parliament House, in the middle of what appeared to resemble a sort of civilised riot.

Horse went before Kane, pushing past: 'Scuse me, sir; 'scuse me, madam; out of my way, you little tinker!'

As they pushed their way through the thickening throng and passed the great statue of Charles II on horseback, Kane thought that he saw a separate crowd surrounding a young man whose face he recognized. The man was smiling and calling to passers-by, taking money and handing them flat, square objects in return.

'Horse – that young fellow under the statue. I'm sure that we have encountered him at some point.'

Horse screwed up his eyes and examined the man's face from afar. 'It's the young fella, Mr K. The artist one. The one what wanted to take your likeness. The one what liked my tea…'

Of course, the young artist Simon Culp. That was the name. But why was he here, calling out to passers-by under a statue? And what was he selling?

Kane's thoughts were interrupted by Horse: 'Mr K – give us your papers, sir.'

'Sorry?'

Horse motioned to the bag containing the case papers.

'Your bag, sir. Just give us it.'

'It is not that heavy, Mr Horse…'

Despite Kane's protestations on the paucity of paper in his possession, Horse grabbed the bag and held it close.

Nearly at the court entrance now, and the crowd could not be more dense as Kane and Horse waded through.

Dozens and dozens of gentlemen stood jostling before door eleven of Parliament House. The sea of top hats reminded Kane of corks bobbing up and down on the water; ladies in bonnets and crinoline were attempting to retain dignified poses while being jostled; a tiny boy was hawking newspapers. The reason for the throng became obvious to Kane, as the paperboy hollered: 'Get yer paper here – Parlour Maid Murderer Trial – all the news of late! Get your paper here…'

The crowd was there to see the trial, although only a fraction would be admitted to the court.

Horse carved his way to the front entrance, Kane huddled behind him.

And then, while going through the entrance door, Horse was seized on each arm by two uniformed police officers.

'And where do ye think you're going, boy?'

In his foggy state, Kane mused that the officers looked like two toy soldiers produced by the same factory, the one indistinguishable from the other. Both wore tall, stovepipe hats with jackets secured up to the chin with brass buttons.

Then Kane heard Horse's voice, except on this occasion, it sounded uncommonly polite: 'I am sorry to trouble you officers, but I am here for to assist Mr Kane, the Advocate...'

The officers looked at each other in a 'so-what' fashion. Horse was more insistent now: 'That is Mr Edward Kane, the Advocate. The Advocate what is defending The Parlour Maid Murderer...'

Both officers immediately looked chastened and unhanded Horse. Horse smiled and held up Kane's bag: 'And as you can see, gents, I am assisting the Learned Counsel by carrying his papers and whatnots.'

One of the officers then gave a low bow and addressed Horse and Kane: 'Begging your pardon, sirs, but we've had all sorts trying it on today. Please, just go in...'

Kane led Horse into the corridor so that he could study the Rolls of Court on the walls, which would tell him which court to attend for the trial. First, he looked for the appointed judge's name - 'Lord Scott', the Dean had told him - but no sign. Then he looked for the name of the case - 'Her Majesty's Advocate versus Patrick John Phillips Macnair' - no sign. Then Kane caught sight of a passing Macer, Andy Andrews.

'Oh, Mr Andrews. Mr Andrews?'

The Macer turned around and smiled. 'Yes, Mr Kane. Good morning, sir.'

'Good morning, Mr Andrews.' Kane indicated the Court Rolls on the wall. 'I'm looking for the case of...'

Andrews laughed and held up his hand. 'I know what case you're looking for, sir. Problem is Lord Scott. Taken unwell in the night, Mr Kane. Bad oysters, they're thinking. They've been scrambling about looking for someone – any other judge – to take his place, but so far, sir, no joy. Good luck to you, sir.'

Kane stood looking blankly at the Rolls of Court on the wall, when he became aware of a silent presence beside him. Before he looked around, he could sense who it was: Manville.

★★★

'What in heaven's name do you think you are doing, Kane? And what the deuce is this... this abomination?'

Dean of Faculty Rab Lennox – his face apoplectic with rage – hurled a hard, flat, square object in the direction of Kane, narrowly missing his head.

When Kane looked around to retrieve the item, he found that he was being handed it by Mr Whittle, who had already burrowed into a corner of the Dean's room.

Kane thanked The Mole and examined the item.

It proved to be a hand-coloured illustration. An extremely comical caricature.

Of course, the work of that young artist – Simon Culp.

It portrayed Kane – a very good likeness – riding on a horse marked 'Justice' – the face of the horse, Kane noted, bearing a very strong resemblance to his own Mr Horse. They were being challenged by an Advocate in wig and gown holding a blunderbuss. In the background was a scowling figure reaching through a barred window (presumably Patrick Macnair, but not a likeness) holding the throat of a parlour maid. The Advocate holding the gun was a good likeness of the prosecutor in the case, Jon Hunter. And at the bottom of the page, the caption read: 'The Hunter and The Lady Killer.'

Kane's examination of the work was interrupted by the voice of the Dean: 'What do you have to say for yourself, eh? Why on earth would you demean yourself by posing for such a display of blatant mockery?'

'I did not pose, Dean of Faculty...'

'Then how do you explain the likeness?'

'The artist in question came to my home and asked me to participate. I refused. He must have taken the likeness from that very short encounter.'

Kane thought it best at this point to omit the detail that the artist had also sat at his table and happily scoffed some tea and toast.

Kane pointed to the figure with the gun: 'Also, Dean of Faculty, you will have noted the true likeness of my colleague, Jonathan Hunter. I cannot imagine that Jonathan would have modelled for this. Again, he must have been the victim of some trick on the part of the artist.'

The Dean appeared to calm down somewhat at this suggestion. He growled: 'Yes. That is what he says. Well, at least you both have arranged your stories to match...'

Kane stood, waiting for the next onslaught, but the Dean paused for a moment, then spoke now with a different sort of intensity: 'I've spoken to Whittle here, and he tells me that Macnair will now tender a plea of Not Guilty. Is that correct?'

'That is correct, Dean.'

'And when did this change of position come about?'

'Yesterday morning, sir. He was visited by an old army friend, and that friend persuaded Macnair to change his mind and plead Not Guilty.'

There was silence in the room for a moment, then Kane added: 'It had nothing to do with me, sir.'

Again, silence in the room.

Then the Dean asked: 'And what new evidence has emerged, then, from the plea.'

Kane thought for a moment, then: 'Nothing, sir. Apart from the plea of Not Guilty, I have nothing.'

This seemed to satisfy Lennox, who smiled and nodded: 'Then you will not be asking any questions, will you?'

'I fear, Dean of Faculty, that it will be an uncommonly short trial.'

Lennox nodded and, again, Kane had the impression that Rab Lennox now thought that he and Kane had entered into some sort of unspoken pact.

'Capital, Kane, capital. Of course, the only obstacle now is that we have lost one of our judges. Old Wallace Scott, up all night regurgitating his sea food, I hear. In any event, we have found a replacement. John Blake. Lord Blake will take the chair.'

'I am not familiar with that name, Dean...'

'Nor should you be. Retired before your time, Kane. Best that could be found in the circumstances, I'm afraid. In his day, John Blake was one of the best prosecutors I had ever seen. And then, as a judge, he would hand down Death Sentences as lightly as a man scattering breadcrumbs to the birds. Just the right judge for sentencing in this case...'

★★★

In the Gown Room, the Faculty Servants buzzed around the Counsel who were getting dressed for court.

A number of cheval mirrors stood angled at the walls serving Advocates, old and young, thin and round, tall and small, while the Servants helped them on with their jackets and gowns and handed them their wigs.

Kane was standing before one such mirror, tying his white bow tie, when he was joined by his opponent, Jon Hunter, who came to dress beside him. Hunter was smiling. He spoke, mimicking the voice of the Dean: 'Well, Mr Kane – how do you explain the likeness in this abominable caricature, eh, eh?'

They both laughed.

'Good morning, Jon. In my case, the starving artist arrived at my door begging for food. You?'

'He feigned a delivery of instructions to Parliament House. Then, when I was summoned, he pretended to have forgotten the papers in question. But only after he'd examined me up and down. The rogue!'

'A likeable chap, though.'

'As many rogues are, Edward, as many rogues are. And speaking of likeable rogues, how goes it with a certain Mr Macnair?'

'I was able to see him again yesterday, Jon. At Calton Jail. But could only begin the visit proper when not just one, but two ladies of the night required to be removed from his bed.'

Jon Hunter laughed as he tied his white bow tie: 'One can only admire the sheer vigour of his amorous pursuit of women – of a certain class.'

They laughed. Then, perhaps with a little too much insouciance, thought Kane, Hunter focused the subject: 'And, again, he makes no plea. And I take it that that remains his position this morning?'

Kane stopped what he was doing and turned to Hunter: 'Matters have progressed, Jon. Macnair is now pleading Not Guilty.'

Kane detected a near-imperceptible pause in Hunter tying his tie as the news was communicated. Hunter smiled, but without warmth: 'And when did this happen?'

'Yesterday morning.'

Hunter was angry now, but spoke in a controlled fashion: 'Edward, I should like to have known that.'

'I'm sorry, Jon. My understanding is that even if the accused were to plead Guilty in such a case, the Crown still requires to lead its evidence and prove the charge against him. Because of the... of the serious nature of the consequences here.'

'The rope, you mean, Edward.' Hunter was visibly irked now. 'I cannot believe, Edward, that you thought that it made no difference that your man was now pleading Not Guilty. Can't you see, in the eyes of the jury...' Hunter threw his head back, closed his eyes and then exhaled slowly '... this may make all the difference.'

Hunter collected himself and looked at Kane again: 'You must excuse me. It's this case. You understand...'

'Jon – I assumed that you would be told...'

Hunter smiled: 'It is difficult enough, Edward, and then we find that we have lost our judge into the bargain.'

'The Dean appears to think that we have secured a replacement.'

'Not something he chose to share with me.'

Kane nodded: 'A Lord Blake. A retired judge, apparently. Drafted in as a matter of urgency. A noted prosecutor in his day, by all accounts...'

Hunter thought for a moment, then: 'John Blake?'

'Yes. John Blake.'

'I thought that Lord Blake was dead?'

'Then, it appears, Jon, that he has been resurrected for this trial.'

A cloud appeared to pass over Hunter's face: 'As I understand it, his conduct in the courtroom led to a rather unfortunate soubriquet – 'Lord Bleak'. And so, Mr Kane, we find ourselves in very different straits. I am to conduct my very first criminal trial under the watch of one of this country's greatest prosecutors, and you are to navigate your first case where the penalty of death is now a certainty.'

Hunter placed his wig on his head, adjusted it, regarded himself in the mirror for a moment, then turned to Kane: 'One of us is about to lose badly, Edward. And it is not going to be me.'

And he strode off.

***

It was easy enough to enter the nurse's stairwell without being seen.

Fat Dode Soutar stood outside the door of Nurse Lily Parker's lodgings as he fingered the bristles of the rope in his coat pocket. No response to the knocking, yet she had not left the building and it was now after nine-thirty in the morning.

Soutar heard movement behind the door and the voice of a young woman from inside: 'Hold on, just coming.'

Soutar gripped the rope. The door opened slowly.

Soutar was presented with a young woman, but one that could not be described as petite. This young lady was around two feet taller than

Soutar and, for a lady of her age and station, very powerfully built.

'Yes?'

'Uh, sorry, miss. I was looking for the nurse.'

'Yes, I am the nurse.' The giant girl frowned: 'What's the matter, sir? Has there been an accident? Does someone need help?'

Soutar began to sweat: 'It was the other one, miss, the other nurse I wanted. Nurse Parker.'

'I'm afraid that she is still asleep. Shift work, you know. We get in at all hours. Can I help?'

'No. It was her that was needed.'

The large lady at the door stood back in the doorway and looked Soutar up and down: 'I'm afraid, Mister... Mister...?'

'Mr Smith. John Smith.'

'I'm afraid, Mr Smith that I am under strict instructions not to disturb Nurse Parker until later this morning. She needs her rest for this evening's shift. Apologies to you, sir.' She balled her considerable fist.

Soutar thought for a moment, then: 'I've got a package for her. She needs to sign for it.'

'I can sign for it.'

'Sorry, miss – it needs to be her.'

'Where is it then?'

'What?'

'The package, Mr Smith. The package that requires the signature.'

Soutar felt the rope in his left pocket. He then felt the knife in his right pocket. He could feel the sharpness of the blade against his fingers. This would have to be done fast. And done now, or not at all.

'The package? It's in the cart downstairs, miss. Didn't want to lug it up all these stairs in case nobody was in. If you give me a minute, I have the chitty here somewhere...'

He pretended to fumble in his right-hand pocket and took hold of the wooden handle. He rehearsed the process in his mind: a lightning-fast lunge; a stab to the heart; push the harridan inside; finish her off; and then see to the other one while she was still asleep. Then make it look like a robbery....

★★★

When Kane arrived at the courtroom, it was already full and noisy and as bustling as a busy marketplace.

Kane looked upwards towards the raised judge's bench – no Lord Blake yet.

Immediately below the judicial bench stood a long, rectangular table jutting out into the middle of the courtroom. At the head of the table, sat the Clerk of Court, surrounded on both sides by Advocates, all casually chatting.

Kane noted that the courtroom was filled with Advocates, not to attend to their own cases, but to observe the trial of The Parlour Maid Murderer.

He looked out into the packed public area behind the dock. Two-hundred-and-fifty or 300 people sat waiting for the trial to begin. The palpable excitement, the clamour of the crowd reminded Kane of his visits to the theatre as a child before the rising of the curtain. All that was required now was the Villain of the Piece - Patrick Macnair - but there was no sign of him in the dock as yet.

The space for the accused might have been empty, but behind the dock sat a whole row of gentlemen of the press, peering around themselves and scribbling furiously into their notebooks.

At that point, Kane realised that he had absolutely no idea where he should be sitting. He felt a hand on his shoulder. It was Collins, also in wig and gown: 'I have come to witness your High Court debut and keep you company, Edward...' He motioned to the hundreds of people inside the courtroom '... but, perhaps an enlarged audience is not what you require at present.'

'My dear friend, Collins. A friendly face in a sea of strangers is all the company that I require.'

'Edward, my own diary at present resembles a blank sheet of paper, and so I wondered if you would like another Counsel to act as your junior for these purposes. I am a very good note taker, sir, and I am happy to follow the Leader.'

For the first time in a long time, Kane felt a sense of relief wash over him. A friend by his side during these proceedings would make his defeat the more tolerable. In addition, Collins, was a man of detail and missed nothing. Kane nodded and smiled his thanks to his friend.

Kane studied the lawyers' table and there, on the right-hand side, until now obscured by the comings and goings of the Advocates, stood Mr Whittle motioning to Kane to approach the table.

'Mr Whittle. Good morning to you, sir.'

'Morning, Mr Kane. I have your bag and your papers here. Your man, Mr Horse, left them with me. I encountered him in the great Hall, sir.'

'And where is Horse now, Mr Whittle.'

The Mole motioned way upwards, towards the front row of the gallery. And there, upon high, sat Horse, squeezed in between two pretty ladies and regaling them both with some exploit or another, to their obvious enjoyment.

Kane spoke to Whittle: 'And this, Mr Whittle, is my junior: Mr Collins, Advocate.'

Collins gave a low bow: 'How do you do, sir.'

Whittle looked flushed and flustered now: 'I had no idea... your own junior... this is hardly acceptable... on the day of the trial, to be told...'

Kane had to be firm: 'Mr Whittle. Our joint enterprise here is to provide Patrick Macnair with the best possible defence. Mr Collins here is both an excellent Advocate and a first-class taker of notes. He will prove invaluable in this case.'

Somewhat churlishly, The Mole let Kane's bag drop on the table and muttered: 'Well a fee for Mr Collins will be quite out of the question...'

Collins, pouring oil on troubled waters, was quick to respond: 'Mr Whittle, I do not expect a fee here, sir. Enough for me that Justice is served.'

It struck Kane that he would ask a question now that he ought to have asked long before: 'Whittle, you have raised an issue here that I should like to have resolved. Who is paying for this?'

The Mole – if such a thing were possible – looked sheepish: 'You are not being paid any fee for this, Mr Kane; you agreed with the Dean of Faculty...'

'No, no, no, Mr Whittle. Not me. I recall that you told me that you were being paid and paid handsomely. I have a right to know, sir. The knowledge may have some bearing upon the evidence of the case.'

Whittle thought for a moment, then: 'In faith, Mr Kane, I do not know, sir. I am acting as correspondent for Malcolm and Company. The instructions came from there. From Mr Malcolm himself.'

Kane did not know why, but he was not surprised: 'Mr Whittle – John Malcolm is the lawyer who acts for Sir Charles Irving.'

'Mr Kane – John Malcolm is the lawyer who acts for every great family in this city. In any event, I was told that, regarding the funding of the Macnair murder trial, Mr Malcolm was acting for a new client, a Mr Angelo.'

Mr Angelo? Kane now felt as if his brain had been filled to overflowing. As if a pint pot had just been emptied into a half-pint mug.

'I assumed, Mr Kane, that it was the generous gesture of an old army friend, perhaps?'

Their conversation was halted abruptly by the shout of the Macer: 'Court all rise!'

Emerging from a side door on the raised level beside the judicial bench, the Macer walked into the centre of the area and hung the ceremonial mace on the wall behind the judge's chair.

The court was now in session.

Behind the Macer, a tall, bowed figure followed. Dressed in a horsehair wig, white falls dropping from his neck and wearing a bright red coat and white cape dotted with blood-red crosses, Lord Blake strode to his chair.

To Kane's surprise, an identically clad figure soon followed Lord Blake. Then a third scarlet-robed judge emerged from the door on the other side of the raised area. All three judges stood before their seats, gave a low bow to the assembly and sat down.

The several hundred people in attendance stood up, bowed in return, then sat again.

While the judges arranged their papers, Kane sat down and hissed to Collins: 'There are three of them?'

Collins whispered back: 'Of course.'

'Why do we require three judges?'

'Edward, it's a murder trial. There are always three judges. I thought that you said you had recently watched a trial?'

'I was peeking in from the side door. I could only see Norval Norris...'

Having sat down, Kane noted that all of the surrounding activity at the table had stopped and most of the other Counsel had now taken their customary places two rows behind the dock, leaving only the Clerk of Court, Kane and Collins and directly across the table Jon Hunter, Advocate Depute, accompanied by two juniors.

Hunter and his helpers had arranged their copies of the various productions in the case in neat, regimented piles of paper, in meticulous preparation.

Collins was digging into Kane's bag and attempting to put the Defence papers into some kind of order.

The Clerk of Court called the case: 'Her Majesty's Advocate versus Patrick John Phillips Macnair.'

Despite Kane's belief that the event could hardly become more theatrical, on the floor of the dock area a large trap door flew open and the tall, black tip of a stovepipe hat bobbed up slowly, followed by a lanky police officer.

Given the configuration of his slightly-raised right arm, the officer was clearly pulling on something. Kane watched as the officer surfaced, and now saw that the officer's right hand wore a handcuff and that the other manacle of that handcuff was attached to Patrick Macnair. A second officer followed, handcuffed to Macnair on the other side. The great door from which they emerged then slammed shut.

Macnair stood straight-backed between the officers, shaved and well-dressed now, pale but boyishly handsome.

The Clerk of Court confirmed his identity: 'Are you Patrick John Phillips Macnair?'

'Yes, sir.'

'Sit down.'

Lord Blake looked down at Kane: 'Yes?'

Kane stood up. He could feel his hands trembling and his voice quavering: 'My lords, I appear for the Pannel, Patrick Macnair, and...'

He was interrupted by Lord Blake: 'And how are you?'

Kane was not expecting such a civilised and gentle introduction to the practice of Criminal Law, but responded in kind: 'I am very well, my lords, and I trust you are too?'

Lord Blake looked puzzled for a moment, and then: 'No, no – not how are you, sir, I said who are you? What is your name, sir?'

Kane felt at this point as if his brain had just been mashed into the consistency of stewed apple, '... My name is... is Kane, my lords, and I am enlisted... I mean to say, I am assisted by my Learned Friend, Mr Collins...'

Kane's head then emptied of every word that he had ever learned.

Lord Blake looked down: 'And?'

Kane noticed the eerie silence in the court. There must have been several hundred people in attendance watching, and yet there was no sound other than the gargling of his own throat and, somewhere in the room, the ticking of a distant clock. He became aware of a sheet of paper that had been slid in front of him by Collins. It read: *AND THE PANNEL PLEADS NOT GUILTY.*

Kane found his voice: 'And the Pannel, Patrick Macnair, pleads Not Guilty.'

Lord Blake smiled at the two other judges around him: 'I was under the impression that Justice was Blind...' he indicated towards Kane '... not Deaf.'

The judges laughed.

'Mr Kane, I am sure that we could readily locate an ear trumpet for your use, if it proves that you – and thus Mr Macnair – are labouring under any form of physical disadvantage.'

Kane bowed: 'That will not be necessary, my lords. I am obliged to you.'

Lord Blake smiled and turned to Jon Hunter: 'Now, Advocate Depute, the first thing that I should ascertain is: can you hear me?'

Everyone laughed at this point. Everyone except Kane and Collins. And the man facing the rope, Patrick Macnair.

***

Fat Dode Soutar stood there at the front door of Nurse Lilly Parker and continued his conversation with her giant room-mate. Soutar rummaged in his right-hand coat pocket.

The giant girl, Nurse Nancy Campbell, stood at the door and watched.

And now Soutar had the handle of the blade clutched in his right hand and he was ready.

He smiled at Nurse Campbell: 'Just getting that chitty, miss...'

One hard and fast strike would do it. It would have to be now...

And then he heard the voice from within the lodgings: 'Nancy? Nancy, who is it?'

Soutar let go of the knife. As he did so, a man came to the doorway. If anything, the gentleman was even bigger than the giant nurse Campbell. They were obviously related. The giant addressed Soutar: 'What's your business here, mister?'

Soutar was tongue-tied at the emergence of this mountainous obstacle. Nurse Campbell addressed the giant: 'Angus, he has a package for Lily.'

Big Angus Campbell spoke: 'I'll take it. Where is it?'

Nancy indicated the stairway: 'He has it in his cart downstairs. I think he wants a hand up the stairs with it.'

The gentle giant offered: 'I'll help you. What is it?'

The moment had passed now. Soutar needed to get away from the scene. He doffed his hat: 'No need. It's not a problem for me to come back. I need that signature, you see, or my boss will be on my back. I will return at a more convenient time. When Nurse Parker is awake. Thank you for your assistance here. Good day to you.'

And he turned around quickly and hurried down the stairs.

Sister and brother Nancy and Angus Campbell stood in the doorway and looked at each other. And then, from within the house, they heard the voice of Lily Parker: 'Nancy? Nancy? Is that someone at the door?'

Nurse Nancy Campbell called back: 'Get back to bed, you silly sausage. It was some wee fat fellow looking for you.'

There was silence for a few moments, then Lily Parker emerged from her room, dressed in a housecoat.

Angus Campbell averted his eyes to preserve the girl's modesty.

'Looking for me?' The brother and sister were suddenly aware of a certain concern in Lily's voice.

'And what precisely did he look like?'

***

The courtroom was hushed.

'And what did he say then?'

'Nothing.'

Prosecutor Jonathan Hunter, Advocate Depute, stood across from the witness and continued his examination-in-chief of Sheriff-Substitute Dow, the judge who had examined Patrick Macnair immediately after Macnair's arrest.

Hunter turned towards the fifteen men of the jury to make his point.

'And what plea did he make?'

The Sheriff shook his head: 'He made no plea.'

'And did he make any declaration, Sheriff Dow?'

'He made no plea and no declaration, sir.'

Hunter continued the questioning with relish: 'And it was at that point, Sheriff Dow, that the Pannel Patrick Macnair could have pled Not Guilty, could he not?'

'Of course, sir.'

'It was at that point, Sheriff Dow, that Macnair could have declared his innocence to the world – but, instead, he chose to say nothing. Am I correct?'

'Perfectly correct, sir.' The Sheriff nodded towards Macnair in the dock.

Hunter looked towards the jury, smiled ruefully and shook his head: 'And instead, we have a man being given every opportunity to put forward his account of what happened, and he says nothing for weeks and then – on the day of the trial – he decides to tender a plea of Not Guilty. What should we make of that?'

Sheriff Dow pondered for a moment and then, as he was about to answer, he was interrupted by the judge, Lord Blake: 'Advocate Depute, your Learned Friend, Mr Kane has not objected to that question – I rather think that the question 'What should we make of that?' in this case would be better left to the good men of the jury, don't you?'

Hunter bowed and smiled: 'I am rightfully chastened, my lords. The question was perhaps best understood as a form of rhetorical flourish.'

Blake grinned at the judges surrounding him, then: 'Advocate Depute, you are a Scottish Advocate addressing a Scottish jury...' He leaned forward in his seat '... not Cicero addressing the Roman Forum.'

Hunter bowed, smiling: 'I am well rebuked, my lords. I am obliged...'

Kane studied the faces of the men of the jury. They seemed engaged and contented and – thought Kane with no little alarm – they liked Hunter. A number of them nodded whenever Hunter made a valid point against Macnair, as if they were grateful to Hunter for confirming their own prejudices against The Parlour Maid Murderer.

Lord Blake motioned towards the clock on the wall. It was ten minutes before one o'clock: 'In any event, Advocate Depute, I note the hour. A tardy beginning to these proceedings has resulted in considerable delay. Do you have a great deal more for this witness?'

Hunter looked at his papers, then shook his head: 'I have nothing further, my lords.'

'Very wise, Advocate Depute.'

Blake turned towards Kane: 'Mr Kane?'

Kane stood up: 'My lord?'

'Do you have any questions for this witness, Mr Kane?'

Kane could think of nothing to ask. In fact, Kane could think of nothing to say.

'Mr Kane?'

Again, he attempted to assemble some words onto the blank page of his mind.

'I... I...'

And at that point, he became aware of Collins slipping a hastily-scrawled note in front of him. Without thinking, he automatically read this aloud: 'Ask for more questions after luncheon.'

Blake frowned: 'I beg your pardon, sir?'

Kane came to: 'I do have a number of questions, my lord. I should be grateful if I could begin my cross-examination after the luncheon period.'

Blake shook his head: 'Can't you ask them now, Mr Kane?'

'I could begin the process now, my lord. However... it would take some time to conclude... and I am sure that the gentlemen of the jury would be appreciative of...'

Kane motioned towards the men in the jury. On closer examination, however, they seemed hostile to anything that Kane had to say, and they were obviously keen to proceed, having been kept waiting for the greater part of the morning.

Lord Blake studied the jury members and shook his head. 'Well, Mr Kane, we have already ascertained that your hearing is defective, and that your ability to speak is questionable – but looking at these members of the jury, and their obvious willingness to press on, I now have grave concerns about your eyesight...'

Waves of laughter from the public gallery. Lord Blake was now clearly enjoying himself. It seemed to Kane that the whole court was one great jest of which he was the constant punchline.

But when the laugher died down, Kane was saved by an unexpected sound. The sound of snoring.

Kane looked up and there, to the left of Lord Blake, sat retired judge Lord Flood with his head thrown back, his eyes tight shut and his mouth wide open. And, from the back of his throat, a sound resembling the mating call of an excited pig.

Lord Flood was not in the first blush of youth. In fact, in recent times, his ability to act as judge had been frequently compromised on account of the fact that he would appear to be sound asleep on the bench. The Advocates who appeared before him had devised various ruses to rouse the sleeping judge: a very loud clearing of the throat, a fake and entirely theatrical sneeze, the dropping of a great number of books, the crash of which would lead to the opening of one judicial eye and a sleepy muttering of 'Very warm for this time of year...'

Lord Blake stared at the judge in repose and then turned to his other side to gauge the response of the other judge, on his right-hand side. The third judge of the bench, Lord Piper, sat covering his mouth with his hand, affecting a judicial pose of deep thought, although those close to him thought that they saw the twinkling of eyes that was more suggestive of holding back tears of laughter.

Blake looked back at Kane: 'Well, Mr Kane, it appears that my brother Lord of Justiciary here would appreciate the opportunity to rest his eyes for a time. I understand, then, that you are moving the Court to adjourn now for luncheon...'

Kane smiled cautiously: 'Well, my lord, I am minded of the wisdom of the Book of Proverbs...' he motioned towards the sleeping Lord Flood '...

open thine eyes and thou shalt be satisfied with bread.'

Kane had excavated this proverb from somewhere in his memory. When he was a child, his father would sometimes rouse him with it in the mornings with the promise of breakfast.

Lord Blake looked puzzled for a moment. It seemed to Kane for a very long moment. Then the judge smiled.

'Ah – another Son of the Manse is lured to the Scottish Bar. Mr Kane, I was also blessed with a father who was a Man of the Cloth. Your motion is granted, and we shall resume at two o'clock.'

Lord Blake stood up, immediately followed by Lord Piper on his right.

The third judge – Lord Flood – still fast asleep, remained seated in his chair, his head bobbling slightly as he inhaled.

Kane wondered for a moment how the sleeping judge might be roused – respectfully – but the question was soon answered when the Macer, Mr Andrews, stood at Lord Flood's side and bellowed towards the judge's ear: 'Cooooo-u-rt all rise.'

The old judge's eyes opened sharply, and he was heard to mutter 'I concur' before he looked around himself, stood up, made a hasty bow towards the auditorium – then scuttled off to the exit door on his left.

All of those attending in the courtroom stood and returned Lord Blake's bow. As Kane watched the judges leave their places, he looked up towards the gallery again to see what Horse was making of the whole situation.

But Horse had already left. There was business to be done at Mrs Bennett's Bar. Business that involved the recovery of money and a certain lanky individual who had ordered steak and was wearing dead men's teeth.

***

'Mrs Bennett?'

'Who wants to know?'

Horse stood, cap in hand, and examined the face of the old lady before him. She might have resembled one's benevolent grandmother, except for the deep scar on her left cheek and the eyepatch over her left eye.

'The name's Horse, madam'

Old Mrs Bennett stood on her doorstep and eyed the stranger up and down: 'Horse'? 'Horse'? Goad blissus, whit kind of name is that for a grown man?'

'I was told I could get a drink here, madam. In private, if you know what I mean.'

The old lady seemed reluctant to engage: 'Aye, well, maybe ye can and maybe ye cannae. I dinnae like the look of you, son...'

'I was hoping...'

'Ye talk awful funny as well. Are ye the polis?'

'No, madam. But I am no stranger to the Edinburgh Force – if you get my meaning...' Horse looked around himself, as if he were checking for the presence of the police.

'Are ye by yerself?'

Horse nodded. Mrs Bennett smiled, then stood aside: 'Ye'd better come in then...'

Horse gave a short bow and entered Mrs Bennett's drinking establishment.

'I dinnae hae any licence or anything o' that nature, son. But I'll share what I have with ye, and if you want to leave me a wee bit o' money on the table there, then that'll do just fine.'

Mrs Bennett's rather quaint disavowal of running a drinking establishment was disproved immediately when Horse noted a long bar area running along the left-hand wall, complete with a tall beer fount. On top of the counter lay a number of bottles of hard spirits, whisky and gin, surrounded by an array of what looked like silver thimbles, some small, some large and in the shape of hourglasses.

'Will ye have a wee dram, son?'

'I'll have what you're having, Mrs B.'

The old lady threw her head back and laughed. Horse could hear a faint wheezing sound from her lungs: 'Oh, son – I huvnae touched a drappie in years.'

Mrs Bennett went to the bar and poured some whisky into one of the silver thimbles, and then decanted it into a glass, which she handed to Horse.

'Get that down ye.'

Horse raised his glass to her – and downed the drink in one gulp. It was immediately apparent that this was not whisky of any great quality, and Horse felt his eyes water, but he was moved to thank his hostess: 'Well, Mrs B, thank you for a very fine snifter.'

Mrs Bennett smiled: 'Ach – yer too polite, son. This is the stuff I gie the navvies. I keep the good stuff under lock and key in the back. Now, can I get you another something else?'

The quality of that first measure was not an experience that Horse wished to repeat: 'Some beer, madam, some beer would be appreciated.'

The old lady giggled: 'Aye – I dinnae blame ye. And it'll take away the taste of the dram that you just had...'

The old lady repaired once again to the bar area.

While Mrs Bennet was tending to the beer engine, Horse looked around. Despite being one o'clock in the day, the shutters were drawn and the room seemed dingy, illuminated by few candles. Tables and chairs were scattered around, and through the gloom Horse could discern around ten or a dozen other men, some sitting alone and nursing their drinks, others whispering to their companions.

The old lady returned with the beer: 'You'll like this.'

Horse put the tall glass to his lips and drank. He wiped the foam from his lips: 'I thank you, Mrs Bennett. Just the ticket.'

The old lady beamed.

'Now, Mrs B, I wonder if you could help me. I'm looking for a friend. A Billy Brown. Have you seen Billy Brown?'

There was a change in the old lady now. Horse had difficulty reading her, but it was clear she knew something.

'Look around you, son. Do you think I keep a school register here? Some of these boys have been drinking here for years and I still dinnae ken their names. When the polis turn up and say, 'Have ye seen so-and-so?', I say, 'I don't know anybody cried that name.' And that's no lie, son. Anyway, I think ye'd better drink up and go now. And don't forget tae leave me a wee present on the table there.'

Horse did not move to leave: 'It's just that I got something for him here in me pocket.' He patted his left breast pocket with his right hand.

The old lady smiled. She appeared undecided now.

Horse persisted: 'Billy Brown – you'd know him because he come into a bit of money recently and he got himself some new clothes. And some new teeth...' Horse pointed at his mouth.

It was obvious from her face now that Mrs Bennett was mulling something over in her mind. She looked around to see if they were being watched.

Horse raised the beer mug high to his lips and gulped down the rest of the beer. He wiped his mouth, looked around, then looked at her and then muttered something under his breath.

The old lady looked up: 'What did you say there?'

'I said I'll just tell Dode that you wouldn't help...'

She screwed up her face: 'Dode'?'

He could tell by the look on her face that he had her now.

'Yes – Fat Dode – You know. George. George Soutar...'

For the first time in their conversation, Horse felt a genuine emotional response from the old lady, and that response was fear. At the sound of the name – and barely conscious of doing so – Mrs Euphemia Bennett shut her one good eye and began to re-trace the deep scar on her face.

'But you don't know any names, do you, Mrs Bennett?'

The old landlady emerged from her reverie: 'He's in the back room, in the snug...'

'Who?'

'Billy. Billy Brown'

Horse felt his breast pocket. 'And who is he with?'

'Nobody. He's just ordered his food.'

'Don't tell me: a nice piece of steak?'

Mrs Bennett nodded.

'Thank you, Mrs B. Dode will be very pleased with you. We're just going to have a little chinwag now with our friend with Waterloo teeth...'

'You told me you were by yourself...'

'I swear I am, ma'am. I mean you and me. It should only take a couple of minutes. Oh, and before we go in, can you fetch us a bucket of water, a mop and a couple of old bedsheets.'

The old lady frowned: 'What for?'

'Just to be on the safe side. You and me – we might just have to do us a bit of cleaning up afterwards, Mrs B.'

'And what are the bedsheets for?'

Horse placed his hand on his breast pocket: 'Ah, Mrs Bennett, that would be telling, wouldn't it? Now, my dear – show me – where is Billy Brown?'

***

'Well, the good news, Edward, is that I have seen worse.'

'Not Proven' Norris puffed on his pipe as he, Kane and Collins strode along Parliament Hall during the luncheon adjournment.

Norris had been one of those Counsel who had witnessed Edward Kane's torrid christening in the Criminal Courts.

'And the bad news is that I have not seen much worse.'

Kane submerged into despair once again.

'May I remind you, Edward, that you are not a physician – you are a lawyer. The Hippocratic Oath does not apply here. There's merit in the 'First do no harm' approach if your question would harm your client, however – simply to sit there in imitation of a deaf mute is never a strategy that I would recommend.'

Kane came to an abrupt stop: 'Then I fear that Macnair is doomed...'

'Edward, you are still in the early stages of this great voyage of discovery. Think of the prosecution case as a great big ship. Take whatever tools you possess and start fashioning large holes into the side of that boat. The moment the jury members realise that that ship is sinking, they will desert it like rats.'

Kane laughed for the first time that he could remember: 'And what, pray, Mr Norris, might I use as my tools?'

Norris puffed on his pipe for a moment: 'That old Sheriff, the old fool who seemed to take so agin the accused making no plea or no declaration...'

'Sheriff Dow...'

'That's the one. Since this is your maiden voyage, Edward, let's smash that sheriff's head against the side of the boat, as the defence voyage gets underway. Now – here's what to ask...'

***

'Effie! Effie!'

Billy Brown banged his knife on the table. A smoky pipe rested on the edge: 'Effie – what have you done with that steak? Have I got to kill that cow myself? I'll maybe pay you a visit after.'

No response.

Louder: 'Effie!'

Mrs Euphemia Bennett appeared at the door of the snug area. She was holding a mop and a bucket; some old sheets were thrown across her shoulder. Brown took a look at her: 'Get in here, you old baggage! Where's my grub?' He took another look: 'And what's all that stuff for?'

The old lady looked at Brown: 'William – you've got an English visitor.'

An odd introduction, perhaps, but at this point, Horse appeared beside the old lady: 'Hello, Billy, me old chum. How you doing?'

Maybe it was the sheer gloom of the place, but Horse detected no surprise on Brown's face. The hairs on the back of Horse's neck began to prickle. Something wasn't right here. For one thing, Billy Brown remained seated, with no attempt at escape or hint of being threatened. Brown sat there, a broad grin on his face sporting a set of teeth that were at least two sizes too big. He reminded Horse of a drawing he'd once seen of Prehistoric Man grinning in a murky cave.

Far too calm, far too calm. What's going on here? What have I missed?

Billy Brown sighed: 'Sit down, sir.' He laughed and lifted up the pipe: 'Will you join me in a pipe? You never got the chance last time...' he pointed to his mouth '...too busy smashing my teeth in.'

Horse took his seat on the other side of the table from Brown. A bottle of what looked like whisky stood on the table, surrounded by glasses.

'You done well, Horse, you done well. You deserve a drink. Here.'

Brown took the bottle and poured a large measure into one of the glasses. He pushed it across the table to Horse.

'You'll understand that Mrs Malone, the landlady, told me all about you – an inheritance from my old Irish grandmother. You remember, the one in Kerry – wherever that is. Very clever, Mr Horse. Very fly.' Brown raised his glass: 'Here's to all of our imaginary Irish relations.'

Brown took a good drink from his own glass of whisky.

'And then, prowling about the Doric Tavern. Asking folk about me. Do you think they're not going to tell me that somebody is looking for me?'

He took another drink from his glass.

'And so, here we are, Mr Horse. The end of the road. Just you and me. And wee Effie, of course...'

Brown nodded towards Mrs Bennett, who was still standing in the doorway, mop in hand, sheet on shoulder.

'... and I said to her: 'Effie, when the Horse turns up here – as he will – call me 'William' when he comes in, and I'll know that he's here.' Good girl, Effie.'

He raised his glass high to Mrs Bennett, finishing the contents. He gave out a long sigh, then ran his index finger across his mouth and licked it.

'Now what can I do for you, Mr. Horse?'

Horse replied immediately: 'I want my money back, Billy.'

Brown laughed and poured himself another drink: 'Have a care now, Mr Horse, have a care. Remember, we're dealing with lawyers here, aren't we. So it was not your money, was it? That money belonged to a certain Mr Kane, Advocate. If I'm not mistaken.'

'Where's the money, Billy? Give me what's left and I won't hurt you.'

Brown laughed: 'Do you think for a minute, Horse, that I kept all that money? No – I was just paid for the job, that's all. Although, I admit, paid handsomely.'

Brown reached for the bottle: 'You see this, Horse? You see this whisky here? Fifty years old. Can you imagine that – fifty years? I don't think I'll live that long.'

He held his glass of whisky to the candle and the light gave the glass an amber glow.

'This is the good stuff that Effie keeps locked away. I've poured you a glass – try it.'

Horse looked at his glass; then he raised it to his lips and tasted a small quantity. Brown was right. This was a dram that Horse had rarely experienced. Brown watched Horse drink and then he took another gulp himself.

'Do you feel that, Horse? Do you feel the sheer warmth of the old aquae vitae as it goes down? Old Meldrum's finest. I just couldn't afford it before, but since my meeting with your man, Kane...'

Horse took another sip. Without knowing why, he knew he had to get out of there quickly: 'Tell you what, Billy, I'll leave you the bottle. Just give me what's left of the money and nobody will get hurt here.'

'Two mistakes, Horse. Two careless mistakes. One – to think that I'd go back to drinking the cat's piss that is normally served to folk like me...' he looked behind Horse now '... no offence, Mrs Bennett...'

Horse heard the old lady behind him say: 'None taken, Billy.'

'...and the second mistake, good Mr Horse – some would say the fatal mistake – is not keeping a lookout behind you...'

Horse frowned – then looked behind.

And there stood old Mrs Bennett, the kindly-looking little grandmother, no longer carrying a mop and a bucket, but a shiny pistol pointing at Horse's face.

★★★

Kane was on his feet in the crowded courtroom: 'Sheriff Dow – how long have you been a Sheriff, sir?'

The prosecution witness, the old Sheriff, shifted on his feet. He narrowed his eyes and calculated: 'Twenty-six... twenty-seven years this year.'

'And you will have examined many, many accused persons in that time.'

'Possibly hundreds, sir.'

'And in the vast majority of those cases, in the early stages, where the accused has appeared before you – as Patrick Macnair did...' Kane now motioned to the man in the dock, '... the accused person also made no plea. Isn't that correct?'

'Yes.'

'And made no form of declaration, am I correct?'

'Yes.'

'And in a number of those cases, the accused was later found to be not guilty of the crime alleged. Isn't that right, Sheriff?'

'Of course.'

'Those individuals made no plea, as Macnair did; no declaration, as Macnair did; and they finally benefitted from the presumption of innocence, just as Macnair does today, isn't that right?'

The old Sheriff thought carefully for a moment, but before he could answer, Jon Hunter was on his feet: 'Don't answer that question.'

Lord Blake poised his pen over his papers: 'Advocate Depute – you have an objection?'

'Yes, my lord...'

In truth, Jon Hunter had no actual idea what his objection was. Pure instinct had brought him to his feet at that point as he felt control of the proceedings slipping from his grasp, but the particular nature and content of any objection had yet to crystallise in his mind.

'I... my lords... the question...' Hunter floundered. Then, finally: 'This is trite law, my lords.'

Lord Blake looked at Hunter, closed his eyes, opened them again and looked at the ceiling for a moment, then turned to Kane: 'Mr Kane, I will repel the Advocate Depute's objection without the necessity of being addressed by you. It appears that he has only recently become aware that the accused person in every case benefits from a presumption of innocence. Please continue...'

***

'Drink up, Horsey – drink up.'

Billy Brown sat forward in his chair, grinning, his big teeth glistening in the candle-light. Horse did not move. The pistol was cocked behind him and the gun barrel pointed right at his head.

Brown laughed: 'You see, Effie. What is it they say? 'You can lead a horse to whisky, but...' and he laughed again, clearly enjoying every moment of his victory.

Horse lifted his glass, put it to his lips and drank a little, then turned and nodded behind: 'That is a very impressive firearm, Mrs B.'

Brown butted in: 'It's from the Americas, Horse. Brand new it is. This one will give you five in the head. One straight after the other...' Brown cocked his hand to imitate a gun and pointed it at Horse: 'Bang. Bang. Bang. Bang. Bang – with no re-loading, they say. They call it 'The Dragoon'. You'll know all about it, a military man like you...'

'I fought alongside The Dragoons, Billy. Served at Waterloo. But I never shot anybody in the back...'

'Come on, Horse. We're not any different, you and me. We both kill when we have to. Now, finish your drink, and we'll do what we have to here.'

Horse raised the glass to his lips again.

Brown smiled: 'You ready, Effie?' The old lady nodded her assent. Brown laughed again: 'Oh, and thank you, Horse, for suggesting the bucket and the mop. They will come in very handy.' Brown's face became deadly serious: 'Now, drink up...'

Horse lifted his glass, but all that he could think of at that moment was the face of Mrs. Bennett behind him. Which eye was it had the patch? The right? No, no – it was the left, wasn't it. So, the right eye was her only good eye. If anything were to happen to that good eye, then the old lady would be plunged into darkness, wouldn't she?

★★★

Court finished early that day. Two brief prosecution witnesses identified some formal court documents and plans of Sir Charles Irving's house, then Lord Blake thanked the fifteen men of the jury and adjourned the trial until the following morning.

Kane and his friend Collins walked up and down Parliament Hall.

'Collins, my friend, I fear that the gentlemen of the jury do not care for me. Every time I smile at them, I receive nothing but a scowl in return.'

Collins smiled: 'My dear Edward, this has nothing to do with you. It is your client that they resist, not you, my friend. Whenever they look at you, they see him and – beyond peradventure – they have already convicted him in their minds.'

Kane nodded: 'Thank you, Collins. It does feel at times as if I am in the middle of defending Blackbeard the Pirate...'

The two friends stopped and laughed for a moment, but then, without warning, Kane bent over and clutched his head. Collins grabbed his arm to steady him: 'Are you unwell, my friend?'

'I think... I think that it is simply... exhaustion. At some level, I suppose, I did not think that the trial would ever start, and now...'

Kane then stood up straight and exhaled loudly: 'I must get home, Collins.' He smiled weakly, 'I expect that my man Horse will have some magical potion or other to cure me of whatever it is that ails me...' He motioned to the wooden benches at the side of the hall. 'Perhaps If I were to sit down for a moment...'

But as Kane was making his way towards the benches, he noticed someone on the other side of Parliament Hall, waving to attract his attention.

He narrowed his eyes to see Florrie Forbes-Knight. But he also noted that standing at the fireplace was an odd figure, wearing a huge hat and long coat. The face of that person was, somewhat bizarrely, hidden behind what looked like a carnival mask from Venice.

Kane began to walk over, and Florrie came to meet him half-way.

'Edward, are you unwell? You look positively ashen.'

'Florrie, as they say, this too shall pass...'

Florrie smiled: 'Well, Edward, I hope you do not mind...' She nodded towards the fireplace. 'I have brought you a visitor.'

They walked over and Kane examined his visitor more closely. Yes, a Venetian mask, being held to the face by a thin stick. The shoulders of the figure appeared to be trembling.

Kane addressed the stranger with something of a weary bow: 'Good afternoon, sir...'

The figure stopped trembling, then pulled away the mask to reveal – with a happy shriek – Amanda Forbes-Knight.

'Edward, my Edward!'

And with that, Edward Kane – Advocate, defender of the Parlour Maid Murderer – passed out.

***

'Well, Billy boy, I got to admit it, son, you got me fair and square.' Horse raised his glass of whisky, as if in a toast. 'And just before I finish my drink...' he turned towards Mrs Bennett '... and can I just say, my dear, that I have never tasted a finer drop...' he took a sip '... and please do not think me wery impolite, my dear, but...' he motioned towards the patch over the old lady's left eye '... what's the story with the old blinker there?'

Billy Brown butted in: 'Shut it, Horse...'

Horse raised his glass to her: 'Sorry, Mrs B. I meant no offence...'

The old lady began blinking her one eye now.

'... but it must have been sore, love. And you would have been a wery handsome woman in your day, Mrs B. Wery handsome.'

Brown picked up the knife from the table: 'Shut it, Horse.'

'I saw it happen at Waterloo. Sometimes it was the knife what done it. And sometimes, when you was fighting at close quarters, like...' He mimicked sticking his thumb into his eye, '... it was the thumb what gouged it clean out. Is that what happened here?'

Brown shouted now: 'Horse!'

The older lady looked more and more fragile as Horse spoke: 'And I know who done that to you, Mrs B...'

'Horse!'

'It was... it was... Soutar, wasn't it?'

As before, at the name Soutar the old lady closed her eye for a second, a reflex against the memory of what had happened to her at his hands.

And in that split second, Horse threw his glass of whisky into the old lady's good eye. The impact of the glass was painful enough, but the whisky in that one good eye was stinging even more. The old woman was totally blind as she started to fire shots into the darkness.

CLICK. BLAM! Horse had jumped from his chair and was trying to scurry along the floor without making a noise.

CLICK. BLAM! This time, the bullet whizzed past the head of Billy Brown: 'No – ye stupid woman, he's getting behind you, behind you...'

Mrs Euphemia Bennett spun round, furiously rubbing her good eye with her left hand while pointing the pistol with her right.

CLICK. BLAM! Through the door.

Far too close. Horse couldn't get out the door. Maybe, if he got closer to Brown, she'd stop shooting. But Brown had that steak knife and was coming towards him.

***

It was like a garden. Warm enough that Kane would require to unfasten his collar to breathe more easily. And in that garden she was stroking his head with a cool, soft handkerchief. It was Miss Amanda's voice, but that gentleness of touch did not seem like hers. The garden began to fade.

Now Kane felt as if he were a bucket of water being drawn up from a deep well. Up, up, up.

Is that light? Light at the opening of the well? And what is she saying? What is Amanda saying? Something about salt? Smelling salts. Smelling salts?

Kane opened his eyes and found himself not in a garden but in a candlelit room. One of the basement rooms below Parliament Hall. Kane had been laid out on a table there. He looked around. Florrie was standing back, dampened handkerchief in her hand; Collins was also standing back, concerned, blinking through his horn-rimmed spectacles and holding a tiny opened bottle in one hand and a minuscule cork in the other; and around the table stood Manville with two other Faculty Servants, who had – as discreetly as possible – lugged Kane downstairs. And there – her face still hidden behind the Venetian carnival mask – stood Miss Amanda.

Kane moved to speak, but the muscles in his mouth were reluctant to comply with the orders from his brain. 'Whu... whu...'

Amanda was pointing at him and speaking from behind the mask: 'There! Smelling salts. I told you. The only sure remedy for the vapours. I know this. I am an artist, as you can see. It is a part of my own temperament. Smelling salts are also efficacious for people of defective body. And mind. People like Edward.'

Kane was conscious again of his head being dabbed with a handkerchief. A beautiful, cooling salve in this strange world. Florrie spoke gently – but firmly – to her sister: 'Amanda, Amanda – please stop. Edward requires rest...'

The masked figure was furious now and hissed: 'Florrie! What have I told you? Never address me by my true name. Not before...' and at this point she made a sweeping motion directed at those in the room '... my public!'

Florrie's face flushed. She bit her bottom lip, then resumed the dabbing. 'Temperament? Stuff and nonsense. This is all because you haven't eaten today, isn't it, Edward?' She smiled and raised her eyebrows at Kane to elicit a positive response: 'Isn't it?' Kane understood that good, kind Florrie was attempting to preserve his reputation. He nodded his head.

Florrie looked around at the others: 'And he is so dedicated to his work, he hasn't had the time to eat. That is what makes him such an excellent Advocate. As you will have seen today from his sterling performance in the courtroom...'

Florrie smiled at Kane and he smiled back at her, grateful for this judgment on his courtroom christening.

Collins placed the cork back onto the tiny bottle: 'Well, the smelling salts seem to have done the trick. Shall I order a carriage and we'll get you home, my friend?'

Florrie shook her head. 'That will not be necessary.' She nodded towards Amanda. 'My sis...' Before she could complete the word, Amanda hissed. Florrie paused, then continued: 'My companion and I already have a carriage waiting. We will deliver Mr Kane to his home. We require no further help, thank you.'

Manville, ever alive to his cue for an exit, jerked his thumb at the other two servants and they scuttled out of the room. Manville himself left with a low bow.

Collins gave a nervous laugh: 'Then, ladies, I shall leave you to your business.' He turned to Kane: 'Edward, I will return the papers to your box with my own notes from today. I shall be in the library at eight o'clock tomorrow morning, and we can discuss the evidence at that point. Until then...' And Collins bowed to the ladies and left.

Florrie looked after Collins: 'He seems a decent fellow, Edward.'

Kane nodded: 'Florrie – he is the best friend a man could have.'

At that point, Kane heard a sob from the other side of the room. Miss Amanda had let the mask drop and was holding it by her side. Her other hand was spread over her face now and she was sobbing.

Kane called over: 'Amanda, Amanda, whatever...?'

The girl let out an anguished howl: 'Time was when I was your best, Edward. I was your best...' She began to howl again.

Kane was flabbergasted. He wished to go over and comfort the girl, but remembered that she had written to him only recently and had stated expressly that any romantic attachment between them was at an end.

'Oh, Amanda...'

'Oh, Edward. If only my great talent had not come between us. If only you were competent in your own work. But here we stand, star crossed lovers, like Romeo and Janet. And I came today, Edward, to apologise. I came to say that I am sorry for what I wrote. When I wrote that you could not expect to buy tickets for my concert at a discount, it was wrong of me to do that. Of course, you may do that. Only this morning at breakfast, Father said that despite his best efforts to encourage an audience to attend, the Assembly Rooms resembled, resembled...' She turned to Florrie. 'Florrie, what did he say it resembled?'

'A deserted barn.'

'A deserted barn', do you hear that, Edward? My epiph... epiph...'

Florrie assisted: 'Epiphany.'

'My epiphamy. Thwarted. Mr Brookes says...'

At the mention of the name, Kane gave an interior sigh.

'Mr Brookes says that sometimes it take hundreds and hundreds of years for the people – the common people that is – to recognise genius...' Amanda raised her eyes wistfully, as if she expected to find her tortured artistic soul somewhere on the ceiling.

She looked again at Kane and began to sob again: 'A barn, Edward. A great, big, deserted barn...'

Decorum be blowed! Kane let himself down from the table, walked over to Miss Amanda and he put his arms around her. She collapsed into him and nestled into his chest, like an injured little bird. He rested his cheek on the top of her head. Then he held her out at arms' length and looked into her eyes. And those waif-like eyes sparkled and glistened as the tears ran down her cheeks. Kane smiled: 'My dear Miss Amanda, I would not miss your concert for all the world. And even if that room is not entirely full, it will, at least, be filled by those who truly value you.'

Amanda wiped the tears from her eyes.

'Oh, Edward, Edward, you simply cannot understand the great responsibility that I bear...'

And then Kane became aware of a head peering through the doorway.

'Kane! What the Dickens...?'

Kane did not have to look up to know that it was the voice of the Dean of Faculty, Rab Lennox.

★★★

Horse had, of course, faced a number of difficult situations in his life. He had often remarked that he could write a book on the subject. That said, as Horse was holding Brown's flailing wrist in an attempt to keep a steak knife from slashing his throat, all the while endeavouring not to be shot by a one-eyed crone now apparently randomly discharging the contents of a repeater pistol in his direction, this episode would certainly deserve, thought Horse, more than a mere footnote. If he survived to write the tale, that was.

CLICK. BLAM! Brown shouted at the old woman: 'Mind what you're doing, ye stupid woman! Ye nearly hit me there...'

Horse and Brown were now face to face as they wrestled for control of the knife. Horse could feel Brown's warm, stale, whisky-stinking breath on his face now. And those great oversized teeth, like tombstones each bearing the inscription *Here Lies Horse*...

No time to retrieve Aunty Betty without being stabbed in the process. But maybe there was another weapon here. Horse snapped his teeth at Billy Brown's arm, letting them glance along Brown's arm without doing any damage. Snap! Same again.

Brown laughed: 'Are ye that desperate, Horse? Are ye? Trying to bite me? I'll show you a bite, boy!'

Brown immediately sank his teeth into Horse's arm. Painful, yes. But all according to plan. What Brown had forgotten in the heat of the struggle was that those great teeth – those veterans of the Battle of Waterloo – were not, in fact, his own.

Horse pulled away his right hand from Brown's grip and stuck that hand into Brown's mouth. Inside, under the lips. Brown released his biting grip from Horse's arm and snatched at Horse's hand. Horse did not pull away but, instead, let the teeth cover his hand – before he gave those teeth a mighty yank.

And with that, the Waterloo teeth fled another grim (if not so illustrious) battlefield – as they flew out of Brown's mouth.

Billy Brown stood frozen for a moment: 'Uh?' Just enough time for Horse – in a well-practised motion – to remove from his pocket his Aunty Bettie. The steely maiden aunt soon re-acquainted herself with the contours of Billy Brown's face. Brown's eyes blinked furiously before he fell to the floor.

Horse looked down at his handiwork. He let go a long, laboured sigh of relief. And then he heard a CLICK. He looked up. Mrs Euphemia Bennet had regained her sight and was now pointing the pistol directly at Horse's head.

★★★

Rab Lennox was being so polite that Kane barely recognised him. He attributed the veneer of civility to there being ladies present.

'Ah, Kane, I was merely seeking to be apprised of how... how... the first day of trial...' Lennox seemed tongue-tied.

Florrie spoke up: 'It was an excellent first day, Mr Lennox. You should be very proud of Edward.'

Amanda spoke up now, too: 'Yes, Mr Lennox. Edward was embarrassing at first, and then a bit better. And then he fainted.'

Lennox frowned: 'Perhaps, Mr Kane, you can come to my room when you have finished with the ladies, and we shall have a little chat...'

'Quite impossible.' Said Florrie.

'Miss Forbes-Knight,' Kane was sure that he could a hear a distant rumble somewhere inside Lennox's voice, a volcanic rage ready to erupt. 'I would remind you that I am the Dean of the Faculty of Advocates. If I instruct a Member of Faculty to attend at my room, miss, then he shall do so.'

Florrie was unperturbed: 'Mr Lennox, I know very well who you are, since you appear to have been making almost daily visits to my father's house...'

'On matters that are of no concern to you, Miss Forbes-Knight.'

'I'm afraid, Mr Lennox, that your writ does not run there, nor does it compel a sick man to jump through hoops, sir.'

'This is quite outrageous...'

Florrie motioned to the door: 'I observed, Mr Lennox, that there were still a great number of members of the press upstairs in the hall. Shall I inform them that Edward's ability to continue the trial is being compromised by his own superior?'

Lennox pursed his lips for a moment, then spoke to Kane: 'I shall expect a full report tomorrow morning, Kane.' He then gave a shallow bow on leaving: 'Ladies...'

Kane and the ladies waited until they heard Lennox pass through the hallway door outside. Kane studied Florrie's face. Her eyes were red and moist: 'Well, Florrie, so much for 'When in doubt, be Anne of Cleves'.' He smiled at Florrie. Florrie smiled back, then burst into tears.

Miss Amanda produced a lace handkerchief from her coat pocket and handed it to her sister: 'Oh, Florrie – you are such a shrew. Small wonder you have no suitors.'

If this remark was meant to be of a consoling nature, then it had, in fact, the opposite effect on Miss Florence Forbes-Knight and her tears fell faster and more copiously. 'Oh, Edward, I am so sorry. I do not know what comes over me at times. It is just that...' She cried harder.

Kane took her hand and smiled: 'Florence Forbes-Knight – today, you have been my guardian angel...' No sooner had he uttered these words than a pathetic wail arose from the direction of Miss Amanda. 'But, Edward – I used to be your angel. Oh, my sweet – I miss you...'

And so, in that cramped and darkened basement room, Edward Kane, Advocate – although entirely devoid of energy, drained of colour and feeling more than a little nauseous – held the hands of two very different sisters, both inconsolable, while he waited for an opportune moment to venture that they might mount the stairs and take a carriage home.

★★★

Horse was standing with his hands raised up high as the pistol pointed at his face.

'Effie, I don't know you that well...'

'Then don't call me 'Effie'...'

'A wery good point my dear. Wery well made. But one thing that I have to admire about you...'

The old lady cocked her head and looked skeptical.

'... is that, here you are, a lady not in the first blush of youth – if you don't mind me saying so...'

Mrs Bennett pointed the gun closer to Horse's face.

'... but having to fend for yourself at your time of life. A lady like you. A lady of quality...'

Had Euphemia Bennet still the ability to blush, then that observation might have brought the crimson to her cheeks.

'Having to deal with the lowest of the low – like young Billy Brown here.' Horse pointed to the inert, slumped figure on the floor.

The old lady looked grim: 'Believe me, son – Billy Brown is no' the lowest.'

'And having to quibble about the bill with these men. I can just see you now – 'Was that six drinks you 'ad, or was it seven?'

'I ken them all here, son, and I ken how many glasses they've had, don't you worry. I keep the count here in my head.' And she tapped the side of her head with the index finger of her free hand.

Horse nodded, a serious look on his face now: 'You see, Mrs Bennett, counting glasses of whisky and counting coppers is one thing – but counting bullets is another thing altogether, ain't it?'

The old lady frowned. Horse continued and nodded towards Brown on the floor: 'And when our sleeping friend here was telling me all about that shiny new pistol you got there in your hands there, he managed to say that you got five shots in it...'

'So?'

'So you're out of bullets, my love.'

A look of shock passed over the old lady's face: 'What?'

'You wasn't counting, Mrs B. You was firing that gun like a mad thing, you was, but you wasn't counting the bullets, was ya? All done, Mrs B. All the bullets in that gun have been fired.'

The old lady considered this and kept the gun pointed straight at Horse's face. She gave a short laugh, but Horse though that he detected a slight tremor in her voice now: 'Yer a liar. Look at you, you've got your hands up because you know I've got bullets left.'

'I've got these 'ands up out of respect for me elders, that's all, Mrs B. You see, what's going to happen is this: if you pulls the trigger then I will know then that you are me sworn enemy forever – and I will 'ave to set about you with this nine-inch metal bar...'

The old lady's jaw dropped. Horse lowered his hands and pointed to the patch on Mrs Bennett's eye.

'... and I know that you 'ave already lost the use of that one eye, my dear, but I promise ya, if you pull that trigger you will then require the services of a cane and a guide dog. Permanent.'

Horse stared unblinking at the old woman. He dipped his head and raised his eyebrows. Slowly, he held out his hand, inviting the old woman to hand over the weapon: 'Come on, me old love. I'll even help you clean up the mess...'

The old lady said nothing. Just stood there, pointing the gun.

***

Kane's apartments seemed eerily empty without the presence of Horse. The space was so small, it was easy to look through each area in a matter of seconds. No sign in the sitting room, no-one in Kane's bedroom, the larder was empty, Horse's alcove was undisturbed, no fire in the grate. Where on earth was Horse? The whole place had a cold and clammy quality to it, like a corpse that had exhaled its last breath.

Kane stumbled into his bedroom. Fully clothed, he lay down on top of his bed.

'Come sit you down upon this flowery bed...' That was what his father would say to him when Kane was a child and father was trying to get him to bed. The boy Kane would kiss his mother on the cheek, then jump upon his father's back and be ferried to his bedroom. And when the boy was tucked underneath the covers, he would put his hands together, fingers and thumbs interlocked, and they would say prayers. And at the end of prayers, his father would kiss the boy's head and whisper:

'Be strong and of a good courage, Edward, for the Lord thy God is with thee wherever thou goest.'

And the candle would be blown out.

And now as an adult, lying there, fully clothed, after that long day, Edward Kane could still hear his father's voice: 'Be strong and of good courage...'

Kane smiled at the memory.

I'll rest my eyes. Just for five minutes.

***

'A very wise decision, Mrs B, very wise...'

Horse placed the five-shot repeater on the table and began the process of turning out Billy Brown's pockets to see what, if anything, was left of the money. He had spread out one of the bedsheets on the floor and was dropping items into it.

Some notes, some coins. Still a decent sum. But, as Brown had said, nowhere near the full amount.

Horse began to take off Brown's boots.

Mrs Bennett – in the process of mopping up the blood from the floor – looked over: 'What are you doing now?'

Horse held up the boot, turned it upside down, and a crumpled ten-shilling note fell to the floor. Horse opened it up, smoothed it out and, with a grin, he exhibited the note to Mrs Bennett. The old woman shook her head and resumed her mopping.

Horse began to strip down the unconscious figure and make a silent inventory of the items to himself. Jacket (good quality material), shirt, cufflinks (not real silver – but worth something), neckerchief (silk?), handkerchief, trousers (no underwear), socks, until Billy Brown was lying there entirely naked.

Horse examined each of the items. He scooped up the notes and coins and put them in his pocket. Placing the corners of the sheet into the centre of the sheet, he tied a knot, creating a small pack. He put the boots and clothes in the pack and slung it over his shoulder.

He went to the table, lifted up the gun and put it into his pocket. 'Well, Mrs B...'

The old lady stopped her mopping and looked up at him.

'... can I just say, it was an adventure, my dear.'

The old woman pointed at Horse's pocket. 'Leave the gun. It's no' Billy's, it's mine.'

Horse narrowed his lips and thought for a moment: 'Sorry, my lovely. Can't leave that here. Somebody might get hurt. And that might be you, Mrs B. Wouldn't want that, now, would we?'

Euphemia Bennett thought for a moment, then: 'Was it true, though?'

'Was what true?'

'The bullets. Ye'd counted the bullets and there was no bullet left. Was that right enough?'

Horse reached into his pocket and produced the pistol. He slowly raised his arm and placed the gun against his right temple. He cocked the gun. CLICK. He held it there for a moment, then pointed the gun towards the ceiling. And pulled the trigger. BLAM.

A small mist of grey masonry fell from the ceiling.

Horse placed the gun back into his pocket.

'Looks like I was mistaken in my counting, Mrs B. 'Rithmetic never was my strong point.'

Mrs Bennett stood frozen.

'The gun is still mine...'

'Yes, but you was trying to kill me with it, my dear, so I reckon you owe me something. Still...' Horse reached into his pocket, took out the money, peeled off two pound notes and placed them on the table. 'Fair exchange, Mrs B...'

The old lady shook her head and pointed to the unconscious, naked Billy Brown on the floor: 'And look at the state of that one. How is he meant to get home like that?'

Horse smiled: 'That was what the other sheet was for, my dear. He don't live far from here. Just tell them he's lost his wits and he thinks he's Julius Caesar...'

Horse slung the makeshift knapsack over his shoulder. 'And when he wakes up, you can tell him – just like that Roman bloke – he'd better watch his back. And remember...' He patted the pocket with the pistol '... I got five chances of getting him with this alone.'

Horse gave a shallow bow and made towards the door. He was stopped by the old lady's voice: 'Mr Horse?'

He turned around: 'Yes?'

The old woman pointed to something under a chair: 'Ye forgot the teeth...'

Horse looked round and there, under a chair, almost luminous, sat the Waterloo teeth. Hard to tell if those dead men's teeth were grimacing, or grinning at the absurdities of the living.

Horse took his handkerchief out of his pocket, scooped up the teeth, put them in his pocket, made a quick bow, then left the drinking establishment of Mrs Euphemia Bennett.

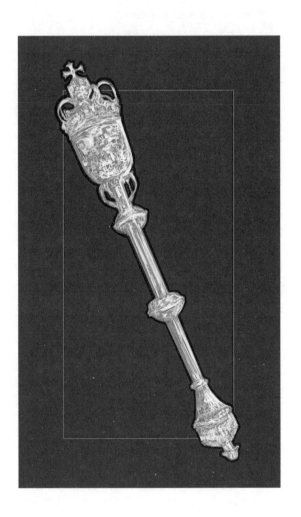

Chapter Nine

Leaning over the bed, Mr Moss, the surgeon, held one of the sleeping boy's eyelids open. He stood back from the bed. 'How long was he awake for?'

Nurses Nancy Campbell and Lily Parker stood at the foot of the bed. Nurse Campbell spoke up: 'Maybe two minutes, Mr Moss. He seemed to wake with a start, and then he was babbling. I sent Nurse Parker to inform you immediately, sir.'

Mackintosh asked again: 'But what were his exact words?'

Nancy Campbell frowned: 'Just gibberish, sir. I couldn't really make it out.'

The surgeon Moss stood back from his sleeping patient's bed. 'By rights, this young buck should be dead and buried by now. Heaven only knows what it is that is keeping him alive.'

***

Horse was whistling as he climbed the tenement stairs. On the way home, he had visited Mrs Ratchett and secured some very good prices for the items retrieved from Billy Brown. The old teeth, mused Horse, were icing on the cake.

And as he passed the first landing, he heard the voice of the landlady, Mrs Thomson: 'Mista Hort... Mista Hort...'

Mrs Thomson – or as the street knew her 'The Widow Thomson' was never one to pass up the opportunity of telling whomsoever she met that she was sure that she was afflicted by some certainly fatal disease. This terminal condition, however, did not appear to impede, in any way, her ability to harangue her tenants regarding any rent owed or about to come due.

Horse was not sure if he had ever seen the widow without a large handkerchief at her nose, as she battled through her latest complaint.

'Mista Hort – ah thought that was you whistling as ye came up the stair...'

'Yes, Mrs Thomson, despite your struggles with serious illness, your powers of detection are undiminished.'

'The rent.'

'What about it?'

'It's due the morn's morn...' Horse knew from dealing with the The Widow Thomson that this meant the following morning.

The old lady's eyes narrowed behind the handkerchief over her nose: 'Ah mean, ah mean, last month I had to ask ye fower times, fower times...' The widow held up four fingers.

Horse held up his hand, as if he were signalling a carriage to stop: 'And that is why, Mrs Thomson, today it is my intention to pay you in advance...'

The widow eyed Horse with suspicion, but softened her tirade somewhat: 'Ye doh me, Mista Hort, ye doh me, ah was never wan tae moan, but I've no' been well, and last month...'

Horse interrupted the inventory of ailments by producing a thick wad of pound notes from his coat pocket. This appeared to quiet the landlady, whose eyes widened. Horse licked his right thumb and started to peel off the notes from the bundle: 'Yes, Mrs Thomson, and because you 'ave not 'ad your troubles to seek in recent months, I am instructed by Mr Edward Kane to pay you three months' rent in advance.'

This was, of course, complete fabrication on Horse's part, since the last discussion between Kane and his man relating to finances had revolved around whether or not there was enough money for milk.

Horse proffered the money, which the Widow Thomson took and counted out carefully. She smiled and placed the money into her shawl. 'That'll be the money from the killer, then.'

Horse frowned: 'I beg yer pardon?'

'The man that throttled that wee lassie at the Irving hoose. Ah seen it in a' in the papers. Everybody kens he's guilty. And Mr Kane is just trying to get him off wi' it.'

***

Kane awoke to the smell of cooking and realised that he was lying on his bed still fully clothed. He sat up. His head felt as if it was stuffed with cotton wool. His joints were stiff. He heard the sound of whistling and he smiled. Mr Horse's whistle was a melodious sort of trill, and often accompanied cooking.

Kane opened the bedroom door slowly. Horse looked over: 'Ah – Mr K, you're awake. I thought I'd leave you 'til you swam to the surface, sir. I'll get you a nice bowl of hot water and you can freshen up before dinner.'

Kane peered into the frying pan: 'Is that steak, Mr Horse?'

Horse beamed: 'Steak and onions, Mr K – and some nice new potatoes. In the pot there. I just finished mine. I got some butter to spread on them, an' all.'

Kane became conscious that his mouth was watering now and remembered that he had not eaten that day. Still: 'Mr Horse, I'm afraid that the purchase of steak is an extravagance far beyond our means...'

Horse interrupted him: 'Billy Brown, sir. One of them blokes what nicked your money. Me and him – we had a little chat today, we did. And he handed over his share of what was stolen from you.'

Kane was incredulous: 'He simply handed over the money?'

'Well...' Horse shuffled his feet a little '... he would have handed it over if he hadn't been unconscious, but...'

Kane raised both hands: 'No, no, Mr Horse. I have heard enough. If you are satisfied that you have recovered what was stolen from me, then we shall say no more on the subject...'

There was silence between them for a moment, as Horse stuck a fork in the sizzling steak. The blood ran from it, and he turned it over.

'Oh, and I meant to say, Mr K, that I met the Widow Thomson on the stair and she was asking about the rent...'

Kane covered his face with both hands.

'... and so I paid her three months in advance. I trust that was acceptable, sir?'

Kane released his face from his hands. 'Of course. Well done, Mr Horse. Very well done.'

'Right, then, sir – basin of water here. You get yourself sorted and we'll get this dinner down you, shall we?'

And what a dinner it was. The finest rump steak cooked to a turn, and beautiful, sweet new potatoes. To cap it off, afterwards, Horse poured Kane a small glass of spirits and that dram was – beyond question – the finest whisky that Kane had ever experienced.

Kane and Horse sat down at the table together and Kane related all that had transpired in the afternoon.

Horse sat back in his chair: 'You done well, sir, considering.'

'Considering what?'

'Considering Macnair is guilty as sin.'

'Do you really believe that, Horse?'

'Well, Mr K – who else is in the chair?'

Kane frowned: 'The chair?'

'What was it that other bloke said?'

'Norval Norris...'

'That was him. He said something like, 'If you don't get Macnair's arse out of that chair, then he's done for'.'

'I'm not convinced that those were the actual words used, Mr Horse, but the meaning is plain. If it wasn't Patrick Macnair, then who was it? At whom may we point that accusing finger and shift the focus of suspicion?'

Kane drummed his fingers on the table for a moment. Horse broke the silence.

'What about the butler done it?'

Kane nodded: 'Yes. Mr Hand...'

'Remember, Mrs Ratchett seen him with the dead girl about two weeks before the girl got done in – and they was together and trying to sell the family silver – and we know now what that money was for.'

Kane took a sip from his glass: 'All excellent points, Horse. I shall devise a line of questioning on that point...'

Horse shook his head: 'Begging your pardon, sir. Don't see much questions there. Just say to the butler: 'You filthy old rascal, you put a bun in that young girl's oven, and you throttled her to keep her mouth shut' The jury will understand that, sir.'

Kane laughed: 'That they would, Mr Horse, that, they would!'

Kane looked at the clock on the mantelpiece: 'I thank you, Mr Horse, for an excellent dinner. And now, I shall retire to bed. Early rise, tomorrow, Horse, early rise.'

Each headed for their own sleeping spaces, but before Kane went through the door to his bedroom, he turned back and called to Horse: 'Mr Horse, I meant to ask. What was in the sleeping potion that worked so well last night. I'm bound to say, it snuffed me out like a candle.'

Kane heard Horse's voice from the cubbyhole: 'Oh, that, sir? That would have been the laudanum...'

***

Amazing the effect of a good night's sleep and a hearty breakfast. The next morning there had been the unusual sight of toast and eggs *and* bacon on the plate. And all accompanied by a cup of tea so strong that it threatened to arm wrestle anyone who dared to lift the cup.

Edward Kane and Mr Horse made their way along Edinburgh's Royal Mile towards the courts. It was well before eight in the morning, but the crowds were already forming to gain entry to that notorious murder trial.

Kane and his man passed the King Charles statue. Again, a small crowd had formed around the base and the young artist, Simon Culp, was doing roaring trade selling his latest etching. Horse grinned at Kane: 'I'll just do the honours, sir.'

Horse pushed his way through the crowd. Kane could see him reach Culp and speak to the young man. Horse pointed towards Kane, and Culp looked over and gave a cheery wave in his direction. Kane returned with a little nod, not entirely free of embarrassment.

Horse pushed his way back to Kane, holding a rolled-up paper in his hand. 'My, Mr Kane, you are the talk of the town!' He unfurled the paper and they examined the illustration.

Again, very good likenesses of Kane and the prosecutor, Jon Hunter. But the scenario was different. This time, it showed the judge – Lord Blake – angrily waving a stick at Hunter, who was wearing a dunce's cap. In the centre of the picture was a sleeping judge (a fair representation of the old Lord Flood), his mouth open and distorted with drool falling onto his chin. The saliva was falling onto a piece of paper and forming words: *obviously guilty*. In the centre of the page, stood Kane carrying an enormous ear-horn, obviously straining to hear what was going on. And a banner ran above the illustration declaring: *Avoiding the DEAF Sentence*.

Horse nodded: 'Well, Mr K – you can't say that it don't look like you, sir.'

Kane sighed: 'Let's get in, shall we?'

They made their way to the door of the court. The same police officers were on guard, but this time, as Kane and Horse sought entry, the officers stood to attention and barked: 'Sir!' as they passed.

Horse turned to Kane: 'Ah, look at that, sir. Yesterday, you was nobody. Today, you're the Advocate what defends the notorious murderer.' He pointed to the police officers: 'And these boys will get home tonight and tell the wife and children that they was talking to you. That makes them famous an' all.'

They went into Parliament Hall and pushed through the crowds waiting to enter the courtroom.

Kane and Horse visited Kane's box where, as promised, his friend Collins had left the notes and summaries of the evidence from the previous day. It was a slim volume.

'My Horse, I will let you take my things to court. I'll have a look at these papers and get dressed...'

Horse frowned: 'Ain't you forgetting something, Mr K?'

Kane frowned.

'The Dean, Mr K. He wanted a word this morning, you said.'

Of course. Florrie had fended off the Dean yesterday, but there was no escaping him today. Kane sighed: 'Of course, Horse, of course. Very well. I shall see you in the courtroom then...'

Kane walked through the Advocates Library to the Dean's Room. He knocked on the Dean's door. No answer. Knocked again. Nothing.

'May I assist you, sir?'

Manville.

'Oh, Manville.' Kane pointed to the Dean's door. 'The Dean of Faculty expressed the wish to see me this morning.'

'That will not be possible today, sir. The Dean has been called away on business.'

'But Manville, the request was made only last night...'

For no reason, a thought flashed into Kane's mind. This had something to do with the trial. Something to do with Irving.

'Of course,' Kane bluffed now, 'the business to do with Sir Charles Irving...'

To the casual onlooker, Manville might have appeared unperturbed, but Kane was certain that he detected a ripple of discomfort.

'I am not privy to the reason, Mr Kane.'

An obvious lie. Manville was the kind of man who was privy to the answer to the Riddle of the Sphinx. Kane pressed on: 'I mean to say, Manville, that the pressing nature of the Dean's attendance will be related to the failing health of Sir Charles...'

Manville cut in: 'You will forgive me for interrupting your speculation, Mr Kane, but I am merely here to instruct you that the Dean will not be available today. Now, I further understand that our Mr Collins has been asking for you this morning. He is at present in the Law Room.'

Manville took Kane's arm in a manner that was simultaneously forceful and polite: 'Let me escort you there, sir.'

★★★

It was just a momentary event, but Kane's meeting with Jon Hunter that morning could hardly be described as cordial. Not so much a meeting, in fact, as an encounter that lasted mere seconds, but was somewhat sour in nature.

As Kane was entering the Gown Room to prepare dressing for court, Hunter and his juniors were leaving. They met at the door.

Kane smiled: 'Good morning.'

Hunter, realising it was Kane's voice, looked away, gave a small nod and moved on quickly, his prosecution juniors scurrying behind. It struck Kane as more than a simple snub. There was something wounded and furtive about Jon Hunter this morning.

Of course. Kane recalled the latest caricatures in the illustrations being sold outside the front doors. Kane had been portrayed as hard of hearing, but Jon Hunter had been drawn as an incompetent dunce, being told off by the judge. Not the kind of critique that Hunter would have wished in his first outing as a prosecutor.

★★★

Again, the courtroom was, as Horse would later describe it, 'full to the gun-holes'.

The good citizens of Edinburgh of every age and class were represented in those straining for a good view of the event. When Kane entered the courtroom, there was a sudden intensity in the buzzing conversation, as people pointed and whispered to their neighbours.

The prosecution team, Jon Hunter in the centre, were huddled and in deep conversation. Hunter was shaking his head and pointing at something in his papers, his acolytes scribbling as he spoke.

Kane looked down at his own papers. These had now been arranged in rows neatly and in order by Collins, who was already seated at the table. Kane smiled; he motioned to the prosecution team: 'Have they indicated which witnesses are to be called today?'

Collins leaned forward, so as not to be heard: 'I spoke to one of Hunter's juniors this morning. Not a happy crew. Apparently, after the trial yesterday, the Lord Advocate himself took Hunter into a room and tore several strips off him. Accused him of 'dawdling' and so forth. The repeated refrains as I understand it, were 'Just get on with it' and 'You are losing the jury'.'

It struck Kane that that the only way that the prosecution could 'lose' this jury now would be to place a blindfold on them individually and drop them – without the benefit of a map – into the middle of the continent of Africa.

Kane nodded: 'And is there any indication of the identity of their witnesses today?'

'I'm told that they have the housekeeper, Mrs Trent, then the butler – a Mr Hand.'

'Mr Hand? I have not seen anything in the way of a statement by Mr Hand...'

'Nor have I... There is nothing in the papers here.'

A new voice interjected. It was Mr Whittle, who, somewhat out of breath, was just joining the table: 'I do apologise for my tardiness, gentlemen – those crowds outside...'

Kane looked up: 'Mr Whittle, they are calling the butler, Hand, as a witness – did you know this?'

'It would appear to make sense, sir. After all, he is the house butler.'

Kane's tone became firmer: 'Mr Whittle. If the butler is to give evidence, then he would have provided a statement, perhaps?'

Whittle thought for a moment, then shook his head: 'I have never seen any statement, sir. As I understand it, preliminary enquiries revealed that Mr Hand had nothing to contribute. He appears to have been asleep at the relevant time. Thus, no statement was taken.'

There was silence for a moment, then Collins spoke: 'If Hand has nothing to contribute, then we have nothing to fear. In any event,' Collins continued, 'I was told that Hand will not be arriving until later. In the meantime, they have the Police Surgeon on stand-by and the housekeeper first, I think.'

Collins handed Kane the statement of Mrs Trent, the housekeeper. Kane had read over each statement so many times that he was sure that he could recite them now while asleep.

On the night in question, Mrs Trent, the housekeeper, had awoken to an argument between Macnair and the parlour maid at the top of the back stairs. She then heard a scream and a thud. The housekeeper ran to the bottom of the back stairs to see what the commotion was about. She found Patrick Macnair over the dead girl's body. She asked Macnair what had happened. He shook his head, said nothing, got up and ran away.

'Court rise!'

***

Mrs Trent was a very good witness for the prosecution. She stood erect in the witness box and gave her evidence clearly and without prompting from the prosecutor. Hair pulled tightly back into a bun, she was a thin, severe woman in her mid-sixties, with a stern, forbidding aspect. Kane could imagine her barking orders at the parlour maids or scolding the cook on account of the inadequate warmth of the Scotch Broth.

She proceeded to give evidence, repeating her statement, more or less word-for-word. Jon Hunter smiled: 'I have no more questions for you, madam. Thank you.' And he sat down.

Lord Blake turned to Kane: 'Mr Kane?'

Kane rose from his chair and walked across the courtroom floor to face the witness. Mrs Trent stood tall and imperious, causing Kane to feel as if he were about to climb a great mountain.

'Good morning, Mrs Trent.'

'Good morning, Mr Kane.'

Kane pretended to leaf through his papers. He looked above for inspiration.

Lord Blake interrupted Kane's thoughts: 'Mr Kane – may we assume that you have a question for this witness? A question other than an affirmation that the 'morning' is 'good'?'

Kane snapped out of his reverie, 'Thank you, my lord.' He turned to the housekeeper in the witness box: 'Now, Mrs Trent – something that my Learned Friend, the Advocate Depute did not ask you about – where was the butler of the house, Mr Hand, at the beginning of all of this commotion?'

The housekeeper looked stunned: 'I beg your pardon, sir?'

Kane repeated the question. He was conscious now that an entirely different kind of hush had fallen over the courtroom. For the first time, Mrs Trent was hesitant in her answer: 'He was in bed, sir.'

'And where were you?'

'I was also in bed.'

Somehow, and unexpectedly, the event had taken a salacious turn. Kane turned to look at the men in the jury. They were sitting forward in their seats now, and one or two of them were smirking.

'Then how do you know that Mr Hand was in bed?'

'Sir, I don't know what you are suggesting.'

'I have suggested nothing, Mrs Trent. What are you suggesting?'

Mrs Trent blushed and looked down. Kane pressed on: 'You heard a commotion and you went to the foot of the stairs.'

'Yes, sir.' The housekeeper breathed a sigh of relief to be back on script.

'And Mr Hand also attended there.'

'Yes. But not until later.'

'How much later?'

'Two or three minutes perhaps.'

'So Mr Hand was never far from the scene?'

The witness paused for a moment, then: 'Mr Hand has rooms at the top of the house.'

Kane repeated: 'And so he was never far from the scene.'

Pause, then: 'Yes. But it was not his voice that I heard.'

'In the argument?'

'Yes.'

'How many times have you spoken to the accused,' Kane pointed to the man in the dock, 'Patrick Macnair?'

'Never, sir.'

'So you don't know his voice, do you?'

Mrs Trent was silent for a moment, then: 'That is correct, sir.'

'Then, you cannot say that it was Macnair's voice you heard during the argument with the dead girl, can you?'

No response.

'Can you, Mrs Trent?'

A pause, then: 'No, sir.'

Point scored. Kane looked down at Collins. Collins raised his eyebrows, nodded, smiled and continued writing.

'The argument, Mrs Trent, what did the argument concern?'

'I don't know, sir. It was all very… very muffled'.

'And you were in bed?'

'Yes…'

'And it was the argument that woke you up.'

'Yes.'

'So, what were the parties saying to each other?'

'I don't know, sir.'

'Are you telling us that you could not make out a single word that was said?'

'That is correct, sir.'

'Then, Mrs Trent, how do you know it was an argument?'

She considered this for a time.

'The voices were angry, sir. The girl's voice was high and then very low, and the man's was very, very angry...'

'And that angry man's voice could have belonged to any man in the house – because at that point, you could not see its owner. Am I correct?'

The witness thought for a moment. Then she nodded and gave a gentle shrug: 'That must be true, sir.'

Kane pressed on: 'For example, it could have been Sir Charles Irving at the top of those stairs...'

The housekeeper snapped back: 'Oh, it was not Sir Charles...'

'How do you know that?'

'He was in bed...'

'And how do you know that?'

Mrs Trent looked as if she was drowning now. She struggled to find a response. Kane continued: 'You were in bed too – were you not?'

At that suggestion, Kane felt sure that he heard sharp intakes of breath from several of the ladies in the in the public gallery.

'Mrs Trent, the question is a simple one: if you were in your bed, then how can you be sure that Sir Charles Irving was in his?'

No answer. Kane began to sense a broken quality about this witness now: 'I don't know, sir. I assumed he was in bed at that time. He has been a bit unwell of late.'

Kane leapt on this: 'Unwell – and with a temper shortened by illness, I venture...'

Mrs Trent said nothing, but nodded.

At that point, the judge, Lord Blake, who had been noting the exchange and writing rapidly, looked up from his papers and peered at Kane: 'I'm sorry, Mr Kane, did the witness give an answer? I did not hear one.'

Kane looked up from his papers: 'She did, my lord and she acceded to the proposition that Sir Charles Irving has had, of late, something of a short temper, and that the angry man's voice she heard could have been his...'

At this point, Jon Hunter leapt up: 'I am sorry to interrupt my Learned Friend in what appears to be a premature speech to the jury, my lord, but this witness has accepted no such thing! Sir Charles's indisposal apart, she has never accepted that the voice that she heard could have been his...'

Lord Blake examined his own notes, then turned to Kane: 'The Advocate Depute appears to be correct Mr Kane. There has been no explicit concession...'

Kane came in quickly: 'Then I will ask her, my lord.'

Lord Blake nodded and resumed writing. Kane turned to the broken housekeeper: 'Mrs Trent, you were awoken from your slumber by the voices of people arguing. The sound was muffled. You could not distinguish a single word of what was being said. You formed the view that it was an argument by the tenor of the voices heard. It was impossible to identify the voice of the man. Am I correct so far?'

'Yes, sir.'

'The male voice could have belonged to any of the men in the house at that time. Correct?'

'Yes, sir.'

'And present in the house at that time, as far as you were aware, were Sir Charles Irving and the butler, Mr Hand. Yes?'

'Yes.'

'The voice could have belonged to Sir Charles or Mr Hand.'

Mrs Trent thought carefully for a moment, then she bowed her head in defeat: 'Yes.'

Kane looked up at Lord Blake: 'I trust that that purifies my Learned Friend's concerns, my lord. May I continue?'

The judge did not look up, but nodded and kept writing.

'Now, Mrs Trent, turning to Mr Hand: when he arrived on the scene, what was he wearing?'

The lady seemed aghast: 'What was he wearing?'

'That was my question, madam.'

Mrs Trent stood frowning for a moment.

'I can't really recall, sir. I think that he was just dressed normally.'

'By 'dressed normally', you would mean wearing a collar and tie? Waistcoat, morning coat and so forth?'

'Of course, yes.'

'And do you recall this, Mrs Trent, or are you simply assuming again?'

The housekeeper recovered her composure, resolved and responded tartly: 'Now that you mention it, sir, I remember it well – he was dressed in a normal fashion, collar and tie and the rest. No assumption this time, I'm afraid.'

Kane said nothing for a moment, then: 'No nightcap or bedsocks, then?'

The witness shook her head and had a disgusted look on her face: 'Mr Kane, I have no idea what you mean...'

'Mr Hand was not dressed in bedroom attire, was he?'

'No.'

'And he attended, more or less immediately, did he not?'

'Yes.'

'And you saw for yourself that he was fully dressed in his day-wear.'

'Yes.'

'Then why on earth, madam, would you tell the police that Mr Hand was in bed at the time? Did you assume he was sleeping fully-clothed?'

Laughter from the auditorium.

The housekeeper's face turned a bright shade of crimson. After what seemed like a long time: 'I don't know, sir.'

'Well, he could not have roused himself from his slumber and dressed himself entirely properly in one hundred and twenty seconds, could he?'

'I don't follow you, sir...'

'You said he attended after a couple of minutes...'

She began to stutter: 'Perhaps it was longer. I don't know. Two or three minutes...'

'Two or three minutes? To get out of bed? Get fully dressed? Find his collar? Apply his collar studs? Find his cufflinks? Tie his tie? Two or three minutes?'

Kane turned around and looked at the gentlemen of the jury. Some were nodding now.

'I don't know, sir.'

'But there would have been enough time for Mr Hand to have a dispute with the girl, run upstairs to his quarters and return shortly afterwards presenting as if nothing had happened?'

'I did not hear anyone run upstairs, sir.'

'But you wouldn't, Mrs Trent, would you? Because Sir Charles has laid thick carpeting on those back stairs, hasn't he? I saw it myself recently...'

Again, Jon Hunter leapt to his feet: 'Don't answer that question.' He turned to the judges: 'My lords, I have not so far objected to my Learned Friend's irrelevant and entirely unfounded line of questioning. I had thought better of him than to drag the names of other, I dare say, better men into the mire of suspicion here. That is concerning enough. However, he now appears to be giving evidence himself.'

On each side of Lord Blake, Lords Flood and Piper nodded. Blake addressed Kane: 'Mr Kane?'

'My lords, the questioning merely seeks to set out the whereabouts of other parties in the household...'

Lord Blake interjected: 'I have no difficulty with that, Mr Kane, despite the Advocate Depute's comments. The substantive concern would appear to be that you, yourself, are now giving evidence relating to the nature and quality of a piece of carpeting...'

Kane nodded: 'I apologise, my lords. I will take the evidence from the witness...'

'Thank you, Mr Kane. The objection is repelled.'

Kane turned to Mrs Trent and resumed the questioning: 'The back stair is carpeted, yes?'

'Yes.'

'And where did the carpet come from?'

Lord Blake turned to his colleagues: 'I hoped it's not India, or we'll be here all day…' He glared at Kane. Kane smiled up weakly, then continued: 'Am I right in saying that the same carpet formerly covered the staircase of the main house?'

'Yes.'

'And it was still thick and luxurious?'

The lady nodded. Her face was no longer red, but beginning to turn a shade of green.

Kane thought he heard the judges chortling. He looked up. The judges were staring down at him. No-one was writing.

'So – coming back to my original point, someone could have run up and down those back stairs and you would not hear them.'

She looked ill: 'That must be correct, sir.'

'Thank you.'

Now, thought Kane, it was time to put that butler, firmly 'in the chair'. Kane looked down at his papers and said casually: 'Madam, the butler, Mr Hand, he has something of a reputation with the young ladies, hasn't he?'

Pause, and then a shriek from the ladies in the gallery; a sudden buzz of the men's voices in the courtroom; yet no answer from the witness. Kane continued to stare down at his papers, then – with a new hardness in his voice, he pressed his point: 'Do I have to repeat my question, Mrs Trent?'

Kane looked up. The housekeeper had vanished from the witness stand. Kane looked around quickly. Lord Blake was glowering down at him from the bench: 'Mr Kane, sir, you may perhaps repeat your question when the lady in question recovers…'

Kane looked again at the witness box. No sign of Mrs Trent, but a leg peeping out at the bottom of the box. Mrs Trent had fainted.

***

Edward Kane and Jonathan Hunter were standing in the room of Robert Lennox, Dean of the Faculty of Advocates, but they might as well have been standing tied to a tree and wearing metal boots in a lightning storm, waiting for the flash that would incinerate them both.

Lennox held his head on his hands: 'In all my years in this building, I have never – I say never – witnessed such a degrading circus as the events in that courtroom today.'

He turned to Jon Hunter: 'Hunter! If you accepted the role – the responsibility, sir – of being one of the Lord Advocate's Deputes, then would it not have been wise, sir,' he was almost shouting now, '... to learn the basic rules of criminal procedure? Instead, the Lord Ordinary requires to school you like an infant, and the public are treated to the spectacle of you wearing a dunce's cap!'

He turned to Kane: 'And you! You, sir. I entrust you with an important matter because I, myself, have required to refuse instruction. And the result? A common and vulgar exhibition of theatricality. That poor witness. Subjected to such vile and degrading... I should have listened to your Devilmaster. You clearly cannot be trusted...'

My Devilmaster? The man who trained me as an Advocate? Why?

'...and so I will conduct these proceedings from here on in. Return the papers to your agents, Kane. I want you nowhere near this case, sir. You are dismissed.'

Kane stood still for a moment taking in what had just been said.

Lennox leaned forward and barked: 'Did you hear what I said, sir? You are dismissed. Now, get out of my sight.'

***

'Chin up, Mr K, chin up – you done well, sir.'

Kane sat back in his chair, nursing a glass of whisky: 'If I have done so well, Mr Horse, then why am I suddenly unemployed?'

'Nothing to do with you, sir. It was all the hidden things that was against you, wasn't it?'

Horse attempted to pour more whisky, but Kane put his hand over the glass: 'I am trying to keep a clear head, Horse...'

'What for, Mr K? You ain't in court any more, are you?'

Kane nodded. And sipped.

Their conversation was interrupted by a knock on the door.

'Have you ever noticed, Mr Horse, that every time there is a knock on this door, it is invariably bad news.'

Another knock.

'Perhaps if we do not answer, then the bad news will be taken to an altogether different door instead...'

More knocking, this time more intense.

'Or maybe, Mr K, you're just putting off today what will come and bite you tomorrow, sir.'

Kane nodded. Horse went to answer to door. A few seconds later, Horse re-emerged with Mackintosh of the Detective.

Mackintosh took off his hat. 'Sorry to disturb you sir, but there's been some developments with young Willie Cullen.'

Kane raised his hand to interrupt: 'Mackintosh, I am grateful to you for taking the trouble to come to see me, but I fear that the matter is academic to me now. I have been dismissed as Counsel for Patrick Macnair.'

Mackintosh was taken aback: 'I am surprised to hear that, Mr Kane. My own intelligence was that you were making significant inroads into the Crown case.'

'In any event, thank you for coming, Mackintosh.'

'Then before I leave, I should tell you that the matter is truly academic now, not just to you, sir. The boy, Willie Cullen, died in his sleep this evening.'

Kane, Horse and Mackintosh were silent now. And then there was another knock at the door.

They did nothing. More knocking. Mackintosh motioned towards the door: 'Sorry, sir, but shouldn't you answer it?'

Kane remained seated in his chair: 'I fear, Mackintosh, that I lack the strength.'

More knocking. Horse spoke up: 'Still, Mr K, it's a long road that has no turning in it, sir. Shall I just get it?'

Kane nodded. Horse went to answer the door.

Kane heard some conversation at the front door, then Horse re-emerged – followed by the Faculty Servant, Manville.

Kane rose from his chair and greeted Manville, not entirely without irony: 'Manville. What a pleasant surprise. And what brings you to my humble abode, sir? More instructions from the Dean of Faculty, perhaps?'

Horse made a mental note not to serve strong liquor to his master so early in the evening.

'The Dean of Faculty wants to see you, sir.'

'I find that surprising, Manville, since it was that same Dean who – not three hours since – told me to get out of his sight.'

Manville shifted on his feet and looked around at the others: 'I would be grateful, Mr Kane, if you did not discuss private Faculty matters in front of others. Now, the Dean wishes to see you, and to see you now, sir. I have told him that I would wait and accompany you back. I have a carriage downstairs, sir.'

Kane downed the remainder of the contents of his glass: 'And if I am otherwise engaged at the moment, Manville?'

'Then that would be a source of great disappointment, Mr Kane. Not only to the Dean of Faculty, but additionally, to Lord Blake, who is also waiting in the room for you, sir.'

★★★

'Come in, Edward, come in.' The voice was a friendly one that Kane recognised.

He looked up and saw the smiling face of Lord Blake, beckoning him in. The Dean sat glowering at his desk, like a ruddy, malevolent toad. And in the corner, sat The Mole, Mr Whittle. Whittle gave a small nod of acknowledgement; Kane nodded back.

'Sir down, young fellow – over here.' Blake pulled over a chair and motioned for Kane to sit.

Kane sat, utterly baffled at this impromptu conference.

'Now, Rab here,' Blake indicated the Dean, 'has told me all about your predicament, and I'm sure that we can – as gentlemen – overcome this impasse.'

Kane had no idea what the old judge was talking about, and his head was not entirely clear of the generous dram of whisky that Horse had recently served up. He resolved to stay quiet.

Blake continued: 'As we all appreciate, the taking of instructions can be a delicate matter, especially when a life is in the balance...'

'Lord Blake...'

The old judge smiled and interrupted, 'Call me John, young fellow. We're all Members of Faculty, after all.'

'Lord... John... I apologise if my somewhat heavy-handed attempt at advocacy has caused any difficulties here, sir, but you will appreciate that I was only trying to do my best...'

The old judge frowned, looked quizzical and began to stroke his chin. There was something unspoken in the room. Blake looked at Lennox, as if for some kind of answer, but the Dean remained silent and stared resolutely out of the window. Whittle raised his hand, like a timid schoolboy venturing an uncertain answer. Lord Blake nodded to him to proceed.

The Mole spoke: 'He doesn't know, sir.'

Blake frowned. The Mole repeated: 'He doesn't know. Mr Kane has not been informed of the recent... developments.'

Silence for a moment, then Blake laughed out loud. The Dean of Faculty remained silent and stony. The old judge nodded to Whittle: 'Of course, Mr Whittle. I will let you pick up the narrative here since you were present during the events in question.' Blake folded his arms, placed his chin on his chest and sat back in his chair.

The Mole turned towards Kane: 'Well, sir. After the trial today, I was informed by the Dean of Faculty that you were... you had been... you were no longer with the case. Patrick Macnair was still in the court building and had yet to be taken back to the Calton, so I arranged that we would consult with him in the cell area below. And so, we went down to tell him that – begging your pardon sir – the young Advocate that had been causing the disturbance had been dismissed and that the Dean of Faculty himself – one of the foremost pleaders in the country – would now take over his case. Personally.'

Whittle paused his account at this point, his lips still moving nervously, almost as if to rehearse the words to come. He ventured a timid look at Lennox, who was still looking out of the window.

Kane raised his eyebrows: 'And then?'

Whittle looked at the ground: 'Suffice to say that Mr Macnair indicated an alternative preference – an Advocate other than the Dean.'

No wonder the Dean looked so affronted now. Kane ran through the alternatives in his head. He thought that he would throw the Dean a bone of reconciliation at this point: 'Well, I am surprised to hear that, Mr Whittle, since the Dean is – unquestionably – the pre-eminent Advocate of our times. Who, then, was ultimately instructed?'

Whittle looked up from the floor. His face had an expression of horror: 'I hesitate to say, sir.'

Lord Blake, who had been listening to the tale with a smile on his face, re-joined the conversation: 'As I understand it, Edward, when Macnair was told the glad tidings, he threw his cup against the wall and cried: 'Damn the Dean – get me Kane!'

The old judge savoured the words now: 'Damn the Dean – get me Kane'.

★★★

Was it day three of the trial already? The crowds were even larger at the King Charles statue today. Still, there was a lightness of heart this fine morning as Kane and Horse pushed through the crowds.

The din of the courtroom lulled when he entered. Collins rose to greet him: 'Good morning, my friend. Glad to see that you are still aboard. Now, let's see if the housekeeper can remain upright this morning, shall we?'

Kane looked across the table. Jon Hunter sat in silence, his juniors around him. He was studying what looked like a letter.

'Court rise!' The Macer; the three judges; the bows; the case was called; Macnair put in the dock.

Lord Blake set down his pen and addressed Hunter: 'Advocate Depute?'

The prosecutor rose, the letter in his hand: 'My lords, I regret to say that while it was the intention of the Crown to continue with the evidence of the housekeeper, Mrs Trent, it would appear that the lady has been deemed unfit to continue.'

He handed the letter to the Clerk of Court, who handed it to Lord Blake. Blake looked down at the defence side of the table: 'Have you seen this, Mr Kane?'

Kane stood up: 'I have not, my lords.'

Blake studied the letter: 'It is a communication from the lady's physician opining that the lady is in no fit state to continue. This declaration is made, explicitly, on his soul and conscience. What would you have me do?'

Kane thought for a moment, then looked down at the table. Collins had scribbled a note and had placed it in Kane's view. The note said: 'Not our witness; she can be excused now.'

Kane looked up: 'My lords, I am in the hands of the court. The witness is unwell. In any event, the lady is a Crown witness...'

Blake looked down at Hunter: 'Advocate Depute, will you have any re-examination for this witness?'

For the first time in the proceedings, Kane thought that he saw Jon Hunter lost for words, then: 'No, my lords, at present, I have no further questions for the lady.'

Kane quickly rejoined: 'Then nor do I, my lords.' And sat down.

The judge turned to Hunter: 'Then your next witness, Depute?'

'That would be Dr James Stanton, Police Surgeon, my lords.'

At the defence end of the table, Collins leaned over and whispered to Kane: 'A very good outcome for us, Edward. The last thing that the jury heard was you asking the lady if the butler, Mr Hand, was a ladies' man, and she fainted on the spot. They will not soon forget that.'

Dr James Stanton was not quite what Kane had expected. He had provided a report on the injuries of the dead girl, including the cause of death. But despite the morbid and, at times, gristly nature of his work, Dr Stanton was himself an entirely cheery individual. One could imagine him chatting away to the dead body on the slab while he was examining their open liver for signs of poison. He was questioned about his report concerning the late Martha Cunningham: female; aged late teens; abrasions and contusions on the arms; asphyxiation; neck broken; pregnant, around two months.

Jon Hunter hit upon something that stopped his progress: 'And so, Dr Stanton, what is your final conclusion regarding the cause of death?'

'The ultimate cause of death was asphyxiation, sir.'

Hunter turned to face the men in the jury for maximum impact: 'What you are telling us, Dr Stanton, is that this girl was strangled, then thrown down the stairs...'

There was a pause, while the witness considered this, then the doctor replied 'No.'

Hunter turned round to address the witness: 'I am sorry if you misunderstood my question, sir. It says clearly in your report, this girl was strangled.'

'My report does not say that, sir.'

Hunter flicked through the pages, and stabbed at a certain paragraph: 'Page four sir, 'Conclusion: Death by asphyxiation...' It says it here in black and white.'

'Yes, sir.' Replied the doctor cheerfully.

'And bruising on the neck area...'

'Yes, sir.'

'She was strangled!' insisted Hunter.

'No, sir.'

Hunter slammed the report onto the table. He looked up at the judges: 'My lords, I wonder if the Court could direct this witness to answer the question.'

Lord Blake sighed and shook his head: 'It would appear to me, Advocate Depute, that the difficulty here is not the answers, sir, but the questions...'

Hunter stood still for a moment, struggling to comprehend. Lord Blake took over the examination of the witness:

'Dr Stanton...'

'Yes, sir?'

'You appear to be drawing a distinction between the girl being 'asphyxiated' and the girl being 'strangled' – is that correct?'

'Yes, my lord.'

'Explain the difference, sir.'

'Well, my lord, they are not precisely the same thing. If the girl had been asleep, for example, and I had covered her face with a pillow, then that might asphyxiate her – but not strangle her, if you get my meaning...'

'Why do you say that there was no strangulation in this case?'

'Well, there are none of the usual features of strangulation here. For example, no fingertip or thumb marks around the neck area. No sign of a rope burn or a scarf being used to constrict breathing.'

Lord Blake invited Hunter to continue: 'Yes, Advocate Depute?'

Hunter pressed on: 'But your report notes bruising to the neck, doctor'

'That would relate to the angle of the neck when it was broken. Probably in the fall, sir.'

'Then if she was not strangled, how could she be asphyxiated?'

Dr Stanton smiled as if explaining to a child: 'It's all a bit of a mystery, and it relates to the brain, sir. The thinking is that the brain tells the other parts of the body what to do. That would make sense, when you think about it.' The doctor smiled and continued blithely on: 'Take Mary Queen of Scots, as an example. Once her head was severed from the rest of her, then her body was hardly likely to go for a stroll, was it, sir?'

The doctor's cheerful nature was infectious now. Kane saw some of the jurymen were smiling.

Hunter was growing impatient: 'I fail to see, doctor, how Mary Queen of Scots...'

Dr Stanton, an experienced witness, amicably rebuked the prosecutor: 'If I could finish my point, sir?'

Hunter pursed his lips and nodded.

The witness continued: 'You will forgive, I hope, the crude analogy here. But the point is this: once the line of communication has been broken between the brain and the rest of the body - in my example, the beheaded queen - then the rest of the body, including the vital organs, such as the heart and lungs, they no longer receive instruction from the brain to carry out their functions.'

There was a pause, while Hunter's own brain processed this information. After a few moments of silence, Lord Blake resumed the questioning: 'And how, Dr Stanton, is that example relevant to the death of the girl in this case?'

The doctor smiled and looked up at the judge: 'In this case, my lord, rather like a set of ivory dominoes falling, one injury caused another. In simple terms, the girl fell down the stairs. In the course of the fall, she broke her neck.' The doctor grabbed his own neck: 'And when the neck breaks, this may sever the line of communication between the brain and the vital organs. And without the instruction from the brain, effectively, the poor creature forgot how to breathe. Thus, she was asphyxiated.'

There was silence now, while Hunter tried to work out how to pick up the pieces of broken glass that were formerly his case theory. He gave a smile, without warmth: 'But of course, doctor, you are not in possession of all of the facts in this case.'

'Of course.'

'And if we hear evidence that the girl was thrown down the stairs...'

At this point, Kane suffered a very pronounced punch on the arm. He yelped: 'Ow....'

The judges looked down; Hunter looked over; Dr Stanton peered over his glasses from the witness box. Collins hissed: 'Stand up, Edward!'

Kane jumped up immediately.

Lord Blake, pen poised in his hand, looked down at Kane. 'Are you in pain, Mr Kane?' He pointed to the witness: 'If so, we have a physician at the ready.'

'No, my lords...'

Kane looked down at the desk before him. Collins had scribbled the answer. Kane continued: 'What I meant to say, my lords is that...'Ow.... how can that question be answered if there is no witness to speak to it?'

'I take it that is an objection, sir?'

'My lords, the learned Advocate Depute has put to this witness that we may hear evidence that the girl was thrown down the stairs...'

'Yes?'

'But there is no witness who can speak to this. No one else was there, except the dead girl and the man whose voice was heard. There will be no evidence of anyone being thrown anywhere. The very question creates a false impression in the mind of the jury.'

Kane sat down. Lord Blake addressed Hunter: 'Advocate Depute?'

'My lords, the Crown position is that the Pannel, Macnair, argued with the deceased girl and threw her down the stairs, and in the whole circumstances caused her death...'

The judge interrupted: 'Yes, yes – I think that we have ascertained the Crown position, Mr Hunter. The objection here is that you have indicated to this witness that they may hear evidence that the girl was thrown down the stairs.'

Hunter stood thinking for a moment, then: 'Very well, my lords, I will withdraw the question and take the evidence from this witness.'

The judge nodded and began to write. Hunter turned to the witness again: 'Now, Dr Stanton, you would agree with me, sir, that this girl could – possibly – have been thrown down those stairs.'

'Yes, sir.'

'The injuries are consistent with someone's who has been thrown down the stairs.'

'On the whole, yes.'

'And when she was thr...' Hunter stopped himself. 'It was the... the... tumble down the stairs, that led to a broken neck that led to her asphyxiation and death.'

'That is the most likely conclusion in this case, sir, yes.'

'Thank you, doctor.'

Hunter smiled and sat down. Lord Blake looked down at Kane: 'Mr Kane?' Kane rose and readied himself to question this witness, reminding himself of 'Not Proven' Norval's words: Misdirection is the conjuror's greatest gift...

'Good morning, Doctor Stanton.'

The witness gave an enthusiastic reply: 'Good morning, sir.'

'Now, you'll be aware that Mr Patrick Macnair here,' Kane pointed to the man in the dock, 'was arrested on suspicion of murder in this case.'

The witness replied cheerfully: 'That'll be why he's in the dock, sir.'

Some of the jury members laughed.

'Precisely, Dr Stanton. And he was arrested immediately after the girl's death.'

'Yes, sir.'

'And he has been remanded – for some months now – and kept in the Calton Jail.'

'That is my understanding, sir.'

'And he has been nowhere near Sir Charles Irving's house since the girl's death.'

'If he has been in the Calton, sir, then that must be correct.'

Kane paused. 'And how many people have been killed in Sir Charles' house while Macnair has been in custody?'

Jon Hunter shot to his feet: 'Don't answer that question...'

Lord Blake barked down at the prosecutor: 'Sit down, Advocate Depute!' The judge looked at the witness: 'Please continue, doctor.'

Dr Stanton narrowed his eyes as if counting. 'I think, only the one, sir.'

Of course, Willie Cullen has also died, but that was only yesterday evening. This witness does not know that yet.

'Only the one death, doctor?'

'Yes.'

'Shot in the head by Sir Charles Irving.'

'Yes, sir.'

'But he was not the only person recently shot in the head by Sir Charles, was he?'

'No, sir.'

'In fact, Sir Charles shot another individual there too, who required to be taken to Infirmary Street and have a bullet removed from his brain. Is that not correct, doctor?'

'You'd have to ask the surgeons about that, sir. I generally examine the dead, not the living.'

Kane turned to the jury: 'A dangerous and deadly house – when Patrick Macnair is not there...'

Hunter rose to his feet again: 'My lords...'

Lord Blake interrupted and shouted at Kane: 'Mr Kane, that was not a question, sir. It was a conclusion. Now, either ask a proper question or sit down.'

Kane bowed. Hunter sat down. Kane continued: 'Now, doctor, there were also scratches on the girl's arms, weren't there?'

'Yes, sir.'

'And those scratches could have been caused by long, bony fingernails.'

'No, sir.'

'No?'

'Fingernails are never bony, sir. Begging your pardon, they are made of a very different material altogether, sir, not bone.'

Not quite the best answer, but when Mr Hand came into that witness box later, the first thing the jury would notice would be those long, bony, scratchy fingers.

Kane resumed his cross: 'Now, finally, doctor, is it not fair to say that, at the end of your very thorough examination of the body, that there is absolutely no proof that the girl was thrown down the stairs.'

'That is correct, sir.'

'She might simply have slipped and have fallen.'

Dr Stanton replied cheerfully: 'Sir, for all we know, she might have been doing the dusting...'

Chapter Ten

'Not Proven' Norris puffed on his pipe. Kane and Norris walked along Parliament Hall: 'Good show, my young friend, good show! As I told you: short questions, paint the picture, sit down. A job very well done with that Police Surgeon. You almost had me believing that Macnair is innocent. Who is their next witness?'

'That would be the butler, Mr Hand.'

Norris chuckled: 'Of course. Mr Hand. The mysterious figure who – in the minds of the jury – sleeps fully-clothed, is never far from the scene and likes to scratch young parlour maids with those long, lecherous fingernails.'

They smiled and walked. 'But,' said Norris, 'I fear that our informal tutorial must come to an abrupt close, my friend.'

Kane stopped: 'How so, Norval?'

'I understand that the Dean of Faculty is keen to speak to you.'

'How on earth would you know that?'

Norris chuckled, puffed on his pipe and nodded at a figure following close behind them.

Manville.

★★★

'Come in, Edward, come in.' Rab Lennox rose from the chair behind the table in his room.

The Dean's Room seemed crowded now as Kane entered. Others were sat around the table; it seemed to Kane that he had disturbed a meeting that had already been in progress for some time. And it soon became clear that this would be no ordinary conversation. Sitting across from the Dean was the solicitor, Whittle. And in the other chair arranged around the table sat Kane's adversary, Jon Hunter.

'Sit down.' Kane sat down.

'Now, Edward, you will recall that you came into this case as a favour to me. And despite your many difficulties, I have allowed you to retain instructions here...'

That was not quite Kane's memory of their last conversation, but he said nothing and allowed the Dean to maintain face.

'Yes, Dean of Faculty.'

'Well, Edward, as you understand it, I retain an interest in the case...'

'Yes, sir...'

'So I have had an informal discussion with the Lord Advocate himself, and he has indicated that he is willing to amend the charge. Perhaps better if I let his Depute explain it for himself.' He turned to Jon Hunter: 'Jon?'

Hunter did not look directly at Kane, but addressed his remarks to the table in front of him: 'The Lord Advocate has indicated that I have the power to accept a plea of Guilty to a lesser charge...' Hunter continued: 'And so, in the circumstances, I am empowered to accept a plea of Guilty to Culpable Homicide.'

Kane nodded his head slowly, trying to process precisely what that meant. The Dean read his mind: 'What that means, Edward, is that Macnair pleads guilty, let us say, because there was a 'tiff' between two lovers and the whole event simply got out of hand, then Macnair avoids the noose. What the English call Manslaughter. Now,' Lennox nodded towards Whittle, 'I have directed your agent, Mr Whittle, to attend to Macnair in the cells downstairs to inform him of the news.'

There was a pause, and then Kane spoke: 'And if he refuses to plead guilty?'

The Dean sat back in his chair: 'I have had dealings with Macnair. He is stubborn, but he is not stupid.'

★★★

Kane and Collins sat in the Reading Room, where the taking of coffee was interrupted by one of Manville's Men.

'Begging your pardon, Mr Kane, but there is a young lady in the hall asking to see you.'

Kane's heart sank. Miss Amanda.

But when Kane walked out into Parliament Hall, there was no sign of his former fiancée. Instead, by one of the fireplaces, smiled Florrie Forbes-Knight.

'Florrie!' Kane joined her.

'Edward, I was waiting outside the courtroom, but I overheard that there would be a later start for the next session.'

Kane bowed his head: 'There appear to have been developments, and a certain matter requires to be clarified...'

'And does that matter relate to carpeting... or dusting?' Both friends laughed.

'Oh, Florrie...'

'Edward, you are doing a magnificent job in that courtroom. I have been watching the jurymen closely and I see them coming around – slowly, mind you – coming around to the possibility that Patrick Macnair did not kill that girl. Or not intentionally, at any rate.'

For the first time in some time, Kane felt how good it was to smile and laugh with a friend.

'And, my dearest Florrie, how go the preparations in the Forbes-Knight household for that great 'Epiphany' this week?'

Florrie shook her head and frowned: 'Mr Brookes attends every day. Matters between the singing master and Amanda can be... strained.'

'It is certainly an ambitious enterprise...'

'Father says that it is as ambitious as a blind man playing a game of darts...'

They laughed. Then Florrie became serious: 'Edward, you must know that – wherever the outcome of the Macnair trial – no man could have done a better job than you.'

Good old Florrie. Preparing me for disappointment.

Kane became aware of a figure running across the hall towards them. It was Horse: 'Mr K - you're wanted back in the court, sir.'

★★★

There was something of a lull in the buzzing courtroom as he entered, and the onlookers seemed to sense that something momentous was about to happen. Kane looked toward the dock. Macnair sat, arms folded, an unhappy look on his face. Kane sat down at the table and faced Collins and Whittle.

'Well?'

Whittle was clutching his hat tightly with both hands and stammered as he spoke: 'Well, sir, as directed by the Dean, I put to Mr Macnair that he was now to plead guilty to Culpable Homicide and that would be a means of avoiding... of avoiding...' Whittle began to rub his neck nervously.

'And?'

'He was not... not happy, sir. And he said... he said...' Whittle pursed his lips while he recalled the exact words used: '... he said 'Damn the Dean... damn the noose. Get on with your job and get me Kane.'

Kane pondered this for a moment and then looked at Collins: 'And where does that leave us?'

Collins smiled: 'Once more unto the breach, dear friend...'

And at that point, the Macer cried: 'Court rise!'

★★★

Mr Hand was every bit as cadaverous as Kane remembered. As the witness raised his right hand to swear the oath, Kane thought that he saw some of the men in the jury study the butler's hand.

The butler gave his evidence-in-chief in an aloof manner. 'And on the night in question, Mr Hand, where were you?' asked Hunter.

'In my quarters, sir.'

'At the top of the house.'

'Yes, sir.'

'And what were you doing?'

'I was sleeping, sir.'

'It may be suggested to you that when you attended at the bottom of the stairs, you were, in fact, fully dressed.'

'That would be correct, sir.'

Hunter raised his eyebrows to encourage a fuller answer. The butler continued: 'What you must understand, sir, is that rest and sleep are purely relative terms in relation to the duties of a butler. I know from my experience that the activities of a household will never fully die down until well into the early hours of the morning.'

'And how does that affect you, Mr Hand?'

'I have a practice, sir, that as the evening progresses, I might enjoy some light sleep in the armchair in my quarters. That way, if there is a summons from the bell-pull at, for example, eleven o'clock in the evening, then I can attend, immediately and fully dressed.'

'And why might you be summoned at such an hour?'

'Sir Charles has been known to work into the early hours in his study, sir. As you will be aware, he is a man of property and his affairs can occupy much of his time. He may require tea or other sustenance at that late hour.'

'So, what happened that night?'

'I was sitting in the armchair, sir, I confess dozing somewhat. I was awoken by the sound of two raised voices. At the top of the back staircase.

A male and a female person were in the middle of a loud disagreement. I recognised the voices immediately. The female voice was that of the parlour maid, Martha Cunningham.'

'And the male voice?'

Hand pointed a bony finger: 'That was the voice of the man in the dock there, Patrick Macnair.'

Jon Hunter paused for a moment to let the identification sink in with the men of the jury.

'And how can you be certain that you identified the voices accurately?'

'In the case of the young girl, Martha, she was someone I saw every day. Regarding Mr Macnair, I had heard his voice on a great number of occasions when he visited the house, sir.'

'And had you ever spoken to Macnair directly?'

'On numerous occasions. Mr Macnair was conspicuously at ease with the lower classes, having risen from the lower orders himself. Especially in the case of the younger, perhaps more impressionable, members of the female staff.'

Hunter continued his examination: 'And so, what happened then?'

'Well, sir, I heard Mr Macnair shouting at Martha. I could not quite discern the wording being used, something like 'Not mine, it's not mine...' and she was shouting back at him and...'

At that moment, the witness stopped. He bowed his head and the long, pallid face looked disturbed. Hunter looked up from his papers: 'Are you well, Mr Hand?' The butler said nothing for a moment, then: 'I was... very fond of the girl, sir.'

'Are you fit to continue, Mr Hand?'

The witness collected himself, nodded and replied quietly: 'Yes, sir.'

'And what happened then?'

'The commotion continued and there was more shouting. It seemed to reach a peak, then it stopped. Quite suddenly, sir. What sounded like a struggle followed by a thudding noise. Then, silence. And at that point, I rose from my chair and attended.'

Hunter nodded and continued: 'And as you were coming down, did anyone pass you on the back stairs?'

'No, sir.'

'And what happened then?'

'I reached the bottom of the stairs and I saw...'

'Yes?'

Again, the butler seemed as if he was struggling to speak.

'Excuse me, sir, I was very fond... I reached the bottom of the stair and I saw the...I saw the girl. And the cook, Mrs Bolton was standing there. And I saw Mr Macnair leaving the area.'

'And what was Macnair's demeanour, Mr Hand?'

'Impossible to say, sir, because he was running.'

Hunter turned to face the jury: 'Running from the body of the dead parlour maid.'

'Yes, sir.'

'Thank you, Mr Hand.'

Hunter sat down. Lord Blake motioned towards Kane. 'Mr Kane?'

Kane got up and straight into it: 'Now, Mr Hand, you have quite a reputation with the young ladies, do you not?'

If the courtroom had been quiet at that point, it was doubly silent now.

Hand had not expected this question. He frowned: 'Reputation, sir?'

'With the young ladies, Mr Hand. You are considered something of a – how shall I put it – a 'ladykiller', I think is the common, if unfortunate, term.'

Kane thought that he heard a gasp from those observing. The prosecutor shifted in his seat. He glanced up towards the bench and saw that the judges were sitting back in their chairs, listening intently.

Hand considered the question for a moment, then: 'As I understand it, sir, it is the nature of reputation that it exists in the mouths of others, not your own. You would perhaps better direct that question to others.'

It struck Kane that he was now playing a verbal tennis match and he was not quite sure who had won that last point.

'And Martha Cunningham was a young girl in your charge, was she not?'

'Yes.'

'You could, as the butler, dismiss her from her employment at any time, could you not?'

Hand thought for a moment: 'There would have to be a reason...'

'If she did not... please you, Mr Hand.'

'If her work was, in some way, below acceptable standards, sir.' There was a silence, then he added: 'But the girl's work was always of a very good quality.'

'And in the main, she... she satisfied you.'

'Yes.'

'And you were very fond of her?'

The butler nodded: 'Yes, sir.'

Kane looked down at his papers.

'And I note from the documents in the case that she came into Sir Charles' household from your recommendation.'

Locked in an unspoken battle now, the Advocate and the butler. Kane knew what the questions meant and Hand knew what the questions meant. The fifteen men in the jury knew what the questions meant, and they sat forward in their seats. Who would falter first?

The butler responded: 'She was one of a number of girls who graduated, as it were, from Sir Charles' factories.'

'Graduated?'

'It is human nature, sir, that some individuals are more disposed to work than others. Martha was a hard worker. It has to be accepted that she had somewhat of a lively exterior, but in her own way, she was fastidious about her work.'

'And that attracted her to you... as an employee?'

'Yes, sir. A number of the girls from Sir Charles' factories are identified and assessed as suitable for household service.'

'For household service?'

'As kitchen maids. Scullery maids. Laundry maids and the like, sir. In Martha's case, a parlour maid. I venture that you will find a great number of Sir Charles' girls in many – if not most – of the great houses in Edinburgh.'

'Chosen specially by Sir Charles?'

'Yes, sir.'

'But you chose Martha Cunningham.'

'It was certainly my recommendation, sir. I knew her family somewhat and I'm afraid that they rather importuned me.'

'So, she came through Sir Charles – like many other girls – and then she came through you.'

Kane looked at the men in the jury. They well knew Sir Charles had a wider reputation in the community for 'improving' his young female employees.

'Yes, sir.'

'And you grew to be particularly fond of her.'

'That is fair, sir.'

'And she fell pregnant.'

The witness narrowed his eyes before he replied: 'It would seem so, sir.'

'You would keep her company sometimes, away from Sir Charles' house in Heriot Row, would you not?'

'My duties frequently take me away from the house, sir. Often accompanied by various members of the staff.'

'Some weeks before her death, you and Martha took a stroll together, did you not?'

The witness shifted on his feet: 'It is possible, sir.'

'And you accompanied her to an address in the Old Town, and to the home of a certain lady who acts for a local pawnbroker, did you not?'

A pause, then: 'I don't recall, sir.'

'I find that surprising, Mr Hand. You are telling the gentlemen of the jury that you do not remember that day when you and Martha were seen in the Old Town. Only weeks before her death. And between you, you were carrying a valuable candlestick. Does that assist your memory, sir?'

Hand was clearly uncomfortable now.

'It is possible, sir.'

Kane pressed on: 'A candlestick that the pregnant girl was desperately trying to sell because she required to raise money. To raise money, sir, in order that she be – how can one put this delicately – that she be no longer be in 'the family way'.'

'The candlestick was a gift from Sir Charles...'

'That you were trying to sell to get the girl out of trouble.'

'No.'

'Because, if anyone argued on the stairs on the night in question and shouted, 'It's not mine' that night, then it was more likely to be you, Mr Hand? Because that baby might have been yours?'

'Ridiculous! I resent...'

'Is that not why poor Martha ended up dead at the bottom of those stairs, Mr Hand? Your stairs. The stairs that lie at the bottom of your rooms...'

The butler shook his head violently: 'No, no, no...'

'Because that baby was yours, sir!'

'No – impossible!'

'The girl chosen by you – to be under your thrall, Mr Hand.'

'No.'

Kane turned to face the jury: 'Wandering the streets of Edinburgh, desperate for the money to avoid the disgrace of a child out of wedlock.'

'No.'

'With you, sir, skulking around in the background. Because that baby might have been yours.'

'Impossible.'

'Again – the word 'impossible', Mr Hand – when the whole affair is perfectly possible...'

The witness looked exhausted now: 'No, sir.'

'And, pray, why is it not possible, Mr Hand?'

'Because Martha Cunningham...'

'Yes?'

'Because Martha Cunningham was my daughter.'

★★★

Retching. The sound of retching.

Horse held Kane's shoulders as the young Advocate retched again into the bucket.

'Who would have thought it, eh, Mr K? The butler – being the father of that dead girl. The dirty old blighter. I wonder how many other maids in the town have his long fingers, then. And you was doing so well at the time. You had him by the throat an' all. Until, well, you know...'

Kane vomited again.

Horse studies the interior of the bucket: 'Can't be much left now, sir.'

Kane surfaced: 'How can I have been so wrong, Horse? How could I not have seen it?'

'How was you supposed to, sir? You was doin' a good job putting somebody else into that chair instead of Macnair. Turns out it was the wrong bloke, mind you...'

Kane handed the bucket to Horse. 'Thank you, Horse. I think the worst is over. What time is it?'

Horse pointed to the marble clock on the mantelpiece: 'Just after nine, sir.' He indicated the bucket: 'I'll just take this downstairs, Mr K, and give it a good washing out outside.'

Kane shivered: 'Horse – why are all the windows open?'

'Begging your pardon, Mr K, but with you being ill at both ends, sir, it's no rose garden in here...'

★★★

The mantle clock struck four and Kane lay awake, not feeling quite so wretched.

The obvious answer was that Macnair had killed that girl. The existence of his child would be the end of all of Macnair's aspirations to live amongst and be accepted by his betters.

But if that was the truth, what of it? Kane's responsibility remained to defend Macnair honestly to the extent that Macnair would defend himself. At this hour, neither day nor night, Kane's thoughts ran like colours bleeding into each other. What was it that 'Not Proven' Norris had said? Find a different truth. Was he simply being facetious? Place another in that chair of suspicion. Who was left? Martha Cunningham had been one of Sir Charles Irving's 'graduates'. Was it time to place the old man, that old, sick man into the chair?

★★★

The crowd was noticeably more hostile this morning. Following the surgical – but in many minds, unnecessary – unmasking of the butler, attitudes appeared to have shifted. Kane had also besmirched the character of Sir Charles Irving – a man who, according to his supporters, had helped create prosperity in that great city, a philanthropist who had provided significant employment for the community.

It now seemed as if certain members of the crowd were determined to stand in Kane's way as Kane and Horse walked towards the courts. Some even spat onto the path in front of him.

'Do you think, Mr Horse, that we should enlist the help of a police officer to escort us for the remainder of the journey?'

Horse shook his head: 'They'd just as likely arrest you today, sir. I'll get in front and we'll just push on, Mr K.'

And so they did – and arrived at the (comparative) safety of Parliament House.

Kane was relieved this morning to assume the anonymity of the wig and the gown as he walked towards his box.

Perhaps Macnair would see sense now? Following the events of yesterday, the best outcome possible would be to accept the offer to plead guilty to Culpable Homicide – and at least avoid the noose.

In Kane's box he found a letter, which he tore open and read:

Dear Sir

Please note that the offer of a plea of Culpable Homicide in the case
of her Majesty's Advocate versus Patrick Macnair is withdrawn.
Yours faithfully

Jonathan Hunter, Esq
Advocate Depute

★★★

Mrs Bolton stood, shrivelled and hunched, in the witness stand. The old cook was clutching a well-worn set of rosary beads in both hands, which she seemed to be counting as she was giving her answers.

Hunter was coming to the end of his examination: 'Now, you have told us, madam, that when you attended at the scene, Macnair was already there.'

'That's right, sir.'

'Did you speak to him?'

'Aye, sir.'

'And what was said?'

'I says to him 'What have you done, son? What have you done?'

'And did he reply?'

'No, sir. He just looked panicked. And he ran out the room, sir.'

'Thank you.' Hunter sat down.

Kane rose and faced the witness.

'Good morning, Mrs Bolton.'

'Mornin' sir.'

'Now, I want to ask you something that the learned Advocate Depute did not seek to address, if I may?'

The old cook nodded.

'Now, I should first clarify with you: you gave a number of statements in this case, did you not?'

'Aye, sir.'

'And you gave them soon after the event.'

'Yes.'

'And you were telling the truth when you gave the various statements.'

The witness held up her rosary, as if to prove her credibility: 'As true as God, sir.'

'And your memory of those tragic events at the time you gave the statements would be better than it is now, some months later? Yes?'

'Yes, sir. Of course, sir.'

'Then, perhaps you can help me with the statement that I have.'

The witness nodded. Kane held the statement before him and read aloud: 'You said in your statement: 'I woke up because I could hear them arguing. I knew it was Martha's wee squeaky voice straight away because she had been in Sir Charles' service for some years. It was at the top of the back stair, the argument.' Did you say that?'

'Aye, sir.'

Kane continued: 'I got up and I lit a candle and I put on my gown. All the time, there was more arguing and a rustling and swishing like a struggle.' You said that?'

'Yes.'

'And then there was a kind of gasp. And a thumping noise on the stairs. And I heard Martha say something and I went out to see what was happening. But by the time I got there, she was lying dead. And Patrick Macnair was leaning over the girl's body.'

'That's right, sir.'

'When you say, 'I heard Martha say something' – what did you hear her say?'

'I don't know, sir. I couldnae really make it out.'

'But you did hear her say something?'

'I was half asleep, sir.'

'But you were up and getting dressed at the time.'

'Aye, sir.'

'And you can tell the difference between a woman's voice and a man's voice.'

'Yes, sir.'

'So, what did she say?'

'I'm not sure.'

'What do you think she said?'

John Hunter was quickly on his feet: 'Don't answer that question.' He addressed the judges: 'My lords, learned counsel is now inviting the witness the engage in speculation.'

Kane quickly answered: 'Not speculation, my lords. Clarification. It is the witness' understanding of what she heard that I seek to establish.'

Lord Blake looked around at the other judges. They nodded. Blake spoke to the prosecutor: 'The objection is repelled.' He looked at Kane: 'Please continue.'

'What do you think was said, Mrs Bolton?'

The old cook clutched her rosary beads, looked at the judges and spoke carefully: 'I've been thinking a lot about that night, your worships, and the more I think about it, it just makes me sick tae my stomach. I dinnae remember why I said that about Martha. She didn't say anything after she fell, and that's the God's honest truth here.' Tears began to fall down her face; 'Martha said nothing, and that's the truth.'

Kane continued, exercising more care now: 'I am sorry, madam, if you find this upsetting. I have a mere handful of questions remaining for you. Are you content to continue?'

They witness sniffed and nodded and clutched her beads closer.

'Now, I think – as we all understand – you were very fond of Martha?'

'Aye, sir.'

'She, perhaps, reminded you of your own children?'

'I have... I had three bairns, sir. I lost them all to the cholera. A girl and two boys, I had.' The old cook seemed to fall into reverie now. 'Maria, the first, then my wee Eddie...' she nodded towards the Advocate, 'Then my youngest, Richard. And then, sir, and then...'

She stopped speaking and started to sob again. She produced a handkerchief from her coat and dabbed her eyes. Perhaps time to change the subject for the moment.

'Mrs Bolton, if I could just ask who attended at the scene after you saw Mr Macnair leave.'

'Well, everybody, sir.'

'I mean, who arrived and when?'

'Oh, it was just a real stramash, sir... Mr Macnair walking, backwards, sir, towards the door, and then I saw a light on the stair, and it was Mr Hand coming down with a candle.'

The witness thought for a moment: 'Then there was Mrs Trent, the housekeeper.'

'Yes?'

'Somebody screamed.' She gave a hollow little laugh: 'I think it was probably me, sir.'

'Did Sir Charles attend at the scene?'

The voice of the witness changed now, became harder and was very definite on this point: 'No. He never saw any of it. He was in his bed, sir.'

'But surely, as the master of the house, he would have attended...'

'No' really, sir. He keeps a housekeeper and butler to deal with this kind of thing.'

'To deal with this kind of thing'? What a curious way of putting it. A dead girl at the bottom of the stairs. 'To deal with these this kind of thing'?

The witness continued: 'And then Miss Cordelia came in. I think she had been out at one of her events. I remember she had her new ballgown on.'

'Yes, but with reference to Sir Charles – how do you know that Sir Charles was in bed?'

The witness looked uncomfortable now: 'I dinnae like to speak out of turn, sir, but I think that it's well-known now that the maister has been a bit poorly in recent weeks...'

'Sir Charles' study is directly across from the spot where you heard the argument.'

'Aye, sir.'

Kane looked at his notes from Mrs Trent, the housekeeper: 'And he has been described as being 'short-tempered' of late. Is that fair?'

'Aye. That's fair. Sir Charles has been that bit more... carnaptious...'

Lord Blake interrupted: 'Carnaptious?' He looked at the other judges and they shook their heads, equally as puzzled.

The old cook continued: 'Aye, 'carnaptious' – it's like 'crabbit' – only worse.'

Lord Blake resumed writing and muttered to himself: 'Short-tempered...'

Kane continued: 'And Sir Charles knew the dead girl well.'

'No' really, sir. She was just a parlour maid... one of the household help...'

'More than that, Mrs Bolton. Martha Cunningham was hand-picked by Sir Charles to service him at his home...'

A different kind of silence from the public gallery.

'I didnae ken that, sir...'

'Hand-picked after her service in one of his factories...'

'I heard she came from the factories, right enough.'

'Because Sir Charles could have sent her anywhere. To any of the great houses in Edinburgh.'

'Aye, sir.'

'But he chose to have the girl in his own house – beside him?'

'Must be. But, remember, sir, she was a good wee worker, was Martha. And she was a friendly soul.'

Kane began to focus the point: 'Now the court has heard that, at the time of her death, she was expecting a child.'

'Aye, she was in the family way, sir. It happens to mony a poor lass, sir.'

'And she was a very friendly girl. Especially with Sir Charles...'

The witness thought again, then: 'Very friendly with all men, sir. In fact, I mind the time when I found her and your Mr Macnair playing a game of 'hide and seek' in one of the downstairs cupboards...'

Lord Blake cut in at this point: 'Must have been a jolly large cupboard...'

Everyone in the courtroom laughed. Except Kane.

'Mrs Bolton, that's what the dead girl told you. You did not see that for yourself...'

The old cook laughed: 'Oh, I did sir. I was the one that heard her squealing behind that door, that squeaky wee voice of hers. And I opened it and the twa of them were laughing and giggling like bairns, sir.'

Kane didn't know what to do with this piece of unfavourable evidence, so he turned to the judges: 'My lords, I wonder if the gentlemen of the jury could be directed to disregard the recent answers of this witness...'

Lord Blake sat back in his chair and shook his head: 'Mr Kane, the relevant answers are in complete response to the questions asked. Perhaps you should direct your objections to your own questions, sir. Please continue.'

Kane felt like a dog scrabbling at a door, trying to escape. He affected a none-too-convincing laugh: 'All that you are telling us, Mrs Bolton, is that – on one occasion – you discovered the dead girl and Mr Macnair, and they were engaging in a childish game.'

'Aye, sir.' Kane breathed a sigh of relief. Then the witness continued: 'Aye, and I said to Martha afterwards: 'Lucky you weren't playing games with Macnair in the kitchen, because, knowing what that boy is like, you'd get a bun in your oven...'

Kane stood speechless for the moment. Lord Blake looked down: 'Any further questions, Mr Kane?'

***

Kane and Collins stood before one of the fireplaces in Parliament Hall. Collins was consoling his friend: 'Edward, Edward – no-one could have done more than you.' Collins frowned: 'But it might just be time to let go, my friend. I fear that another such mis-step may damage your own reputation. And permanently...'

The case had been adjourned since the old judge, Lord Flood, had been parlously close to entering The Land of Nod for the last fifteen minutes.

Kane shook his head and looked at the floor. Through the hubbub of the hall, he heard a gentle voice speak his name: 'Edward?'

Kane looked up at Florrie Forbes-Knight.

Kane laughed – but ruefully. 'Florrie, I'm afraid that your welcome visit has coincided with an unwelcome chapter in my great book of trial-and-error...'

Florrie nodded: 'I was there, Edward. I saw what happened.'

Kane pursed his lips and looked at the floor. Collins spoke to ease the moment: 'A pleasure to see you, Miss Forbes-Knight. No doubt there is still much in the way of preparation for tomorrow evening.'

Collins rummaged in his papers and held up a ticket: 'I have not forgotten.'

Kane recalled that he had instructed Horse to secure two tickets for the concert, one for Kane and one for Collins. But he did not recall receiving them. Collins noted Kane's puzzlement: 'Found it in my box just now.'

Florrie placed her hand on Edward's arm: 'You'll find one in your box too, Edward. The uptake of tickets for the event was somewhat disappointing. Father has now decided to distribute all tickets without an admission cost...'

'He is giving the tickets away?'

Florrie spoke with a straight face: 'Father says that he is ensuring a more discerning audience.'

There was a short silence, then Florrie began to giggle: 'Father thinks it better to guarantee a generous attendance at the event, than Amanda look out into a wilderness of empty seats.' Florrie pointed across the hall, where the great woolly-bearded figure of Sir John Forbes-Knight was barking orders at two housemaids. 'He has enlisted our household staff to place a ticket in every Advocate's box.'

Florrie smiled: 'Next stop, as I understand it, is the Infirmary – of course, Father has friends and colleagues there.'

Sir John Forbes-Knight looked up and saw Florrie. He began to stride over to the fireplace.

Collins – anticipating that the conversation to come might take some time (and be of some intensity) – made his excuses, gave a short bow, then hurried off into the Advocates Library. His fears proved to be not without foundation. Bellowing ensued: 'Florence, Florence – what the deuce are we to do with these girls? I offer a simple instruction to place a ticket into each Advocate's box and I receive nothing but blank stares...'

'They are, perhaps, overwhelmed by the grandeur of the surroundings, Father. I shall speak to them.' Florrie gave Kane a smile and made her way across the hall.

Kane found himself stranded at the fireplace with the man who had deemed Kane not fit for purpose as a son-in-law. Then the old surgeon broke the silence between them: 'Rum business, I must say.'

Since that utterance could have related to any of the events in Kane's life at that moment, Kane ventured to clarify: 'Rum business', Sir John?'

'The old cook, Mrs Bolton... I was there, Kane. Saw the whole thing today. Heard so much about the whole blasted thing that I thought I would pay a visit and observe your circus.'

Kane did not know how to respond. 'Thank you, Sir John.'

Forbes-Knight continued: 'Of course, she is lying through her teeth, the old witch.'

'About what, sir?'

'About everything. It's as plain as the crooked nose on her face. It is a wonder that she has endured so long in the service of Sir Charles. From what he tells me, the old baggage cannot even cook.'

There was another silence as Sir John squinted to get a more focused view of some figures who were walking up and down Parliament Hall: 'I say, isn't that Cordelia Irving? Walking with your Dean of Faculty?'

Kane looked over. Walking across the hall and in deep conversation, Cordelia serious and explaining, Rab Lennox nodding. Cordelia looked up and saw the mis-matched pair at the fireplace. Her face went blank for a moment, then Kane saw her break into a smile at them. The glow was bright, but not warm. Cordelia Irving said something to Lennox to conclude the conversation and walked over to Kane and Forbes-Knight.

'Well gentlemen, has the engagement been re-instated?' She gave a deep-throated laugh.

The gentlemen at the fireplace looked embarrassed.

Cordelia Irving purred in her low voice: 'Perhaps, Sir John, it is you who have had – how shall we term it – an 'Epiphany'?'

The old surgeon ignored the jibe and grunted: 'I trust that we shall see you tomorrow evening?'

Cordelia smirked: 'I would not miss such an artistic event for all the world, Sir John. I did not know – nor, apparently, did anyone else – that Miss Amanda could sing...'

Sir John raised himself up to his full height: 'Miss Amanda has received expert tuition for a number of years now. And tomorrow night, we shall hear the fruits of that.'

Cordelia Irving cooed: 'Oh, doesn't the Good Book tell us that the plucking of fruits is an extremely dangerous business, Sir John? Ask Mr Kane here – his father was a Man of the Cloth.'

Kane smiled: 'Only when the fruit is forbidden, Cordelia.'

The girl looked out onto the crowded hall: 'Such a lovely creature, Miss Amanda. But she seems to have depleted the family larder of beauty, Sir John, leaving not a crumb for your other daughters. What a pity...'

Cordelia nodded towards the approaching figure of Florrie Forbes-Knight.

Cordelia Irving and Florence Forbes-Knight had known each other since infancy. Despite living only several minutes' walk from each other, despite parental encouragement that they should be friends during their childhood years, despite a shared and acknowledged station in life, the seeds of friendship never bloomed. Rather, both women developed a certain wariness of each other, calm and smiling on the surface, but locked in some subterranean struggle for ascendency.

Cordelia called over: 'Florrie – we were just talking about you...'

'Then fortunate that I arrived when I did...'

'No, I was just remarking that Amanda was so beautiful. Lovely as a swan. You know, they say that some swans sing before they die. My own view is that it would be better that some people should die before they sing...'

Kane thought that he saw Florrie bristle, ever so slightly. Then she responded: 'It's always lovely to see you, Cordelia. I expect you are looking for your father? He appears to be sued here on a daily basis...'

'No,' replied Cordelia cooly, 'I am here to witness your friend, Mr Kane, and his... his attempts at advocacy...'

'His attempts,' retorted Florrie, 'to exonerate your fiancé, I understand. We all feel so sorry for you, Cordelia, that the man you were sworn to marry was driven to seek pleasure – in the arms of a parlour maid.'

Kane, who had been following the exchange as one follows a game of tennis, noted that Cordelia failed to reply to that last shot and so – as was understood by all in attendance – she had conceded the point. Advantage Forbes-Knight. Except, now Kane noted tears welling in Florrie's eyes. This was not a game that she enjoyed. It was apparent that rain would soon stop play. He motioned in the direction of the Advocates' boxes: 'Florrie – I'm sure that I have just seen one of your maids requesting your attention. I would attend, if I were you.'

Without saying a word, Florrie turned on her heels and made her way over to the boxes. Cordelia followed her with her eyes and shook her head: 'Well, Sir John, as you have often said yourself 'Too shrewish to marry'...'. And with that, Cordelia Irving walked away.

Sir John reflected on that recent skirmish: 'She was always a difficult one, Cordelia Irving. How could she be otherwise, with Sir Charles as a father?'

'Yes, Sir John.'

'The fruit' – as they say – 'does not fall far from the tree'. Never a truer word was spoken. Look at my own daughters. Each one of them bears my own stamp...'

This last proposition was too preposterous to Kane to merit vocal response, so he merely pursed his lips and nodded.

'I have known Sir Charles for many years and have spent many happy hours in his company. But in some ways, he is quite mad.' Sir John stood more erect: 'And I say that as a medical man...'

Kane silently wondered how the surgeon's facility for cutting open people's bodies qualified him to comment so authoritatively on the condition of their minds.

The surgeon continued: 'All types of outlandish ideas. He is a Marlovian – did you know that?'

'No, Sir John – I assumed he was Scottish.'

Sir John Forbes-Knight turned his head towards Kane and stared into the Advocate's eyes, as if he wanted to do him harm. Having examined Kane's face for some five seconds, the old surgeon exploded into laugher and repeated Kane's reply: 'I assumed he was Scottish'! Oh, Edward, young man, you're a decent fellow at core, and I do so enjoy your sense of humour. And can I say, young man, that you are doing such a good job with that Macnair case that we'll have him hanged in no time. So, well done, sir.'

Kane nodded feebly. 'Thank you, Sir John.'

The old surgeon's praise was interrupted by the sight of Florrie, who was now walking back to them. Kane could see that she was smiling at him now. The cloud had passed.

'Father, the girls appear to be working well now. The whole enterprise should take a further twenty minutes or so – who would have thought that there would be so many Advocates and so many boxes!'

The surgeon nodded: 'Capital, my dear, capital.'

'I have instructed them to meet us at the Infirmary when they have finished, and we can start the process there...'

But the old surgeon was somewhat distracted. His eye had caught the figure of Rab Lennox walking in the hall by himself. 'If you'll excuse me...' And with a cursory bow, he was gone.

Florrie gave an embarrassed smile to Kane: 'And Edward, I wish to apologise for my unforgivable behaviour with Cordelia Irving...'

Kane held up his hand to stop her speaking.

Florrie laughed: 'It is just Cordelia. She has always been the same. One of my earliest memories is being placed in a nursery with her to play.'

'That sounds pleasant enough...'

'It was. Until she stabbed me with the bayonet of a toy soldier.'

'An unusual choice of toy for two young girls to play with, perhaps.'

'Her father had been expecting a boy. The nursery was full of such items.'

The unexpected sharing of the painful memory was such that Kane found it difficult to pick up the thread of the conversation. They stood in silence for a moment and watched Sir John and Rab Lennox walk up and down Parliament Hall.

Kane mused aloud: 'Your father was opining on the mental state of Sir Charles Irving. Apparently, Sir Charles is quite mad because he is... I did not recognise the term... 'Mullovian'?'

Florrie screwed up her eyes for a moment, then smiled: 'Marlovian.'

Kane laughed: 'That's the one! I had no idea what he was talking about.'

Florrie rolled her eyes and shook her head: 'Father and Sir Charles and all his other cronies sit around and smoke cigars and drink brandy and argue endlessly that Shakespeare was not really Shakespeare. And that Shakespeare did not write the plays of Shakespeare.'

Kane recalled the study of Shakespeare at school. 'Twelfth Night' and 'The Merchant of Venice'. 'If music be the food of love – play on...' and 'The quality of mercy is not strained...'?

The Advocate smiled: 'Then, Florrie, I can appreciate why brandy is required. In copious amounts. And so, if Shakespeare did not write 'Richard the Third', then who did?'

'Christopher Marlowe, apparently.'

'I am happy to say, Florrie, that I have never heard of him...'

'Oh, I am sure you have, Edward. A playwright of the Tudor period...'

'Ah! Your father's interest is suddenly apparent. But I'm afraid that obscure Tudor playwrights are not my strong point.'

'Marlowe is hardly obscure – you must have heard of 'Edward the Second'?'

Kane shook his head.

Florrie searched her memory and ploughed on: 'I know! 'Doctor Faustus'! You must have heard of 'Doctor Faustus' – the man who sold his soul to the Devil.'

Kane laughed now: 'Of course. I have heard of that. And it does seem highly apt that Sir Charles Irving would appear to be so enthusiastic about such a scenario.'

The friends laughed. Florrie continued: 'Sir Charles – and many others – say that it was, in fact, Marlowe who wrote his own plays and also wrote the plays of Shakespeare – thus the adjective 'Marlovian'.'

Kane suddenly looked downcast. Florrie noted this: 'Edward, has our conversation made you sad?'

The Advocate closed his eyes and shook his head slowly: 'Oh, Florrie. For the luxury, the simple luxury of sitting with brandy and cigars, debating the authorship of some play written hundreds of years ago. 'Edward the Second' or 'Richard the Third'. But today, here I am with a man's life in my hands and instead of shepherding him to safety, I appear to be ushering him towards the gallows.'

Florrie pretended to rebuke him: 'Mr Edward Kane, Advocate. You are hereby instructed to raise your chin from the ground and take credit where credit is due. You have inherited a man who will not give you instructions to save his own life, and a group of witnesses resembling a menagerie of fantastic creatures, each one of which seems more determined to convict him than the last. No-one – look at me, Edward...' Florrie placed her finger under Kane's chin and raised his head. She looked into his eyes. '...

No-one could have done as well as you in these circumstances. If Macnair is truly guilty – as it looks as if he surely must be now – then he could not have had a better defence.'

Kane looked into Florrie's face. Cordelia Irving was wrong. The family store of beauty had not been depleted. Florrie was beautiful. Kane smiled: 'Florrie... I...'

But that thought was interrupted by Collins, who had come out quickly from the Advocates Library.

'Edward, we are back. The Court is ready to resume.'

Kane looked at Florrie. She kissed her gloved fingers and tapped Kane on the head: 'For luck.' She smiled. 'And remember: the quality of mercy is not strained...'

Chapter Eleven

Kane sat at the table and readied his papers for his last few questions for Mrs Bolton. He looked over at Patrick Macnair in the dock and mused over what Florrie had said: 'a man who will not give you instructions to save his own life'. But what could be more important than life itself? Collins reached over and handed Kane his own notes of the old woman's evidence.

Court resumed. Mrs Bolton took the witness stand. Lord Blake looked down kindly on her: 'You are still under oath, madam, you understand that?'

The old cook held up her rosary beads: 'Aye, sir.'

The judge looked at Kane: 'Mr Kane?'

Kane nodded. There was a hush over the court as Kane walked across the courtroom and laid out his papers on the table before him.

Just a few questions more. This old lady had been through enough in her life already. No need to prolong her agony. Perhaps not mention the children again...

He picked up Collins' notes. And there it was. Staring Kane in the face. In Collins' notes. The answer – or at least part of the answer – to this whole puzzle. Kane stood there, and then, suddenly, fully formed in his mind, the answer was complete. The answer to everything. As if someone had woken up one day and found a whole new house in their garden. The answer. The complete answer. The complete construction, From basement to roof. Sitting there.

Lord Blake noted the delay and called down: 'Mr Kane, are you ready to continue your cross-examination?'

Kane felt as if he was standing underwater and the judge's question seemed to bubble down towards him. Of course. Of course. Kane nodded.

'Now, Mrs Bolton, we have heard that you were particularly fond of Martha Cunningham because she reminded you of your own daughter.'

'Yes, sir.'

'You referred in your evidence to your late daughter as 'Maria, the first'.'

'Aye, sir – she was my oldest.'

Kane indicated the rosary beads: 'And should we understand – from the use of the beads that you are holding there – that you are Catholic?'

'Aye, sir. Cradle Catholic. Like my father and mother before.'

Kane started to focus. This would require some subtlety – and the judges would not care for the approach – but it was necessary.

'Your three children. Were they christened before they died?'

'They were baptised, sir, aye.'

'And that would be to place them in a state of grace?'

'Aye, sir.'

'And fit the children for Heaven.'

'Aye, sir.'

Lord Blake stopped writing, was staring down and looking puzzled at this line of questioning. The prosecutor, Jon Hunter was shaking his head.

'And you hope to join them one day.'

The old lady nodded: 'Aye, sir. If I can die in a state of grace and get to

Heaven myself, sir. I go to Mass every day, sir.'

'And you have sworn an oath in this court to tell the truth. An oath that may imperil your very soul.'

Jon Hunter had had enough: 'Don't answer that question.' He turned to the judges: 'My lords, while my Learned Friend might be admired for undertaking what is – demonstrably – a hopeless defence. I fear that we are now being treated to the sight of a man who is fishing in an empty pond.'

Lord Blake looked down at Kane: 'Mr Kane, the Advocate Depute makes a valid criticism. Your exploration of the tenets of Catholicism appears to have no bearing on the issues in this case.'

Kane bowed, accepting the rebuke. But his work had been done. The old cook had been reminded that to tell a lie on oath now would separate her from her deceased children for all eternity.

Kane resumed his questioning: 'Now, you live in Sir Charles' house and you hold the position of head cook.'

'Yes, sir.'

Kane recalled Sir John Forbes-Knight's comment that Mrs Bolton could not actually cook.

'Did you receive any training for such a post, Mrs Bolton?'

The old lady seemed puzzled by the question.

'For example, did you work under another cook in learning your trade, Mrs Bolton?'

Mrs Bolton clutched at her rosary: 'No training, sir. I just picked up bits and bobs as I went.'

'And when was the last time that you cooked for the Irving family?'

The witness frowned and knotted her eyebrows, as if doing complex mental arithmetic. Then: 'I don't think I've ever cooked for them, sir.'

'And yet, you were appointed head cook.'

'Aye, sir.'

'By Sir Charles Irving himself.'

'Aye, sir.' She paused, then: 'But just tae let you understand, I look after the kitchen. I keep the other lassies on their toes. I make sure that everything is clean. That the soup tureens have been properly washed and that.'

'Now, you have told us that you had two sons.'

'Aye, sir.'

'Edward and Richard.'

'Correct, sir.'

'In that order.'

'Aye, sir.'

Kane paused, then: 'Why did refer to your daughter as 'Maria, the first'?'

The old lady thought for a moment, then: 'Because she was my first born, sir.'

'Who chose her name? Was it you, or was it the girl's father?'

'We both had a hand in it, sir. I always wanted to call a girl 'Maria' – after the Holy Mother of Our Lord.'

'And the father of the girl saw the name 'Maria' as acceptable because – for example – it is the name of a character found in a play by Shakespeare. In 'Twelfth Night' – 'Maria' in that play is a domestic servant, like yourself, Mrs Bolton.'

'I wouldnae know, sir. I've never saw a play. I've never even been in a theatre...'

'But your understanding was that that was why the name was acceptable. To the father of the girl.'

Mrs Bolton stared at Kane and went silent for a number of seconds. There was a changed quality to her; a sort of crumbling inside. Then she answered: 'Yes, sir.'

'And your next child after that, after 'Maria the first' – we have 'Edward the Second'?'

Some of the jurors laughed. A glare from Lord Blake soon silenced them.

The old witness seemed weary in her answer: 'Yes, sir.'

'And without straining the point, Mrs Bolton, your third child – Richard – would be 'Richard the...' what?'

The prosecutor, Jon Hunter, sensed that in some way this case was spinning out of his control. But he did not know how or why. He jumped to his feet: 'I regret that I am on my feet, once again, my lords...'

Lord Blake shook his head slowly: 'I agree entirely, Advocate Depute.' He turned to Kane: 'I fear, Mr Kane, that your enthusiasm for this endeavour has clouded your judgement entirely, sir. I fail to see of what possible relevance this discussion of Shakespearean characters and the kings of England could be to the issues before this court.'

'My lords, I have a mere three questions more – and I then I undertake to the court that I will sit down.'

Lord Blake threw his head back and rolled his eyes. Then he turned to the judges around him. They nodded.

'Very well, Mr Kane. Three questions only. Question Number One?' He started to write on his papers.

Kane resumed: 'Mrs Bolton – the reason why the three children are called Maria, Edward and Richard is because their father chose those names because they are characters and titles in plays by Shakespeare and his contemporary, Marlowe – is that not correct?'

The old cook was struggling now: 'Yes.'

Lord Blake looked down: 'Second question, Mr Kane?'

Kane looked directly at the witness: 'And who was the father of those children, Mrs Bolton?'

The witness flared up at this point: 'I was a married woman, sir!'

'Then the answer to my second question should be simple, madam. The question is this: who was the father of the children? The children born in the Irving household with their names drawn from the work of Shakespeare and Marlowe?'

Jon Hunter was on his feet: 'My lords...'

Lord Blake barked: 'Sit down, Advocate Depute, the court has already allowed this and a final question.'

The courtroom was deathly silent now. The only sound was the ticking of the court clock. Kane spoke gently: 'Mrs Bolton – you have sworn an oath today. On the peril of your soul, madam. On the hopes of seeing your three children again in the life to come. You must answer truthfully: who was the father of those three children?'

The old cook stood for a long time saying nothing. Then she shook her head, then looked up towards Lord Blake. 'I made a promise, your honour, in the Lord's name. To the bairns' father. That I would never tell.'

Silence for a moment, then Lord Blake responded in a steely voice: 'And you have sworn an oath, today, madam. A solemn oath. You swore by Almighty God to tell the truth, the whole truth and nothing but the truth. Now, what is the answer to the question, Mrs Bolton?'

The old lady said nothing. Everyone in the courtroom waited for her to answer that question. But everyone in that courtroom knew the answer: Sir Charles Irving was the father of those children. And why retain a cook who could not cook? Because Sir Charles owed Mrs Bolton for the three children that she had lost.

The old lady remained silent, wrestling with promises made in the past and in the present.

Edward Kane turned around and looked into the public gallery. And there, among the rapt faces, he saw the face of Sir Charles' daughter, Cordelia Irving. She was staring into Kane's face, and her face was disfigured by hatred.

★★★

Of course, the old lady did not answer. Despite a number of severe warnings by Lord Blake that she would be found in contempt of court and sent to prison – she remained obstinate. The cook who could not cook, the unwitting mother of Edward the Second and Richard the Third, was remanded in custody and the case was adjourned until the following morning to decide what to do with her.

Kane stood at the fireplace with 'Not Proven' Norris. Norris puffed on his pipe and chuckled: 'Excellent work, my young friend. Masterful misdirection. Of course, everyone knows now that Sir Charles has always had a taste for – how shall we put it – 'downstairs'. But we still have a problem, don't we?'

Kane looked up. Norris continued: 'It still looks as if Macnair killed that girl. Talk about ancient history as much as you like, but it is Macnair who is present at the event and is heard arguing with the dead girl, then seen running away from her body. Those are the facts. And despite your good work, the men in the jury are far from stupid.' Norris looked into the great Hall: 'Ah, and Edward, I see that we are about to have a visitor. And I do not think that I am the one she wishes to speak to.' Norris gave a short bow as the figure of Cordelia Irving came into view: 'Until tomorrow, my young friend.'

Cordelia Irving stood face to face with Edward Kane. Her eyes were red and wet. In a deliberate and slow motion, she removed the lace glove from her right hand, finger by finger – and then slapped Edward Kane full across the face. Kane said nothing. He could feel the welt begin to rise on his cheek. Carefully, he turned his face to the side and offered Cordelia Irving his other cheek.

Cordelia Irving replaced the glove and spoke in a cracked voice: 'I suppose that's something you learned from your father. Well, Kanemiss, my father has taught me a different way to deal with the enemy, as you will soon appreciate.'

Edward Kane and Cordelia Irving looked into each other's eyes, saying nothing until Kane spoke: 'It was you, wasn't it?'

Cordelia Irving said nothing in reply. She stood there, no expression on her face.

Kane continued: 'I honestly do not know how I did not see it. What was it that would make Macnair say nothing in his own defence? Not a single word. What could it be that was worth to him more than his own life? The first time we met in the Calton Prison, he told me: 'I love Miss

Cordelia more than life itself.' Because it was you there at the top of those stairs that night, wasn't it? Watching your fiancé argue with that poor girl. Shouting that he wasn't the father. Mrs Trent heard a woman's voice – 'high' then 'low'? It was little Martha Cunningham's squeaky voice and then yours. That's what she heard. And the old cook heard 'swishing' – it makes no sense. Unless it is the sound of the ballgown that you were seen wearing later.'

Cordelia Irving walked past Kane and began to stare into the fire.

'And didn't you tell me that you - how did you put it - you 'missed all the fun that night' because you were in bed. In bed - wearing a ballgown? You see, the things that made no sense then, make perfect sense now, Cordelia. Scratches on the dead girl's arm? The prosecutor made nothing of this because it did not fit with his theory that Macnair did it. But a soldier - and a good one like Macnair- does not fight by scratching, Cordelia, but a woman does. It was you. And the greatest mystery of all becomes simple now: how did that dead girl speak after she was thrown down those stairs? What did she say? Her neck had been snapped. How could she speak? The simple answer is that she didn't. You did. The woman's voice that Mrs Bolton thought that she heard was yours, wasn't it. And what you said to Macnair - to poor, lovestruck Patrick Macnair was 'Promise you won't tell.' And with that, you placed the man you professed to love in the shadow of the gallows. And you were home and clear.'

Cordelia Irving stared into the flames: 'If Patrick had truly loved me, then he would not have been interfering with a common little trollop, would he? So, the gallows it is and no more than he deserves.' She looked at Kane: 'And, of course, you have no evidence whatsoever for any of this.'

Kane looked into Cordelia Irving's eyes: 'You forget, Cordelia – I have one question left. And when old Mrs Bolton is brought back into that court tomorrow, my last question is a simple one: 'When you thought that you heard a woman's voice after Martha had come down those stairs

– was that the voice of Cordelia Irving?' And I predict that she will not hesitate to answer that question truthfully.'

Without another word, Cordelia Irving walked away and across the great Parliament Hall and out into the street.

★★★

'How's the welt on that cheek coming, Mr K? Will I put a bit more lard on it?'

Horse was pouring some warn milk into the old, battered metal mug. He poured it from a height, so the milk was frothy at the top. 'There you go, sir. This is how my nan used to make it for me. When I couldn't sleep.'

Kane sat in the glow of the fire. He sipped the milk and could feel the warmth of it as it went down. Better now. And – inevitably – his thoughts returned to the case. Of course, Norris had been right. The fact that it had now been demonstrated that Sir Charles Irving had been a philanderer in the past, did not exonerate Patrick Macnair as a philanderer in the present. And once that old cook had spent the night in a prison cell, there was no telling what she would come up with in court later that morning. Kane looked up from his cup. Horse appeared to be laughing to himself. Kane smiled: 'You seem particularly merry, Mr Horse...'

'I was just laughing to meself, sir. Hide and Seek. In the downstairs cupboard...' He then imitated Lord Blake in an exaggeratedly plummy voice: 'Oooh – thet must have been a jolly big cupboard, Mr Kane – a jolly big cupboard, dontcha know!'

Kane couldn't help it – he threw his head back and laughed: 'And then, Horse, and then I was invited to object to my own questions. Oh dear, oh dear...' They laughed. Horse continued in his mock-plummy voice: 'That's because they were jolly bad questions, Mr Kane... jolly bad...' More laughter. Then a knock at the door.

The laugher stopped. Kane sighed. 'What time is it Horse? Is the clock correct?'

Horse nodded towards the clock on the mantelpiece. 'I wound it at midnight, sir. It's fifteen minutes after three...'

Kane smiled ruefully: 'In your experience, Mr Horse, when the door knocks at a quarter past three in the morning, does that tend to be a good or a bad sign?'

'Well Mr K, you was threatened earlier by a lady what has some influence in this town, so I will answer the door.' Horse smiled and picked up an object from the table. 'And, just in case, I will take with me this jolly big knife.'

Horse went to answer the door while Kane sat by the fire, sipping his milk. He heard a low conversation, and then Horse emerged followed by Mackintosh of the Detective, who had a serious look on his face.

Kane stood up and addressed him light-heartedly 'Mackintosh – always a pleasure. Even in the middle of the night. You look serious, sir. Have you come to arrest me? If so, would you mind if I finished this milk? I have enough trouble sleeping in my own bed, never mind the cots at the Calton.'

Mackintosh removed his hat. His face remained serious as he spoke: 'I've just come from Sir Charles Irving's house, Mr Kane There's been another shooting.'

Kane sat down in his chair.

The detective continued: 'It's Sir Charles. He's shot himself, sir. And he's left a note. And a confession...'

★★★

Mackintosh told the entire story of the evening. A call had come to the police office just before midnight. A gunshot had been heard inside Sir Charles' study. The butler, Mr Hand, attended and the body of Sir Charles Irving was found slumped in his armchair, an antique pistol dropped nearby. He was holding a crumpled piece of paper in his left hand. The Police Surgeon, Mr Stanton, later concluded that the old man had died from a gunshot wound to the right temple at point blank range. A number of documents were neatly arranged on his desk. These included a handwritten Will, leaving the majority of his estate to his daughter, but in a series of complex trusts of which she was the sole beneficiary. No husband could ever claim a share of that estate. There were also significant annuities to the servants, Mr Hand and Mrs Bolton.

But the document that most interested Mackintosh and the Police Surgeon was the paper found crumpled in Sir Charles' hand. It was a suicide note and confession. It narrated how he had discovered that Martha Cunningham was expecting a child. According to the note, the father was not Patrick Macnair, but was instead, a young man introduced to her through one of the scullery maids. Irving had challenged her about the situation, and he had, in a fit of temper, pushed her down the stairs during an argument. Any male voice heard that night was his. No-one else was involved. It had been unfortunate that Patrick Macnair had been the first to find the body at the bottom of the stairs and had attempted to assist the girl. The fault lay entirely with Sir Charles. The confession ended with a quotation: 'The evil that men do lives after them. The good is oft interred with their bones.' Mackintosh thought that this was probably a quote from Shakespeare, but could not confirm it at this stage.

Mackintosh, Kane and Horse sat silently around the fire. Horse broke the silence: 'Well, that means, Mr K, that Macnair is off the hook then, doesn't it, sir.'

'I am not entirely sure.'

Kane looked at Mackintosh: 'What do you think of the whole thing, Mackintosh?'

'It is all very neat, Mr Kane. In fact, I don't think I've ever seen a case wrapped up so neatly in one fell swoop, sir.'

'The handwriting on the paper found in his hand, Mackintosh,' asked Kane, 'does it match the handwriting on the other documents?'

The detective nodded: 'It all seems in order, sir.' But he looked glum.

'You will forgive me for saying so, Mackintosh, but you do not seem to be particularly happy about this development, even though you now have a neat solution to your case. Perhaps you yourself can start to get some sleep now.'

Mackintosh said nothing.

★★★

Kane met Collins early that morning in the Advocates Library, and Collins quizzed him on whether the rumours about Sir Charles were true. Kane related the whole story.

Collins rested his chin on the palm of his hand and listened. 'Then, Edward, what is the position of the Crown today?'

'I have no idea, my friend. I had rather hoped that one of Jon Hunter's Crown Juniors had approached you this morning.'

Collins shook his head: 'I have heard nothing.'

Kane saw someone approach them; it was a smiling 'Not Proven' Norris: 'Well, Edward – is it true?'

Kane nodded. Norris chuckled and puffed on his pipe: 'And has the Crown done the decent thing and raised the white flag of surrender?'

'I have heard nothing.'

Norris nodded towards the door: 'Then something is afoot. That is possibly why our Learned Friend Mr Hunter is, as we speak, walking up and down Parliament Hall with the Lord Advocate himself...'

★★★

By the time the three judges entered the court they had also heard the rumours, as had everyone in the crowded gallery and – most importantly – the fifteen men of the jury. Several of them were sitting, skeptically, with their arms folded. Kane thought that he saw traces of friendliness in their faces today – and a certain animosity directed towards the prosecution side of the table.

The case was called. Lord Blake addressed Jon Hunter.

'Yes, Advocate Depute. Might you have a motion to make?'

The prosecutor stood up: 'Yes, my lords. Certain information has come to light, and I wonder if the case might be adjourned for fourteen days to consider the import of that information. And perhaps for further investigations...'

Lord Blake looked down at his desk and smiled. He invited Kane to respond: 'Mr Kane?'

Kane stood up: 'My lords, if by 'certain information' my leaned friend is referring to the fact, the fact that Sir Charles Irving – now a clear suspect in this case,' Kane turned towards the jury, 'last night shot himself in the head...' There was a gasp from the auditorium from those who hadn't heard, 'and left a note confessing to the murder – while explicitly exonerating the man in the dock here, Patrick Macnair, who has been held in appalling conditions in Calton Prison for many months now,' Kane turned back to face the judges: 'If that be the 'information' to which the learned Advocate Depute refers, then what possible 'further investigations' can he be suggesting?'

Lord Blake looked down at Jonathan Hunter: 'Advocate Depute – what investigations are you referring to?'

Jonathan Hunter stood up. He had nothing to say but, ever the Advocate, said something: 'The precise nature of the investigations is not clear at this stage...'

The judge cut in: 'You mean you don't know.'

Hunter paused for a moment, then: 'Those are my instructions, my lords.' And sat down.

Lord Blake sat back in his chair and thought for a moment. Then he spoke to Kane: 'And in the event, Mr Kane, that there were to be no more trial, then what do you propose that we do with yesterday's reluctant witness, the cook – Mrs Bolton?'

Kane had already considered this question very carefully. In the last analysis, his responsibility was to secure the acquittal of Patrick Macnair, not the prosecution of Cordelia Irving.

'My proposal, my lords, is this: if this case is to go no further, then I will withdraw the offending question. Thus, Mrs Bolton will not be required to answer it and she may be excused.'

The judge considered this for a moment, nodding as he listened.

Kane sat down.

Lord Blake summoned the other judges to him; they huddled together, their backs to the lawyers and the public gallery.

After some animated minutes, the judges resumed their seats. Lord Blake spoke to Jon Hunter: 'Advocate Depute...'

The prosecutor stood up: 'Yes, my lord.'

'Advocate Depute, your motion for an adjournment is refused.'

Hunter tried to object: 'But, my lords...'

Lord Blake snapped back: 'A decision has been made, sir. Why are you still speaking?'

Hunter, cowed, sat down.

The judge raised his eyebrows: 'Shall we resume the evidence, then, of your witness – Mrs Bolton...'

Jon Hunter said nothing and remained in his seat. Blake continued: 'Or do you have an alternative proposition, sir?'

Hunter let his pen drop on the table. Then he stood up.

'My lords, I have discussed the matter this morning with the Lord Advocate himself...'

Lord Blake looked down, pen in hand: 'As was proper, sir.'

'... and I am instructed that if an adjournment is not to be permitted, then...'

Blake was smiling: 'Yes?'

'...then the Crown withdraws the libel against the accused.'

'Very well. Thank you, Advocate Depute.'

Hunter slumped down into his seat.

Lord Blake spoke to the man in the dock: 'Patrick Macnair, stand up. As you heard, the Crown has withdrawn the libel in this case. What that means is that they are no longer seeking a conviction against you. In those circumstances, Patrick Macnair, I find you 'Not Guilty'.' The judge smiled: 'And you are free to leave the dock, sir.'

At that point, two things happened simultaneously: the three judges got up from their seats, bowed quickly, and beetled out of the courtroom – and, as they were doing so, a great, deafening cheer rose up from the public gallery.

Kane was still sat at his desk as other Counsel came over to shake his hand or pat him on the back, and members of the public swarmed across and tried to touch him, as if that would impart to them a measure of his great success in the matter. People were throwing hats in the air and nodding and smiling and gabbling that they had 'never seen the like' in all their lives. Journalists sitting in the front row were scrambling over each other and pushing through the crowds now to get their copy to their newspapers and journals.

And in amongst the motion and the noise and the frenzy, Kane looked across the table and saw the disconsolate figure of Jon Hunter. Sitting alone now, his eyes were closed and motionless, his face pale and smooth. Like a death mask.

PART FOUR: THE EPIPHANY

ASSEMBLY ROOMS GEORGE STREET

On THURSDAY EVENING, Sept. 25.

Epiphany

The DIRECTORS beg to announce that

MISS AMANDA FORBES~KNIGHT

will perform THE WORLD PREMIER

in the form of a number of

UNFORGETTABLE DRAMATIC and MUSICAL RECITALS

TICKETS NOW READY

ADMITTANCE ONE SHILLING

FOR ONE NIGHT ONLY

The Performance to commence at Half~past 8 o'clock precisely, and to conclude about 9

Chapter Twelve

'Hold still, Mr K, hold still.'

Horse fiddled and fussed with Kane's white cravat. And after more detailed pinching and tightening – success. 'Aha – perfect, Mr K.' Horse stood back to admire his handiwork.

There stood Kane, approved now for his evening engagement.

'Now, Horse, we appear to have two extra tickets for Miss Amanda's event...'

Horse nodded to himself that as, predicted, it had been a waste of two bob.

'... and so I was thinking, perhaps you would like to attend yourself, and invite one of your lady friends. I'm told that the Assembly Rooms has adequate seating at the rear of the auditorium.'

Horse thought for a moment: 'Begging your pardon, Mr K, but I don't think that the young ladies of my acquaintance enjoy the opera, sir.'

'It's not opera, as I understand it.'

'Then what is it?'

Kane considered this: 'It is... it is... actually, I have no idea what it is, Horse.'

Horse helped Kane on with his black overcoat. 'Shall I wear my cloak, Horse?'

'No, sir. You'll be walking down to George Street. Don't want you getting too hot, now, do we, sir?'

'Didn't you send for a cab, as I asked?'

'No, sir. Got to make that two bob back somehow...'

Kane began to button up his coat. 'Well, I hope I am not too conspicuous arriving on foot.'

Horse brushed down Kane's coat. 'I wouldn't worry about that, Mr K. It's all rich people. They don't notice anything but themselves, sir.' He pointed at the mantle clock. 'Now, if you're ready to go, Mr K, then that will be a wery pleasant stroll down the hill, sir.'

★★★

Horse was right. As he walked down the hill towards George Street, Kane noted that the roads appeared to be getting more and more dense with cabs of all descriptions. All seemed headed towards the same destination: the Assembly Rooms – and Miss Amanda's 'Epiphany'. Clearly, given the exertions of Sir John Forbes-Knight to avoid an empty house, this now had to be one of the social events of the season.

The Assembly Rooms was one of the perfect social hubs of Edinburgh, where the great and the good could congregate and parade in all their finery.

As he approached the entrance, he chuckled that Horse was right again. Kane was essentially invisible. The whole road was a riot of police officers moving the crowd along, and of coaches, with the coachmen shouting at each other and the occupants of those coaches alighting. The pavements were transformed into a veritable ocean of gentlemen in top hats, cloaks, notch collars, cravats, kerseymere trousers and scented handkerchiefs, all accompanied by ladies in swooshes of crinoline, puffed sleeves, bell-shaped skirts and impossibly complex hats. Kane smiled to himself that a passing farmer might be tempted to take a pot-shot at the sheer volume of feathers on display.

The only surprise to Kane was a makeshift market stall placed at the side of the entrance. Under those grand pillars and to the side of those entrance arches, Kane became aware of even more intense activity. He recognised a certain face at that stall. It was the young artist Simon Culp selling prints of his version – his 'truth' – of yesterday's court proceedings. No proceedings today, of course, since the trial was now at an end, so what better location to guarantee sales of those final events in court than at the social event of the year? Kane watched for a moment and – by all indications – Culp was doing a roaring trade. At one point, the young artist looked up and caught Kane's eye. The Artist gave the Advocate a shy little wave. Kane responded with a smile and a doff of his top hat.

Through the arches passed that slow moving throng, and Kane saw many familiar faces filing in. There was Rab Lennox and his wife. There was Mr Moss, the surgeon. And there was 'Not Proven' Norris, with his particular friend, Mr James Blades. And was that... it couldn't be... it was Patrick Macnair. To all appearances, in the company of a young lady. A young lady with beautiful, long red tresses. A young lady who was not Cordelia Irving.

Kane heard someone call his name: 'Mr Kane... Mr Kane...' On turning around, Kane saw that it was Mackintosh of the Detective – accompanied by Mrs Mackintosh.

'Mackintosh,' Kane bowed. 'And Mrs Mackintosh. A pleasure as always.'

'Likewise, sir. Likewise.'

Mackintosh seemed cheerful enough, but the detective's wife had her usual glowering demeanour, like a cloud about to burst. Kane tried to lighten the mood: 'Well, this event has certainly attracted the most notable of worthies in this great city, Mackintosh. And that, of course, includes you and your fair lady here.'

The lady was not smiling, but Mackintosh leapt in. 'It's the free tickets, Mr Kane. Not often that you get an invitation to the Assembly Rooms for nothing, sir.'

'Quite so, Mackintosh. And – from what I have heard – it is likely to be a singular event.'

'As long as it's not The Opera, sir. I don't care for The Opera, sir. Nor does Mrs Mackintosh.' Mackintosh looked down at his spouse for agreement. Her face remained stony.

'In The Opera, sir, some poor fellow gets stabbed in the heart, and what does he do? He sings for the next twenty minutes. That's not my experience of these things, Mr Kane...'

There was a lull in the conversation, then the detective's wife stared at Kane for a moment, then blurted out: 'He's guilty, you know.'

Mackintosh tried to placate her: 'Now, my dear, Mr Kane here was only doing his job...'

Mrs Mackintosh ploughed on: 'I mean, we all know he did it.'

No name was mentioned, but the subject of conversation was clear to all.

Mackintosh tried to smooth matters: 'My dear, my dear...'

She turned her wrath on her husband: 'Don't you 'my dear' me, Mackintosh.' She pointed to Kane: 'He's not the one who has to lie beside you night after night, a-tossing and a-turning in your sleep. If old Sir Charles had done it, then you'd know it, Mackintosh, you'd feel it in your bones.'

'My dear...'

'... and then the scoundrel Macnair turns up here – among good God-fearing Christians – flaunting his latest... his latest blowsabella...'

Mrs Mackintosh's bellicose harangue was interrupted by Mackintosh, when the detective tried to change the subject: 'I say, Mr Kane, isn't that your man, Horse, over there? I didn't know that he cared for The Opera...'

★★★

In ordinary circumstances, Nurse Lily Parker would be difficult to follow – such was the density of the crowd on George Street.

This evening, however, accompanied by Nurse Nancy Campbell and Angus Campbell, two exceedingly tall individuals, Nurse Parker's progress towards the Assembly Rooms was clear for anyone who wished to follow her: simply follow those two tall heads above the crowd. And following those tall, tall heads was George - 'Fat Dode' - Soutar, who had unfinished business here.

A knife in one pocket and a rope in the other. Soutar knew Nurse Lily Parker could link him to the boy Willie Cullen because of that aborted visit to the hospital. A slim chance, but better if she were removed from the picture. Among the jostling of the crowd, if Soutar could just get close enough for a lightning-quick slash of one of the main arteries, then the young nurse would be dead in a matter of minutes. Amid the confusion in the throng, it would take a certain amount of time for anyone to appreciate what was happening.

Soutar was close enough to the girl now. Nurse Parker's friends were several steps in front of her. He grasped the sharp blade in his right hand. He felt the sharpness against his fingers. Then: 'Well, if it isn't George Soutar – Fat Dode himself. Didn't take you for a theatre-goer, Georgie. What you doing here?'

Soutar turned around and was confronted by two police officers, dressed in their buttoned-up coats and stovepipe hats. He recognised one of them as an officer he had had dealings with in the past. That officer – for a substantial financial inducement – had provided inside assistance with an investigation into the business affairs of Sir Charles Irving. The investigation was later dropped, when certain essential evidence went missing from the police office. It was Soutar who had acted as the go-between.

The policeman chuckled: 'Thought you'd be at home, George, crying in your beer...'

If there was a joke here, Soutar did not quite get it. He assumed a bluff cheerfulness, but responded with an edge in his voice: 'Been a long time officer. I thought you'd still be looking for certain documentation that the force seemed to have mislaid. Remember?'

The police officer held up his wooden truncheon and pointed it at Soutar as he spoke: 'Oh, I remember, Georgie. I remember it well, son. But I think that some people would be better to forget it – if you know what I mean.'

Soutar nodded and turned behind him. Nurse Parker and the two tall heads were gradually receding into the crowd. The police officer pulled Soutar back: 'Not so fas,t George.' He motioned with his truncheon: 'You seem awful interested in those ladies there. Are those nurses' caps? Not your unusual type, wee George...'

And then it struck him: a fatal stabbing in the crowd, and Soutar seen by two police officers in the vicinity at the time? And seen following the victim? The door of opportunity had closed. He turned to the police officers and gave a laugh that was almost convincing: 'Ha – just out for a wee walk, officer...'

The police officer frowned: 'Ah, but you're looking awful nervy tonight, George. Still upset about the old man, are you?'

'The old man?'

'Sir Charles Irving – your old boss.'

Soutar looked perplexed and shook his head. In planning the dispatch of the young nurse, he had scarcely left his rented room in the last two days. He had spoken to no-one. He had read no newspaper. It may have been that George Soutar was the only person in Edinburgh who did not know that Sir Charles Irving was dead.

'You'll be upset that old Irving shot himself and confessed...'

This stopped Soutar in his tracks. Sir Charles – dead? And confessed? He became anxious now: 'Confessed to what?'

The policeman leaned into Soutar's face, enjoying the cat and mouse exchange: 'To everything, Georgie, to everything. So where does that leave you, my boy?'

Soutar stood frozen. He had no idea. His brain huffed and chunted like a steam engine as he tried to process what he had just heard. If Charles

Irving was dead, by his own hand, then wasn't it better to get out of Edinburgh? What was the point of killing Nurse Parker now? Why create the splash? And now a police officer – two police officers – had seen Soutar follow Nurse Parker. No. Time to leave – and leave soon.

The policeman's voice stirred Soutar from his thoughts: 'But look at you. You're looking very shady tonight, George. Very shady.' The officer pointed at Soutar's coat. 'I think that my colleague and me are going to have to search you, my boy, and we'll see if there's any stolen property in those big pockets of yours.'

Soutar put his hand into his right pocket where the knife was ready. But he looked up. There were two of them. And they were police officers. No guarantee of success. He put his hands in the air: 'Well, officers – caught red-handed. I suppose I will have to give up my ill-gotten gains then...'

Soutar unbuttoned his overcoat, then undid his jacket and held the sides of the jacket wide apart, displaying the inside breast pockets. And – sticking out, conspicuous in the left-hand breast pocket – was a white five pound note. As expected, the police officer seized the note and examined it: 'Oooh – look at this, Georgie, look at this – a Bank of England fiver. Very impressive...'

Soutar smirked: 'And it's the full five pounds. I suppose you'll have to take it as evidence... before you let me go...'

The policeman studied the note carefully, then shook his head: 'It's no good to me, George. It promises to pay you – not me.'

Of course. The handwritten banknote would have to be redeemed at a bank by Soutar in person.

The policeman pointed with his stick: 'What else have you got in those pockets, son?'

Soutar fumbled in his right-hand coat pocket and produced a gold fob watch. The policeman's face lit up: 'Ah, that's more like it, Georgie, that's the ticket...' Soutar handed it over with a forced grin: 'I suppose you'll have to confiscate this...' The officer held up the item to examine it, smiled, nodded, then put it in his pocket. 'Alright, George, I'll just keep this as evidence then.' He waved his truncheon. 'You'd better be off before you get into any trouble. And a piece of advice – stay away from the nurses, George.'

Soutar gave a short bow, and started walking away while buttoning up his coat: 'Always a pleasure, officer, always a pleasure...'

He looked around. Lily Parker and her tall companions were out of sight now. Soutar pushed back against the oncoming crowd and headed towards his lodgings. He would wait until the early morning, when a coach would take him far, far from the city.

And so, with that chance encounter between the police officer and the would-be executioner, the unspoken death sentence against Nurse Lily Parker was lifted.

***

'Mr Horse – I do believe you've shaved.'

Horse, kitted out in his last remaining respectable suit of clothing, rubbed his chin as if to demonstrate the unusual smoothness there.

'Well, Mr K – can't let the side down, can we? Anyway, I had to be here to make sure that you didn't get into any bother, didn't I.'

Kane smiled. 'Horse, look around you. We are in the midst of one of the busiest social events of the season. What on earth could happen here?'

Horse shook his head: 'Mr K – sometimes I worry about you...'

Their conversation was interrupted when Kane caught sight of another familiar figure in the crowd. It was Florrie Forbes-Knight. Kane waved over until he caught her eye: 'Florrie!'

Florrie negotiated her way through the crowd towards them. Kane took her arm as she approached: 'Florrie, so lovely to see you. And can I say, how lovely you look this evening.'

Horse concurred: 'Evening miss. And I hope that you don't mind me saying that Mr K here is right – you do scrub up very nice...'

Florrie was radiant. Shining hair parted in the centre, gentle ringlets around her ears, she glowed in her silken pink evening dress. But, on closer examination, it became obvious she had been crying. She was trying to speak, but was having trouble.

Kane took both of her arms: 'My dear, gentle Florrie – whatever is the matter?'

Florrie spoke, tears in her eyes: 'It's Amanda. Something dreadful has happened. The concert cannot go on...'

***

Florrie led Kane and Horse into the backstage area. As they walked past the auditorium, they saw that many members of the audience had already taken their seats: there had to be five or six hundred people.

They reached the rear room where Amanda would be getting dressed into her costume. Kane gently knocked on the door. The voice that bade them 'Come' was not that of Amanda. Rather, it was the booming voice of Sir John Forbes-Knight. Kane, Horse and Florrie entered and saw Sir John pacing up and down the room, his eyes bulging in that great hairy face like a distracted bear. And sitting in the corner, dressed in a cotton gown, arms wrapped around herself, was the tiny figure of Miss Amanda, eyes closed and shivering. She reminded Kane of a kitten that had just been dunked in freezing water.

Sir John looked at Kane and barked over: 'I take it that Florrie has told you everything?'

Kane replied that Florrie had told them nothing.

Sir John stopped and starred at Amanda for a moment, then: 'It's the singing teacher, Mr Brookes. That blackguard. He has stolen everything. Everything...'

The old surgeon went on to recount how – on the advice of that singing teacher – a quantity of valuable jewels had been obtained to be sewn into Miss Amanda's dress. These – according to Brookes – would make the figure of Miss Amanda sparkle and shine in the footlights during the concert. As planned, the jewels had been sewn onto the dress by an established and trustworthy seamstress, and Mr Brookes had insisted that he himself collect the item for inspection on the day of the concert. In the event, Brookes had collected the jewel-studded dress – and had promptly vanished. When enquiries were made at his lodgings, his landlady told visitors that young Mr Brookes had left with a large suitcase that afternoon and had said that he would not be returning. When Miss Amanda and Sir John called in at the Assembly Rooms later that afternoon in the hope of a final rehearsal (or an explanation), it became apparent that no preparation had been made for the event. No music. No scenery. A thick curtain gauze was still stretched across the front of the stage from a previous production. The only musical instruments evident were an old, discarded tympanum drum and an out-of-tune piano.

Kane and Horse listened in silence, then Kane volunteered: 'Sir John, I am shocked. I'm sure we all are. Now, I have seen Mackintosh of the Detective outside and I am sure that if you were to tell him...'

Sir John cut in: 'Are you mad, sir? The loss of the jewels is merely financial, Mr Kane. It can be borne. No. It is the disgrace to the family, sir. To my daughter...'

Kane tried to salve the surgeon: 'Sir John, I am sure that no-one...'

He was cut off by the angry bluster: 'That 'no-one' what, sir? That no-one will laugh at the old fool who took that cutpurse into his house? That no-one will laugh that the thief stole not only the old man's jewels but also the affections of his... his imbecilic daughter? We shall be a laughing stock the remainder of our lives.'

Sir John slumped down onto a chair. He leaned forward and held his head in both hands. After a moment, he looked up: 'Well, nothing for it, I suppose. I shall have to take the stage and tell... how many are there? Eight hundred? Tell eight hundred people waiting that there will be no, no... what in blazes did that charlatan call it? No 'epiphany' this evening. We shall tell them that Miss Amanda has been taken unwell...'

Horse – who had remained silent throughout – frowned a little at that point. Sir John – now conscious of any slight, even the most miniscule, barked at him: 'Who the blazes are you, sir? And what gives you the right to frown!'

Kane stepped in: 'This is my manservant, Mr Horse, Sir John. I am sure that he meant nothing by it...'

Forbes-Knight was determined to compound his woe: 'Ah, so now we will have the lower orders gossiping about it to boot!'

'I assure you, Sir John, my man Horse is the soul of discretion...'

Horse came in at this point: 'Begging your pardon, sir, no disrespect was meant. I was just thinking that if you was wanting to avoid people laughing at you, then it was not the best idea to have the daughter of a famous doctor not going on – because she's sick.'

Sir John considered this for a moment, then nodded. Horse continued: 'I'm looking at the clock, sir. Don't we have about fifteen minutes before the whole thing is meant to start?'

The surgeon removed the fob watch from his pocket and examined it: 'Twenty-two minutes by my reckoning...'

Horse continued: 'Then, I wonder, sir, if me and Mr Kane might put our heads together and see if we can't come up with something.'

The surgeon frowned: 'Such as?'

'Well, I don't know yet, sir – 'cause we 'aven't put them heads together yet, 'ave we...'

★★★

Horse and Kane stood inside the auditorium. The din was growing greater now as the remainder of the eight hundred people took their seats. Kane was shaking his head: 'Mr Horse, that was a very gallant thing to do. To volunteer to try to save this event. But – as you yourself have said on many occasions – you know nothing of the arts. You have expressed the view, more than once, I'm bound to say, that such enterprises are – and I quote: 'A waste of two bob.'

'You're right, Mr K. It's all stuff and nonsense to me. But this is different, sir, and what I do know, is that when your friend needs help, then you put your best foot forward.'

Kane exhaled slowly: 'Mr Horse. You know nothing of the arts; I know precious little more. What shall we do in our remaining fifteen minutes?'

Horse smiled: 'Well, sir. Didn't you once give a bit of tea and toast to a bloke what does a bit of drawing...'

★★★

'Set design?'

The young artist, Simon Culp, had been in the middle of taking down his outdoor stall as he was approached by Kane and Horse.

'Of course. If you remember, Mr Kane, I showed you some examples of my work when we met that day.'

Kane was silent as Horse proceeded to lay out the Forbes-Knight predicament. Given the time constraints, this was done with remarkable brevity and with one or two curse words to underline the seriousness of the situation. At the end of the narrative, Culp stood still and muttered, 'Gosh!'

They stood silent for a moment, then Horse spoke up: 'Well, sir. What do you think? Can you help us?'

Culp frowned: 'What is the actual nature of the event?'

'Nobody got a bleedin' clue, sir.'

Culp nodded. 'Well, that could be helpful. What is it called?'

'It's the 'Ee-puff...' eh, the 'Ee-piff...'' Horse was struggling and looked towards Kane.

'The title of the evening is 'The Epiphany'.' Helped Kane.

Culp nodded: 'The Three Wise Men and the stable and that sort of thing?'

Kane shrugged his shoulders: 'It's far from clear, Mr Culp, but that is the title of the event that the audience is expecting to see.'

Culp pondered this: 'How long before the curtain is due to rise?'

'Around ten minutes...'

Culp laughed: 'This is the theatre, Mr Kane. Attending the theatre late

– and to be seen arriving – is part of the game here. That will buy us another ten minutes, at least. Alright – I have an idea. Help me to stow this gear into the foyer, and then we can examine the set-up of the stage.'

Horse and Kane helped Culp carry the dis-assembled market stall into the theatre foyer for safekeeping.

Culp brushed his hands together to shake off the dust: 'Now, gentlemen, I should be very grateful if you could find me two very large Bibles...'

***

Precisely fifteen minutes later, behind the closed curtain, shielded from the audience, and assembled on the middle of the stage, stood Culp, Kane, Miss Amanda, Florrie and an increasingly irascible Sir John Forbes-Knight.

Culp smiled: 'Now, Mr Kane, did we manage to obtain those Good Books?'

Kane looked towards the stage exits: 'I tasked Mr Horse with that exercise, but I fear, that at such short notice...'

At that point, Horse entered, stage right, hugging two extremely large black volumes. He smiled at Kane: 'Got 'em, Mr K, got 'em...'

'Excellent, Horse, excellent. But where on earth did you...?'

'Church across the street, Mr K. Saint Andrews...'

Kane wrinkled his nose in disbelief: 'And they simply agreed to lend two great, valuable bibles to a stranger?'

Horse looked shifty, then: 'I'll get them back before they know they're gone, sir.'

Their conversation was interrupted by the clapping of Culp's hands to attract their attention: 'Very well, everyone, take your places.' He nodded in Florrie's direction: 'Now, miss, are you quite certain that you can play without the music?'

Florrie Forbes-Knight stood at the piano and nodded: 'I will try my utmost, Mr Culp. I have played these hymns many a time – but never in the dark...'

Culp laughed: 'I would not be overly concerned, miss. That piano is so far out of tune, I doubt that the odd wrong note here or there will make much of a difference.'

Culp lifted the bibles from Horse and handed one to Kane and one to the surgeon. 'Remember what I told you – slow and stately, just keep following her.'

Culp then took Horse by the arm, led him to the back of the stage and pointed to a large piece of brass machinery there: 'And you, sir, will be entrusted with this.'

Horse scrutinised the machine. It looked to him like the lens of a telescope attached to an accordion: 'What the bloomin'...'

Culp twiddled with some knobs, struck a match and held the match to a small nozzle. The nozzle began to burn and blow. The flame licked against what looked like a large piece of white coal. And suddenly, the coal began to glow with a blinding intensity. A focused shaft of light emerged from the lens and shone towards the front of the stage.

Culp smiled: 'And that, Mr Horse, is the limelight – and you will direct that, at all times, at our diva here.' Culp pointed towards Miss Amanda. He then produced a stage pistol from his pocket and held it above his head. 'Take your places. Ready...'

***

The next morning, the following review appeared in The Scotsman newspaper:

The People That Sat in Darkness Have Seen a Great Light

Miss Amanda Forbes-Knight (of whom the writer was not previously familiar) last night made her debut at The Assembly Rooms in the personification of 'Epiphany', and it proved to be a debut of admirable facility and effect.

The loud report of a pistol was the harbinger of the opening of the curtain on a veritable tour de force of Biblical allegory. Behind a thick veneer of gauze stretched across the front of the stage, the strains of a distant pianoforte – eerily remote and out-of-tune – underscored the presentation of Miss Forbes-Knight in a stately progress across the bare stage.

And at her heels, two figures followed: the first, bearing the shaggy beard on an Old Testament prophet, and declaiming loudly from the Book of Isaiah; the second figure, slighter, and somewhat struggling with his oversize Bible, piped in periodically with passages concerning the Three Wise Men. On close examination, in the darkness, a third Magus was present behind the blinding limelight, focused always on the figure of Miss Forbes-Knight. The complete effect was, at once, charming and disconcerting. The whole event became a meditation on the ineffable nature of epiphany itself: the robust Old Testament followed by the faltering New, the music of the chapel, recognisable, but faded and discordant, and at the head of this Progress of History, the shivering, shimmering figure of Epiphany herself, exposed, but hidden behind the gauze of Time, always under the intense Limelight of Scrutiny, a glare that simultaneously illuminates and blinds.

Miss Forbes-Knight's style of acting is, if we may use the expression, more significant, more pregnant with meaning, more varied and alive in every part, than any we have almost ever witnessed. She expertly conveys the futility of human understanding as the character of Epiphany appears to wander aimlessly the length and breadth of the stage; there is no vacant pause in the action; the eye is never silent.

Her performance was quite equal to anything we have seen on the stage. Her singing voice, too, deserves distinct consideration: at times, a full-throated contralto, expertly intoning discord on well-known hymns, while at other times, expressing Divine Despair, skilfully modulating her singing voice to resemble the sound of a seagull trapped in a hempen sack.

For depth and force of conception, it must be conceded that in the presence of Miss Forbes-Knight's 'Epiphany', we required to acknowledge that we were in the presence of Genius...

***

'Well, that was a load of old gammon and spinach, wunnit!' Horse sat grinning in his chair in the dressing room, shaking his head.

'It may be nonsense to you, Mr Horse, but just listen to that audience.' Simon Culp giggled as he cupped his ear towards the auditorium.

Despite the event concluding some minutes before, the members of the audience, many on their feet, were still applauding and calling out: 'Brava' and 'Author'.

Kane approached Miss Amanda who appeared, to all intents and purposes, to be in a state of shock. Kane smiled kindly at her: 'And how are you, Amanda? Now that it is all over?'

Amanda seemed distracted, in a daze, then: 'I feel... I feel... I'm afraid that I am going to be sick...'

Sir John Forbes-Knight leapt up from his chair, grabbed his youngest daughter by the arm and led her outside: 'There's a sink out here somewhere. I'm sure of it. Deep breaths, my girl, deep breaths...'

Horse and Culp (who seemed to have conjured up a sandwich from somewhere) then left to make sure that the lime was not still burning in the machinery on the stage, leaving Kane and Florrie alone.

The Advocate sat down across from the older sister. Nothing was said for a time, but they looked at each other and smiled. And then, with a sort of mutual understanding, like two naughty schoolchildren who had just got away with something secretly, they began to laugh.

'How did your man, Horse, put it again?' Florrie mimicked Horse's

Cockney accent: 'A load of old gammon and spinach'?'

The friends burst into laughter again. Kane wiped his eyes: 'Oh, Florrie – if only the event itself had contained that much substance.'

They laughed once more. Somewhere in the back of Kane's mind, he had the thought that if it were possible to stop time, just for a moment, then he would do so now. In that bare, theatre dressing room, sitting across from Florrie, Kane realised that at that moment he wanted for nothing else. Sitting with Florrie, whose eyes shone and sparkled now as she laughed; Florrie, who had never looked so beautiful, sitting there before him in her ringlets and silk gown, radiating sheer joy and decency, Kane had the feeling, akin to that deep relief of the man who had finally come home.

Kane looked up: 'Florrie?'

'Yes.'

Kane hesitated for a moment, then: 'You understand that... that your father has broken my connection with Amanda...'

Florrie placed her hand gently on Kane's arm: 'Yes, Edward, I'm sorry.'

Kane gave a shy smile: 'I confess, Florrie – I am not.'

They sat in silence for a moment, then Kane stammered: 'I am a free man, Florrie.'

Florence smiled. Kane looked up: 'And you, Miss Forbes-Knight, as I understand it, are similarly un-attached.'

Florrie gave a broad smile, and answered with an exaggerated mock-courtesy: 'Why, this is true, Mr Kane.'

'Then,' Kane place his hand on top of Florrie's, 'then, I wonder if you would... if you would consider... you would consider doing me the honour of...'

And they were suddenly interrupted by the booming voice of Sir John Forbes-Knight: 'Remarkable, sir, quite remarkable...'

Kane and Florrie stood up automatically.

'The sheer turnaround of events!'

Horse and Culp also returned to the room in time to see the old surgeon grab Kane's hand and begin to shake it vigorously: 'Remarkable. Just listen, sir. That audience is still cheering and clamouring about the whole affair. Kane – you have saved the day. And more importantly, your resourcefulness has preserved the honour and dignity of this family.'

Kane attempted (correctly) to attribute the success – and the narrow escape – to the artistic flair of the young artist, Simon Culp, but Sir John was having none of it. 'Poppycock, sir. This evening, you were like the young Raleigh. I sent you from our shores empty-handed and you, sir, returned with the riches of tobacco.'

Kane mused for a moment that the *older* Raleigh had had his head cut off. But he said nothing.

The old surgeon bellowed on: 'And in the same week, you exposed Sir Charles Irving as the old fraud that we all knew that he was. You're a dark horse, aren't you, Kane? But this affectation of modesty does you no good, sir, no good at all. You will never prosper as an Advocate if you persist in assuming the character of a wallflower.'

Kane could think of nothing to say, so he said: 'Thank you, Sir John.'

Sir John then took Miss Amanda by the hand: 'Now, Kane, I must acknowledge that I have underestimated you, sir. And so, you will be delighted to hear,' he tried to place Amanda's hand into Kane's hand, 'that the connection that I had formerly forbidden is now in place once more...'

He couldn't help it, but Kane recoiled: 'No, Sir John... I don't think that you understand. I...'

Forbes-Knight laughed: 'Of course, I understand, my young friend. I understand now – 'The course of true love never did run smooth' and all that...'

Kane shook his head: 'Things have changed, Sir John...'

The old surgeon nodded furiously: 'Of course they have, sir, of course they have. The scales have fallen from my eyes. So, let me announce it publicly: Edward Kane, Advocate, you are free to marry my youngest daughter.' And with that, Sir John Forbes-Knight took the hand of his youngest daughter and placed it into the hand of Edward Kane.

Both Kane and Miss Amanda looked stunned.

'Now, it must be accepted that I was somewhat at fault here, and allowed Miss Amanda to form a quite inappropriate attachment to that blackguard, Brookes. But I have had stern words with her, sir, stern words. And, of course, you yourself have your faults, young Kane, but at least you are not a musician...'

Sir John chuckled at his own witticism.

Kane tried to look at Florrie, but she had already turned her face away...

Chapter Thirteen

'Just look at that box of yours, Edward. I do not think that I have ever seen one quite so full.'

It was the following morning in Parliament House, and Kane's friend Collins stood back and smiled at the mound of papers in Edward Kane's work box, all sealed with letters of instruction presenting compliments to Counsel and bound with pink ribbon.

Kane nodded. 'I fear, my dear friend, that all of these instructions will relate to the pushing of various parlour maids down flights of stairs...'

Their conversation was interrupted by their sudden awareness of the presence of Manville, the Faculty Servant, who – as far as anyone could tell – appeared to have been conjured from thin air.

'Manville?'

'Begging your pardon, Mr Kane, but there's a young lady asking for you at the fireplace.'

'Thank you, Manville.' The Faculty Servant gave a small bow, and then evaporated into the main hall.

Collins looked at his friend: 'Edward, you did not ask who it was?'

'Collins, I, I...' Kane shrugged his shoulders. The events of the previous twenty-four hours seemed to catch up with him at that instant. 'To be perfectly honest, Collins, if it is Miss Amanda, then I do not know what to say. And if it is Florrie, then...'

Collins put his hand on his friend's shoulder: 'Edward, at every stage, you have done the right thing. That being so, you must trust that all will be well in the end.'

Shoulders down and eyes on the floor, Kane made his way into Parliament Hall, and when he reached the fireplace, the figure waiting for him was neither of the Forbes-Knight sisters. Instead...

'Well, Kanemiss – aren't you famous now.'

There at the fireplace stood Cordelia Irving.

'Oh, Edward, Edward, you look surprised to see me. Of course, in my book, better a look of surprise than of disappointment.'

She gave a low-throated laugh. Kane said nothing.

'And I understand that congratulations are in order. Again. You and Miss Amanda. I would have thought, Edward, that you might prefer someone more blue in the stocking. Amanda has an older sister, you know...'

Kane sighed: 'Cordelia, I have work to do...'

'Of course you do. You'll be very busy now. 'Some have greatness thrust upon them,' as my father used to say. You'll remember my father, Edward. He was the man whose reputation you ruined...'

Kane held his tongue.

'Did you know that Papa had a gift for you. Near the end. Said he wanted you to have it. Did you receive it?'

Kane shook his head.

Cordelia Irving closed her eyes and was silent for a moment. 'Well, anyway, Edward, the reason I am here today is to consult with your Dean, to see if we can't resolve all of these ridiculous legal fights between Papa and his old enemy Sir Michael Coates.'

'Then, you could not be in better hands, Cordelia. Now if you will excuse me...' Kane began to move away, but Cordelia Irving took him by the arm. 'And... and I wanted to apologise, Edward. For striking you. I should not have done that.'

Kane thought for a moment, then nodded: 'I hardy think that it matters now.'

'And, I came to say goodbye. We leave tomorrow. For Boston.'

'We?'

'Patrick and I. We are to be married there. Unlimited business opportunities for a man like Patrick Macnair, apparently. According to Patrick Macnair, of course. He says that a change of scenery will help. Although, I do suspect that Boston has as many coquettish parlour maids as Edinburgh.'

'Then, I wish you well.'

'It's luck you should wish me, Edward. Six weeks on a boat, with stinking water and stale bread...'

Kane felt a suddenly wave of exhaustion: 'Then, I wish you luck, Cordelia.'

Cordelia Irving stared at Kane and smiled: 'And did you know, Edward, that they still have slaves there? Can you imagine? The power of life and death over another human being.'

And as Edward Kane looked into the eyes of Cordelia Irving, he realised that nothing, nothing could warm the frozen landscape that was her soul. And he walked away.

***

'You seem glum tonight, Mr K. What's the matter? Too much beef?'

As Horse started to clear away the dinner dishes from the sitting room table, Kane sat, rubbing his temples.

'I fear, Horse, that I am still giddy from the merry-go-round of recent weeks.'

'Fair enough, Mr K, but look on the bright side, sir. You get a bloke off with murder, you get back your woman, and now you got lots of work an' all.'

Kane shrugged and nodded. Then he looked up and smiled: 'And now that I think of it, Mr Horse, didn't you tell me that you knew that Patrick Macnair was guilty?'

'I was only saying that, Mr K, for when you was going to lose the case and he was going to get the noose, sir. I'll just put the kettle on, shall I?'

Horse scurried to the larder to fetch the kettle. Kane got up from his chair and went to the window. A full moon shone above the rooftops of the Old Town.

A rap at the door. Horse frowned and popped his head out of the pantry, but Kane waved him away. 'You will proceed with the making of tea, Mr Horse, while l deal with our mystery visitor.'

Kane opened the door to find a large, red-faced boy, out of breath. He was leaning on what looked like a beautiful antique desk. 'I'm looking for a Mister Edward Kane?'

'Yes, I am Edward Kane.'

The boy rapped on the desk: 'Delivery for you, sir.'

Kane examined the desk. It looked familiar, but he could not place it: 'I'm sorry to tell you that I have not ordered such a thing. Beautiful as it is.'

The red-faced, out-of-breath boy was not happy: 'Begging your pardon, sir, but this is the third time today I've lugged this thing up these stairs. You're never in during the day, so I thought I'd try at night. And I looked up and saw the light in your window, sir.'

Kane frowned at the object. Beautiful, neat, waist-hight, a leather writing section, a series of drawers down the side. In many ways, more a work of art than a piece of furniture. 'Well, young fellow, as I say...' But when Kane looked up, the young fellow was already halfway down the stairs. Kane called after him: 'Excuse me... hello?' only to hear the increasingly distant and echoing response call back: 'Thank you, Mr Kane...'

Kane realised what was before him. It was the Davenport, the writing bureau that he had admired that evening in the study of Sir Charles

Irving. This must be the gift from the old man that Cordelia Irving had referred to.

Kane lugged the bureau intro the sitting room.

Horse emerged from the pantry. He saw the bureau and whistled: 'Well, Mr K, you don't take long to spend your money, do you.'

'I didn't buy it, Horse. It is a gift. A gift from Sir Charles Irving.'

Horse looked puzzled: 'But what for, sir?'

Kane shook his head. Then he began to open the series of drawers at the side of the Davenport. And in one of the drawers was an envelope. It was marked: *Edward Kane, Esq., Advocate.* Kane tore it open and inside was a single piece of paper. Scrawled, in a hand that was obviously infirm, Kane read:

Stephano Tempest. Act III. Scene II.

He handed the paper to Horse, who read it and handed it back: 'Well Mr K – how are you supposed to make head or tail of that, sir? The old man was off his head at the end, I suppose. And who was this 'Stephano Tempest' bloke?'

Kane studied the paper: 'Horse, there are some volumes of Shakespeare in the small bookcase in my room. Could you bring them here, please?'

Horse went into the bedroom and returned carrying three bound leather volumes. Kane opened the volume marked 'Comedies' and leafed through it.

Horse enquired: 'Mystery solved, Mr K?'

Kane handed him the open book: 'The Tempest by William Shakespeare, Act Three, Scene Two – and here is what the character 'Stephano' says.'

Horse took the volume and read aloud: 'He that dies pays all debts...' Horse handed back the book: 'Very deep, Mr K.'

Kane started at the volume: 'I wonder what he thought he owed me?'

Horse laughed: 'He was just trying to give you back what he knows was bilked off you by Billy Brown and Fat Dode. That's all there is to it, sir.'

Horse began to study the Davenport now, as if appraising it: 'And I'd say that you got the better deal here, Mr K. This little beauty must be worth a bob or two. Shall I put it in your bedroom, sir?'

Kane said nothing, but sat down and simply stared at the bureau.

'I confess, Mr Horse, that the thought of Sit Charles sitting at that desk all those years, possibly writing that suicide note – at that very desk – and then that same desk in my home...'

Horse thought for a moment: 'I could speak to my friend Mrs Ratchett, sir, I'm sure that she could do us a price...'

Kane shook his head: 'And transfer the bad luck, the horror, from one house to another, Horse?'

Horse nodded: 'Now that I think of it, I had an old girlfriend that used to say that she would never have some bits of furniture in her house. The empty rocking chair, she used to say, was somewhere where the devil could park his bum. Mind you, she was Irish...'

They both stared at the Davenport in silence. Then Horse piped up: 'I think we should tip it.'

'Tip it', Horse?'

'Tip it out the winder.'

Horse began to drag the antique bureau towards the window.

Kane got up from his chair: 'Mr Horse, we cannot simply throw a valuable, antique Davenport out of a third-story window.'

'Why not, sir?'

Kane realised that he was, in fact, lost for words at this point, but struggled on: 'Because... because... well, for one thing, it might hit somebody...'

Horse went to the sitting room window, opened it, stuck his head out, examined the street below and darted back: 'No-one there, sir. The coast is clear...'

'Mr Horse – I am not convinced...'

Horse interrupted: 'Well, sir, you're either going to keep it – which you are not going to do – or pass it on – which you do not want to do, because you think it's cursed or something, sir – or we can tip it and the lucky passers-by can get some good quality firewood.'

Kane stood in indecision.

'It's now or never, Mr K.'

Kane thought for a moment, then: 'Let's do it, Mr Horse.'

Kane and Horse dragged the bureau to the window. Horse looked out again. The street was still empty. 'Alright, Mr K – on three.'

One on either side, Kane and Horse lifted the heavy walnut Davenport and balanced it half-way out of the window. Horse nodded at Kane and counted: 'One, Two, THREE...' and on that count of three, the rare and valuable finely-carved desk was hoisted out of the window. Kane and Horse immediately put their heads out to see. They watched it fall and then shatter on the pavement below. So loud was the sound of the Davenport's demise that those in neighbouring houses looked out of their windows to see what on earth had caused such a crash, and within minutes, the street was full of neighbours examining the debris, some collecting the valuable brass handles, others – as predicted by Horse – gathering wood for the fire.

They watched for a while, then came in from the window. Horse resumed his duties at the kettle: 'Feeling better about it now, Mr K?'

Kane sat down and smiled: 'Strangely enough, Mr Horse – I do feel a kind of relief.'

The door knocked again. Kane and Horse looked at each other. Horse smiled: 'I'll get it, sir. Who knows? It might be a wardrobe this time...'

Horse answered the door and returned a few moments later – accompanied by Mackintosh of the Detective.

Kane stood up: 'Mackintosh. What a pleasant surprise.' And then he became somewhat nervous: 'Now, if it's about... about the Davenport... can I just say...'

Mackintosh narrowed his eyes and cocked his head: 'I'm sorry, Mr Kane. Davenport? I don't know him, sir...'

Kane smiled in relief: 'Of course, Mackintosh. Nice to see you, sir.

Would you like a cup of tea?'

'I'm afraid that I am here on business, Mr Kane. There's a young lady been found dead at The White Hart Inn...'

'Yes?'

Horse interrupted: 'The White Hart, Mr K, that's where some of our military men go looking for a bit of female company, if you know what I mean, sir.'

Kane looked at Mackintosh: 'I see, Mackintosh. You will excuse me for asking, but what has this to do with me?'

'Well, when the body was found, Mr Kane, she was in the company of a gentleman, sir.'

'Yes?'

'And he has been arrested, Mr Kane. And when he was asked if he was going to have a lawyer, sir, he asked for you.'

Kane smiled and leaned back in his chair. He laughed: 'I fear, Mackintosh, that my recent success in the Macnair case has led to an unwarranted demand for my services.'

The detective shook his head: 'No, sir. It's not that. He says that he knows you personally, sir. And his name is...'

Mackintosh removed a small notebook from his coat pocket and read: 'Regimental Sergeant William McNaughtan.'

Kane said nothing. Mackintosh continued: 'He remarked that you would probably better remember him as...'

Horse interrupted: 'Mad Dog McNaughtan.'

★★★

'And just think, Mama, in a mere six weeks or so, we shall all be in America. And your daughter shall be married. And we shall be happy.'

Anyone looking at the scene would have sworn that Cordelia Irving was speaking to herself. On closer examination, however, she would be seen clutching the locket around her neck and speaking to the picture of her mother. The mother who had lost her life giving birth to her daughter.

'And then, like the princess and the prince in the fairy stories, Patrick and I will live happily ever after...' As she held that locket tight, Cordelia Irving smiled, and the tears streamed down her face.

***

'They say that it is bad luck to look at a full moon through a pane of glass, Miss Florence.'

Florrie Forbes-Knight turned from the window to see the household butler, Mr Chambers, set down a glass of warm milk on the table.

'Thank you, Chambers.'

Chambers the butler presented, at times, as icy to the outsider, but his loyalty to the Forbes-Knight family was never anything less than unwavering. Inevitably, butlers would have their favourites within every family group, and Chambers had always held a tender affection for the decent, unfussy nature of Miss Florence Forbes-Knight. And he knew precisely what was troubling her heart at that moment.

'Having difficulty sleeping, miss?'

'It has been an instructive few days, Chambers.'

'Oh, I am aware of that, Miss Florence. The household has been turned upside down at times, what with the preparation for Miss Amanda's concert. But I trust that all has now been restored to its usual state.'

Florrie said nothing, but sat down and lifted the glass of warm milk to her lips.

Chambers made to leave, and then stopped and turned to speak to Florrie again.

'I wonder if I might be so bold, miss...'

Florrie looked up: 'Yes, Chambers?'

'It is commonly said that it is a long road that has no turning.'

'Yes?'

'The secret, as I understand it, is to keep going. One foot in front of the other, being the preferred method, I'm told. From my long observation of these matters, matters of the heart, miss, these things have a way of working themselves out to the satisfaction of all.'

Florrie nodded and smiled: 'Thank you, Chambers.'

'Good night, miss.'

Florrie drank her warm milk and looked out at the moon.

***

'I might have known he'd get hisself into trouble, The Dog.'

Horse, Kane and Mackintosh stepped down from the carriage at the Police Office beside St Giles Church.

Parliament Square was empty now, and the buildings and cobblestones were bathed in the bright, silver moonlight.

Horse looked at Kane. 'Still glum, sir? Cheer up – it might never happen...'

Kane gave a rueful smile and gazed towards the shining face of the moon. He was reminded of his dear, beautiful Florrie: 'That is precisely what I am afraid of, Mr Horse. It might never happen.'

And the detective led the way, as the Advocate and the Horse followed. And the full moon shone over that great city of Edinburgh, as some stories were coming to their end, while others were just beginning.

Acknowledgements

My Good Angel, Sandy McCall Smith, who pops up in my life every few decades and always lights the way ahead - il miglior fabbro.

Alistair Johnson, Faculty of Advocates Librarian, for his patience and skill as a researcher.

Mark McGuire, who fields my hardest questions with ease.

Colin Sutherland, Mike O'Grady, Gordon Liddle and Douglas Fairley. Don't ask...

Donald Findlay and Simon Collins for my shameless appropriation of their best qualities to furnish my fiction.

Katie Jowett for our friendly arm-wrestling over the text. It's a better book for your input, Katie.

And Jean Findlay. The Boss. End of.

THE AUTHOR

Ross Macfarlane QC is a Supreme Courts lawyer based in Edinburgh, Scotland. His articles and short fiction have featured in national newspapers including The Guardian, The Scotsman and Scotland on Sunday. Ross's short story 'Charles Dickens and the Tale of Ebenezer...Scroggie' was chosen as the featured work of The Dickens Fellowship in 2017. This is his first full-length novel.

THE ILLUSTRATOR

Lesley-Anne Barnes Macfarlane is an academic
and illustrator based in Edinburgh. Her work has
appeared in The Scotsman, Scotland on Sunday,
The Edinburgh Evening News and The Dickens
Fellowship online.